MISSING REELS

MISSING REELS

A NOVEL

FARRAN SMITH NEHME

OVERLOOK DUCKWORTH
NEW YORK • LONDON

This edition first published in hardcover in the United States and the United Kingdom
in 2014 by Overlook Duckworth, Peter Mayer Publishers, Inc.

NEW YORK
141 Wooster Street
New York, NY 10012
www.overlookpress.com
For bulk and special sales, please contact sales@overlookny.com,
or write us at the address above.

LONDON
30 Calvin Street
London E1 6NW
info@duckworth-publishers.co.uk
www.ducknet.co.uk
For bulk and special sales, please contact sales@duckworth-publishers.co.uk,
or write us at the address above.

Library of Congress Cataloging-in-Publication Data
Nehme, Farran Smith.
Missing reels / Farran Smith Nehme.
p. cm
ISBN 978-1-4683-0927-0 (hardback)
I. Title.
PS3614.E43M57 2014
813'.6--dc23
2014034174

Book design and type formatting by Bernard Schleifer
Manufactured in the United States of America

FIRST EDITION
2 3 4 5 6 7 8 9 10
ISBN: 978-1-4683-0927-0 (US)
ISBN: 978-0-7156-4990-9 (UK)

For Jad, Zane, Alida and Ben

"When John was twenty-one he became one of the seven million that believes New York depends on them."

—KING VIDOR AND JOHN V. A. WEAVER, *The Crowd*, 1928

SEPTEMBER

1.

THE WOMAN HAD LIVED IN THE BUILDING SO LONG THAT IT WAS HER own name, Miriam Gibson, on the buzzer label, and not some forgotten former tenant. She must have been in her seventies, but she was the most beautiful old lady Ceinwen had ever seen. Her face was barely lined, with fine features and pale brown eyes; she wore her hair coiled at the neck. Miriam stood straight. She wore tailored dresses and suits with scarves, everything perfectly pressed and matched. None of the elastic Ceinwen had quietly shuddered over as Granana wheezed around the house.

Miriam lived on the floor below them. Talmadge, Jim, and Ceinwen hated the climb to their place so much that if someone forgot to buy coffee or cigarettes on the way in, it would take half an hour of arguing to decide who had to run to the bodega. Miriam climbed slowly, but when she reached her door, she seemed no more ruffled than if she had just crossed the hall.

Their apartment was a sixth-floor walkup, but it had two real bedrooms and a double living room with a large alcove that could be closed off with screens for another roommate. There were no closets.

Ceinwen had moved in with Jim and Talmadge early that spring. Jim had the side bedroom, Ceinwen the back, and Talmadge was behind the screens. Ceinwen and Talmadge worked at Vintage Visions, an antique clothing store on lower Broadway where Talmadge was the star floor salesman, and Ceinwen was queen of the accessories counter by default. When they met, Jim had been working there, too, but now he had a better job managing a tiny costume jewelry store on the Upper East Side.

She told herself that living with two men made Avenue C safe, even if Talmadge was short and Jim was skinny. It took only a month to learn which hours were fine and which demanded a cab, which buildings were normal and which should be passed at top speed, which men deserved a greeting as they bought beer in the bodega or sprawled all day on the stoop and which ones were best dealt with by a sudden interest in something twenty yards down the street, no matter how emphatic their cries of "Hey, Blondie!"

Miriam, with her good clothes and comings and goings, worried Ceinwen. Weren't old people apt to get mugged, especially if they looked well-kept? But after a couple of months, it became clear that the other locals treated Miriam with the same brusque respect she showed Ceinwen.

Ceinwen, though, got less of a greeting from Miriam than the stoop-dwellers did. Every time they passed each other in the dank, cramped lobby, she marveled at Miriam's ability to stroll by with a nod on a good day and indifference on a bad. "Boy, is it hot out there," "Could you believe how long the street music went on last night?," "Great scarf"—all of these were met with "yes," "no," and "thank you" as Miriam continued to walk to wherever it was she went.

"Whoever heard of an old lady who doesn't want to talk?" she wondered to Jim. "At the nursing home the problem was getting them to stop. All you had to do was say 'Did you see *Nightline* last night?' or 'So when do you think they'll finally fix that stretch of I-55?'"

"This is New York, honey. Not Yazoo City."

"Or if you were really desperate, I mean *really*, you could ask how the nurses were treating them."

"And yet," said Jim, shutting his book on his finger to mark his place, "like I said, this is New York. Even the old people have actual lives. That's the beauty of this town."

"Uh-huh," she said. "So Mr. Rodriguez over at the Thrifty Mart wanted to tell me all about getting his mole removed on account of he's got such a full life."

"Maybe she's just a bitch." Jim opened his book again. "Why do you care?"

"She seems . . . interesting," she muttered with false hesitation.

"Ever thought," asked Jim, "that's she's got nothing to say?"

Together they had suffered through the summer without air conditioning, the heat drilling through the roof and the fans searching for a breeze that wasn't there. But the first Saturday in September the heat broke, and the sun no longer fought through the haze. Ceinwen touched up her roots that morning and put on a new dress. Talmadge dated it to the mid-thirties: dark blue silk, ruffles at the hem, and a matching fabric belt. It had cost half a week's salary and brought her cash supply down to a truly dangerous level, but it was cut on the bias and she thought it was pure Jean Harlow. And she was sick to death of antique dresses with a missing belt.

Talmadge was on the morning shift, Ceinwen didn't work until the afternoon. Jim was upstairs in the apartment trying to scrape paint off the transoms. Ankle straps adjusted, red lipstick blotted, she clacked down the last flight of steps and into the lobby, where Miriam was getting her mail. The day held too much promise to be marred by courting a snub, so she set her eyes on the street door, which had a busted lock. Her last attempt to discuss this fact with Miriam had produced only, "I have a deadbolt."

"Young woman." The voice came just as Ceinwen opened the door. Miriam was locking her mailbox. "I'm sorry, but I've forgotten your name."

"Ceinwen." Miriam had, of course, never asked her name, but Ceinwen had gotten used to social lying back in Yazoo City.

"Ceinwen." Miriam repeated it like she'd said "Mary." "Would you mind my asking you a question? If it isn't inconvenient. I can see you're on your way out."

"It's all right, I'm early for work." Now she was lying, too, but this was important. Miriam speaks! Sentences! And she had a great voice, low-pitched and classy, almost like Audrey Hepburn. She let the door swing shut.

"Forgive me, but I had to ask what you're wearing."

"It's antique." Miriam liked the dress. It had been worth going broke before payday.

"So it *is* old," said Miriam.

What kind of a comment was that? As a matter of fact, lady, this dress is way younger than you. But as usual, Ceinwen's Southernness emerged when least convenient. Hit by an urge to be rude to an old woman, what she came out with was, "It's a collector's item."

"I see. You collect old clothes." This was said in the same carefully neutral register that Ceinwen had used when discussing plate collecting with Granana's pals at the nursing home. Knowing she was being patronized stung Ceinwen into her sales spiel.

"I work at a store that sells vintage clothing. I like vintage for the beauty and the style. It's your own little personal bit of history," she said.

"Depression history. Ah." Miriam nodded as though this explained everything. Before Ceinwen, whose Mississippi training did have its limits, could reply, Miriam continued, "I was just curious why you always seemed to be in costume."

"It reminded me of Jean Harlow." Why did she have to defend 1930s clothing to a woman who'd worn this stuff when it was new? At least for once she didn't have to explain who Jean Harlow was.

"Did it really. Then I'm afraid the effect's incomplete." Miriam was smiling. Sort of. Had she smiled at Ceinwen before? Did she smile at all? She had no smile lines, so maybe not. Ceinwen remembered that her bag was from the sixties and pulled it closer. "She didn't wear bras," continued Miriam. "Or slips or underwear. A dress, shoes. That was usually it."

Hard to say which was more extraordinary, the information or the source. Granana occasionally had brought up the topic of Ceinwen's underwear, but she would have had a word for a woman who just never wore any. "Well, I don't want to keep you. Good-bye."

As Miriam walked away Ceinwen managed to say, "It isn't a costume. It's a *look*."

Miriam turned and really smiled this time. "It's very pretty. I'm just not used to seeing young girls in old dresses." And vanished up the stairs.

Ceinwen roared down the streets avenue by avenue, pausing to light her last cigarette in a doorway. It was fifteen minutes past one when she reached the store, and she hotfooted it along the sides to avoid the customers, down the length of the entire sales floor. After clocking in, she checked herself in the wall mirror that hung in the tiny back room. Sweat shone on her forehead, wet patches bloomed under her armpits, and she'd gotten herself into this state in order to stand in a lobby that smelled of urine and converse with an old woman who was insulting her taste.

The store was crowded, and she eased behind the long counter, in search of an activity that might make her look as though she had been there since one o'clock. She opened a case and began to straighten necklaces.

"Ceinwen," a voice snapped. "Do you just not notice anything?" Lily was inches away. Her eternal black dresses and black hair always made Ceinwen think of the thunderstorms she used to watch rolling in over a field back home. Except you could always see a squall coming from far off. Lily dropped on you like a chicken hawk.

"Notice what?" She scanned the counter quickly; there didn't seem to be a new shipment.

Lily came closer. Ceinwen hated having her space invaded, and she stepped back. "The note. In the clock room. Go back and look."

She shut the case and walked to the clock room to check the walls. The only note she saw was the sign-up sheet for time off. She went back to the counter, where Lily was pushing a sale. "Lily," she said, "I signed up for my vacation slot last week."

Lily whooshed down about a foot from the customers, just far enough to pretend they weren't supposed to overhear. "I meant the time card," she said, loudly. "The note on the fucking time card. Go back right now and look at it."

She walked to the clock room. At the top of her card, her name was circled in red and an arrow pointed to a note: "See Lily."

Jesus Christ, she thought. She walked back to the counter. Lily had talked a woman into buying a brooch and was ringing it up. Ceinwen slipped back behind the counter and waited. "Did you see the note?"

"Yes," said Ceinwen. "You wanted to see me?"

"You're damn right I wanted to see you. You're late."

"I'm sorry. I got a call . . ."

"Don't you give me your excuses. This is the third time this week." It was the second time this week, and the time before she had clocked in at two minutes past. Trouble was, Lily was the owner as well as the manager. You took two extra minutes, that was food Lily couldn't eat and dates Lily couldn't pay for. "You screw up everyone's schedule when you come in late. Now here I am filling in for you, and everyone's lunch hour is off. Not that you care. You seem to think because you sell a lot you can't be fired. Well, think again. This is your warning. Are we clear?"

"Crystal," said Ceinwen, holding up a faceted bracelet, as if it were worthy of closer examination.

"Good." Lily never got a pun or really any joke at all; she was the most humorless person Ceinwen had ever met. It even took the fun out of mocking her to her face. Lily stomped toward the entrance for a cigarette that Ceinwen could only pray would calm her down.

None of the people milling about were asking to see anything yet, and she went back to straightening. The counter was so long there were six different cases to fix. She loved arranging the jewelry, old pieces and new ones done in an old style, but Lily never liked the results. Ceinwen threw in scarves, mixed up styles and periods. Lily wanted everything by decade and designer, lined up so you could see every surface of every item. Ceinwen would get a case looking pretty, and the next morning Lily would redo everything, until it had about as much chic as a drugstore Tampax display.

Talmadge waved on his way to the men's side, which was separated from the women's by a wide, mirrored passage. She beckoned him over. Before she could say anything he sang out, "Ask-me-how-lunch-went." He was so happy he didn't need a rhetorical response: "I saw George." George was the handyman at the discount clothing place next door. He was dark and muscular, exactly Talmadge's type. Ceinwen preferred blonds, when she roused herself to prefer anything.

"Was his girlfriend with him?"

"Me-ow. He likes me."

"Did he show you his supply closet?"

"Not yet." Talmadge cast a look toward the front register. "I need to get back to my side. Not that anybody's buying anything. Buncha joyriders today. Show me this, show me that, oh no not for me. And Lily is on the warpath."

"Tell me about it. Listen, Talmadge—"

"Make it quick."

"She's out having a cigarette, I saw her go. Do you think it's possible Miriam knew Jean Harlow?"

Too abrupt for Talmadge, who still had one eye out for Lily. "Who? Harlow? What?"

"Our neighbor. Miriam. Could she have known Jean Harlow?"

"Ceinwen, you're obsessed."

"I'm not. But today she wanted to talk to me about my dress."

Talmadge was elated. "I told you that was a great dress. I told you to buy it. There you go."

She diverted the torrent of Talmadge back to the topic. Miriam had said Harlow didn't wear bras, or even underwear. Was it possible she had known her? Talmadge said Miriam probably just looked at that stuff in the movies more than Ceinwen did; "you made me watch *Red Dust* and even I noticed she didn't have on underwear." Or maybe Miriam read it somewhere. "I don't see her in Hollywood. She's way too New York."

"But fifty years ago who knows what she was like?"

"There's nothing California about her. You always forget I'm West Coast."

"You're from Tacoma."

"I know what I'm talking about. There's a whole different vibe out there. Miriam's too proper." The front door to the store opened and Lily stepped in, and in the time it took Ceinwen to turn her head back toward Talmadge, he had slipped away to the men's side.

He's wrong, she thought. I bet Miriam did know Harlow. Old Hollywood was as good a setting for Miriam as any.

Talmadge was right about the customers, though. Once they realized she was there to show things, they kept her on the hop, wanting to see everything in the case and on the shelves. Then, if they bought anything, it was those thin, jangling metal bangles the store sold three for a dollar.

She had no time to consider her imaginary Miriam biography until her lunch hour, which didn't happen until five. Lily prized her arbitrary lunch-dismissal authority. Breaks were timed according to whether or not Lily liked you at the moment, how many customers were in the store, and whether Lily herself was on a diet and therefore jealous of anyone else's eating. That made three strikes today, so Ceinwen counted herself lucky to be getting a lunch hour at all. She devoured scrambled eggs at the coffee shop and sucked down a couple of cigarettes to keep her brain going. Miriam had been Jean Harlow's assistant. Miriam dated someone who dated Jean Harlow. Miriam was childhood friends with Harlow—though that would mean Miriam was from Kansas City, and if it was hard to picture Miriam in California, Kansas City was impossible.

All right, she'd been an actress and she was in a movie with Harlow. Then why had Ceinwen never heard of her? I, she thought, have heard of everyone. And I've seen everything of Harlow's. I've even seen *Saratoga*. Wait, could that be it? *Saratoga*! What was the name of that lady who stood in for Harlow when she died during filming? The one hiding her face behind binoculars and hats.

She couldn't remember the name, but in any case that didn't work. Harlow was tiny, Miriam was tall.

Lily was in such a bad mood that Ceinwen came back five minutes early just to be safe. But Lily wasn't going to like it when she counted out the register and saw how low the day's take had been. It was after eight and the sales probably weren't going to get any higher.

She dreaded the looks of the couple poring over the low-slung case at the end. The woman was wearing a tight leopard-print dress, and leopard-print clothing was a sure sign of a mean disposition. The man was wearing a rumpled, untucked linen shirt that looked expensive but was all wrong for September. But when the woman gave a snappy little wave—I'm not a cab, thought Ceinwen—there was no choice.

"I want to see that," said the woman, tapping one brown-polished nail against the top of the counter. Oh goody, a glass tapper.

"Earrings? Bracelet? Necklace? Pin?" She forced a smile.

"The earrings," said the woman, in some sort of accent. "No, not those." Tap, tap. "Those. No, in the back. The back."

"The blue ones," said the man.

She whipped out the velvet tray and set the earrings down. The woman picked up an earring, said something to the man in whatever language she spoke, and put it down. "No, I don't like those at all. They look cheap."

"Maybe," said Ceinwen, "if you told me what you're looking for, I could suggest something."

"I'm going back to Italy tomorrow," said the woman. "I'm going to a party this week and I want something new."

La. Dee. Da. "That sounds wonderful. Where in Italy?"

"Modena." Spoken in a slow, bored drawl that meant, of course, you've never heard of it. This was basically a dare.

"Oh, just like Mary of Modena."

The man took his eyes away from the case and looked at Ceinwen. The woman said, "Who?"

"James II's wife. He was king of England. Mary was a princess from Modena."

"I know James II." She sounded irritated. "I don't know his personal life."

"She was Catholic," said the man, "just like James." He had an accent too, British from the sound of it. "Bedwarmer affair. Mary helped get him chucked out." Definitely English. He was looking at Ceinwen in that annoyingly surprised way English people always did when an American said something intelligent.

"The English," said the woman, suddenly flirtatious. "Always persecuting the Catholics. Even the English Catholics."

"Oh yes. We've suffered."

Oh please. The man kept glancing at her, maybe wondering if an American who'd heard of Mary of Modena should be a museum exhibit, so she couldn't check her watch to see how much longer she had to suffer along with the downtrodden Catholics. "Let's move down here and see what we've got."

Another case, more tapping, more picking up and discarding, more Italian, more opinions—too old-woman, too flimsy, too heavy. One more case and one more set of taps. "Those."

"She needs a little more info, love," he said softly. Maybe he was trying to be nice. Longish hair and some lines on his face. Probably too much sun. English people were bad about that.

"I'm pointing at them." If nice was the idea, what was he doing with this woman? She was tapping at the back of the case. Ceinwen's eyes followed the nail. Oh no. Not those. Please not those.

"Which color?"

"The silver, with the enamel." Those. Goddamnit. She had put them on hold two weeks ago, waiting until she had the money, and in two more weeks they could have been hers. Lily had put them back in the case, and she'd been running around so much, she hadn't noticed.

"They're a hundred." They were more expensive than most of the other jewelry, and sometimes people recoiled from paying that much in a store that sold old clothes.

The woman rolled her eyes, said something in Italian, and then, "We don't care about the price." Ceinwen took the earrings out slowly and set them on the counter. No velvet. Maybe they'd look worse that way. And they wouldn't look good on this woman, either, not with that olive skin and long narrow face.

"Now those I like," said the Englishman, and Ceinwen was back to hating him.

"Miss." There was a pair of women at the other end of the counter. "Can we see that?" One was pointing at the back wall. She checked her watch as she walked over. 8:25. They wanted to see a hat, the black one with the net veil. Hats were a pain in the neck. People tried them on, giggled a lot, and never bought them. She took it down. Yes, it was wonderful that people used to wear hats. No, nobody knew how to wear them anymore. This one looks better if you tilt it forward a bit . . .

A hand closed on her elbow. Once again Lily was dragging her away, so that all parties could pretend that this exchange wouldn't be noticed. "What are you doing?"

"I'm showing a hat."

"Not them." Lily jerked Ceinwen's elbow so she turned to face the couple. "Them." The woman had put on the earrings and was absorbed in her reflection in the countertop mirror, angling her face this way and that. "What's happening there?"

"She's trying on the earrings." The Englishman was standing back, observing his girlfriend's varied pouts. Maybe he'd have the grace not to listen in.

"I know that. I see that. They're pierced. Pierced earrings." Her voice was rising. Answering Lily's questions was always like this. She got mad if you said nothing, because the answer was in front of your face, and she got mad if you responded, because you were stating the obvious.

"I was helping those ladies with the hats."

"And did you not tell her before you handed them over? Did you mention that there's a regulation, a fucking health regulation that says she can't try on the pierced earrings?"

The Englishman had turned and was easing closer. Yeah, your girlfriend got me yelled at. Now drop dead.

"Who are we supposed to sell them to now? Do we even have any peroxide or anything back there? I don't know what is going on with you, but what I do know—"

"Excuse me." The Englishman was in front of them.

"We'll be with you in a moment, sir." Back to Ceinwen. "You are in charge of what goes on behind this counter, and I should be able to trust—"

"I'm sorry, but it seems there's a misunderstanding." He wasn't going away.

"If you just give us a minute sir—"

"I wanted," he interrupted again—kind of nice to have someone interrupt Lily for a change—"to explain about the earrings. You see Seen When said—"

"What?"

"Seen When," he said, affably, "isn't that the name on her tag?"

Ceinwen hated her name tag for that very reason. "It's KINE-wen," she said.

A chuckle. "Sorry. Ceinwen." Awfully glad you think my name's funny, old bean. The woman hadn't glanced their way once. She was still at the other end of the counter, checking out the way the earrings laid against her neck. He lowered his voice. "Ceinwen did in fact tell my girlfriend she couldn't try on the earrings."

Lily rounded on Ceinwen and demanded to know why she hadn't explained. "I was trying to," said Ceinwen. Before Lily could go into why Ceinwen needed to try harder, the Englishman leaned in and spoke lower still. "Anna's Italian," he said, with an apologetic little grimace. "Bit of a language barrier. And when I tried to tell her, she said I must be wrong because she couldn't see how they looked without trying them on." This, she thought, is one smooth liar. "Anyway, no harm done. I think Anna's going to take them."

Ah-nuh, he pronounced it. She even hated his vowels.

"All right then," said Lily. "We're always glad when people find what they need. Ceinwen will ring you up." She walked past Anna and paused to check out the earrings. "Those are lovely. Art Nouveau. Very Mucha."

You bitch, thought Ceinwen helplessly, as Lily left to harass the men's side. She ran his credit card and gave the earrings a last pat as she put them in a box. Anna was still browsing the case, but the Englishman was watching Ceinwen as she twisted the tissue paper around the box and handed over the bag.

"Have a good evening." She couldn't bring herself to say thank you.

"You too," he said, then, lower, "and good luck." Ceinwen twitched her mouth into a half-smile and turned her back as they walked out.

Granana would have made her say thank you. The longer she stayed in New York, the worse her manners got. Then again, he'd stood right there while his girlfriend hadn't bothered to say thank you or please or anything else. Maybe in Mississippi she'd have been grateful. In Manhattan she'd had it with people who could act like that and worse, buy her earrings at full price.

The hat women had left during the earring episode. At least they hadn't taken the hats, which would have given Lily a reason to yell about security, along with punctuality and hygiene.

There were no more customers after that. They counted out the register in Lily's office downstairs, Lily remarking that the last sale of the night certainly helped. Ceinwen clocked out and walked home, wondering if whoever wore her dress before had had the same kind of luck with it.

The winding stone stairs to the sixth floor might once have looked like marble before years of pounding feet had worn a slope into the middle of each. They weren't that narrow, but they were steep even for the Lower East Side, and on a night like this she had to concentrate on not tripping. She was winded by the time she reached the top.

Jim was in the kitchen, cigarette dangling and coffeemaker going. How he could drink coffee all day and night mystified Ceinwen. She reached into a cabinet and grabbed a half-finished bag of Dipsy Doodles.

"Is that dinner?"

"Yep." She reached into the fridge for some seltzer. "I can't help it. Lily's been killing my appetite."

"You smoke too much and you don't eat enough." He ran his cigarette under the faucet and tossed it in the trash. "And what happened to your dress?"

He pulled at a side seam. It had ripped about two inches straight up, showing Ceinwen's torso almost to the edge of her bra. She didn't know when it had happened or how long she'd been flashing skin. For all she knew, this was why the Englishman felt sorry enough to lie for her. The little match salesgirl.

"Shit." She was almost in tears. Jim looked alarmed.

"It's not that big a deal, honey. That's what happens with these old clothes. The fabric holds up but the thread gets weak." He patted her shoulder. "Take it off."

She thrust a hip forward and said huskily, "What are you saying?"

"Take it all off, baby," purred Jim. He examined the dress again. "I can fix this. It's right on the seam. I'll do it now."

"Thank you, Jim." She undid the belt and the hooks on the side. Jim had seen her in her underwear or stark naked so many times that she didn't bother with formalities. Dress halfway over her head she said, "Want to watch a movie with me while you sew?"

A sigh. "Oh, all right. I'll mostly be looking at the needle anyway." He took the dress from her and turned it inside out. "I might stitch up this whole side."

"*The Ox-Bow Incident*? I just got it."

He looked suspicious. "I read that in high school. It's a Western, right?"

"More of a morality tale. Only," she admitted, "with cowboys."

"So a Western. You know I don't like Westerns. Neither does Talmadge. And wait, it's got lynching, doesn't it?"

"Talmadge would like Anthony Quinn."

"No."

"Dana Andrews was handsome."

"I'm not watching a lynching Western and that's final."

"How about *The Old Maid*?" He wanted to know the plot. Told that it involved Bette Davis' sacrificial mother love, he demanded to look at her video stash himself.

Ceinwen followed Jim through the living room where Talmadge was realigning the couch. It was a low-slung, high-backed, mauve-brocade affair that Jim had found in the street one Sunday night. The couch was beautiful, in a Victorian whorehouse sort of way, but it was missing a leg, which was how it ended up in the junk pile. After the three of them had pushed it upstairs—an operation that took nearly an hour and pissed off every neighbor they had, except Miriam, who was out—Jim positioned two cinder blocks where the leg should have been. This worked, but the couch was a touch shy of level. When they sat on it—and it was the only sitting option in the living room, aside from some floor cushions—the couch slipped a bit on the blocks. Every day it had to be moved back, and Talmadge had taken over this task.

Pushing the couch into perfect harmony with the blocks had become one of his rituals. Talmadge had a lot of rituals.

"Oh looky, it's another Ceinwen lingerie show." Jim didn't care if she wasn't dressed, but Talmadge kind of did.

"I'm getting my nightgown. And a movie."

"Which one?"

"I'm picking," called Jim, who was already in her bedroom running his finger down the rows. "Ceinwen wants all the depressing stuff. Because she obviously had a great day and she wants to make it even better."

"It's called perspective," said Ceinwen, grabbing the slip she wore as a nightie.

"It's called masochism." Jim pulled out a tape. "All right. How about this?"

"Yes!" hooted Talmadge from the doorway. "Marlene!"

She always sat in the middle of the couch where the back was highest; she pulled over an ashtray and propped her feet on the coffee table. Talmadge put in the tape and sat down with a pint of ice cream and a spoon. Jim went to work on the dress.

Ten minutes in, Ceinwen was blowing smoke at the ceiling and wishing she were on a train, reeling in the suckers with Anna May Wong. She felt so much better that she didn't even mind when she remembered Marlene Dietrich's name in *Shanghai Express* was Lily.

2.

I T WAS WEDNESDAY. PAYDAY WAS THURSDAY. THE RAIN STARTED SOON after Ceinwen arrived, and there were few customers. When Lily told her to go to lunch, she laid her assets on the counter and totaled them up. $1.28 in small change and half a pack of Marlboro Lights. As expected, Ceinwen was broke.

She could stretch the cigarettes until tomorrow, but food—food presented a problem. There was almost nothing in the house; she'd had the last of the pasta that morning. Talmadge, she knew, was also broke. He had some ice cream in the freezer, but he'd kill her if she ate it. Talmadge's ice cream was another nightly ritual. She could have hit up Jim before he left for work, but Jim seemed out of sorts, and she didn't want to bother him. Now she was regretting that decision. She had enough for a cup of coffee and a buttered roll, and that was it until 9:00 p.m. and a second chance at Jim.

She swept the coins back into her change purse. Time for Smelly Deli. She looked out the door—still raining. She pulled her coat over her head and dashed across Broadway.

Smelly was the name they'd given Demeter Deli, because of its Pine-Sol fragrance, which varied only in intensity—sometimes it was strong, most of the time it was unbearable. Smelly was a defiantly ugly place with lighting that made everyone look green. There were a few rows of junk food displays and a counter that made huge, cheap sandwiches, so it was always packed with NYU students. There were a handful of tables and chairs in the back, and seats were hard to come by, but the rain had kept the crowd down a bit and Ceinwen found a single empty table near the bathroom. She uncovered her coffee, spread out the paper wrapping for the roll and began tearing off one tiny piece at a time, hoping the bits would expand in her stomach. The problem was not chewing everything at top speed.

"Hello there."

That voice. Mr. Rule Britannia from Saturday night. His hair was damp and his shoulders were spotted with rain. An Englishman with no umbrella. "Is that place taken?" He had a sandwich in one hand

and a Coke in the other. She would much rather have had Coke than Smelly coffee.

"Go ahead." Too late to pretend she didn't remember him. She didn't want to be openly rude, but she didn't want him watching her eke out the roll, either. He was running a hand through his hair and putting his jacket on the back of the seat.

"I never did introduce myself," he said. "Ceinwen, isn't it? Matthew." He stuck his hand across the table as he sat down.

Both her hands had crumbs on them. She shook his hand, and he rubbed his fingers against his thumb to get the crumbs off. She was supposed to say something, and "Why are you people always named Matthew?" probably wasn't ideal. Well, she'd be damned if she was going to say "Where are you from?" She wasn't such a hick as to make a fuss over every accented jerk who said hello to her. Besides, she had an accent, too.

"You live around here?"

"Live and work. I'm at Courant. Over on Mercer."

"What's Courant?"

"NYU maths department."

Ceinwen took a sip. There was always something off about the coffee at Smelly, like it had absorbed the pine ambiance. "You look kind of old for a student." That was openly rude. For once she didn't care.

"I'm a postdoc. Been here since June. I teach a class, and I'm working on some papers with a professor there."

From the depths of her memory she dredged up the one question she could ask about mathematics that didn't involve counting out a register. "Pure or applied?"

"Applied," he said. "Probability." She was eating this roll too fast. It was more than half gone. She tore off another bit and popped it in her mouth, so that he wouldn't expect her to talk for another minute. He didn't say anything, just started eating his sandwich. It looked like roast beef, and at the moment it was considerably more interesting than he was.

"That isn't much of a meal," he remarked. "Did you eat earlier?"

"It's fine. It's all I wanted."

"Are you sure? You look a bit pale." So he could be rude, too. Although maybe, unlike her, he wasn't trying.

"I'm Irish. I'm always pale."

"If you're Irish," he said, sticking a straw in his Coke, "by which I assume you mean Irish descent, why do you have a Welsh name?"

"*How Green Was My Valley*. The book, Ceinwen's barely in the movie. My mother loved it." Wait a minute. "You know it's a Welsh name?"

"Yes."

"Then how come you didn't know how to pronounce it?"

"I do know how. I've even read the book." He smiled. "I was trying to lighten the mood." Down to one-quarter of the roll. Maybe she should just forget trying to stretch it out and gobble the rest so she could get out of here. "Did I?"

"Did you what?" And it was hard to make decisions while he kept looking at her.

"Lighten the mood?" He waited a moment, then, "Because it didn't seem that way." She chewed another piece. "It doesn't seem that way now. I don't know, I suppose I was expecting something else."

She swallowed. "Like what?"

He wasn't smiling anymore. "Like thank you."

"Thank you." She stuffed three pieces in her mouth at once.

"That was heartfelt." Not only was he not smiling, this was pretty much a glare. "See here. You're making it rather obvious you don't like me. Did I or did I not save your job?"

She shrugged. "Probably."

"Then please, tell me. How did I manage to offend you? You don't like the looks of me? You wanted to get fired and I ruined everything?"

The roll was gone and the words boiled up and out of her: "You bought my earrings."

He was lost. "You sold us your own earrings?"

"I mean I was going to buy them. I had them on hold. For myself. And that morning that c—*cow* I work for put them back in the case. And now they're with your girlfriend. In *Modena*," she added, with emphasis, to show she still knew how to pronounce it. And they didn't even look good on her, she thought.

"I'm sorry." He did look sorry. Good. "Why didn't you say anything?"

"You saw my boss. Would you cross her?" You could smoke at Smelly, thank god. Ceinwen grabbed the metal ashtray and pulled out her cigarettes.

"No," he said, "I don't suppose I would." She lit up and blew the smoke away from him. "Can't you get another pair?"

"They're one-of-a-kind. That's this designer's whole thing. Never the same design twice." She took another long, slow drag.

"You know, you shouldn't smoke while people are still eating."

Granana had always told her the same thing. She stubbed it out. "Sorry, I just do that automatically when I'm done."

"Why don't you eat something with me, then." He put a sandwich half on the paper in front of her. "Here. I can't possibly finish this."

"I'm not hungry."

For the first time, she was holding eye contact. His eyes were blue, and little lines fanned out from the corners. "That's odd," he said. "Because you've been staring at the sandwich ever since I sat down."

She looked down; it was roast beef. She took a bite so big she knew she'd left lipstick on her chin, covered her mouth with her hand and spoke behind it. "Thank you."

"You're welcome."

"For the record," she said, finally swallowing, "I don't think there really is a health regulation about pierced earrings. That's just Lily's thing." God this sandwich was good. Maybe he wasn't as irritating as all that, even now that he was trying not to laugh. "My friend Jim runs a little jewelry store uptown. They let everybody try on everything."

"Germ freak. She seems the type."

"I think she's paranoid about AIDS."

That killed the talk for a moment. It always did.

"So," he said, "did you read history?"

He asked the strangest questions, and he never looked away. "Like when, last night?"

"Sorry, I meant your major. History?"

"I didn't go to college." Ugh, a pickle. She drew it out of the sandwich and looked for others. "I work at Vintage Visions full time." He was feeding her, and trying to be friendly, but if he followed up by asking her what she *really* wanted to do, she was leaving and taking the sandwich with her.

"But you read history books, on your own."

"Sure. I like them better than novels. Well, I do read novels sometimes. Old ones." Three more pickles. Did anybody want that many? Had he asked for them?

"So you sell jewelry and you read history and old novels." He'd pulled his straw out of his Coke and was chewing on the end. "And hats. You sell hats."

Put like that, it sounded skimpy even to Ceinwen. "I also go to the movies a lot." She realized she was sucking the mayo off the side of a finger. Granana wouldn't have liked any part of her table manners today.

"Mm. Popular movies?"

What? "I don't try to pick the ones that people hate."

Everything she said was funny to this man. "As opposed," he said slowly, "to art-house stuff."

"Old," she said. "I watch old movies. Revival houses. That's what I like."

His eyes dropped to her suit. It was 1940s, padded shoulders, and she'd pulled her hair back to go with it. "Well then. You should talk to my co-author. He loves old movies too. Quite the buff. And he's almost seventy now. He met some of those people."

She leaned in. "Really? like who?"

"Don't know, not my sort of thing. I go to popular movies." Cute. "But Harry's famous, if you're a mathematician, and he's traveled. He told me he knew one director, did a movie with Cary Grant."

Ceinwen was almost bouncing in her seat. "Howard Hawks?"

"No, him I've heard of. This was a comedy. Married people."

Gee thanks, that narrowed it down. She remembered her watch. Six minutes left, just when things got interesting. "I have to get back to work," she said, and took her last bite.

He pulled a napkin out of the dispenser. "You should wipe your chin. Lipstick's a bit smudged." She didn't have a mirror with her, she'd have to check when she got back to the store. She swabbed at her chin. "That reminds me," he added. "Did you fix that dress?"

She looked at the red smear on her napkin. "Yes, it's fixed. You could have said something. I didn't see the rip until I got home."

"You seemed to have enough troubles." She got up and put on her coat. "Are we all right?"

"We're fine, why not?"

"You were scowling at me again." He grabbed his jacket.

"I just don't want to be late."

"Yes, I imagine that's a catastrophe." He was holding the door for her; the rain had slowed to a drizzle. "I go this way."

"Happy mathematics."

"Why, thank you."

She had made it to the corner when a name zoomed into focus. She turned to see if she could still see him on Broadway. Nothing. She ran down the wet sidewalk, trying not to slip in her heels, and saw him turning from Fourth Street onto Mercer.

"Hey!" He was still walking. "Matthew!" she bellowed. He stopped across the street from the brown glass and even browner brick of Courant. She waved her purse at him and ran across the street, earning a horn blast from a taxi trying to roll through the stop sign.

"Forget something?"

"No," she panted, "I remembered. Leo McCarey."

"Do I know him?"

"The professor, he knows him. Leo McCarey, was that the name of the director?"

"Um. Maybe."

"Could you ask him? *The Awful Truth*." No reaction. "Comedy. Cary Grant. Married people. Leo McCarey directed it. Didn't you see it?"

"No, Harry just told me about it." The rain was starting again. "I take it you like this movie."

"It's a great movie." She was late, really late, but she had to make sure he didn't forget, because if she could talk to someone who knew Leo McCarey, that would be even better than Miriam knowing about Jean Harlow's underwear. "You'll ask the professor, won't you? What's his name?"

"Harold J. Engelman."

"Great. I have to run now."

She was already halfway down the block when he called, "Once I find out, what do I do?"

"Bring him by the store," she yelled. "I'll sell you some hats."

3.

$\mathcal{S}$HE'D PLANNED TO LEAVE THE APARTMENT EARLY THURSDAY, BUT SHE stayed up late to watch *The Ox-Bow Incident*—by herself; Talmadge and Jim had gone dancing at the Pyramid—and she overslept. Now she would have to beg Lily to send her to lunch in time to cash the paycheck. Otherwise she'd be sponging off Jim again. She was barreling into the store when Roxanne the cashier stopped her. "There's a guy waiting for you over at the counter."

"Did he give a name?"

"Nope. Cute accent, though."

Good grief. What now? She started to walk away, then went back. "Where's Lily?"

"No worries. She's downstairs arranging some stuff for a shoot. Should be good for a half-hour."

She clocked in and went over. He had his back to her and was showing keen interest in the bangles.

"Hey," she said. She wondered if she should warn him about the bangles, even though Anna deserved them. "Those things are hideous." Honesty had won again. It always did.

"They are, at that." He held up a stack. "But I see them all over the students. Makes quite the racket in class."

"You could go for the rubber ones. We just got in orange."

"Those are worse." He might not know which earrings looked good on which women, but at least he had some sort of taste. She planted herself in front of him and waited.

"My colleague Harry wants you to come to dinner. So you can discuss Leo McCarey."

He was waiting for a reply, but she was trying to picture what led to this extraordinary invitation. He went back to his office and said, Guess what, professor. I've met a girl who's just as strange as you are. And she eats rolls for lunch. How's about we feed her?

"You asked him." She didn't mean to sound quite so pleased, but she was.

"Yes, and you wouldn't believe how excited he got. No, I suppose *you* would. I couldn't believe it. He says he has a hard time finding people who care about this sort of thing. And he loves having people for dinner. So he's insisting you come over so he can talk to you about this director and about a half-dozen movies. All of which he is now angry with me for not seeing, I might add."

Was she being set up with an elderly math professor? "Just me and him?"

He forced the corners of his mouth down for a second, then said, "No. You, me, Harry, and his wife. I think Donna is making garlic. There's some chicken as well. Usually."

A foursome. Was this in any way a good idea? She couldn't know whether Harry was as weird as she'd always assumed most mathematicians to be, but asking strange salesgirls to dinner suggested he might be an unusual sort of person. And the man in front of her who was running out of hats to contemplate on the back wall was basically a complete stranger, was years older than she was, had an uncommonly bitchy girlfriend, and she didn't know what he was up to, although she was beginning to get an idea.

"What night does he want to do this?"

"Up to you," he shrugged.

Maybe Harry lived on Washington Square. She'd heard NYU stashed some of its bigwigs in the houses on the park, and she'd always wanted to see inside one of those places. She needed more time to decide than she was probably going to get. "Do you want to see a hat?"

"No. Does anyone wear those things?"

"I do, sometimes, behind the counter. To get people to try them on."

"Do they?"

"All the time. And then they don't buy them."

"Harry talks a lot, but he's interesting." Matthew was hard to distract. She'd need more than hats. There was a great scene in *The Awful Truth*, where Cary Grant put on a hat and looked in the mirror, and it slid almost to his eyes, because the hat belonged to Alexander D'Arcy. The problem with the shot was that she wasn't sure she believed Alexander D'Arcy had a bigger head than Cary Grant. "Still deciding?"

"I was thinking about *The Awful Truth*."

"Of course you were," he said gravely. "I'm sorry I haven't seen it."

"No, you're not."

"No, I'm not, and yet I've spent the greater part of twenty-four hours hearing about it. For heaven's sake, come talk to Harry so I don't have to anymore."

Their eyes locked, and this time he went ahead and smiled. She told herself she hadn't turned down a free meal since arriving in New York. "I'm off work Mondays and Tuesdays."

"Tuesday then? Harry likes to eat around 8:30." He grabbed a card off the register and wrote down the address.

4.

IT TOOK HER AN HOUR AND A HALF TO GET READY TUESDAY NIGHT.

They all had their clothes on rolling racks that Ceinwen was reasonably certain Talmadge had boosted one by one from some downtown store dumb enough to keep leaving them on the sidewalk. Jim had wedged wood under the wheels to keep them stable, but if you yanked too hard, the wood came loose. She must have shoved the wood back a half-dozen times as she pulled out dresses and threw them onto the bed. She rejected velvet, strapless, halter, taffeta—well, taffeta was almost always a mistake. She could go casual, or even modern.

She refused to consider pants. The address wasn't on the park, and it had an apartment number, so it probably wasn't a townhouse, but still, a good neighborhood deserved a good dress.

Usually Jim had plenty of clothing advice, and he'd been helpful at first, but then she mentioned Matthew had a girlfriend. She added that she had no interest, that this was about Leo McCarey, and *The Awful Truth*, and maybe *Ruggles of Red Gap*. Jim said of course he believed her and disapproved from that moment onward. As she dashed out of the bedroom in one dress after another, Jim's disapproval followed one short step behind. It crawled down her zippers and curled around her shoe buckles. It was practically sagging her stockings.

Talmadge, on the other hand, was strongly in favor of dinner with a just-met spoken-for mathematician from Whoknowswhere, England, and his eccentric, movie-mad mentor.

"That's it!" he proclaimed when she came out in the last selection.

Jim was smoking furiously and sitting on the floor, which he did only when he was so fidgety he'd jostle the couch. "Way too fancy," he said.

"What are you talking about? It's gorgeous. I love it. Look at that skirt. Her waist looks tiny."

The dress was black, but there was nothing little about it. It was sleeveless, with a full skirt and a bateau neck, and it rustled. "I like it," said Ceinwen.

"What matters, sweetie," said Talmadge, "is that you feel good in it," which was what he always said to customers.

"She won't feel good," said Jim, ashing so hard he almost missed the tray, "when she gets there and everybody's in jeans."

"I like being a little overdressed," she said. "You know that."

"Then you're all set," said Jim.

Talmadge gave him a look. "Will you calm down? It's just a dinner. Ceinwen wants to make a good impression like the nice Southern girl that she is."

"She always makes an impression," said Jim. "In fact, I think she already has."

"You," said Talmadge, "are an old lady, you know that Jim?"

"Jewelry!" said Ceinwen. Jim went into his bedroom and shut the door. Talmadge helped her sort through her earrings and insisted on rhinestones, although they weren't exactly going to dress things down. At eight o'clock she rustled down the stairs, giving herself plenty of time to walk all the way west without working up a sweat.

She always thought life would be perfect in Greenwich Village, beyond the bars and restaurants, on a quiet street in one of the townhouses, big drapes parted. If you lived in a neighborhood this wealthy, she believed, you needed to be public-minded and let everyone have a peek. She wandered past a house on Grove, which had a grand piano, another on Bleecker with a chandelier that sparkled like something out of a Minnelli movie, and best of all, on Sullivan, the living room lined with bookshelves so tall there was a sliding ladder attached.

Window-shopping was her unalterable habit past Christopher. So was getting lost. She turned one way, turned another, decided she needed to loop back around, tried another side street, hit West Fourth Street at West Eleventh, and could have sworn she met herself coming back in the other direction. Finally she asked a woman walking her dog, got an answer she could use, and fetched up at Charles Street with disappointment; a drab apartment building with a narrow nonlobby that smelled faintly of something cooking. "Is that Ceinwen?" chirped a woman's voice on the buzzer. "Come on up."

The smells got stronger as the elevator climbed and she made her way down the hall. Before she could knock, the door swung open, and as the odor of roasting garlic almost blew her hair back, she faced an apple-shaped man who was sounding out in a stage-ready voice, "So this is the Leo McCarey fan!"

"That's me," she said. "How do you do?" All she could see were his eyebrows. They were the size of staplers, a mix of gray, white, and black, and every last hair stuck up or out. "Wait!" He had his hand out like a cop. "You can't come in yet. First you have to answer the question of the evening. It's very important." His face was square, the top of his skull was round, and his clothes looked as though they'd been thrown at him in a fit of anger. He stuck his hands in the pockets of his cardigan and said, slowly and dramatically, "*Love Affair* or *An Affair to Remember*?"

She didn't hesitate. "*Love Affair*."

The eyebrows lowered. She was going to be staring at those things all night. His voice dropped an octave and he drew the word out: "Why?"

"Charles Boyer and Irene Dunne. They're more romantic." Would he send her home if she didn't go for Cary Grant? Just in case, she added, "I love black and white."

"That," he announced, shaking her hand, "is the correct answer. Dinner will be ready soon." He stood aside and she walked in. "Donna is in the kitchen, and Matthew is sampling the scotch. I'll take your coat."

The hallway was narrowed by a long row of bookshelves. Harry waved her along behind him to a living room covered in books that went on and on without a break, pictures hung from the shelves at intervals as if the books were part of the wall. No ladder, but this was pretty great all the same. Ceinwen was trying so hard to make out titles—Nabokov, Henry James, tons of Trollope, an awful lot in French, though all she recognized was Maupassant, and hey, *The Death of a President*, Granana had that one, too—that she didn't notice Matthew coming over until he was almost on top of her.

"Evening," he said. Matthew was, in fact, in jeans, and he was holding his drink to one side. Did that mean he was going to do that European cheek-kiss thing? Oh lord, would she have to kiss him back? She stuck out her hand so fast she barely missed his drink. His mouth did its usual slight twist, and he shook her hand. He was checking out the dress.

"You like to mix up your eras, don't you," he said. "This is . . . sort of . . . *Happy Days*."

Happy Days? Was the man out of his mind? "It's called a Sabrina dress."

"1954. Billy Wilder," said Harry. "I approve. I'm going to put this in the bedroom. Donna will be right out."

"I'm here," said Donna, walking in. She was about a head shorter than her husband, gray-haired and freckled, wearing an apron and glasses on a cord around her neck. "Ceinwen, so nice to meet you," she said, with a kiss on the cheek. Maybe it was an academic thing, too. "What a lovely dress. Let Harry get you a cocktail, dear."

It hadn't occurred to Ceinwen that drinks might happen before dinner, and she had no idea what to ask for. Coke wasn't going to make her look very sophisticated. "What's everybody having?"

"Gin and tonic for me," said Harry, emerging from the bedroom. "Donna's having a sherry, which I do not recommend, and Matthew's well into the Laphroaig."

"That sounds good," said Ceinwen.

"The Laphroaig? I like this woman," said Harry. Ceinwen had meant the gin and tonic, but what the hell. "Up?" She glanced at Matthew's drink, which was straight. "Sure," she said. Harry poured a terrifying amount of scotch into a faceted highball glass. She took a sip and her tongue clamped to her palate. She'd tried scotch before, but what on earth was this? This was smoke and soil and a disturbing dash of Smelly Deli. She attempted an appreciative "mm" and set it down, hoping it got better as you went along.

"Leo McCarey," said Harry, settling on the sofa. "How does a person your age become a McCarey fan?"

She told him about all the time she'd spent watching cable TV in Yazoo City with Granana. Donna said it was sweet that she had a close relationship with her grandmother, did Granana live near them? Ceinwen said her mother died when she was ten, and Granana moved in to keep house. She was dead now, too.

"What does your father do?" asked Donna.

"He's got a farm," said Ceinwen. "Lives in town and goes back and forth." Harry wanted to know if her father liked movies too. How much more were they going to ask about him? "Not really," she murmured into her glass, and took another sip.

Matthew spoke up. "Aha. Granny was the family auteurist."

He came up with that pretty quick, thought Ceinwen. No, she and Granana were in love with Cary Grant, and Ceinwen would go to the library and check out books about Hollywood, and that was how she knew about McCarey. They finally left Yazoo City, and just as she was afraid they might stop in at Vintage Visions, it was on to McCarey.

Harry had been at City College in the fifties and sixties, and in the early sixties he and Donna had gone to California for a visiting professorship at USC. They'd been staying in Santa Monica and would run into McCarey around the neighborhood. One day, on impulse, they'd asked him to come to dinner and wound up at a restaurant. He wasn't especially warm, but he was witty, and Donna said he had good manners and wore nice clothes. He often had a bad cough, probably heralding the emphysema that would kill him in a few years. He never seemed very happy, Donna said, and Harry said he imagined McCarey wanted to be making movies, not puttering around Santa Monica. At dinner they had asked him about *The Awful Truth*. McCarey had been a bit guarded about Cary Grant, but went on and on about Irene Dunne, who was still his good friend. Dunne had been Granana's favorite actress, but Ceinwen didn't want to bring that up, either.

"I did get him to talk about *My Son John*," said Harry. Ceinwen didn't know that one. It was an anti-communist thing with Robert Walker, Harry told her. Nobody ever showed it anymore. Walker had died a few weeks into shooting, and it flopped. It wasn't much good, in Harry's opinion, but it had something. McCarey always did. Harry had told the director about a couple of scenes he liked, with Walker and Dean Jagger as his father, and McCarey had seemed pleased.

"So when he wasn't making comedies this chap was making anti-communist screeds." Matthew again. "How did your views go over?"

Harry's eyebrows bounced. "I was an academic in the 1950s. Believe me, I know how to stay off politics."

Matthew wanted to know about City College and Joe McCarthy and who was getting fired and what they wound up doing after they left. Harry must be fun to watch in class, she thought, even if he was teaching math. He said everything with big gestures and vocal italics, the eyebrows rising up and down along with the volume. And the blacklist reminded Harry that he wanted to tell Ceinwen about the time he sat next to Elia Kazan at a dinner in New York, before Kazan named names, and about talking to Joseph Losey in London during another stint abroad ("bitterest man I ever met") and another time he'd been at a party in Paris, and Elizabeth Taylor showed up with Michael Wilding. She was so beautiful he wound up excusing himself from the person he was talking to so he could go to the bar and stare at her for ten minutes, and Donna had joined him and stared, too.

The scotch did seem better now. It reminded Ceinwen of her cigarettes, which she hadn't had the nerve to ask if she could smoke after the McCarey discussion. Donna kept jumping up to check the chicken. Harry asked her about *Love Affair*, and *An Affair to Remember*, then a movie she hadn't seen, *Make Way for Tomorrow*. It was McCarey's best. She needed to see it, Matthew did too.

"Don't make them see that one," protested Donna. "It's the most depressing thing in the world. I was upset for days." Harry told her she couldn't just stick with Cary Grant movies all the time, and Donna said why not, and Ceinwen said that most of Granana's favorites were sad, like *Penny Serenade*.

"George Stevens," said Harry.

"Cary Grant," said Donna. "That one's a killer too."

"What's it about?" asked Matthew.

"This couple adopts a child," began Ceinwen.

"Never mind," said Matthew, "I'm depressed already."

When Donna announced that the food was ready, the glass was almost empty and Ceinwen felt pretty much as she had when she walked in. Then she stood up and felt one ankle turn over. This was an alarming development. Her heels were just two inches high.

"All right there?" inquired Matthew.

"Fine!" Would you please take your eyes off me for one minute so I can trip in peace? She made it to the dining room, took her seat without bunching her dress and got the napkin in her lap without dropping it. Matthew poured her some water. Harry poured her some wine.

"Behold," said Donna, setting down the chicken. "We have now arrived in the one room in this apartment without any books."

"I love the books," said Ceinwen. "I think you have just enough." Matthew was serving the chicken, and the portion he'd given her was enormous.

"It's taken me forty years to get a decent library together," said Harry, "and all she does is pester me to give them away." Ceinwen sliced in as carefully as possible—chicken on the bone was tricky—and realized Matthew was tracking each lift of her fork. He really did think she never ate anything.

"Harry used to have films, too," said Donna. "Dozens of them. And a projector and screen. I made him get rid of it all when we moved in here. He's still mad at me."

"When did you move in?" asked Ceinwen. The place looked settled, but maybe that was just all the books.

"1973," said Donna. "Ask him the date we sold the last reels. Go ahead, ask him."

"August 17," said Harry. "Tuesday. Hot as blue blazes."

"There was only one air conditioner," said Donna, "and Harry had it in the room with the all the movies. And then he wondered why I didn't want them around."

"Aren't they dangerous to store?" Ceinwen reminded herself to swallow before speaking. The chicken glistened with butter, the skin was crisp, there was garlic on every surface and in every crevice, and the wine was so good she'd just gulped like a farmhand.

"That's just nitrate," said Harry. "I didn't have any nitrate. It's all 35-millimeter anyway. Mine was all 16-millimeter. Safety film."

"Not everything, Harry. You're forgetting *The Crowd*. All nine reels of it. We only had that one a couple of months, but that was when I reached my limit, right there. Made me so nervous, I can't tell you, lying to customs when we came back from Europe. Can you imagine if we'd been caught? 'Math Professor Nabbed Smuggling Hazardous Goods.' Oh, I was glad to see the last of that stuff. You can't imagine how much room it takes up, too."

"What happened to the movies?" asked Ceinwen.

"Yes, don't forget the key data," said Matthew.

"Sold them to Andrew Evans."

That jolted Matthew out of his cool. "Andy? Are you serious?"

"Bought the lot," said Harry glumly. "I never should have let them go. And would he lend any to me later, or let me see something even for reference? Of course not. Always some excuse."

"Harry," warned Donna. "He's a colleague."

"He's a gibbering loon." Matthew choked. "You aren't going to contradict me here, are you Matthew?"

"Ah, no."

"I don't know why he wanted them anyway. Or maybe I do. Andy's thing is silents. That's his obsession. And I bet my collection is gone. I bet it's all turned into lobby cards and fan magazines and Chaplin two-reelers."

"I like Chaplin," said Ceinwen. She didn't care what they discussed anymore. Matthew could talk about the Red Scare all night. She even liked the salad. Yazoo City salads always seemed to include Jell-O.

"I do too, but some of my movies were valuable. Unless you're Andy. If it's got a soundtrack, he's not interested."

"Not surprising," said Matthew. "He's his own soundtrack."

"He tries hard," said Donna.

"He doesn't do anything of the sort," retorted Harry. He turned to Ceinwen. "When Kevin Brownlow was doing the restoration of *The Crowd*, he came here to New York, did you know that?"

Ceinwen knew nothing of Brownlow or *The Crowd*, let alone that it had been restored, so she said, "Really? Right here?"

"He was trying to track down some elements that were in bad shape. And he'd heard about my copy so he came to see me."

"Charming man," said Donna. "Very easygoing. Not at all like some of these film buffs."

"He's considerably more than a buff, honey. Of course I couldn't help him, so I sent him to Andy. And Andy told Brownlow he got rid of all his nitrate when he moved into Washington Square Village. Ha! I bet he did."

"It's difficult to imagine Andy getting rid of anything," said Matthew, "if you've seen his office."

"Oh, he has it. For sure he has it. That's probably the one thing of mine he did keep. He just doesn't want to give anything up, even temporarily. That's what he's like. He wants to have this stuff, he wants to know that it's his and that nobody else can have it. Screwball." Harry knocked back the last of his wine. "I'm ready for a refill, how about you Ceinwen?" He began pouring without waiting for an answer.

"Maybe he *didn't* have it," Donna reminded Harry. "You told him he should donate *The Crowd*, and he said he was going to after he had it copied."

"Andy says a lot of things."

"I don't see why he has to be lying," said Donna. "He couldn't store that stuff in his apartment, you know."

"He's lying," boomed Harry. "All right, not in his apartment, although he's such a hermit how would anybody know. He's got it at some secret facility." He pondered. "Probably in New Jersey."

"Why New Jersey?"

"What else is it good for?" Harry roared at his own joke.

"Andy's at Courant?" Andy sounded more like her idea of a typical mathematician.

"He's with the pure guys, two floors up from us," said Harry.

"Is he older?"

"You mean older than me? Are you wondering if that's possible?" She started to protest but he waved her off. "No, Andy isn't that old. If you're me and Donna, that is. If you're you and Matthew, he's ancient. Must be 50 now."

"Brilliant, though," said Matthew. "Nonlinear partial differential equations." Then, with a glance at Ceinwen's face, "Really fundamental work."

"Eh, he used to be brilliant," said Harry. Donna eyed his wineglass and shook her head slightly. "You know exactly what I'm talking about, and Matthew doesn't care. He did a big burst of great work in his twenties and thirties, got tenure, and he's been resting on his laurels ever since. Now he goes to collectors' conventions and can barely be bothered to grade his own students. Stores a million journals and papers in that office."

"I admit," sighed Donna, "the office bothers me. Such a nice big space and he's almost never there. And there's poor Matthew, stuck in that little room."

"It isn't bad," said Matthew. "More than I had at Cambridge. And there's always the flat."

"Where's that?" asked Ceinwen.

"Washington Square Village," hooted Harry. "Matthew's three floors above Andy. He can't get away from him."

"I don't see him much," said Matthew. "But when I have, it hasn't been pleasant. I wanted a back issue of SIAM . . ."

"Society for Industrial and Applied Mathematics," interjected Harry. "Ceinwen's going to think you were looking up Rodgers and Hammerstein. Or Irene Dunne. Did you see that one?" Ceinwen nodded. "Rex Harrison as the king. With hair."

"I needed an issue," continued Matthew, raising his voice slightly, "and it was missing from the library. So I asked to borrow it from him, because he must have them going back to the sixties. Not only did he claim he didn't have it, he said some journals were missing, and he really, really hoped people weren't taking them without asking. And as he's saying this, his voice is shaking, and he's looking at me as though I had them stuffed down my trousers."

"Yep. That's Andy all right," said Harry. "What do you think of *The Crowd*?" Ceinwen had to admit she hadn't seen it. Harry was horrified. "Have you seen it?" he demanded of Matthew. "Never mind, I know the answer. What's wrong with you two? Or rather, what's wrong with Ceinwen? I know what's wrong with Matthew."

"There's nothing wrong with Matthew," protested Donna.

"Nothing except his taste in movies. Go on, Matthew. Tell us, please. What was your number-one favorite movie of last year?"

Matthew looked resigned to his fate. "*Back to the Future.*"

Harry put his head in his hands. "Oh grow up," said Donna. "I liked it too."

"Well, I didn't. Cars. Thunderstorms. That crazy Christopher Lloyd running around mugging. Because he's a scientist," yodeled Harry, waggling his hands near his ears. "Did he remind you of any scientists we know? Even Andy?"

"He isn't supposed to remind us of real people. It's a fantasy," said Matthew. "Movies are nothing but fantasy."

"In my fantasies," shot back Harry, "I don't want a bunch of incest gags. And I'll tell you another thing—" he pointed at Matthew's chest.

"Watch out, he's got the finger going," said Donna.

"I'll tell you another thing." Harry waved the finger over his head. "*The Crowd* is not only the greatest silent movie ever made, and I've seen nearly as many as our addle-pated friend from Courant, it's one of the greatest movies ever made in this country, period. It was years before they could replicate some of those shots. It takes the life of an ordinary man and turns it into poetry. Harsh, dark, truthful poetry." The finger was pointing at Matthew again. "It makes that movie with the stomach creatures look like a Porky Pig cartoon."

"Stomach creatures?" repeated Ceinwen.

"*Alien*," said Matthew. "I told him to rent it. And I'll never hear the end of it." Ceinwen started laughing and so did Donna. "Plenty of critics liked that one too. I'm not an outlier."

"Critics and their pets," said Harry, with a hand-wave broad enough to scare off all aliens. He took his last sip of wine. "Are we ready for coffee?"

They moved back to the living room and Harry immediately began saying they needed to see more silents.

"So we can be more like Andy," said Matthew.

"Logical fallacy, my friend. Because Andrew Evans watches silent movies, it does not therefore follow that watching silent movies makes you act like Andrew Evans."

"It doesn't exclude the possibility, either."

Ceinwen ate four cookies and ignored her coffee as Harry talked about King Vidor and *The Big Parade* and asked her what silents she'd seen, and she came up with *City Lights* and *The Gold Rush*. Also *The Birth of a Nation*, which she'd hated.

"I thought all Southerners worshipped that one," said Matthew.

Was he kidding? He better be. "I don't like Klan movies."

"Good girl," said Harry. "Griffith should have ended that one when Lincoln got shot." He was flipping up pictures, pulling books off the shelf, handing them to Ceinwen and insisting she borrow them. *The Parade's Gone By*, by the Brownlow person he'd mentioned. *The Movies*, a huge book that Harry said had a lot about silents. He was reaching for something called *American Silent Film* when Donna stopped him and asked if he'd mistaken poor Ceinwen for a Teamster. Harry said Matthew could carry them, and Ceinwen felt *The Movies* almost slide off her lap. She better go home before she did something embarrassing. Harry went to another room for another book, and Matthew went to get her coat. He was going to walk out with her. She hoped she didn't trip.

Donna patted her arm. "It's been wonderful having you, dear. We're so glad Matthew brought you over to meet us."

That sounded funny. What was Donna thinking? Ceinwen tried to work out a pithy way to clarify, and came up with, "Matthew's nice." Then, "Have you met Anna?"

"Oh yes. She's lovely."

Donna didn't like her either. So that was why they didn't mind Ceinwen coming to dinner.

Matthew wanted to carry the books as Harry had instructed—"Bring them back anytime, I've read them already"—but Ceinwen wanted something to do with her hands and she flat-out refused to hand them over. She clutched the books and tried to figure out the right walking space—arm's length? Half an arm?

"You're a hit," said Matthew. "I haven't seen Harry that animated in yonks."

"He's wonderful," she said. Harry made her feel normal. "He's really famous?"

"Invented half the things we're working on."

"Funny how brains work," she said. "He's a genius, but he couldn't remember the title of *Alien*."

Matthew let out the biggest laugh she'd heard from him. "Of course he remembered. He was taking the piss." She hadn't heard that expression before, and she didn't think she liked it. "Harry was a child prodigy. He could read the front page of the *New York Times* once and recite it back almost word for word. His parents used to have him do it at parties."

"Did Anna like him?"

That was a mistake. "Yes, she did."

She'd already messed up, might as well do it big. "What does she do, is she a mathematician too?"

"Economics."

Mathematics and economics. Fun couple.

"The two subjects do rather go together." Damn, she'd said that out loud. She really was drunk. And here was Washington Square Village. "How much further do you have to go?"

"A few blocks that way." She jerked her head east. She didn't want to have the Alphabet City safety discussion, especially not with him mad at her.

"How many is a few?"

"Three," she lied.

"What's that, near Third? Not Bowery, surely? I'll walk you there."

"It's a little past Third . . ."

"Ceinwen. Is there a reason you don't want to tell me where you live? I'm not going to mug you."

She never got away with anything. "I'm on Avenue C."

"*Avenue C*? First of all, that's quite a bit more than three blocks."

"It isn't that far."

"Second, isn't it dangerous at this hour?"

"Of course it's not dangerous." She drew the books close to her chest and stood tall. "I," she announced grandly, "am friends with all the derelicts."

"What does that mean? Do you buy their beer?"

"They say hello to me. Every day."

"Lovely. And that doesn't worry you."

"It does, a little," she confessed. "Like, I worry one day there'll be a derelict who doesn't like me."

"You're taking a taxi."

"I walk home all the time." Because I can't afford a taxi. Why do you think I put earrings on hold?

He was already out on Third Street looking down the road. He got a cab almost immediately and opened the door for her. She thanked him for inviting her, he said, "Pleasure" and "I'll stop by the store again" and then they were pulling away. She shoved the books to the other side of the seat and felt around in her bag for the first cigarette she'd had since leaving Avenue C hours ago. She'd insulted his girlfriend and strongly implied that mathematics was boring; she might as well have smoked all night.

5.

HER STOMACH WAS BURNING AND HER HEAD SWELLED WITH PAIN every time she turned it on the pillow. She threw on her slip and headed for the kitchen, but paused near the door.

"I was snarfing all night. I'm still congested." Talmadge was blowing his nose, but even from the door he didn't sound that bad.

"So wash your hands," Jim said evenly, "and cover your mouth."

"But you know the guy from the Crisis said it wasn't safe."

"He said it wasn't safe if you had flu or something. Are you trying to tell me you're feverish?"

"I don't know, I can't find the thermometer."

"You broke the thermometer two weeks ago when you took your temperature to try and get out of going that time. Will you stop?"

They were arguing about going to see Stefan. This was another one of Talmadge's rituals, and Ceinwen always tried to let it play out without her in the room. She leaned against the wall and waited quietly; it wouldn't take long.

She had met Stefan only twice, at the store, a tall man with a shock of blond hair and a wide mouth. He had been polite, but he was nothing like Jim and Talmadge, who had started flirting and cracking jokes within minutes of meeting her. "He likes you," Talmadge apologized, "but Stefan isn't all that crazy about girls." He was Talmadge's oldest friend, the first friend he had made in New York. Talmadge was always vague about exactly what he did when he went out with Stefan in the early days, and she never pressed him. "I don't ask him either," said Jim.

But the early days ended when Stefan joined AA, at which point Talmadge started to see less of him. Talmadge wanted to keep drinking, and did. "I loved him, but I'd never have moved in with him then," said Jim. "Never. Drunk he was doing Marlene imitations and coming on to everything but the swizzle sticks. Hungover he was Baby Jane Hudson."

Talmadge might have kept on forever had he not fallen asleep one night on the Q train, which wasn't even his line, and woke at dawn in Brighton Beach, still a bit drunk, his wallet and big topaz ring missing and, he told Ceinwen, "it took me half an hour to figure out why the fuck everyone was speaking Russian."

He called Stefan and they went to a meeting, but Talmadge didn't take to the process. "Oh god, sweetie, it was brutal," he told her. "Brutal. I don't know what to compare it to. Sunday school. Or Lily telling me about one of her dates." Stefan argued, but Talmadge objected to everything—the endless talking, the chairs, the lighting, the insufficient number of sufficiently attractive men.

Most of all, he objected to the Higher Power business, which wasn't something you got to skip. "Everybody insisted, and I finally came up with one," said Talmadge. "Marlene Dietrich. Especially *The Scarlet Empress*. I thought that was a great idea. That's power." She gathered that despite Talmadge's sincerity—he really did think Marlene would have been happy to help him out—his bad attitude remained. After about a half-dozen meetings he stopped going, and no amount of Stefan's pleading could get him to return. Instead of going to AA, he'd call Stefan, and they would go out for macrobiotic food, and Stefan would talk him down.

Bit by bit Stefan made Talmadge go through the steps, eventually getting to all of them, or so Talmadge claimed. "Even Marlene?" she'd asked. "Especially Marlene," said Talmadge. "She's very understanding."

He tried to make amends with Jim. "He wanted to tell me all about how sorry he was for leaving me in the men's room at Limelight when he met some dockworker, and that he was sorry for all the times he stole my customers," said Jim. "Be glad you didn't know him while this was going on. It took days. He kept coming back with stuff he'd blacked out, like the time I left a big tip for a cute bartender, and when I turned my back, he used it to buy another couple of margaritas. I hadn't even realized how often he screwed me over. And then he went back to Stefan, and Stefan told him that he knew damn good and well he'd done bigger things to me than that, and Talmadge started apologizing to me about those, and I told him to tell Stefan that Marlene understood and so did I."

Talmadge hadn't had a drink in three years, but now Stefan was sick. The conversation in the kitchen had paused, and she needed coffee in a bad way, so she walked in.

"Good morning, starshine," sang Talmadge.

Jim peered at her. "There's still some coffee. Talmadge and I are just leaving."

"I want to hear how everything went!"

"My head hurts," said Ceinwen. "I guess professors drink a lot."

"You've had NYU students in the store. Do you blame them?" said Jim. He was pouring coffee for her.

"Which professor was drinking?" said Talmadge. "The old one or the one you like?"

"They both were. The old one is sweet. The other one's okay. Kind of annoying at times." She tasted the coffee and wrinkled her nose. "Cafe Busted?"

"It was all I could get last night," said Jim. Cafe Busted was Cafe Bustelo, a lethal Cuban coffee that none of them liked, but which was cheap and effective.

"All right, the annoying one you wore your best dress for. Is he going to call?"

"I didn't give him my phone number," said Ceinwen. "He has a girl-friend."

"Talmadge," said Jim, "get your jacket. We're leaving."

"Ceinwen looks all in," said Talmadge. "We should get her some breakfast. Something good and greasy."

"Talmadge," said Jim. "We're leaving. So get your fucking jacket."

When Jim swore, you moved. Talmadge edged toward the kitchen entrance, then stopped.

"You didn't do anything dumb like ask about the girlfriend, did you?"

"I mentioned her at the end of the evening," she admitted.

"No, no, you didn't! Oh, sweetie . . ."

Jim threw up his hands. "Why shouldn't she mention his girlfriend? He's gonna have one whether Ceinwen brings up her up or not. We're leaving. You know the earlier we make it there the better he is."

Talmadge went to get his jacket. Jim said, "He's really pushing it this morning. If you ask me, he should give those meetings another try."

"He always goes in the end, you know that. This is his way of psyching himself up." Jim was picking at something stuck to the kitchen counter. "I could come too," she said, "before work. Maybe he'd like seeing someone different."

"That's sweet, honey, but right now I'm not sure he'd even remember you." Talmadge reappeared, clutching a tissue to show he wasn't dropping the cold-in-an-AIDS-room issue. Jim kissed her and headed for the door. Talmadge kissed her too and said, "I bet you anything he shows up at the store today. You just watch. Now go get some eggs and bacon."

She got her eggs and bacon at the tiny coffee shop two blocks away, as well as a Coke that settled her stomach and cleared her head. But Matthew never appeared that day, nor the next. The books, at least, kept her occupied.

At work she kept looking toward the front door whenever she wasn't helping anyone, until Lily caught her and remarked that it was no wonder her sales were down, since she spent all her time in a trance like this was a fucking ashram. Talmadge was still working the early shift so Ceinwen often went to lunch with Roxanne. Roxanne had been her first friend at the store. She was from Trinidad, a stunningly good-looking girl who was also very good-natured, but she really only wanted to talk about her boyfriend, and also apartments.

About a week after the dinner she went to the benches in front of Courant to smoke her cigarette after lunch, and she watched the people filing in and out. A lot of Asians. Not a lot of women. A lot of men, young and old. None of them Matthew. As she ground out the cigarette she reflected on how embarrassing it would be if he found her there, looking at the building like Edward G. Robinson keeping vigil for Joan Bennett in *Scarlet Street*, and she resolved not to go back.

Tuesday afternoon she trekked uptown to a silent movie at the Thalia, Greta Garbo and John Gilbert showing off their love affair in *Flesh and the Devil*. When the ladies room cleared out, she took a stab at a Garbo smolder for the mirror. Only Garbo, she thought, could smolder while she was taking communion. She wished she didn't always have to go to the movies by herself.

That evening it was her turn to buy coffee, and she had enough money to upgrade from Cafe Busted. She was about to turn into the bodega when she spotted Miriam, carrying a pocketbook and walking down the avenue. Ceinwen paused a moment, then followed.

Now here was behavior Talmadge could justifiably call obsessive, but maybe she'd spot Miriam meeting someone and get an idea of where she was always going. She kept following until Miriam turned into the Key Food near Fourth Street. Ceinwen stood on the sidewalk, dumbfounded. Grocery shopping. How's that for boring. Served her right for being so nosy. She was about to turn and go back to the bodega, when it occurred to her that while she'd always been afraid of the big, ill-kept, funny-smelling Key Food, the coffee selection might be worth the risk.

She didn't know how she was going to translate groceries into a conversation about Jean Harlow's underwear, but she'd at least get a chance to try. And what else did she have to look forward to? More books.

Recording more movies off the TV. More cigarettes, more planning her outfits. Tomorrow maybe lunch with Roxanne and a long talk about how Roxanne's boyfriend never wanted to go out anymore because he was studying for the bar. She pumped on her toes in front of the automatic door for a minute, trying to get the sensor to sense her and thinking, I'm not *that* short, when a man swept around her and pushed it open. She followed.

How did Miriam find anything here, wondered Ceinwen, as she surveyed the sad-looking produce and the large, malformed root vegetables she'd never seen or even heard of before. She turned to walk down the back, checking each aisle for Miriam. Lots of mothers with fussy kids, a number of tired-looking men, nobody her age. She turned into the coffee aisle and grabbed a can of Melita, then walked back again and checked another aisle. Back in Yazoo City the Winn-Dixie was huge and spotless, and the aisles were so wide you could fit four or five carts across each of them. Everything in this place was narrow and dirty. So was the bodega, but at least it was manageable: you didn't have to waste all this time trying to figure out where everything was.

There was Miriam, a basket over her arm, running her finger down a row of canned goods. Ceinwen checked the aisle sign to prepare her make-believe shopping mission. Soup. She hadn't bought canned soup since she'd cooked for Granana, but it wouldn't kill them to have some around the apartment. She breathed out, which was what Talmadge always told her actors did to warm up, and walked behind Miriam.

"Hey, Miriam." Miriam didn't jump. It was a good question as to what would make her jump. She turned and gave the slightly friendlier look she'd been giving for a couple of weeks now, the sides of the mouth almost going up, but not quite.

"Hello," said Miriam. And went back to the shelf. Ceinwen checked the cans beyond Miriam's arm.

"Excuse me, I'm trying to reach the"—she scanned—"minestrone." She hated tomato soups.

"Please," said Miriam, and stood aside. Then, "I'm trying to pick out a stock. Do you have a favorite?"

Stock? What—wait, that was a cooking word for broth. She'd heard Jim use it.

"I always get what's cheapest," said Ceinwen. "My grandmother used to say they were all the same."

"She's probably right," said Miriam. She took two cans off the shelf and put them in the basket, next to a quart of milk, onions, and greens. An old lady shouldn't have that much on her arm.

"Let me carry that for you," said Ceinwen.

"Thank you, but I'm fine."

"No, really," insisted Ceinwen, putting her hand on the handle, "we're going the same way, and all I needed was coffee. And soup," she remembered to add.

Miriam hesitated, then handed it over. "That's very kind of you." Ceinwen tossed her coffee and soup in the basket—maybe Jim liked minestrone—and they started toward the checkout line.

"I was talking to my roommate Talmadge the other day."

They'd reached the line, which wasn't long, but the lady ahead of them had a full cart. Miriam turned her head, looking interested for the first time. "Talmadge, did you say? Is he the blond?" Ceinwen nodded. "There were a couple of silent movie stars with that name."

"Norma and Constance," she said. Miriam didn't look impressed. If Ceinwen had brought up Norma and Constance at dinner, Harry would have been floored.

"Yes." It didn't matter that Ceinwen had learned of the Talmadge sisters only a week ago from one of Harry's books—she wasn't getting nearly enough credit here. "Is your roommate related?"

"I asked." Last week, but still. "He doesn't think so. It's just his middle name. He likes it better than Albert." They were close enough now for Ceinwen to start unloading the basket. "Anyway, Talmadge and I were wondering if you knew Jean Harlow." She concentrated on piling Miriam's groceries so they wouldn't get mixed up with the other lady's items. "Because you were telling me about what she wore."

"Yes, I knew her."

How could someone say "I knew Jean Harlow," then, silence, as if that was all the information a normal person would want?

"Did you work with her?"

"In a manner of speaking. I worked on her clothes."

At last, the motherlode. "You were a costume designer?"

"I was a seamstress. At MGM. No, that's separate." The cashier was about to ring Ceinwen's coffee in with Miriam's groceries.

She better not ruin things by blurting out a bunch of questions. Better to ask bit by bit. She'd start easy. "Nice woman?"

"Who, Harlow? Why yes, very. She was always playing tramps, but she came from a good family, and she'd been well brought up."

Except she didn't wear underwear, but this seemed like a bad moment to remind Miriam of that, strategically speaking. Miriam was paying. Ceinwen told her to wait and she'd carry the groceries back to the apartment. She paid for her two cans, and they started back.

A seamstress. I'm an idiot, thought Ceinwen. All I could imagine was actresses and stars. MGM was a huge studio, full of people doing all kinds of jobs. Carpenters. Set decorators. Prop managers. And the seamstresses. And they probably all had stories. "Was it a fun job?"

"If you like sewing."

God forbid Miriam should throw her a bone here. "Do you? like sewing?"

"I suppose. I'm good at it. I make my own clothes still." Ceinwen's eyes darted down to the skirt hem that hit exactly where it should. Of course. You couldn't be old, with every part of your body in a different place from where it was, and have clothes that fit well, unless the clothes were made for you.

"Did you stay there a long time?"

"Until I got married. Right after the war ended."

"And then you moved to New York?"

"Oh no, not then. My husband was a stage manager. We traveled around to regional theaters for a long time. I sometimes did costumes. He got a job here in 1962." They paused for the light.

"What made you pick Avenue C?"

Miriam gave a little half-smile. "It was cheap. You didn't grow up here, did you?"

"No," said Ceinwen. Do I sound like I'm from Avenue C? "I'm from Mississippi. You ever been there?" People who had usually didn't ask why she moved.

"Yes, just once. We did a season outside of Jackson."

"Did you like it?" Miriam, for once, seemed to be searching for words. "It's okay, I never liked it much myself."

"In the fifties . . . the hiring practices were troublesome. So was the seating. Of course it was like that almost everywhere. But in Mississippi they were more . . . enthusiastic about it, I suppose you could say."

That was good news, at least. Miriam was a liberal. Seems like we all wind up in New York sooner or later, she thought. They'd reached the building. The street lock was still broken. Ceinwen stood to one side to let Miriam go up the stairs ahead of her. When they got to Miriam's door, Ceinwen was more worn out than usual because she hadn't gone at her own pace. Miriam unlocked the door and held it open. Ceinwen got a few feet into the hall and stopped.

The layout seemed the mirror image of their apartment, but it was as though she were in a different building, a different neighborhood. The walls were completely smooth, the wood trim was stripped and polished, and she realized that underneath all that paint their molding was probably oak. There was an Oriental runner down the parquet floor of the hall. The transoms were clear glass, and there was a glass-paned door at the end of the hall.

Miriam moved past. "I'll just put this in the kitchen. You can step in for a moment." Ceinwen recovered, continued to the living room and stopped again.

She'd gotten glimpses of other apartments in the building: worn linoleum and bumpy walls painted beige or white. No difference. Miriam had gold wallpaper with a Chinese print, and carpet—old people did like their carpet—that was spotless and still plush. She spied full-length drapes and sheers at the windows, and in front of them was a tufted sofa, with all its legs. Next to that a high-backed chair like in men's club scenes in English movies, and in front of the sofa a low coffee table with an inlaid top. On a sideboard sat a hurricane lamp with a landscape painted on both glass globes. Set by a wall was a china cabinet Granana would have killed for.

"This is beautiful." Look at that, there used to be French doors between the two living rooms in these apartments. We were robbed.

"Thank you," said Miriam. "Wait here, I'll put it away."

"I never knew any apartments on Avenue C looked like this." Since Miriam hadn't told her to leave, maybe she would offer her a drink—sherry? Cognac? Ceinwen walked over to a round table, covered with a thick damask cloth that had a tassel weighing down one corner. On the table were a bunch of photos. Mostly vacation shots, it seemed.

"I've had plenty of time to decorate," Miriam called from the kitchen. Ceinwen didn't reply. She was peering at a large photo in the back, sepia, in a silver frame with leaves and flowers twined around the edges. She leaned in to get a better look, and suddenly the picture was in her hand, so fast she wasn't conscious of picking it up.

It was Miriam, she knew it was. Same features, but young, full makeup, dark hair half up and half down, a glittery ribbon wound through it. She was wearing a high-waisted dress and a pearl necklace, and her hand was posed delicately under her chin.

Ceinwen might not know all that much about silents, but she knew a publicity shot when she saw one. This was Miriam in period costume, sometime in the late 1920s, from the looks of the hair and makeup.

Seamstress, my ass.

Down at the bottom she could see writing, in a high-styled, hard-to-read hand. She held the picture closer. "To my darling Emil—All my love, always—" The "all" and "always" were underlined. And under that, a row of xoxoxos, and the name, Miriam.

"I wanted to thank you for helping me with my groceries." She almost dropped the frame. She put it back and turned around in dread. Miriam was standing there with a face that made Ceinwen feel like a burglar.

"Oh, you're welcome." Should she apologize for looking at the picture, or would that make it worse?

"I don't want to keep you." The same kiss-off she'd gotten in the lobby. Man, Miriam was furious. Why have pictures out if you didn't want people to see them?

She tried to think of a way to say she had nothing to leave for, and said, "Have a good evening."

"Thank you. You too."

She was out in the hall and listening to the snick of the deadbolt almost as soon as the sentence was finished. She'd never been so thoroughly eighty-sixed in her life.

Jim was in the living room, dusting. Talmadge was in the kitchen getting his ice cream. She started to tell him about Miriam, but he didn't seem to care. Marlene was the only old star Talmadge really wanted to hear about, and she'd been at Paramount. Forget it, then. She was going to figure the whole story out by herself and spring it on them. They'd both realize she'd been right: finding out more about Miriam was worth the time.

The news about the French doors, however, was huge.

"How do you like that," huffed Jim. "I bet those junkies sold them."

"The ones before us? How do you know they were junkies?"

"Wax in the sink," said Talmadge. Ceinwen nodded, wondering what a junkie needed wax for. She'd find out some other time.

Jim was running his hands over the molding and muttering about laziness and philistines. "This must have been a nice building once. It's still got the jets."

"The what?"

He led her to the hall and pointed to something poking out of the wall, like a small faucet. "Gaslight," he said. She reached up and felt the bottom—a key that would have turned, before it was crusted with paint. She pictured herself as Ingrid Bergman, twisting the flame up and down while she listened to Charles Boyer's footsteps above.

She went into her room early and started consulting Harry's books. Her first job was to find out who this Emil was. Maybe the man Miriam married? The name Emil Gibson sounded kind of ridiculous (assuming Miriam had changed her last name), but then again she'd heard a lot worse in Yazoo City.

She went through the indexes. Precious few Gibsons, none of them named Emil. Could be a middle name. Or a nickname. No, it probably wasn't Gibson at all. You didn't go all ice-cold over someone seeing a photo you gave your husband, did you? You got upset if it was something you didn't want to discuss. And not like a creepy relative, either. Like a lost romance. Ceinwen decided to go with that assumption, mostly because it improved the plot.

The only famous Emil who fit the time period was Emil Jannings; she knew him from watching *The Blue Angel* three times with Talmadge. She wasn't crazy about him. He had good moments, like after Lola's final betrayal, but other times he was too much, as though he were on stage and playing to the balcony. According to the books, he'd made *Blue Angel* when he returned to Germany after sound came in, and eventually the Nazis chose him to head up the main German film studio during the war.

Miriam in love with a fat, hammy Nazi. In love with him enough, furthermore, to scrawl a bunch of hugs and kisses across the bottom of a photo she gave him, then get the picture back from him—somehow—and keep it in a fancy silver frame for the next fifty-some-odd years.

Even Ceinwen's fantasies couldn't accommodate that much . . . fantasy. It probably wasn't an actor at all.

It was well past 1:00 a.m. when she reluctantly switched off the light.

OCTOBER / NOVEMBER

I.

EACH NIGHT BEFORE BED, CEINWEN SEARCHED *THE PARADE'S GONE BY* and tried to find another Emil—a director, a cinematographer, a producer, an art director, a stunt man. Nothing. Nothing in *The Movies*, nothing anywhere else. She decided to attack the problem from another angle, and went through every actress, looking for a Miriam. There weren't any.

Lily had taken a rare Saturday off, Talmadge was in charge, and the atmosphere was festive, or would have been, had Ceinwen not been stuck with a middle-aged lady who couldn't decide between a choker and a pendant. She gently tried to steer the woman toward the pendant, decided gentle wasn't working, and started saying things like pendants were more youthful (although that wasn't strictly true), at which point, due to boredom, she happened to glance toward the front of the store, where she saw Matthew speaking to Roxanne. She had managed not to think of him all day, or at least only twice, which was very close to zero and thus barely counted, and there he was, strolling down the aisle toward the jewelry cases as if no time had elapsed since their last meeting.

He didn't pretend to look in the case. He leaned against the far counter, gave a wave and waited. Ceinwen's sales patter took on desperation. The necklace was twenty dollars, and this woman was carrying a Chanel purse. If she didn't make up her mind soon, Ceinwen was ready to take down some hats and see if she could keep her occupied that way. She finally decided on the choker, and Ceinwen handed her over to Roxanne.

Matthew was still leaning. He didn't look so hot. In Mississippi, if you finally laid eyes on someone who'd disappeared for a couple of weeks, you'd say, "Where the hell you been?" What would you say in England? She walked over and clasped her hands behind her back.

"To what do I owe the honor?"

At least he looked startled. "Harry gave me homework."

She looked around the counter. "What do you have to buy?"

"A movie ticket," he said. "To *The Crowd*."

He was going to ask her, she realized with a little flare of happiness. But that didn't mean it had to come easy. "Great. Let me know how you like it."

He put his elbows on the counter, which probably foretold an explanation. "I would have stopped in sooner"—yep—"but we were trying to work out this proof together. And it wasn't going well, so I was staying late at the office. And yesterday Harry walked in and told me the whole thing was a nonstarter. He'd been giving a talk up at Columbia, and he got on the subway and started thinking about another idea, and he realized our angle couldn't be done. Four months of work. Poof."

She wasn't sure it worked as an excuse, but she did feel a little sorry for him. "Just sitting on the subway? What was he looking at?"

"No idea. A derelict, possibly. In any event, that's that. We have to start over. So today he came in"—Mathew took a folded sheet out of his pocket—"and said this sod—erm, silent movie is playing somewhere called Theatre 80 St. Marks. He said it's tonight only and ordered me to see it." He paused for a second or two, then continued when she didn't speak. "Threw me out of the office. Threats were made against my job."

"Aw, Harry wouldn't do that."

"Probably not. But he did bring up the word 'recommendations' in an ominous sort of way." Another pause. "So here I am."

"Here you are," she agreed. He needed to suffer some more.

"It's at 9:30." She waited it out. "Would you like to go?"

She put her elbows on the counter. "Did Harry order you to take me?"

"He mentioned it."

Harry's idea. Damn. "He's probably right. It's probably a great movie. There's a whole chapter about it in one of the books he lent me. There's one shot of hundreds of desks—I saw a still—and Billy Wilder stole it when he made—"

"Does that mean yes?"

"—*The Apartment*. I don't know, I'm tired."

"This should buck you up. Almost two hours of poetry. Hard poetry."

"That's harsh poetry."

"Right, my mistake. Harsh, dark, truthful poetry. Got that again tonight. I hate to say you owe me, but you do."

She decided it was time to straighten necklaces and opened the case. She smoothed out one, she smoothed out another.

"Of course, if you already have plans . . ."

"I get off work at nine," she said. "I'll meet you there at a quarter after."

It didn't take fifteen minutes to walk to Theatre 80, so she had some time to kill. She watched Talmadge bring the gates down in front of the store. From his post on the men's side he'd been checking out the conversation with Matthew, and he had opinions to deliver.

"You had me thinking he was forty at least. He's not that old at all. And he's cute. Sort of." Talmadge was trying to get the padlock fastened. "For an English guy, he's incredibly cute."

"I didn't say he was forty, I said he's older than me."

"He likes you." Talmadge finally had the lock through the gates.

"I guess. I didn't think he was going to show up again."

"But he did. He likes you a lot." Talmadge gave her the once-over, taking in the hair that was drooping after eight hours behind the counter, the flats, and the dress hem peeking out from under the iridescent men's raincoat. "Has he seen that dress before?"

She hadn't thought about that. It was the blue dress she'd had on the night she first met him. He was going to think she had no clothes. "No, that's sweet," said Talmadge. "It'll remind him of when he first saw you."

"What he saw was my bare waist when this thing ripped."

"Perfect. I'll walk you to Second." When they got to Astor Place Talmadge stopped in front of a street vendor selling vintage clothing and asked, "What are you going to do about the girlfriend?"

"I'm not trying to do anything about the girlfriend."

"Don't bother, sweetie. I'm not Jim. What's her name again?" The dresses were 1970s. Clothing's worst era, as far as she was concerned.

"Ah-nuh." They stopped at the next one.

"What?" She spelled it for him. "Anna you mean?"

"He says Ah-nuh." The vendor seemed to know his stuff was hopeless, and he kept smoking and drinking out of whatever was in his paper bag. "I guess that's how she says it."

"Screw that. We're gonna say it like normal people. AN-na. Is she pretty?"

"I guess. She looks a little like that girl from *Family Ties*. Bigger nose."

Talmadge thought about that. "All right, that's pretty. But not gorgeous. You're prettier."

"I don't know, we don't look one thing like each other. And she's from Italy, so that's exotic." None of the vendors had anything good tonight. They moved on.

"So's Yazoo City."

"Are you kidding? You've heard me talk about it."

"He's from England, what does he know? Let him think you grew up at Tara."

"That was Georgia."

"*Don't* tell him that. And AN-na's out of the picture. If you play things right, which means you do *not* bring her up again, ever, she may wind up in Italy for good. These long-distance things never work." They'd reached Second Avenue. "What did he say she did?"

"She's an economist."

"Oh my god. If you can't get rid of an economist, it's hopeless. Good night, sweetie." He kissed her on the cheek and turned for downtown.

Matthew was waiting for her outside the theater, examining the small group of celebrity footprints set in the concrete sidewalk outside. "Who is Hildegard Knef?"

"German I think? Not all that famous. She was in *The Lost Continent*."

"Future assignment?"

"I think Harry would let you skip it."

"I was asking about you, not Harry."

She concentrated on covering Gloria Swanson's tiny footprints with her own. "You wouldn't get science fiction homework from me."

He'd bought the tickets already, which made her happy, although she told him he didn't have to do it. It was only Saturday—he needed to know she still had money. He bought popcorn, which he handed to her without a word. The theater was a little more than half full, and she directed him to her favorite spot, a few rows back near the middle—the Theatre 80 sight-lines were terrible if you were too close or on the sides. She put the popcorn bag in her teeth so she could unbutton her coat. Matthew unfolded his seat and sat down. The bottom of it tilted forward, and he grabbed both arm-rests to keep his ass from hitting the floor. She had to take the popcorn bag out of her mouth so she could laugh without dropping it.

"I get it. You're testing me."

"You're laughing too." She moved down one more seat.

"Because I can't believe I fell for that. You knew that seat was there, you told me this was your favorite spot."

"I know it's there, but I can never remember exactly where."

"So you say. First time, foreigner, doesn't watch silent movies, give him the dodgy seat." They threw their coats over the broken seat and sat back down. Matthew put his elbow on the armrest between them, then put his hand on it. The armrest, too narrow for more than one small arm, wobbled slightly.

"You gotta comment on everything, don't you," she said.

"As a matter of fact, I was loudly *not* commenting."

"No, you're just doing some kind of experiment."

"I'm trying to see if this has two hours left in it. It definitely won't support two arms."

She put the popcorn in her lap and folded her arms close to her body. "It's all yours."

"Generous woman." He put his elbow on the armrest and slid down until his head hit the top of the seat.

"Don't mention it. You did buy the tickets."

"True, I did. What do I get for the popcorn?"

She'd been doing well to this point, but now she was staring into her popcorn bag and thinking Theatre 80 needed to do better with starting on time. "King Vidor?"

He'd closed his eyes. He did look exhausted. "No, for that I get Harry no longer greeting me with 'Hey, Michael J. Fox.'"

Hallelujah, the curtains were parting and she didn't have to reply. The titles began to roll. Theatre 80 was rear-projection, and the prints fell somewhere between adequate and shredded. The soundtrack, an organ, sounded warped, there was a black line down the left side, and flecks of black floated on the image. A bad splice caused a sudden jump.

"Fuck me," groaned Matthew, who had opened his eyes but otherwise hadn't moved.

"Shush." She elbowed him, and the armrest wobbled. "The prints always get better further in." If he was one of those people who talked during the movie, this was going to be a short evening.

He wasn't. After the baby on screen started crying, neither said a word. Ceinwen, who'd been worried about sitting so close to him in the cramped seats, noticed Matthew only when he picked his head up a few minutes in.

The lights came up, and people began to file out. She turned.

"If you have one bad word to say about that movie, I'm telling you right now, I don't want to hear it."

"I don't." He reached over and picked up her coat.

"You don't? Really?" That was a squeal.

He stood up and held up the coat for her. "No. I don't."

She was still sitting. "You liked it?"

"Yes. That is what I am saying. I liked it. Happy?"

"I'm thrilled. And Harry will be so pleased."

"No more so than I. My career is safe, until he decides I have to sit through *Napoleon*." He waggled the coat, and she stood up and put her arms in the sleeves. His hands brushed her shoulders. "Was that popcorn your dinner?"

"Um . . ."

"Right. Know anywhere around here?"

She needed to do a better job of thinking ahead. She hadn't once considered what happened after the movie, but then she seldom did. "Kiev? It's right over on Seventh."

"Fine."

She fired up a cigarette as soon as they hit the sidewalk and began going through the movie, walking backwards at one point so she could imitate a movement for him, until he grabbed both her arms to keep her from colliding with a passing mohawk-haired kid. The sandwich board. The office building and the desks. Coney Island. The marriage.

It was a short walk to Kiev, a twenty-four-hour joint famous as a good place to put heavy food in a drunk stomach. They found a table and she was still talking, squinting slightly at the harsh fluorescents after Theatre 80's blue lights. The little girl. The truck. The river. The little boy. The movie theater. Matthew reached over and tapped the menu. "Do you have something in mind, or shall I order while you parse the movie? Because I warn you, I'll make you eat your vegetables."

"Nobody in their right mind orders vegetables at Kiev. Except potatoes." She pushed the menu aside without looking at it. "I'm getting kasha."

"What's that?"

"Wheat."

"Heard about this new food craze? It's called protein."

"This has protein, smart aleck. It comes with gravy."

When he'd finished laughing he managed to say, "I'd no idea. Carry on."

"I like kasha. If it makes you happy I'll get some kielbasa with it."

"Strikes you as a fair trade, does it." She had her hand in her purse. "Here's my idea. You don't smoke during dinner, and that will cover all foodstuffs."

She snapped the purse shut. "All right, deal."

He ordered pastrami, which impressed Ceinwen because it was very New York, and he hadn't been here that long. Then he wanted to know what she was doing on Avenue C. She told him about Jim and Talmadge.

"You live with two men?"

"Yeah. Safer, don't you think?"

"I, ah, guess that depends."

"If you mean are they gay, yes."

"A couple?"

"Nope. Old friends. They knew each other for ages before they met me. They bicker, but we all basically get along. Big improvement over my last place."

It was impressive how he could bite into such a huge sandwich and not have a single piece of pastrami fall out. She realized he was trying to phrase something.

"Tell me. If you don't mind. How does a woman from Mississippi wind up . . ."

"Wind up what, in New York?"

"No, I meant the living arrangements. Aren't people in your part of the country, well . . ."

"This," she told him, as she pushed the kielbasa to one side of the plate, "is my part of the country now."

He seemed to have more on his mind, but all he said was, "Fair enough."

She explained to him about Sandra, the painter who'd been her roommate on Avenue A, and the studio they'd shared: "Never share a studio." She told him about the loft bed in the apartment that Sandra got an ex-boyfriend to build for her, and the curtains they'd hung under it to surround Ceinwen's bed. She'd thought it would be like a Victorian novel, having a bed surrounded by curtains, but Sandra seemed to think the fabric was soundproof, and she kept bringing home different men.

"And that was when you said, time to move in with the gay noncouple?"

"Look, I'm not a prude. She thought I was, but I'm not. I just wanted to walk around my apartment without stumbling over a bunch of guys."

"No, you're not a prude. We've established that. What made you give up?"

"She invited a guy who lived in a squat up to the place, and he took her rent money off the dresser."

"Hasn't she heard of banks?"

"Who uses banks? They cost too much and take forever to clear your checks. She was like me, we just cashed the paychecks and got money orders when we had to." She'd felt sorry for Sandra, and didn't want to leave her stranded, but Jim and Talmadge were looking for a third roommate and they took her out to dinner and proposed. Talmadge went down on one knee. She left the following month.

She did generally feel better on a full stomach; the problem was having the time and the money to fill it. As the waitress slipped the check on the table she said, with new energy, "How about a drink?"

He grinned. "What if you're rumbled?"

"Rumbled?"

"May I see some ID, miss?"

"That's fine," she assured him. "I turned twenty-one all the way back in June." She started going through her purse, but the cigarettes seemed to be hiding from her. "Talmadge and Jim and Roxanne from the store took me to Marie's Crisis. It's this gay piano bar over in the West Village where they play show tunes and everybody sings along. And I don't like to brag, but the guys there were real impressed that I knew all the lyrics to 'Let Yourself Go.'" She finally found the cigarettes and the lighter, too. "Dinner is over, right?" She looked up, cigarette in hand. "Come on, there aren't even any plates on the table."

"You're twenty-one?"

"That's what I said. Why, how old are you?"

"I'm twenty-nine." She'd upset him again, but this time it wasn't her fault.

"You were asking if I'd get carded."

"I was joking."

"How old did you think I was?"

"I'm not sure." Same expression.

"How old do I look?" She was losing patience. Was it her fault he had trouble back-dating women?

"Right now? With your lipstick rubbed off and a spot of gravy on your chin? About twelve."

"So this is good news," she pointed out. She was suggesting a drink, that's all, nothing that could get them arrested, even in Mississippi. She'd been on her own for more than two years, and she could get a drink if she wanted. But not if he was going to keep looking at her like she was a room he'd trashed the night before. He had the check in his hand. If she didn't do something fast she was going to get put in another cab.

"There's a bar right across the street from Theatre 80. We could go there." She'd show him. If one look at the Holiday didn't prove she was a grownup, she might as well go see what Jim and Talmadge were up to. "No singing, but it's an interesting crowd." He had his wallet out, but he seemed to have forgotten what for; he was staring at a twenty like he'd never seen American money before. "Drinks are on me," she offered.

"Are they now?" He looked up and handed her a napkin. She'd forgotten the gravy.

"Sure." Adding, as she wiped her chin, "It's cheap."

At last he was smiling again. "So you're taking me to a dive."

She beamed back at him in relief. "Me and my roommates, we only go to dives. It's a matter of pride." She excused herself to the bathroom so she could reapply her lipstick. It made more difference than she'd realized.

When they arrived at the Holiday the crowd was just as she'd hoped, the punks and the rockers back at the jukebox, the old serious drinkers up front around the bar. The dinginess was mitigated only by skimpy Christmas lights that stayed up year-round, the cigarette smoke was always visible near the ceiling, the floor was always sticky, and everybody gave you a mean look as soon as you walked in. Ceinwen had never liked it, exactly, but she figured taking someone there made you look tough. Like taking someone to the saloon in *Destry Rides Again*.

"Congratulations," said Matthew, under his breath. "This really is a dive."

"You didn't believe me?"

"I thought you might not have much to compare it with."

They found seats at the bar. She thought about Marlene Dietrich and tried to slide onto the barstool in a way that would show off her legs. It was a decent effort, she thought, but once she was seated she remembered that the footrest was at a bad level. She crossed her legs, felt her skirt ride up, and tried to solve this problem with a discreet tug, while Matthew was busy ordering a scotch. She got a glass of wine. She hadn't minded the Holiday wine before, but now that she'd had Harry's, she realized it was terrible. She was determined to drink it anyway, and steeled herself not to make a face, because he was sure to notice.

She decided it was finally time to ask about England. He was from Putney, which he said was sort of like a suburb of London, and he'd had an alarmingly normal upbringing. His parents were still married, even. His father was a barrister, and his biggest problem growing up was that he didn't want to be one, too. He hadn't known what he wanted to do after he finished their version of high school and had taken something he called a gap year, where you traveled and tried to make up your mind. He'd gone to the Middle East and the South Pacific, and by the time he decided he wanted to see Japan his gap year had stretched into two. Now he was behind. In math, you weren't supposed to take time off. Since he'd stopped then, he couldn't stop now, or he'd never get tenure.

Guess I'm having some gap years myself, she thought. "You went to Cambridge straight through?"

He nodded. "This is my first outside post."

She'd have to ask sooner or later, Talmadge be damned. "Did you meet Anna there?"

"Yes. She spent a year there. My third." Ceinwen did the math in her head. Six years. Something like that.

"Would Anna be upset that we're out tonight?" Jim *had* pointed out that the girlfriend was a fact whether she brought her up or not.

"No. Anna and I have an understanding." She hoped it was the concept as much as the cliché that was embarrassing him. Anna didn't understand why you might want to say please and thank you to a salesgirl. Ceinwen didn't buy the notion that Anna would understand that same salesgirl going out with her boyfriend for drinks and a movie. Plus two dinners and half a roast beef sandwich. She waited for the follow-up, and when it didn't happen, she said, "What does Anna understand?"

"When she went back to Italy, we talked about how to handle it. We knew we'd have only summers and holidays and there'd be long stretches in between." He was, for some reason, talking to the beer tap. "And we decided we wouldn't worry about what happened when we were apart, as long as things were the same when we got back together."

"So it's all right to cheat." Talmadge was going to be some kinda pissed off.

"It isn't cheating." He peeled the cocktail napkin off the bottom of his glass and took a swallow. "It's cheating when you lie. This is just . . ."

Nope, she was not going to supply him with a phrase, no matter how long he let that hang. And she wouldn't let him leave it blank, either. "Just what?"

"Fun." He downed the rest of his drink and set it on the bar. "That's the idea, anyway."

Fun. Last year she'd tried to have fun with that guitar player who went to Columbia. She'd met him soon after she got to New York, when she was still forcing herself to go to parties. Flattered by first-time male interest, she wore miniskirts, hid her Duran Duran and Doris Day records, and acted like she loved the Replacements. She talked to his friends about politics she didn't follow and writers she'd never read. His band went on a short tour. She didn't realize how short until she found out he had been back for a month, and never called.

Still, she wouldn't have to stand around dark, airless clubs, her ears pounded by music she secretly didn't like that much. Matthew wouldn't have her out in the street trying to flag down one of the few Checker cabs left in the city because those were the only ones big enough to hold a Marshall amp. NYU was a much easier commute from Avenue C than Columbia.

Besides, she liked him very much.

"After two," she said. "Probably time to think about heading out." She'd already paid for the drinks.

"Probably." He stood up and held out her coat. "I'll walk you to Avenue C. You can introduce me to all your favorite derelicts."

"You could come up for a minute if you want." She slipped her arms in the sleeves and turned around to face him because she didn't know what to do with his hands on her shoulders. "It's getting a little chilly out. I could make you some tea."

"Won't we disturb your roommates?" He put on his own coat.

"Not if we're quiet. Tea isn't noisy." She didn't blush on her face like normal people, she never had. She reddened on her chest and right along the base of her throat. She put up a hand to cover it, but he wasn't looking at her neck.

"Quiet tea, then." He pushed in the barstool. "After you."

The streets got less busy as they headed further east. There were long stretches with no people, except a couple of guys who looked like they were the "hey Blondie" type, though not when there was a man around. She kept one hand on her purse, the other in her pocket, and her eyes anywhere but him, and told him what she'd read about *The Crowd* in Harry's books. Eleanor Boardman was married to King Vidor, but wasn't it great that he hadn't tried to make her glamorous? The actors looked like ordinary people. James Murray though, he drank too much, and one day after his career had gone south, he was scrounging change off passersby and one of them turned out to be Vidor. By the way, the top part of this building is nice.

"The cornice," he said. He didn't seem upset or nervous or anything else.

They arrived and she pushed on the door. "No lock?" he asked.

"Not for the past month. No doorman either." She started up the stairs. "And no elevator."

When they reached the fourth floor Matthew held up his hand and stopped, leaning back on the railing. "How much farther?"

"Two more flights."

"When you invite someone for tea, you might think to mention you live on top of K2."

"How do you think I stay skinny?"

"You're skinny," he said, looking up the stairwell, "because you smoke instead of eating."

"That's what everybody says."

"Dare I suggest this should tell you something." She started up the next flight. He didn't move. "This better be good tea."

"It's chamomile."

"You said tea. That's not tea."

She tapped her foot. "Are you coming, or just complaining?" He gave himself a push off the rails and followed.

As she opened the door Ceinwen put her finger to her lips and pointed to Talmadge's screened-off room. They slipped off their coats and shoes and padded to the living room. She switched on the lamp and he walked to the couch, then bent almost double to check out the cinder blocks.

"It's pretty comfortable," she whispered, feeling defensive.

"I'm sure it is. Clever solution, that." He dropped onto the couch and it shifted slightly on the blocks. "Maybe you should consider glue."

"I'll get the tea. Sorry, I mean the chamomile."

He was pushing back on his feet, checking the couch's movement. "I'll be here."

She had to heat the water in a pan, and the weak burners meant that this always took a while. Usually they used tap water, which came out boiling hot, but an Englishman was sure to notice a shortcut like that. She lit a cigarette off the burner. She could go talk to him while she waited on the water. But then she'd have to sit with him on the couch. She could sit on the floor cushions, though that was kind of obvious. Ugh, but so was the couch. If they both had tea, that gave them an activity. And then they could watch a movie. A quiet movie. What did she have with subtitles?

When she emerged, wondering if he was a leave-in-the-bag or take-it-out kind of person, he was sprawled full length on the couch with one arm over his eyes. She set the mugs on the table and stood over him.

"Matthew?" He'd had only one scotch, but he'd seemed awfully tired.

Must be all that math. She put a hand on the back of the couch and bent toward his ear. "Matthew? Are you asleep?"

"No." An arm shot around her waist. The couch rocked and fell back on the blocks with a slam as he pulled her down for a kiss. She was half on top of him and half off the couch, and if he let go she'd fall to the floor, but he didn't let go, not even when he pulled his mouth away and moved a hand to the side of her face.

"Tea's ready," she whispered. His thumb was tracing the corner of her mouth.

"I hate chamomile." His fingers slid to her collarbone, then slowly down.

"I could get you some water." He started to sit up and she slipped off and knelt in front of the couch. He shifted to kiss her again and began to unfasten her belt. She put her hands on his chest, uncertain where to start.

"Can't seem to manage anything tonight." His hand was moving down her spine. "That seat at the cinema, the stairs, this sofa. Now this dress."

"What's wrong with it?"

"Does it have an opening? Anywhere? How did you put it on in the first place?" She moved his hand to her side. "At last." He tugged. "Hooks. Topology. This I can manage. No, spoke too soon. There's a zipper *under* the hooks. Bloody hell."

"Shouldn't we go to my room," she whispered, "instead of staying out here where they can hear us?"

He had his hand inside the dress opening and his mouth on her ear. "I'm not sure. Is the bed up on sawhorses?"

"It's on the floor."

"Brilliant." He grabbed her arms and pulled her up. They kept kissing and she only stumbled once on the way to her room.

2.

RAIN HISSED DOWN THE WINDOW. IT WAS A TWIN MATTRESS, SO SLEEP had been a series of tight turns and tangled limbs, plus a long kiss at some point in the middle to make up for accidentally pinning her against the wall. And he'd stolen most of the covers. He was on his stomach, one leg thrown between hers and an arm trailing on the floor.

One thing was for sure. She was through with guitar players. A mathematician. Why had she never considered one of those? Trial and error. A sense of method. Process. Not just verse, then pell-mell for the chorus.

She checked the clock. Only 9:30, but she would never get back to sleep. She slid herself from under his leg and he barely stirred. She found her slip and headed for the bathroom. She hadn't washed her face last night, and she didn't want him waking up to smudges. There was no sound from Jim's room or Talmadge's corner as she crept past.

The bathroom mirror revealed a face that was a little punk rock, but not too bad. She washed everything off, then went to the deep windowsill where she kept her makeup. Concealer, definitely. Liner or mascara he might notice, so no. A little bit of blush. Where was the Chapstick?

She walked back to her room, trying to step lightly on the creaky floors. Still nothing from Talmadge and Jim. When she opened the door she saw that Matthew was awake, on his back with his arms behind his head.

"Good morning," she said, closing the door behind her.

"Good morning."

She'd been concentrating so hard on fixing her face she hadn't come up with a snappy greeting, and now she was standing over him like a dope. Frantically she tried to think of a line from a good movie, but none of her favorites had a scene where the heroine woke up with a naked man in her bed. Damn you, Hays Office.

He pointed toward her shelves.

"That's quite a collection there."

"I record it myself or get it second-hand. Getting it all up here was a chore."

He jerked a thumb behind him at the clothes rack. "That must have been a job, too."

She decided to sit on the bed near his legs. "I've bought some stuff since I moved in."

"Now I see where all your money goes." He stretched, sat up and put an arm around her.

She had liked New York right away, but people here were always pressing you for details, always trying to get you to talk. A New Yorker, given a remark about how little you made, would immediately find a way to ask the amount. Not Matthew. When she told him she'd never been to college, he didn't make her tell him why or ask if she still planned to go. When Harry was asking about Daddy and Yazoo City, Matthew had changed the subject for her. When she acted uncomfortable, he let it drop. Were all the English like that, or just him?

"Bad news." She stiffened. "Not that bad, actually. But I have to leave." He scooted to the edge of the bed.

She tried to sound casual, but knew she didn't. "Are you sure? I don't have to be at work until one. I was thinking we'd have breakfast."

"That would have been lovely." He turned her face toward him. "Really, it would have been. But I can't make it. Next time." He kissed her, stood up and pulled on his underwear.

She did like the sound of "next time." Maybe she wasn't as tactful as he was, but she figured she had a right to the question. "Do I get to ask where you're going?"

"Of course." He was putting on his pants. "I'm going to mass."

She ran through all the awkwardness she'd imagined during all the night's multiple awakenings. Matthew not liking how she looked in the morning. Talmadge flirting and him not knowing how to deal. Matthew taking one sip of Cafe Busted and spitting it back in the cup. Or worst of all, Matthew clutching his brow and moaning that he'd betrayed the best woman who ever studied economics. Not once had she considered the possibility that things would be cut short for Sunday school.

His pants had wound up stuffed between the shelves and the foot of the bed. He yanked on them and said, "With a name like Reilly, aren't you Catholic yourself?"

"Nope. By the time my Irish ancestors got to Mississippi, they were Methodist."

"I see." He was shaking the pants, but the wrinkles weren't budging. She watched him sit to pull them on, and spoke carefully.

"I admit, maybe I just don't get it. But I don't think a man should be talking about church services when he's zipping up his fly." He grinned, but he was reaching for his shirt, which had wound up behind the door. "Honest? You're going to mass?"

"Honest. I missed it last week because of work."

Her best friend, pretty much her only friend at Yazoo City High School, had been Catholic, and Ceinwen had learned a few things. "Don't you have to be in a state of grace to receive communion?"

He was impressed. "That's very good."

"Yeah, one thing they teach you down South is religion."

"But only half right. The important thing is sincere contrition."

She didn't like the idea of being something to repent about. He bent over for his socks, then stopped and looked at her. His knees dropped to the bed and he put his hands on her shoulders. "Don't look at me like that. I'll be contrite next time, too." He kissed her and she felt him slide a finger under the strap of her slip. He pulled the strap down, her hand moved to his waistband and for a second she thought mass was history. But then he pushed the strap back and reached for his socks.

"Will you have time to be sorry for that before you get to church?"

"It's a long walk to Washington Square. Do you have any paper, or is everything on videotape? Write down your phone number. I promise I'll call tonight."

She grabbed a pen and paper off the shelf and wrote it down. "You better keep your promise. Otherwise it goes on the list for next week's mass. You never know, by next Sunday you might be so full up you can't repent. You'll have to find a Baptist service or something."

He pushed her hair away so he could kiss her neck. "That's exactly right."

"It is?"

"No." He stood up and picked up his jacket. "But I'll still call."

They were halfway through the living room when Talmadge popped out from behind his screens. He was wearing his best pajamas, so he'd known Matthew was there. He posed for a minute and sang, "Hello young lovers, you're"—pause—"under arrest."

"I'm going to guess you're Talmadge." It really was hard to rattle this man.

"Correct," said Talmadge, proffering a hand. "And you are?"

"Matthew."

"Good morning, Matthew. Oh, look who's here. Good morning." Jim was fully dressed, so he'd heard too. Talmadge swept a hand in his direction. "This is Jim. Oops, should I have let you guess?"

"You've ruined the suspense," said Jim. He shook hands. Talmadge offered coffee, Matthew said he'd have loved some but he had to go. She walked him to the door, he kissed her once more and was gone.

She walked back to the kitchen where Jim was already fixing the coffee.

"Soooo?" trilled Talmadge.

"I like him," said Ceinwen.

"Oh yes. I got that last night. So did the couch."

"Where's he off to?" asked Jim. Talmadge might want the physical details. Jim would not.

"He's going to mass."

Over by the cabinets Talmadge froze with a mug in each hand. "Mass? Church?" Ceinwen nodded. Talmadge exhaled. "That is really, really weird."

"It's what people do on Sunday," said Jim. He stopped measuring and muttered, "Damn, I've lost count." He poured the coffee back in the tin and began again.

"No, it isn't. Normal people do not get out of bed with a girl on Sunday and go straight to mass."

"There's nothing wrong with going to mass."

"Listen, I know you miss being a Catholic and all—"

"I still am a Catholic. Nine, ten. There." Jim pressed the button on the machine.

"Whatever you say. But this is crazy. I don't know about this one, Ceinwen."

"Says the guy," said Jim, opening the refrigerator, "who's so atheist he got kicked out of AA. Did you remember to buy milk?"

"It's in the door, and I did not get kicked out of AA. You *can't* get kicked out of AA. I didn't like it. I said if these people are so big on free will, I'm using mine and I'm not going anymore."

Jim set the carton on the counter. "Free will? That's what you got out of AA, free will? Did you listen to a single thing they said?"

"Of course I listened. That's all you do at those meetings. You sit in these awful chairs under these nasty lights and they talk and you listen and—"

"Because, Talmadge, that is the opposite, the exact *fucking* opposite of what they tell you in AA."

"Oh, so you know all about it, do you, Mr. Two-Drink Maximum."

"I guess I know more than you do. You're supposed to admit you're powerless."

"Oh sure. Sure. One night Ceinwen decides we've all gotta watch *Days of Wine and Roses* and now you're an expert on AA. 'Hey Talmadge! Jack Klugman says you're powerless!'"

"Great theme song," said Ceinwen, and sang: "The days of wine and roses, laugh and run away . . ."

Talmadge started to say something else and Jim put up his hand. "Ceinwen's trying to change the subject." He went to pour the coffee; he never waited for the machine to finish. "He seems polite enough."

"He's a psychopath. What if he turns out to have a thing for virgins?"

"You're incredible. He already has a girlfriend, fine and dandy. He goes to take communion, he's a psycho. Do you realize how backasswards that is?"

"I'm going to talk to Ceinwen later." They could hear the screens scraping as Talmadge retreated to his corner. Jim handed her a cup.

"So," she said, "you like him after all?"

"I met him for all of two minutes. Although," he coughed, "I did hear a bit last night."

"I'm sorry."

"I'll forget all about it after breakfast. Let's send Talmadge out for bagels and see if it calms him down." Jim picked up his cup as she followed.

"But you aren't mad at me."

"I never was mad at you, honey. I just want you to be careful."

"That reminds me," Talmadge called from behind the screens. "You did use condoms, didn't you? I assume he's not too Catholic for *that*?"

"Talmadge, can you get us some bagels?"

"When I'm dressed."

After bagels were consumed, Talmadge and Ceinwen walked to work together in the pouring rain. He had, as predicted, calmed down about mass, but still offered menacing observations about birth control and guilt and madonna-whore hangups, in between trying to find out whether the sex had been any good and whether Matthew was really going to call, since she'd brought up Anna after being told not to.

Talmadge was behind the counter helping her rearrange the hats, and the stereo system kicked into "Diamonds Are a Girl's Best Friend." Ceinwen had never been big on Marilyn Monroe, but she did love that song, and Talmadge had been teaching her some of the moves. Lily had disappeared downstairs to the office, and the rain had kept the store nearly deserted, so while it was risky, they still wound up practicing the big finish together.

"Diiiiamonds . . ."

"Yes diamonds . . ."

"I. DON'T. MEAN. RHINESTONES . . ."

"But diiiiamonds, are a girl's best . . ."

Vamp, vamp, vamp . . .

". . . best friend!"

Somebody was applauding. As Ceinwen dropped the pose she heard Talmadge say, "How was mass?"

He'd come from the men's side this time and had, apparently, been standing behind a tall rack of coats. "Fine, thanks. How are you?" He moved to the side of the rack, one hand on a dripping umbrella and the other in his coat pocket, smiling bigger than she'd known he could. Her hand flew up to her throat, though she knew it was hopeless: she was blushing so much she'd need to cover her entire chest.

"*Grand,*" said Talmadge. He'd been mimicking the accent all day

"You were hiding," she said.

"I was," he said. "Wouldn't you?"

"I'll just let you two chat. About Marilyn. Or something," said Talmadge. He darted around the counter and disappeared to the men's side.

"We were rearranging the hats," said Ceinwen.

"That's exactly what it looked like." He'd come over to the counter, still grinning. "I was going to call later, but then I thought I'd be heroic and rescue you from your boss. Instead here I am, rescuing you from a musical number."

She was ridiculously happy he was here, but he better not do that again. "How long were you there?"

"Since about Harry Winston. Want to get some dinner once you're released?"

"Sure."

"Ceinwen, what are you doing?" Lily was standing a couple of feet behind him. How could she just appear like that? Talmadge claimed she used broomsticks. Matthew shifted his umbrella and stuck out his right hand, for all the world as though Lily were a person who responded to ordinary human politeness.

"Hello," he said. "I don't know if you remember me—"

She let his hand dangle in the air. "I remember. Seems like you're here on a different errand this time." Had Lily heard him joke about her? Maybe not, she didn't look quite that mad, though she was stalking past him to the far counter, hands on her hips.

"As a matter of fact, I did come back for something else." He scanned down the counter and reached over for a stack of the metal bangles. "Thought I could use some of these."

"Great. I'll ring them up. Ceinwen, can I have a word with you first?" She walked over and tried not to cower. "I don't know anything about your personal life and I want to keep it that way, *capisce*? So make your dates outside of work. Store's closing. I came to tell you to clock out."

Okay. That could have been much worse. Lily walked behind the counter and picked up the bangles, then set them back down. "These are three for a dollar. You've got ten here."

He frowned at the bracelets in deep disapproval, as though they were an exam from a particularly blockheaded student. "Oh. So you're saying . . ." He tapped his finger against his chin.

"You need either one less," said Lily, with slow sarcasm, "or two more."

"I see now. Let me think." He fanned out the bangles on the counter. "Hm." He held up a couple to the light. Lily shifted her weight to one leg and folded her arms. "Well." He picked up one, set it down, picked up another and handed it to her. "One fewer, please."

"Fine." She practically slammed it back on the display.

"Thanks. Awfully glad you could suggest a solution." Ceinwen put her hand over her mouth. Lily spotted her and barked, "Are you going to clock out or what?" She retreated to the clock room, disappointed that she was going to miss the finale.

When she stepped outside he was waiting, umbrella up and shopping bag in hand. "She's thrown me out, and no mistake. I won't be stopping by again, I think. Unless you really do decide you want to get fired. At which point I'll be happy to help."

She pouted. "What if someone wants to buy *eleven* bangles?" She had her own umbrella, but she ducked under his.

"You'll have to find a pencil, I suppose."

"Courant is too good for house calls. I get it." With no discussion of destination, they started walking west, toward Washington Square Village.

When she woke up the next morning, she discovered he'd stacked the bangles on the bedpost.

3.

Something about Matthew going to mass had lessened Jim's disapproval, although wisps of it trailed around the apartment. Talmadge still spent the occasional evening with George, and one night, as she lay in bed reading, he came in singing "Lili Marlene." And she heard Jim say, "I've got an idea. How's about somebody around here goes out with a man who doesn't have a girlfriend, how does that sound?"

"You're free these days, aren't you? Should Ceinwen and I fix you up?"

"Great, a mathematician," said Jim. "Because my life isn't boring enough."

"George has a brother."

"Strange as this is gonna sound, I prefer to date men who are actually gay."

"I don't see the problem here," said Talmadge. "Less competition for both of us." And he shoved off behind his screens, having switched his tune to "Black Market."

That was the only time Jim came right out with anything. Otherwise, he watched Ceinwen walk in, or watched her get ready to go out, and reminded her to call if she wasn't going to come home, so they wouldn't think she'd been kidnapped by that weird guy on the corner of B and Seventh. Talmadge told her he'd decided Matthew was all right, unless he tried to talk her out of condoms or into a nun costume. If that happened, she was to consult him on exit strategies immediately.

They still went to see Stefan every week, and Talmadge wasn't trying to get out of it anymore. That didn't seem like a good sign.

Unlike the guitar player, Matthew called when he said he was going to call, and warned her when he had to work. He worked a lot, trying to make up for the wasted time working on a busted proof with Harry.

They fell into a pattern right away, of three nights a week, which nights depending on whether or not he needed to stay at the office. She didn't see him much on Friday or Saturday nights; not only was she usually too tired after the store's busiest days, but he really did go to mass on Sunday morning. They frequented cheap restaurants, and Matthew rarely let her pay, though she often felt guilty about it.

Sometimes he cooked for her, always meat or fish, complaining if she didn't finish her portion, which she almost never did. His apartment had a small balcony, and she smoked her cigarette there after the meal, leaning on the railing and blowing plumes of smoke over the rundown garden next to his building.

The place was almost as large as theirs, one big living room, a kitchen separated by just a counter, and a bedroom. The furniture was a few pieces Donna had made Harry bring over because, she said, "we have too much here anyway," and some things Matthew bought second-hand, on Waverly Place and on Second Avenue.

He didn't have a TV, a fact of which he was way too proud, she thought, so at his place they talked or they played strip poker or Trivial Pursuit. One night they decided to make it strip Trivial Pursuit. She nailed all the movie questions, of course, and more than held her own with history and literature, but she got only about half the science, and was so hopeless at the sports questions that he accused her of playing to lose.

Some nights they just went to bed early.

She went to Courant to see his office, a small space just off the sixth-floor elevators, with a chalkboard on one wall that was always filled with equations. On later visits she asked Matthew to explain them, but that was hopeless, so she had to settle for learning Greek letters—she liked the look of the sigmas, with equations stacked on them, top and bottom—and learning a few ideas, like the gambler's paradox and the prisoner's dilemma.

Harry was usually around, and he always had somebody's revival schedule on him, urging Ceinwen to go even if Matthew couldn't. There was a French New Wave series at the New Yorker, they needed to see *Breathless* and *The 400 Blows* and *Les Bonnes Femmes*. How about Walsh, how about Wellman, check out Ophuls, how much Lubitsch have you seen, how about this Fritz Lang. See here Matthew, you want macho, I'll give you macho. Sam Fuller. Anthony Mann. John Huston double feature at Theatre 80. Ceinwen's seen *Treasure of the Sierra Madre* and *The Maltese Falcon*, but you haven't and you need to shape up, my friend. And silents, any kind of silent. *The Big Parade, Way Down East, The General, Seventh Heaven, Pandora's Box, Battleship Potemkin, Wings*. These were the basics, Harry told her, she could fill in the rarities later.

Matthew fell asleep during *Sunrise* and she needled him endlessly about it. Then she fell asleep during *The Trial* and Matthew crowed for days. He loved *The Fallen Idol* and when he left the office for a minute to talk to a student, Harry lowered his eyebrows and cackled, "British repression. Of course he liked it."

Several times she told Harry she should return his books. He asked if she was still using them, and when she admitted she was, he insisted she hang onto them and brought her more. Mack Sennett's *King of Comedy*, King Vidor's *A Tree Is a Tree*, a book called *Shattered Silents*, about the transition to sound. *A Pictorial History of the Silent Screen*, with what seemed like hundreds of photographs of movies she'd never heard of.

When they went to a silent movie, she scanned the credits for an Emil or a Miriam; on nights she didn't see Matthew, she checked each fresh book, and still she came up empty. It was possible the photograph was from a play, but Ceinwen didn't think so. Miriam didn't work in theater until after the war. She knew for sure Miriam had been in Hollywood in the early thirties, so why not the late twenties, too?

The search had become a habit, like turning to the middle of a movie book to see the photos first. She didn't like the idea, but maybe Miriam was in movies, and Emil wasn't. Maybe Emil was a waiter at the Brown Derby. She knew she was keeping it up out of sheer stubbornness; she was seeing much less of Miriam, and when she did, the greeting was back to square one, as though Miriam had never asked Ceinwen about her dress.

They went to see *Broken Blossoms* and she loved it. She took him to Downtown Beirut afterward, figuring the bar name would give her extra in-the-know points, but they wound up arguing so heatedly over the movie she wasn't sure he had even noticed how debauched the place was. He asked if she didn't think the movie was a little melodramatic, and wasn't it creepy to have a grown man in love with a little girl, and they went on for almost three hours, lingering over the last drinks until the bartender brought them their tab without asking. They decided to go back to Avenue C; we can make a game out of keeping quiet, she told him, thinking that sounded racy. And when they arrived at the building, there was Miriam, getting out of a cab. It was way past midnight, where on earth had she been?

"Thank you," said Miriam, as Matthew held the street door for her. It was still broken.

Too much wine had made Ceinwen frisky. "Hey Miriam," she said, a little louder than she should, waving her arms in Matthew's direction like she was trying to sell him at the store. "This is my friend Matthew Hill. Matthew, this is my neighbor Miriam Gibson."

Miriam hesitated, but he put out his hand and said "How do you do." She took it. "Pleased to meet you."

"Matthew," said Ceinwen, her voice so announcer-sparkly she could have been introducing a Miss Mississippi contestant, "is here all the way from London."

"You don't say. Welcome to Avenue C." That had to be a joke, although Miriam's face was impassive as ever.

"Thank you very much. It's great to be here." Matthew was pretty well lit himself.

"Glad you're enjoying it." Nice going, Matthew, you almost got a smile. "Where in London?"

He stood to one side and they let Miriam take the stairs ahead of them. "Putney."

"I don't know Putney, but I did go to London once, after the war."

"What did you think?" asked Ceinwen, hoping Miriam would come out with a zinger.

"Oh, people were very nice." Come on Miriam, you can do better than that. "We were staying with friends, and I'm afraid what I mostly remember is rationing."

"Before my time, of course," he said, "but I've heard a lot about it." Miriam stopped at her door and said "good night," but at least she didn't say that she didn't want to keep them. As they started up the last flight, she saw Miriam pause to watch. She'd never watched Ceinwen take the stairs before.

She'd left the light on in her bedroom, or maybe Jim had turned it on for her. As they tiptoed in she whispered, "I think she's beautiful, don't you?"

"Mm, your neighbor? For a woman that age, yes, I suppose she is." He threw his coat just past the bed. "Do you know what she used to do?"

"Not really," said Ceinwen.

"She seems interesting." He reached up and pulled the string on the overhead.

By late November she was trying to mix things up, but it was hard without money. She talked Matthew into going to Chinatown, to a hole in the wall Talmadge had told her about. Everybody knew if you wanted good food in Chinatown, you had to go someplace a bit dirty and try not to picture the kitchen. When they got there, it was so run-down he tried to talk her into going down the street, but she wouldn't hear of it. She craved noodles.

She told him Talmadge didn't come here anymore because he got kicked out. He'd brought a date and tried to order chicken's blood tofu off-menu, and when they wouldn't serve it to him he made a scene and accused them of discriminating against Caucasians. Matthew said even his Chinese colleagues thought that dish was disgusting, so why did Talmadge try to order it? She said she imagined he wanted to impress his date, who was straight.

"Surely that would make his date bi."

"Oh no. Talmadge told me *nobody* should ever date a bisexual."

He started to say something, stopped, then settled for, "Didn't you say the man he's seeing now is straight?" She nodded. "Why this odd, ah . . . pattern?"

"There's different theories about that."

"Such as, he can't tell?"

"He can tell all right." Since Matthew appeared wrapped in thought, now was a good time to lay down her chopsticks and subtly reach for a fork.

He said, "Fear of AIDS?"

"I don't think so."

"Has he been tested?"

"Jim has. Negative. Talmadge says he is very in tune with his body and he'd know if there was an alien force inside it."

The corners of his mouth appeared to be fighting an alien force themselves, but he said only, "I take it that's a no."

"Yes. A no." He was pushing his noodles around in a way that seemed disapproving. Defensively, she added, "I know it's obvious he's just scared. Jim told him so to his face." He fished out a piece of chicken with his chopsticks and chewed as though he were expecting it to chew back. "I don't think that has anything to do with his love life, though. If you ask me, it's fear of commitment."

Matthew laid down his chopsticks, began, "Ceinwen," then stopped.

She sucked in a stray noodle; the Chinese ones never would wind all the way around the fork. When she finished, she said, "What?" He didn't answer. "Go on, say it."

"Does Talmadge strike you as normal?"

She was annoyed. "Of course he's normal. What a thing to say."

"The last time I was there he was singing in German. Does he even speak German?"

"No, he speaks Marlene."

"*That's what I mean.* He was singing in German—"

"Come on. Like he's the only gay man on earth obsessed with Dietrich."

"—and he was straightening the furniture. All of it. Twice."

"Saves me and Jim the trouble."

"Then he sat on the cushions and did that thing with his fingers . . ."

"Manual dexterity. They're exercises. Ask him to teach you, you could use it." His eyebrows rose and she added quickly, "All those equations you're always writing out."

"Believe I'll pass, if it's all the same to you. And then he ate an entire container of ice cream and while he was doing it, he kept sucking in his cheeks."

"That's for his skin tone. He says if he does it enough, it makes his cheekbones pop."

"I don't dislike him, you understand. At all. It's just that you and Jim . . ." She waited. "I'm not sure what made the two of you want to live with him."

She thought about it. "He's loyal."

It was a bright, clear night, and when they walked out she could see a few stars. It was chilly, but not too bad, though there was a strong breeze blowing trash along the gutters.

"I've got an idea," she said. "Let's walk down to the Trade Center."

"I've been to the top already."

"Not that. This is really cool."

"The only cool part is that there are two of them."

"That's what you think," she told him.

The wind got stronger the further downtown they went, until she started ducking behind him to avoid the gusts and he told her buck up, this was her idea. When they arrived, she pulled on his arm to stop him and turned slowly, her eyes searching the whole vast expanse of the plaza between the buildings. It was nearly empty, just a handful of people probably working far too late.

"What are you looking for?"

"Cops," she said. She grabbed his hand and pulled him toward one of the big stone benches.

"Sounds promising. What do you have in mind?"

"Here. Lie down." She'd found the perfect spot, near the sphere. The fountain was off.

"On second thought, I'd rather not get arrested, if you don't mind. Looks bad to the students."

"We're lying down, that's it. On our backs. Come on." She stretched out and patted the space next to her.

He didn't move. "Is that clean?"

"Will you stop worrying and lie down?"

"That line never worked for me," he said, but he settled next to her. "Now what?"

"Now we look up." She pointed to the buildings hulking over them.

"What am I looking for, King Kong?"

"Just *look*."

The wind made whistles and gasps around the bench while she waited for him to notice. With one visible star as a marker, she watched as both towers slowly, perceptibly, moved back and forth.

"Do you see?"

"Passive viscoelastic dampers."

Lately all he ever thought about was work. "Are you looking at the buildings?"

"Straight at them. Passive viscoelastic dampers. It's what's in skyscrapers, to keep them from swaying too much in the wind."

Jim had told her about doing this on a date, and she'd hoped for a more poetic response. "And it's cool, right?"

"Very." He pulled her close. "Except I'm freezing."

They lay there until the cold of the bench reached through to chill her skin. He said, "Your Thanksgiving is coming up."

"Yes indeed. The great American holiday." She didn't want to think about it.

"Are you planning anything?"

She rested her chin on his chest. "Sort of. Talmadge and Jim are going out to Long Island, this guy they know is having a dinner. I'm invited too."

He picked his head up slightly to look at her. "Do you not want to go?"

"Not sure." Last year she hadn't felt like she fit in, and she'd spilled the host's green-bean casserole. Matthew dropped his head and looked back at the towers.

"Well. There's a probabilist at Columbia, friend of Harry's. Every year he gives a dinner, for the foreigners and anyone else who doesn't want to cook. Harry and Donna are going. Thought I'd see if you were free."

A big dinner, full of colleagues. She wondered if the force of her heartbeat could be felt all the way through her coat. "That sounds great. As long as—" She stopped just in time.

"As long as what?" Give me a second, I need to change my what. "What?"

"Nobody's going to think it's odd, me being there with you?" She hated herself.

His arm loosened and his voice tightened. "Paru told me to bring a friend if I liked. I don't have to explain anything to anyone."

She rolled on her back again to see the towers. "Okay. It's a date."

About a month earlier, while he was in the shower, she'd spotted a small stack of air-mail envelopes under a book on his desk. She'd flipped them over to see the return address on the back. Italy. She had stared at them a long while, but when she finally decided to have a peek, she heard the bathroom door open. The next night the envelopes were gone. "You can't hesitate when you get a chance like that," Talmadge told her.

Last night she'd noticed a postcard on top of a stack of papers to be graded. The Colosseum. A boring photo, she thought. Looked like a lot more fun in *Nights of Cabiria*. This time she'd been able to read while he made dinner, but it was in Italian. Nothing she could make out, except the close. *Ti amo*. What Ingrid Bergman wrote to Roberto Rossellini, because it was the only Italian she knew.

When they got back to his apartment, she checked the desk as soon as she walked into the bedroom.

No postcard. She decided that was a good omen, too.

4.

TALMADGE FLUNG BOTH HANDS IN THE AIR WHEN SHE TOLD HIM about Thanksgiving. "Yes! The economist is history!"

"This does sound good, at that," said Jim.

"It's fabulous, that's what it is. Up to Columbia. To meet and greet all the math elite."

"A magic evening's in store," said Jim.

"With any luck, no one will be talking math," said Ceinwen.

"We'll have to make sure of that." Talmadge folded his arms. "Dress code. Do we know what it is?"

"Matthew said it isn't formal or anything, but it's okay if I want to get dressed up."

"Better and better." Talmadge posed, one finger pointing at her door. "To the rack!" Jim fell in behind, and they crowded into her room. Talmadge put up both hands as though casting a spell: "What kind of a reaction are we looking for here?"

"Ideally, we're looking to have his eyeballs fall out and roll around on the floor."

"He's English. Let's not ask for miracles," said Jim. "Let's settle for making him loosen his collar."

Talmadge pushed hangers one by one along the rack until he stopped on a dress. "Strapless?"

"Kind of stiff, what with all the bones. I turn, it doesn't."

"That's how they made 'em in the fifties, honey," said Jim. "Shove the good bits in a cage." He pulled on a dress. "Halter?"

"Maybe I don't want to go *that* sexy. The mathematicians might think I was, you know . . ."

"A rental," finished Talmadge. He reached the end of the rack. "We have some possibilities. But we might need something fresh."

She had decided on the halter; it was from the early fifties, and Jim said it wasn't as blatant as all that, as long as she wore a strapless bra, although the white wasn't strictly seasonal and it kind of washed her out. But when she came home the night before Thanksgiving, Talmadge jumped up from the couch and said, "Wait right there!" Ceinwen waited and Jim lit a

cigarette while Talmadge rummaged behind his screens. He emerged holding something behind his back, posed for a second, then whipped it around
and held it up to his shoulders. Jim whistled.

"Talmadge," gasped Ceinwen, "that can't be for me."

Sleeveless, dropped waist, obviously from the 1920s. The fabric was
silk velvet, a greenish bronze that shimmered even under their dim lights.
The neckline was deep and the skirt was gathered a bit in front, the hem
cascading down to about mid-calf. No lace, no trimming, just the gleam
of the fabric. Ceinwen reached to feel the edge of the armhole.

"This didn't come from the store," she said. "This I would have noticed."

"Where did it come from?" asked Jim.

"Bargain Bernie's," said Talmadge. Lily's cross-Village vintage rival.
"Try it on, try it on!"

Talmadge was giving her a present, so she changed in her bedroom to
make him happy. The shoulders were a little too big and might slip, but
otherwise it fit. She put on her highest heels and walked out.

"Wow," said Jim.

"God I'm good," said Talmadge. "Everyone should have me shop for
them."

"Speaking of shopping," said Jim, leaning back and blowing a steam-
whistle of smoke toward the arch of the living room entrance. "How much
was this? Because as we all know, Bargain Bernie's is no bargain."

The price tag was still attached. She flipped it over. "Talmadge! $200!
Have you gone crazy?"

"No, sweetie. I got a discount."

During the ensuing silence, Talmadge walked over and began to adjust
her shoulder seams.

"So," said Jim. "Should Ceinwen wear this to Bargain Bernie's, to show
everybody how it looks on a pretty girl?"

Talmadge stood back to check his work. "Why bother? Such an ugly,
crowded store. That's why I go there, so poor Ceinwen doesn't have to.
You have to know exactly what you're looking for or you never find anything."

"Mm-hm," said Jim, examining the glowing tip of his cigarette. "Wonder if they're looking for this dress right now."

"They didn't understand this one," said Talmadge. He squatted to
check the line of the hem. "They had it crammed on a rack with a bunch

of boring old sheaths from the sixties. It was going to get torn and dirty. I *rescued* this dress."

"Talmadge, I love you so much," said Ceinwen. "Thank you. I don't care if the dress is . . ." She tried to think of a diplomatic phrase.

"Scalding hot?" suggested Jim. Talmadge continued to run his hands around the hem. She didn't see a hole from the security tag; he'd probably lifted a tag-remover from Vintage Visions ages ago.

"Jim," she said, ready to beg.

"I'm teasing, don't worry about it. Bernie's the biggest prick in the business. He makes Lily look like Santa Claus. I got a couple of things from there myself."

"Ooh, what?"

"Not telling." He stubbed out his cigarette with elaborate care. "Like the man said, don't wear it to Bargain Bernie's. They won't appreciate it."

"Promise. Won't even walk down Bleecker."

"I personally think it's way too good for a bunch of math professors, too," said Jim, "but what the hell. Give the nerds a thrill."

The next day she went for the complete effect, putting her hair up in back so that the front looked almost like a bob, adding some finger waves. She met Matthew at the Christopher Street station and they took the subway together. She hadn't been this far uptown since the guitar player; Paru's apartment was even past the Thalia. And it was huge, a big hallway running past what looked like vast bedrooms, plaster molding she wished Jim could see, a double living room divided by arches, a dining room separated by those doors that slid into the walls, and windows that ran the whole length of one wall, overlooking the Hudson River. No wonder Matthew wanted tenure—it was worth all the late nights if you could live like this.

Paru turned out to be approximately nine feet tall, and Ceinwen had to keep even more than her usual distance in order to avoid talking to his shirt button. He offered to take their coats and she handed hers over. Matthew turned to say something and paused, his mouth still open.

"Do you like it?" she prompted eagerly. He'd shut his mouth but otherwise wasn't moving. "Is something wrong with it?"

"Nothing at all," he said, finally. "What, no tiara?"

She didn't care that he was teasing, his expression was more than enough. "You did say I could dress up."

"I did. And if someone wants to give you an Oscar while we're here, you won't even have to change. Listen, I'd like a word with Paru. Do you mind if I leave you a minute?"

She knew he was trying to get some paper going, so she said fine. She scanned the room for Harry. Nope, not in this room, anyway. Something was off, though she couldn't put her finger on it. She spotted a table with hors d'oeuvres and decided to get something to eat before she started introducing herself around. As she piled shrimp on a plate she kept checking out the crowd, until she realized what she was missing.

Women. There must have been more than twenty people there, but she saw only two women, both a fair bit older than she was, with that ineffable wife vibe about them, standing close to a man and trying to look like they were part of his conversation. Where were they keeping the women? This was kind of creepy, like the men's club in *The Stepford Wives*.

She'd never thought of herself as shy, but parties were a bit overwhelming. Back in Yazoo City she'd gotten into the habit of finding someone else who wasn't mingling well and trying to draw the person out. She had a good prospect right here by the table, and he was eating shrimp, too. He looked wary when she introduced herself, but gave his name as Yoshi. He turned out to be from Kyoto. She knew better than to ask about his math specialty, so she contented herself with bringing up Japanese movies, which she actually wasn't that familiar with, and neither was he. Still, she was learning how to pronounce some names from books, at least. He had a way of staring past her at something in the room, and she turned at one point to see what it was, except all she saw was the fireplace mantel. She'd gotten Akira Kurosawa and Sessue Hayakawa down pat, or so she thought, when she decided to get something to drink. She set down her plate, poured herself some seltzer, and turned back to discover he was gone.

Was I that boring? she wondered, feeling hurt. She picked up a piece of bread and wondered if she could smoke. Matthew was nowhere to be seen, but here was Donna, approaching for a cheek-kiss.

"That dress is spectacular. Did Matthew leave you here?"

"He's off with Paru somewhere. I was talking to someone named Yoshi, but he's disappeared."

"Oh, yes." Donna was pouring herself some wine. "I saw him heading out the door."

"Out the door?" She'd driven the man right out of the party? She *liked* Hayakawa, she'd said so.

"Yes. But you mustn't think anything of it, he does that."

"Does what, just—leaves?"

"Yes, exactly. It's nothing personal." Donna leaned closer and lowered her voice. "Harry decided one night to take Yoshi with us and some other Courant people to a movie. Ozu I think. I liked it all right but I couldn't tell you the title, they're all so similar. Late Spring, Early Fall, Mid-Winter, I get lost. Anyhow we're walking to dinner from the Bleecker Street Cinema, and one minute I'm talking to Yoshi, and the next minute all I see is his back, taking off across the park." She started laughing. "And of course, when I asked what on earth was that about, they all acted as though I was the strange one for commenting on it."

"At least I know it wasn't me," sighed Ceinwen.

"No, dear. With mathematicians, *never* assume it's you. Don't worry about Yoshi, he'll be back. He rejoined us on the other side of the park."

Harry was in the kitchen, kibitzing over Radha's turkey, Donna said. They'd been arranging to go to Paris, for all of February. Harry had no classes next semester and the École Normale Supérieure was having a conference, but they were really going to visit their son. Ceinwen blurted that she hadn't realized they had one, then tried to cover by asking if he was a mathematician too.

"No, no, not at all. He lives in Paris, he thinks he's a painter. Oy. But he may be about to settle down. He's living with a woman from Senegal, and I suppose he's serious since he wants us to meet this one."

"Does she sound nice?"

"She sounds employed, so I'm all for her. Works at a gallery. Uh-oh." Ceinwen turned and got a brief impression of hair walking past them into the other living room. "There's Andrew Evans."

"The Andy you told me about?"

"The very one. Ceinwen, I'm sorry to abandon you, but I'm going back to the kitchen to see if I can keep Harry there for a while longer. Trust me, we want those two separate as long as possible. Will you be all right?"

"Sure," said Ceinwen, "I'll introduce myself." This should be good.

"Go ahead," said Donna. "You might find him interesting." Ceinwen spotted the hair by the bookshelf and maneuvered herself into introductory position.

And there he was, Professor Andrew Evans, purchaser of Harry's movies, a man so strange he stood out amongst mathematicians. He was dressed soberly in chinos and a v-neck sweater over a shirt, and he wasn't scratching or talking to himself, but this was clearly a weird dude. His hair was down to just above his shoulders, a wiry mix of brown and gray, and his hairline crawled patchily back on his skull. His ears were so big they stuck out through the frizz.

He also appeared to be slightly pop-eyed, but it was hard to tell. Because Andy was staring at her. From time to time a man his age stared at her in the store, but not quite like this. She realized he had moved to shake hands.

"Andrew Evans," he said, in a weedy little voice. She hated thin, high voices in men.

"Ceinwen Reilly," she said. His hand was cold and slightly damp. She had it. *The Gold Rush.*

"So, how do you know Paru?"

The Little Tramp, she recalled, was in the mountains, snowed in by a blizzard. And his starving companion kept staring and staring, until he began to hallucinate that the Tramp was a giant chicken.

"I'm a friend of Matthew Hill," she told him. Any minute now Andy was going to grab a knife and fork and lunge for her throat. He was certainly looking in that vicinity. No, lower. She pulled the shoulder of her dress back into place.

"Matthew. Yes. I know him. He hasn't been here long. How did you two meet?"

Another social occasion, another lie she hadn't thought to prepare. "I work in the neighborhood and we met . . . around," she said. "We got to talking about old movies and then he wanted me to meet Harry."

"Talking about old movies. That's something of a surprise. I thought he only cared about new releases." His speaking manner was bizarre too, fast, pause, fast, pause, like a cabbie rushing to the next stoplight, then tapping the brakes.

"Maybe he was afraid to bring it up with you. Harry says you're something of an expert on silent movies."

"Afraid. Matthew." Obviously her lying was as polished as ever. Andy repeated her words like she'd told him Matthew had been wearing a toga.

"You know how the English are," she said. "Never want to reveal any kind of ignorance."

"I can't say that's been my observation." Pause. "On the contrary, I find the English are always pretending ignorance, in hopes of gaining some sort of tactical advantage." All righty then. Not exactly president of the fan club. "But I think it's fair to say the silent cinema is something of a passion of mine. Do you know anything about silents?"

"A bit."

He wasn't waiting for a response. ". . . Because you remind me of a silent star, a great one. Vilma Banky. Do you know her?" Becauseyouremindmeofasilentstaragreatone pause. VilmaBankydoyouknowher? pause.

"The name's familiar."

Her input was wholly unnecessary. "She was discovered by Samuel Goldwyn and made a number of high-quality productions in the 1920s. Her acting skills were not inconsiderable, but she was famed primarily as a beauty. She was promoted as the Hungarian Rhapsody."

A no-talent sex symbol. Was this a good place to say thank you? Evidently not, Andy was still going, and while she was dithering she'd missed the tour of Banky's filmography. ". . . with Valentino, and *The Winning of Barbara Worth*, directed by Henry King. When sound came in she had difficulties, however. The accent, and she also had a bad case of what they called mike fright. So she retired. Luckily she'd taken good care of her finances, and she was happily married to an actor named . . ."

And here was another thing about Andy. He was a major space invader. As he talked, he inched closer. "But, like a lot of silent stars, more than half her movies are lost." She took a step back. "I hope you don't think it's too forward of me to mention the resemblance."

"Not at all. I'll have to look her up when I get home. But it's probably just the dress."

"That is a very unusual dress. Quite authentic."

"It should be, it's from the twenties." Where was Matthew?

"So you have an affinity for the silent era."

"You could say that." Another step back.

"That's wonderful, just wonderful in a person your age. Have you seen many movies from the period?"

"Sure," she began. "I saw *The Crowd* at Theatre 80. With Matthew. He liked it too."

"Theatre 80? Oh no, not there! You couldn't possibly have appreciated it there. Rear projection, 16-millimeter, it's horrendous. And the projection speed of course is all wrong."

She'd hoped throwing Matthew back into the conversation might discourage Andy, but instead she had opened the taps. Projection speed, it seemed, was the key to proper enjoyment of silent movies. Andy knew all about projection speed. The silent cameras were operated with a hand-crank and the speeds varied, but projection often didn't. Sometimes it was too fast, and they were screened at sound-movie speeds of 24 frames per second in clips on television, making everything look like the Keystone Kops. But at Theatre 80 the speeds were a hair too slow. If you showed a silent movie at 16 frames per second . . . Where the hell was Matthew? She couldn't see him anywhere . . . 18 frames per second, but Theatre 80 was slower than that, and it killed the . . . something. Undercranking. Over-cranking. Adjusting to the rhythm of music played on the set during film-ing. It was all probably very important, but that voice, and those eyes, and how could anyone who cared so much about projection speed not have any notion of the speed of his own sentences?

Suddenly Matthew was at her elbow, and Andy wasn't noticing: ". . . and I tried to talk to the Theatre 80 management, but they really don't care that much about silents, so . . ."

"Forgive me," said Matthew, "but it seems we're going in for dinner. How are you, Andy."

"I'm well. Thank you." Ceinwen imagined Andy watching *The Crowd* at 24 frames per second. He'd eye the screen the same way he was eyeing Matthew.

"We should go find a seat," said Matthew. "You don't mind if I just borrow her for the duration, do you? I'm sure she'll be happy to go back later to, what was it?"

"Film-projection speeds," she said.

"That's right," said Andy.

"Ah. Sorry I missed that." Matthew made a little after-you gesture and she followed, relieved that Andy was still nursing his drink.

"Where have you been?" she whispered.

"Over by the door, talking to Paru and watching Andy back you up across the room."

"My hero."

"Do you realize you started there"—he stopped to indicate a spot at one end of the bookshelf—"and wound up there?" He pointed to a spot about eight feet away, near the window.

"He kept stepping toward me. Doesn't he realize New Yorkers need their space?"

"New Yorkers need their space. You need Yankee Stadium." He pushed her dress back onto her shoulder. "Have a heart. Andy probably dreams of cozy chats with young Mary Pickford. And there you were, in that dress, with that hair. The answer to his prayers."

"Shows how much you know. He said I reminded him of Vilma Banky." They were keeping their voices low as the others filed into the dining room behind them.

"Who?" He was pulling out her chair.

"Vilma Banky. Silent movies. A sex symbol. They called her the Hungarian Rhapsody."

He let go of the chair and coughed for a second, then resumed pushing her in. "Smooth-talking devil, that Andy."

Harry blasted into the room with greetings for both of them, and he and Donna settled directly across the table. Ceinwen spotted Yoshi sitting way down at the opposite end and reminded herself Donna had said it was nothing personal. She heard Matthew say, "Looking for something?" He was addressing Andy, who was hovering nearby.

"Just trying to find a seat." Andy sounded almost plaintive.

"You're in luck," beamed Matthew. "One right here." He pointed to the empty chair next to hers. Andy quickly leaned past Harry to plunk his glass down at the spot, like he was saving a seat at the theater. Harry's eyebrows shot toward the ceiling. Donna took off her glasses and rubbed the bridge of her nose.

Ceinwen had come to realize that Matthew had an extremely overdeveloped sense of mischief.

Still, things seemed to go all right at first, everyone passing plates and commenting on the food and Donna exclaiming over the cleverness of Radha putting garam masala in the stuffing. They talked about Paris and what it was like in February and whether there were any good exhibits at the moment. That led to Parisian moviegoing, which led to the Cinémathèque Française, which led back to silent movies, at which point Matthew asked someone to pass the wine.

She told Harry that the bad part of his silent-movie books was reading about a movie that sounded great, only to find out it didn't exist anymore. *Four Devils*, for instance, or *London After Midnight*.

"The studios never thought they had any value," growled Harry. "That's what happens when you let raw capitalism determine which art survives."

"I don't disagree with that," said Andy. "But I do think it helps to put things in a broader perspective."

"What kind of broader perspective do you have in mind?" Harry said this way too calmly.

"Lost movies appeal to our sense of doomed artistry," said Andy. It was safer to have him sitting down, thought Ceinwen, though there was still an awful lot of leaning. "The movies in your head are always much better than the movies you sit down to see. We build up heroic concepts of certain directors. Then, when their work is lost, we imagine what we're missing as even better than the movies we have. In that sense, we need lost movies. They fortify our Romantic ideal of cinema, that's cap-*R* Romantic of course."

She was stymied. How did you find a polite way to say, "That's just about the stupidest thing I've ever heard"?

"Postmodern *poppycock*," exploded Harry, pounding the consonants so hard a tiny bit of spit flew in the air.

"It isn't postmodernism, Harry. It's—"

"Rubbish. Nonsense. Have you been sneaking over to the humanities building?" Any minute now, Harry's finger would be launched at Andy's chest. "I'm not F. W. Murnau, I'm not Tod Browning, I'm not interested in my own puny concept of what they'd have done. I want to see those movies. I don't want to get my kicks imagining little scenes with Janet Gaynor."

"You're avoiding the question of—"

"And furthermore"—there went the finger, only it was pointing between Andy's eyes—"I *do* know what happens when some slob tries to reimagine a great movie. I know because I get to sit through the last twenty minutes of *The Magnificent Ambersons* and see just how Robert Wise stacks up against Orson Welles."

"*Magnificent Ambersons*," said Andy, who'd been trying to break in, "is a completely different instance, but now that you mention it, Harry, it actually supports my case. That's a movie where we have fragments of the director's vision. When you can see part of a movie, your imagination naturally fills the gaps. Your interpretation of what it would have been like becomes your experience of seeing it."

"Reader-response theory," said Matthew. "You *have* been playing with the humanities boys, haven't you."

Harry's eyebrows were about to meet his cheekbones. "You've been unfaithful to us, Andy," he intoned.

"Sneaking off at lunch," said Matthew.

"Discussing Barthes at secluded tables in dark little restaurants."

"Meeting Stanley Fish at the Washington Square Hotel."

Andy's hair was vibrating. "It isn't my fault you need a certain vocabulary when discussing the arts."

Ceinwen wasn't crazy about Andy, but she was even less fond of seeing someone ganged up on. "You have to study the arts like anything else," she heard herself say. Her reward was Andy's hand giving her bare shoulder a pat. She pulled her dress back up and caught Matthew leaning a bit closer.

"That's right," said Andy. "We aren't superior to artists—"

"That's exactly what I'm saying."

"And if you'd let me finish, I was going to say that we also need theorists to illuminate what the artist is trying to do. And my original point about lost films isn't—"

"I don't need their stinkin' theories," boomed Harry.

"*Treasure of the Sierra Madre*," said Matthew, like he'd hit the buzzer on *Jeopardy!*. Andy looked stunned. So did everyone else. As they digested the fact that Matthew had referenced a movie made before Watergate, he spoke across Ceinwen, addressing Andy with the air of a patient tutor. "The Mexican bandits, pretending to be officers? Bogart asks to see their badges, and the leader says, 'We don't need no stinkin' badges.'"

Harry's glass went up in a silent toast.

"I know the scene," said Andy. "I didn't realize you were a John Huston fan."

"I'm not." Matthew gave Andy a big smile. "That's Ceinwen."

"I thought maybe Anna took you to see it." She winced. Good grief, who knew professors were this catty. Vintage Visions was more collegial.

"Everybody," said Matthew evenly, "needs a good movie friend."

"I agree," said Donna. "Who wants to go to the movies by yourself?"

Donna then changed the subject, with no attempt at a smooth transition, to Reagan. Politics, apparently, was a much safer subject with academics. Everyone was on the same side.

The party broke up quickly, although Harry and Donna hung back. They took the 1 train at 116th Street. It was cold on the platform, and when they sat down Ceinwen put her feet on the heater underneath the seat. The car was almost empty, just two tired men in down jackets and an old lady in a plaid coat, Bible open in her lap, eyes darting around behind thick-lensed glasses. As soon as the train pulled out she began to speak.

"And seeing the multitudes, he went up into a mountain: and when he was set, his disciples came unto him, and he opened his mouth . . ."

"Wish she'd shut hers," muttered Ceinwen.

Matthew didn't turn. "Done to death, I agree."

". . . blessed are the meek . . ."

"Maybe she takes requests," said Ceinwen. "Go on, ask her for Ecclesiastes."

"Ask her yourself, you're dressed for it. Vanity of vanities, all is vanity."

"Oh, go to hell."

"There's an idea. Revelations. And upon her forehead was a name written . . ."

"Don't you dare."

"Mystery, Vilma Banky the Great. What did you think I was going to say?"

"I'll never hear the end of Vilma. Will I."

"I'm just jealous." She caught herself before the grin spread. "It would take me days to think of a chat-up line that good. I'd have compared you with that woman in the Marx Brothers movie we saw last week."

"Thelma Todd?" She was the only blonde.

"No, the other half of the bill." She shook her head. "The one who hung around Groucho. Similar taste in dresses."

"*What?!?*"

"Although I can't help but point out, *she* had a tiara. Remember, you're fighting for this woman's honor, which is more—ouch! You brat, that *hurt!*" She pulled her foot back. "All right, all right, not her."

"Ye are the salt of the earth . . ." The woman was getting louder.

Matthew moved closer and pushed her hair back, sucking in one cheek as he studied her face. "Maybe Ginger."

"Rogers? I'll take that."

"Gilligan's Island, although the hair—" He put his hand on her knee before she could swing her foot again and they started kissing. After a minute she noticed the subway car had fallen silent and then she heard a shuffling.

They turned their heads to see the Bible lady open the connecting door to change cars. They grinned at each other and kept necking all the way to Christopher Street.

DECEMBER

1.

THREE NIGHTS A WEEK WAS EASING INTO FOUR. EITHER ANNA WAS writing less, or Matthew had found a place to hide her letters. Ceinwen drew the line at going through his desk. She bought a toothbrush and left it in his bathroom. After a week of him saying nothing about that, she added a bottle of cleanser. The ticket-takers at Theatre 80 had taken to greeting them both by name. The bartender at the Holiday had a special grimace just for them.

With less than two weeks left before Christmas, Matthew had decided they were going out to dinner. At the party Paru had been talking about a French place, way east for a good restaurant, almost near First Avenue. My treat, Matthew told her. Don't argue. She ordered veal to make him happy. He ordered an entire bottle of wine. Still not as good as Harry's, but a huge improvement over the offerings at the Holiday.

He was going to London for Christmas. "Aren't you going home?" he asked.

She shook her head. "New York is wonderful at Christmas anyway. The closer you get to the day, the nicer people get. Unless," she added, "you're working retail."

And Jim and Talmadge would be in town, too. Last year Jim had come out to his family in Michigan. His mother was relieved, said he could call more often. Jim's sister, though—she seemed to think New York had done something to him. And his parents were divorced. His father never called that much before, and now he didn't call at all.

Talmadge's father had skipped out when he was a baby, and he was very fond of his mother. He'd never told his mother, in so many words, but then you'd have to be on life support not to realize Talmadge was gay. The problem was Tacoma. "It makes me drink," he said. "I don't even have to feel the wheels hit the runway. They announce that we're starting our descent into Tacoma, and all I can think is please god somebody get me a tequila and Coke."

Matthew refilled her wine. She broke off another piece of bread and ran it around the last of the sauce. "London at Christmas sounds like Dickens," she said. "Maybe you'll have snow. You can sing 'God Rest Ye Merry

Gentlemen' through a keyhole." He was concentrating on laying his knife and fork across the plate. "*A Christmas Carol*?"

"I won't be in London the whole time."

She wrapped her hand around her wineglass. "Where else are you going?"

"Christmas Day I'm flying to Modena."

"Modena." She took a sip. "What's Christmas in Modena like?" Did Anna get nicer at Christmas?

"We won't be there long." She couldn't tell if he was looking at the silverware, the plate or the tablecloth. "We're going to St. Moritz."

"I didn't know you knew how to ski."

"I've done it a few times." The base of her throat was getting hot, but she kept her hand on her glass and her eyes on him until he met them. "We made the reservations before she left. We knew I'd be back in London so of course we arranged to meet."

"That's logical." She could feel her chest moving up and down with the effort not to yell. "When in London, hop next door to St. Moritz. With Anna."

"What's that supposed to mean?"

"It means," she said, relaxing her grip on the glass so the stem wouldn't snap, "it's great you can afford a ritzy ski resort on postdoc pay. Or is it Anna's nickel?"

"Nice." With that accent of his, he could bite off a single word like no one she'd ever known.

"What do you expect me to say?"

"Would you be happier if we were going to sit around the flat in Modena? Why do you have to drag money into it? All sorts of people go there."

"Glad to hear it. I'm glad you and Ah-nuh can go up and down the slopes and say 'Hey, isn't it great there's all sorts of people right here next to us on this ski lift?'"

He put both hands on the table and leaned as far toward her as he could. "Absolutely bloody incredible. You're the most class-ridden person I've ever met, and I'm *English* for fuck sake."

"What, you think you folks are the only ones who know about class?" She swallowed some more wine and dialed up the accent as far as it would go, all the way to backcountry. "Southerners know all about it too, hon. We can tell by the accent, same as y'all. On account of a Southerner would hear me talk and know I got myself a little education, leastwise, enough to where he wouldn't try and tell me, long as he's in London, might as well run next door to St. Moritz—"

"I didn't say—"

"—when that's like sayin' 'I was in Atlanta, so I figured what the hell, might as well swing through Omaha.'"

"I didn't—" He stopped, looked at the startled couple at the next table, and brought his voice down. "I didn't try to tell you it's next door, and I don't appreciate your little digs, when I never imply you're stupid, never. All I said is that we're going to be on the same side of the ocean, so of course we're going to see other."

"In all fairness, not seeing the logic there *is* kind of stupid of me, isn't it?" She snapped open her purse. "And I'm also too dumb to know what I'm supposed to do when you get back. Wait for you in the lobby at Courant?"

"You can do what you want. That's always been the case. I made that clear, didn't I?" She pulled out her wallet and slammed it on the table. He caught her wine glass as it teetered. She grabbed it away from him and drained the last third in one gulp. "Will you calm down? You bolted that. You're making—"

"I'm twenty-one. You just said I can do what I want." She set down the glass, hard, and snatched up her wallet.

"What are you doing? I said I'd pay." She pulled out two twenties. "And that's too much."

She balled up the bills and tossed them across the table. He pulled back as they landed in the last of the sauce on his plate. He put a hand up to the side of his face, as if to hide from the couple just inches away.

"Ceinwen—"

She threw her wallet back in her purse and snarled, "If I need your math help, professor, I'll stop by during office hours."

She picked up her coat and purse and half-ran the short way out to the sidewalk, dragging on the coat as she went and hitting another diner in the head with it. When she got to the corner, she knew he wasn't coming after her, and she started to cry. No tissues in her purse or pockets, and she'd forgotten to take her scarf out of her sleeve. Still walking, she pulled it out and wiped her eyes.

On the corner of Avenue B and Seventh the weirdo called out "Whatsa matter, Blondie, bad date?" She screamed back, "Fuck you," in part because she hated how predictably she was playing the part, and spent the next block checking to make sure he hadn't followed her. He hadn't. But she'd have to avoid that corner for at least the next couple of weeks.

They'd finally fixed the street door, but her key had migrated to the bottom of her purse and she had to pull out half her stuff to find it. She unlocked it, went up the stairs at twice her usual pace and had to catch her breath on the third floor. When she got to the apartment her legs were burning and she was shaking. She walked in, shut the door, and stood face-first against the wall.

"Ceinwen? Is that you?" She didn't turn to see where Jim was calling from. "What happened?" He was standing next to her. She didn't move.

"I'm an idiot. That's what happened." She wiped her nose with her scarf. "You have my permission to tell me. Ceinwen, you're an idiot."

"I'm sorry, honey." She felt him pat her back. "Nobody's going to tell you you're an idiot. Unless you stay here in the hall ruining your scarf." He took her purse out of her hand. "Take off your coat and come sit down."

She started to pull it off, then stopped and leaned her shoulder against the wall, the coat trailing on the floor. He slipped it off her arm. "All right. You stand there till you feel like taking a walk to the living room." She closed her eyes. She heard Jim's footsteps fade away toward her bedroom. Then she heard him walk back and open the door to the bathroom. She walked to the living room, sat on the couch, dropped the scarf on the floor and covered her face with her hands. Through the bottom of her hands she saw something appear on the coffee table. It was a roll of toilet paper.

"We're out of Kleenex," said Jim. "I knew there was something I forgot at Thrifty Mart."

"Where's Talmadge?"

"He called from a pay phone to say he'd gone out with George. He should be home soon."

"Good for him." She peeled off a long strip and blew her nose. "I'm glad somebody is getting some tonight."

"You let me know when you're ready to tell me what happened." Jim put on his glasses and picked up his book from the coffee table, she pulled off some more toilet paper, and they said nothing for about half an hour. Talmadge's keys sounded in the door and they heard him singing down the hall.

"Falling in love again, never wanted to, what am I to do—" Talmadge stopped in the doorway. "What the fuck happened?"

Nobody answered.

Talmadge sat down on a floor cushion, coat still on, and demanded the whole story. Jim put down his book and they both listened.

"Well, one thing I can tell you is Mr. Mass on Sunday isn't nearly as chic as he thinks he is," said Talmadge. "St. Moritz is over. Greg told me so."

"Greg?" asked Jim. "You mean that old investment guy? You still see him?"

"No, not for ages. Now that I'm not drinking anymore I actually have to like them. But he knew, and that's what he said. People go to Gstaad. Or Zersomething."

"Zurich? That's for bankers, not skiers."

"It's not Zurich."

"Then what are you talking about?"

"Switzerland, that's what. I forgot the name, okay? If I was personally familiar with the place, I wouldn't be spending Christmas on *fucking* Avenue C." Talmadge got up. "We need a movie here. I could go to the rental place. It's open till midnight." She pulled her legs up and hugged her knees. "A movie. Right?"

"Let me go," said Jim. "It's two-for-one night. I know exactly what to get."

Ceinwen put her head on her knees. Talmadge took off his coat and went into the kitchen to make one of his famously nasty herbal teas. This one was dried sage and she drank it anyway, trying to wash the taste of veal and wine out of her mouth.

When Jim returned he dumped the videos on the coffee table. She picked up the top one and read the cover. "*The Bridge on the River Kwai.*" Jim was putting his feet up.

"Don't know that one," said Talmadge.

"Alec Guinness," said Ceinwen. "As a prisoner of the Japanese. Along with a bunch of other soldiers. All British."

"Nope, for once you're wrong. You forget William Holden is there too," said Jim. "And some Canadians."

"Nobody ever remembers the Canadians." Ceinwen picked up the second box. "I get the feeling you're making a point here."

"Why, whatever do you mean? Great movie."

Talmadge leaned over and read the spine. "*The Great Escape.* More prisoners of the Japanese?"

"The Germans," said Jim.

"Oh good, variety," said Talmadge. "And Ceinwen, look, they escape. Right there in the title, see?"

"The British prisoners all get shot," said Ceinwen.

Jim crossed his legs. "Because one of them makes an incredibly stupid mistake."

"I vote for that one," said Talmadge. "Not that you two just ruined the ending or anything."

"If you don't like these, there's still time to go back," said Jim. "They had *A Man for All Seasons*."

"There you go, she's almost laughing," said Talmadge. "Who's a prisoner in that one?"

"An English Catholic," said Ceinwen. "He gets beheaded."

"You know you love me," said Jim.

"I do. But you stink."

Four days passed before she picked up the phone. Classes were ending, she knew. He'd be giving his final exam soon. She called the home number and let it ring until she lost count, until she heard the apartment door opening and she set down the receiver, needing two tries to get it in the cradle. That was enough time for Jim and Talmadge to make it to the living room, and to see her replacing the phone on the cardboard table that had been its temporary home since the previous Christmas.

"Uh-oh," said Talmadge. She sat on the couch and stared at the TV, which she hadn't turned on.

"Talmadge," said Jim. "What do we got in the way of tea these days?"

"We got oregano."

"Oregano? Jesus."

"Whole leaves. It's cleansing."

"Fine. Just use the tap water, god knows it's hot enough. Let's cleanse." Jim plopped next to her and offered her a cigarette, which she took even though she didn't smoke menthols. He waited until they were both well into their first drags, and said, "Was he there?" She shook her head. "You can't call him." Silence. "Let me repeat that. Nice and slow. You. Can't. Call. Him."

"I hadn't been planning to," she whispered.

"Hey, nobody ever does. You get weak after a while. I understand. But I'm telling you, I'm a man and I know how our brains work. Worst thing you can do."

"I only did it because . . ." She trailed off.

"I know. You felt bad. It's been a few days, you start to think, maybe I was too harsh. I said mean things. So you figure, I'll call and say . . . well, I don't know *what* you say to this one. 'Hi, I'm sorry I pointed out that you already have a girlfriend.'"

"That's not why."

"'I'm sorry I called you rich?'"

"No." She started to sob. "It's his birthday."

Jim slipped an arm around her waist.

"Sagittarius," Talmadge called from the kitchen. "That is one flaky sign. And you're what, Gemini? Oh dear."

"Let us know when it's ready." The toilet paper had migrated to a spot under the coffee table. Jim pulled it out for her. "I'm sorry, honey. But like I said, I'm a guy, and I'm telling you, if you call him, you look desperate. If you want him back, it'll make him want you less. And if you decide good riddance, you'll feel better leaving it like this."

She blew her nose. "It was just one call."

"One is too many and a thousand wouldn't be enough. Speaking of which..."

Talmadge had come in with the tea. "Are you ready? Because this is something you may not hear me say again for a long, looong time. But—" He picked up her hand and put the mug in it. "Jim is right. Did you hear that, Jim?"

"My week is made."

"My pleasure. I repeat, Jim's right. If Pope John Paul wants you back, he's gotta call himself." She took a sip and so did Jim. "How is it?"

"It's worse than the sage."

"I'll say," said Jim.

"Good. We're cleansing like with like. Bitter with bitter." He waved his hands over her head. "Think of it washing through you."

Talmadge walked to the phone, a heavy, black-metal rotary from the 1940s that Jim had bought refurbished. It had a twelve-foot cord so they could move it around the apartment, and untangling the cord was another of Talmadge's self-appointed duties. This time, he picked up the whole phone. "Observe. Jim keeps saying I know nothing about recovery, but he is so very, very wrong." He carried the phone into Jim's room, walked back out, shut the door on the cord and dusted his hands. "Avoidance? *Works.*"

2.

THREE MORE DAYS WERE ALL SHE HAD TO GET THROUGH UNTIL Matthew left, and she made it without calling. Jim took the phone out of his room. She quit looking down the store to the entrance. Vintage Visions was hopping, and Lily was happy, or at least less nasty. One week before Christmas, Talmadge waited on Madonna and talked of nothing else for days.

She went home every night and watched war movies with Jim until Talmadge rebelled: "I know you're mad at men right now. I know you want to see them suffer. And Jim, he just likes to see *me* suffer. But one more battle scene and I'm buying *Miracle on 34th Street*. Colorized. And I'll play it every night."

They split the cost of a tree, a ratty, lopsided affair that Jim and Talmadge bought on Avenue A and bargained for fiercely, united in holiday stinginess. For two days before that, they had argued about colored versus white lights. Ceinwen recused herself. Jim won. They got white.

She'd bought ornaments here and there, but the tree was bigger than she had reckoned, and it looked even rattier sparsely decorated. They walked around it a bit and debated about where to get more ornaments, until Ceinwen remembered her box of broken jewelry. They finished trimming it with severed strands of fake pearls, necklaces and bracelets with broken clasps, clip-on earrings that hurt too much to wear, mateless earrings, and brooches with missing stones. Jim contributed a few cufflinks. Talmadge strung up some worry beads.

They agreed it was the chicest Christmas tree in Manhattan.

Christmas morning they opened gifts. For Talmadge, Jim and Ceinwen had gone halfsies on a huge framed poster from the Marlene documentary they'd watched together. Ceinwen's gift from Jim was a set of rhinestone dress clips from the 1940s, which she immediately put on her coat. Talmadge had managed to get Jim an entire double-breasted vintage suit, and Jim had the courtesy not to ask where it came from. Nor did Ceinwen question the origin of her gift, a black silk robe with a red-and-gold dragon guarding the back, claws outstretched. "This is a very powerful sign for you right now," explained Talmadge.

Jim's mother had sent him an answering machine. They argued about what to record for the outgoing message, and finally Jim said they'd use the prerecorded one until they reached a consensus.

Jim made a small turkey, basting it every ten minutes like a madman. Ceinwen made the mashed potatoes, and they ate a salad so they'd feel like they'd earned the chocolate ice cream.

After dinner, Talmadge announced he needed to call home. "Do you want to call home first?" he asked Ceinwen.

"No."

Jim was shaking his pack of Newports. "Damn. Forgot to stock up."

"Thrifty's open," said Ceinwen. "I'll run down."

As she descended the stairs she heard music. She was surprised Miriam wasn't out. She stopped and tried to identify what was playing. Classical, that was all she could tell. For Ceinwen, classical was either Beethoven, or Not Beethoven.

When she came back upstairs she deposited the cigarettes on the coffee table. "Miriam's home," she said.

"Wanna invite her up?" came Talmadge's voice from behind his screens. He was trying to decide where to hang Marlene.

"You think she'd come?"

"I was joking," came the voice again. "What are we going to do with Miriam, hold a snubbing contest?"

Jim narrowed his eyes. "Is this about your grandmother?"

"Granana? What do you mean?"

He gathered his words. Then, "She died, and I know you miss her, honey. But if you're looking for a substitute, I don't think Miriam is the way to go. She doesn't even have a dog."

She unbuttoned her coat and went to her room to hang it up. When she returned she sat on the couch. "Granana was barely as tall as me, she weighed about two hundred pounds, and she never wore anything unless it had elastic. She hardly left the house and the only music she listened to was bluegrass and gospel. When she wasn't sitting around watching old movies, she was watching CNN or backtalking William F. Buckley on *Firing Line*. Trust me, Miriam does not remind me of Granana."

Talmadge went into the kitchen and crossed back to his space, a brick in one hand and a nail in his mouth. Jim put down the answering-machine manual. "All right. You want to talk to Miriam. It's Christmas Day. Go take her a gift. Maybe she'll invite you in."

She thought about it. "Not bad."

"Talmadge isn't the only one around here who can come up with something devious."

"I love you too, Jim." Hammering began.

She grabbed Jim's hand. "Help me find something I can give her."

They went to her room and surveyed her shelves.

"How about a scarf," said Jim. "You have what, twenty? You won't miss one." He pulled the stack down and they sat on her bed.

Some were souvenir scarves from the fifties and sixties, which she'd bought because if you folded them right they kind of looked like Hermes. Kind of Hermes surely wasn't right for Miriam. There was a velvet one she used to keep her head warm in cold weather, a couple of plain ones that were too boring, a couple of lace ones that were too young. She drew out a long, narrow scarf, dusty pink chiffon, edged with lace that had aged to dark ivory, dotted with tiny pearl beads. Probably 1930s at least, maybe earlier. It was so delicate she had worn it only twice. She unfolded it and held it up to the light.

"I said you should give her a scarf," said Jim. "I didn't say it had to be your best one."

"This is the only one I think she would like."

"It looks its age," said Jim. "It's beautiful, but she's gonna know it's not new. Didn't she criticize you for wearing old stuff?"

"I think she might like it."

"Suit yourself." They went back into the living room, and Jim picked up the tissue and ribbon he'd saved from Talmadge's present and wrapped the scarf. He'd gotten so much practice at his store that he didn't need tape. "There you are."

Talmadge's head appeared between his screens. "You're really going to do this?"

"She can't lose," said Jim. "If Miriam hates the scarf, it's still hers."

Ceinwen went downstairs and looked under the door. There was a faint light, and the music was still playing. She knocked and listened for Miriam's footsteps. The music stopped, the door opened. Miriam was wearing a big sweater and yet another expression Ceinwen couldn't read for the life of her.

"Hello."

"Hello, Miriam. Merry Christmas." She held out the gift. Miriam took it and picked up the end of a ribbon. "It's by way of being neighborly," said

Ceinwen. "And," she continued after a beat, "I also wanted to say I was sorry. For, you know, offending you a while back."

"You didn't offend me. I'm sorry you thought you did." She let go of the ribbon. "This is a lovely thing to do. Thank you. Would you like me to open this now?"

"Yes, please." She said that too fast, but Miriam opened the door wider. The light in the living room was soft and pretty at night; the glass hurricane lamp gave off a pinkish glow. Miriam gestured toward the armchair.

"Have a seat. I'm afraid I didn't get you anything, but maybe you'd like some coffee. I just made it."

On the coffee table was a tray that held a china pot, a creamer, a sugar bowl, and a cup with a saucer. Everything matched. Ceinwen never drank coffee at night—it kept her awake. But the cup had a gold rim and a gold vine shimmying up the handle, and dark blue and deep pink flowers on the side. She wanted to pick it up.

"Thanks, that sounds great." Miriam went to the china closet and came back with another cup and saucer. Then she walked to the sideboard and reached into the cabinet underneath.

"I'm going to put some brandy in mine. Would you like some too?" She came up with a large green bottle.

"Even better." Drunk, and unable to sleep. At least that would add one twist to all the other nights these past two weeks. She watched Miriam pour out the coffee, then a generous splash of brandy in each cup. Ceinwen took a sip and Miriam picked up the present.

"This is really very nice of you." She pulled on the bow. Of course Miriam wouldn't just rip away. She unfolded the paper and held up the scarf, fingering the lace at the edge. The quiet lingered so long Ceinwen wondered if she might get thrown out again. "It's beautiful."

"It's vintage." Might as well get that out of the way.

"I used to wear scarves like this," said Miriam. "Brings back some memories." She folded it neatly and set it beside her. "You've been making an effort to cultivate me. Haven't you." It didn't sound like an accusation, but it didn't sound like an invitation, either.

"I'm from Mississippi," said Ceinwen. "We're used to knowing our neighbors there." She took another sip of coffee for morale. "But I have to admit, you're the only one in the building who seemed like . . ." Miriam wasn't going to help her out. ". . . like we might have things in common."

Miriam took her first sip. "You're an old-movie buff." Ceinwen nodded. This didn't seem to be going as well as it could have. "I've met a few over the years. I don't think many of them go so far as to wear the old clothes, though. Especially not at your age."

"You'd be surprised," said Ceinwen, seizing a chance to push the conversation somewhere better. "Vintage is really popular."

Miriam sighed. "You seem like a nice girl. Really. But if you think I'm some treasure trove of movie lore, you're wrong. I was a seamstress. Mostly I saw the costumers. When I saw the stars, it was just fittings. Good morning, are you sure this seam is straight. Can you take the bodice in. When will this be ready. Good night. I never did hear much gossip and what I did I've probably forgotten. It's been more than forty years."

This was uncomfortably close to what Ceinwen had, in fact, been hoping for all these months. But it still felt unfair to both of them. "I thought you seemed interesting before I had any idea you'd ever been near Hollywood."

"That's nice to know. Unfortunately, I'm not. I'm a widow living alone on the Lower East Side. I play mah-jongg with some friends uptown. Sometimes we go out to dinner. I read books and I go to museums and lectures. I don't even go to the movies anymore."

She was starting to feel peeved. She'd brought Miriam her best scarf and in return she was getting Irish coffee and a talk about how boring the woman's life was. "I haven't asked you about Garbo or Joan Crawford or anything, and I wouldn't."

"Garbo was a Sapphic." Sapphic? Who says Sapphic? "Crawford was gracious but she hated Norma Shearer and we had to be careful to schedule their fittings so they couldn't possibly run into each other. Is this anything you haven't read before?"

"If I were going to ask you about the old days, I wouldn't ask you about MGM," retorted Ceinwen. "I'd ask you about that." And she turned and pointed to the silver-framed picture on the table.

"That's what you were looking at last time." Miriam set her cup in its saucer and crossed her legs at the ankle, a ladylike pose Ceinwen had never learned to maintain. "You saw that photograph, with me in costume, and decided I'm a forgotten star. Like *Sunset Boulevard*. You must have seen that one?"

"Of course."

"I'm sorry to disappoint you, but that isn't the case either. No mansion, no chauffeur, no stardom. I had only one part where I was on screen for more than a few minutes, and the movie is long gone."

"Lost?"

"Has been for decades. I don't think there's many people alive who ever saw it. I'm not Louise Brooks. Nobody's going to ask me to write for the *New Yorker*."

Ceinwen twisted toward the picture again. "I don't know any Emils from the silents," she said. "Except Emil Jannings."

Miriam began to laugh. It was the first laugh Ceinwen had ever heard from her, and it was wonderful, a low-pitched vibrating cackle. Even her laugh was elegant. And it went on and on, until she picked up her napkin and wiped her eyes with it. "You looked this up, did you? And that's what you came up with? I inscribed a photograph with love to Emil Jannings? Have you seen his movies?"

"Sure I've seen them," said Ceinwen, too sharp, but her viewing chops were being maligned. "I saw *The Blue Angel* like everybody else." Miriam started laughing again. "I didn't think it was him, but he's the only Emil in any of my books. I figured your Emil wasn't an actor."

"No. No, he wasn't an actor. And he'd have given you what-for if you compared him to Jannings." She folded the napkin and laid it beside her cup. "He was a director. German, like Jannings. That was all they had in common, I assure you."

"Your Emil directed your movie. The one that picture's from."

"It was a publicity shot. But yes."

Her coffee was almost gone, and Miriam wasn't offering any more. That didn't seem promising. She kept her cup in her hand, to signal she was still drinking from it and shouldn't be thrown out just yet. "What happened to him?"

"He died in a car accident. About a year after the picture was finished." Then, as if to fend off a follow-up, "He was driving drunk. People did that in the twenties, too."

"I'm sorry." For the first time, she considered that Miriam might feel about Hollywood as she did about Yazoo City.

"It was a long time ago." Back to the "sorry-to-disappoint-you" voice. "Don't worry, I don't go all weepy every time I hear his name."

"I'm sorry," she repeated. "I've been trying to see some silents lately. I've never known anybody who made one. I wanted to hear what it was like."

"Moviemaking's dull. That's why the stories you hear are all about what goes on off set. It's Christmas night. I would think if you weren't with your family, you'd be off with that young man I met."

She set the cup down; if Miriam wanted her to leave now, at least she could go back upstairs and cry. "We broke up."

Miriam reached over and patted her shoulder. "I'm sorry. I didn't mean to be tactless, truly. So that's why you're asking about Emil. You want to hear that life goes on. That sort of thing."

She hadn't expected the pat, but she didn't want the pity. "If I want to hear that time mends broken hearts or whatever, I can talk to my room-mates. They've been telling me that for two weeks."

"That's good of them. But they're wrong." Miriam gave no indication she thought this was bad news. "You sweep the pieces into a corner. And after a while they stay put." She set down her cup and poured in a little more brandy. "You really do want to hear about it, don't you. You want to hear about this old movie nobody's ever seen. You even brought me a bribe."

"It wasn't supposed to be a bribe, exactly."

"No, that's bad of me, it was very kind. This was your own scarf, wasn't it." She tried to think of a plausible denial but Miriam didn't pause. "And if I don't tell you the whole story, you'll be back at Key Food, want-ing to carry my groceries up four flights again until you wear me down. You'll be at my door on Lincoln's Birthday, ready to give me a stove-pipe hat." She poured some more coffee into Ceinwen's cup. "I guess I'd better go ahead and indulge you before you go to any more trouble." She added some brandy. "I'd tell you it's a long story, but I get the feeling that's what you want."

She picked up her coffee so fast she sloshed a bit into the saucer, and said, "All the best stories are long."

Miriam smiled. "You're a romantic." She looked past Ceinwen, at the picture on the table. "You tell me something first. Were you always pretty?"

Ceinwen hadn't felt pretty for more than two weeks, and not that often even before, but a good guest doesn't whine to her hostess. "No. I was skinny as a kid and way too pale and I had glasses and it took a while for the gap in my teeth to close up. Then my eyes got better and so did my looks, I guess. Nobody thought much of me in Mississippi. They like 'em tan and athletic down there."

"They liked them plump and hearty in Milwaukee when I was growing up," said Miriam.

It wasn't Kansas City, but it was close. "I wouldn't have guessed Milwaukee."

"Why not? It was quite a sophisticated town in those days, at least for the Midwest. They tell me it isn't as nice now."

"Nobody liked your looks in Milwaukee?"

"Oh, I wasn't the fashion, but people liked the way I looked. I wasn't one of the ones who start out plain and blossom."

"Yeah, I guess that was me."

Miriam tucked her legs up on the sofa. "Me, I was always pretty. I got tired of it early on. Just about the first thing I can remember is people stopping Mother in the street to tell her how pretty I was, and Mother talking and talking to them about my eyes and my bones and my hair. I heard it so much, it got to be like someone noticing I had teeth. Mother had been a beauty herself, but she had me late in life, after they'd just about given up on having any children at all. By the time I reached my teens, her looks were mostly gone and she'd gotten stout."

"My grandmother used to say that when people can't stand their own looks anymore, they gussy up the kids."

Miriam nodded. "It's natural. But Mother took it further. She kept entering my photo in contests, wanted me to do amateur theatricals and plays. Father wouldn't have any of it."

"Didn't approve of actresses?"

"No, he did not. And his word was law. But the year I turned fourteen there was diphtheria going around. Mother didn't catch it, she never caught anything, but Father caught it, and he died. And I got it too, and I was terribly sick. My hair fell out. I remember Mother standing over me and at first I thought she was feeling my forehead for fever, but she was running her hand over my scalp, trying to see how much hair was left. It did grow back, but it took almost a year. My hair had been pin-straight before, but it grew in with a wave, and when it started getting thick again she'd brush it and say maybe diphtheria was a stroke of luck. The sickness hadn't changed my face at all, and curly hair was much more fashionable. Meanwhile I'd been out of school so long I had to repeat the year.

"And of course with Father gone she could enter me in as many fool things as she liked. She kept making me do plays, but I was lucky to get the ingenue and sometimes I didn't even get that. Then I won a beauty contest in Milwaukee. I'd placed second or third in a few before, but this was a big one, city-wide. Mother figured it would give us some kind of entree in Hollywood."

"You didn't want to go?"

"Heavens no, but there was no question of trying to talk her out of it. I refused one beauty contest and she took to her bed. I was ungrateful, I didn't love her, I was trying to kill her. She carried on for a week until I finally gave in. After that I tried sabotage. They'd tell me to smile and I'd bare my teeth. I'd slouch when I was supposed to be graceful. I'd fake stage fright. I don't know where I went wrong with that last contest, but somehow I did win. And there we were in Hollywood, with probably a thousand other girls from a thousand other contests. Didn't matter to Mother. As soon as we got off the train she started gushing on about the sunshine and the oranges and the ocean. I had to wear a hat to ward off freckles, citrus still gives me an acid stomach and neither one of us could swim. I don't even like stucco. But she sold our fur coats the first week we arrived, and I knew what that meant. We had to stick around until she came to her senses.

"Every little bit part I got made her think I was ripe for discovery. She took me to every casting call. I even met with Chaplin."

Now that was impressive. "How did it go?"

"Badly. Like everyone else we'd heard he liked girls innocent and young. I was eighteen, and that was actually a bit old for him, but Mother thought I was a sure thing. Then when he came in I crossed my legs at the knee, pulled my hem up a bit and asked him for a cigarette. Mother tried to tell him I didn't smoke and this was my idea of being comical, but he couldn't get me out of that office fast enough. I think that was the closest she ever came to slapping me."

She couldn't believe it. "Why? Why did you blow it like that? It was Chaplin."

"Because I knew how it would go. At best I'd get another bit, like all the other bits I got now and again. Simpering on the sidelines, handing the star her powder puff. Only if it was Chaplin it would be worse, because Mother would be more sure than ever that I was going to be a big noise. I knew it wasn't going to happen. And I was getting letters from my friends in Milwaukee, and they were going to parties and getting engaged, and some girls were even going to college. And Mother and I were living in furnished rooms, and every day we weren't on set waiting for my few pitiful shots we were in offices, standing in line with girls my age, a lot of them with parents just like mine."

"Stage mothers."

"They're a cliché, I know, but Mother was as typical as they come." She paused and smoothed a lap crease, then continued, a little more gently. "That isn't fair. Believe it or not she was better than most. And what people don't mention is that the girls were just as bad. They wanted to be stars, too, and they hated any competition. It wasn't as though we offered one another any comfort. I tried to befriend a few and gave up.

"So it had been about a year and Mother got wind of a new project over at Civitas. It was a small studio but the head, Frank Gregory, was trying to make it bigger. And he'd brought over a director from Ufa to make a costume picture. It was going to give them some prestige, some clout with the big boys. Nobody here had seen this fellow's movies, he'd only made two as director, but whatever Gregory's people saw in Germany they liked."

"Did you like them?"

"I never saw them. After the war I thought I might get a chance, but they'd been stored in Berlin."

Ceinwen thought of the aerial shot of Berlin in *A Foreign Affair*, not a building intact, and didn't have to ask more.

"When Mother heard Emil Arnheim was casting she sent him my pictures and the next thing I know she's shoving a book at me, which she'd certainly never done before, and demanding that I read it because I have an interview with the director who was going to film it. An old Gothic romance called *The Mysteries of Udolpho*, which even then hardly anybody had read. And everyone thought the choice was crazy, because it's a perfectly terrible book."

"I read that one. I liked it."

"I can't imagine why. Most people know it only because Jane Austen made fun of it."

"*Northanger Abbey*. That's why I read it. But I still liked it. I thought," said Ceinwen, trying to phrase things with finesse, "it had a lot of atmosphere."

"What sort of atmosphere?"

"It was sexy," admitted Ceinwen. "To me at least."

She'd never seen this before—Miriam was delighted. "That's what Emil thought. Sublimated sex, the whole thing. He thought he could bring that out in the movie, and he wouldn't have to bother with the prose, which didn't exactly sing on the page. I didn't know that, of course. I just knew Mother wanted me to read it. Which I did, although I skipped big sections and snuck my own books between the covers when she wasn't looking. And then when I went to meet Emil, I wasn't supposed to tell him I had read the book, because that would look overeager, but I should be as much like Emily St. Aubert as possible. I had to remember to be sweet and high-toned and I'd better not embarrass us by talking about Milwaukee or modern authors. If he asked me if I had read the book, I was to say no, and bring up Ouida and Baroness Orczy. Then he'd think I was too romantic to be ambitious."

"That's kind of clever."

"She was diabolical. But I'd had it. I had a notion that if this one fell through, I could persuade her to give things up. We'd run through most of the money Father left us and were living on what little I earned and some sewing Mother did on the side. I could sew too, but she wouldn't let me do it for more than an hour or so at a time, because it would make me squint and I'd get lines around my eyes. I'd just turned nineteen without a single friend to share a slice of cake with me, and I told myself that would be the last birthday I'd have in Hollywood.

"We went to Civitas and waited outside his office and right away I thought things were different. There was only one other girl ahead of me, a different type altogether, very blonde, like Emily in the novel. The secretary told her to go in and she stayed a bit longer than I expected, and Mother didn't like that at all. Then it was my turn.

"And we walked in and it was just him, no assistants. He was rather handsome and a bit younger than I'd expected. And he takes my hand and he shakes it—I was used to having it kissed by the Europeans, which I always hated. He kept calling me Fraulein, which I thought was dreadfully affected. His English was excellent and anyway, how hard is the word 'Miss'? And he didn't want to know about what I had done before, instead he asked me questions about myself. At first I answered yes and no and right around the time I thought Mother was going to kick me he switched to questions that required real answers. Impertinent things, I thought, like what was my favorite fabric for a dress.

"We hadn't been there very long when he sat on the edge of the desk and said, 'You don't want to be here, do you, Fraulein Clare?' And I snapped, 'No.' That was when Mother really did kick me. But I didn't care, I was sick of it all. He said, 'Where would you rather be?' I said, 'I wish I were at home reading a book.' He asked, what would I be reading, then? And Mother jumped in and said I'd been reading *The Scarlet Pim-*

pernel all week. He gave her a look and said, 'Why, that's exactly the sort of the thing a romantic heroine should be reading.' And she said yes, that was the sort of thing I read all the time, she couldn't stop me. I was the most romantic girl in the world, all day long I dreamed of finding a soulmate.

"And he asked if he might speak to me alone. She didn't like that. Mind you, I don't think she was worried about my virtue at all. She was worried I was going to tell him I hated the movies and I hated Mrs. Radcliffe and I hated him and that would be that, I'd never be the next Lillian Gish. She said surely he understood that a mother had to think about even the appearance of impropriety. And he said he understood of course, but still, 'Frau Clare, I can't tell whether your daughter is suitable if I can't see how she is without her mama around.' He was putting it to her plainly; she left us alone, or else.

"She was stuck, and she left. He shut the door behind her and went back to sit on the desk. The only other time I was left alone with a director he'd asked to see my legs, and I'm sure I wasn't looking very friendly. He said, 'All right Miriam'—not Fraulein, not Miss Clare, Miriam—'what are you really reading?'

"I said, 'I'm reading *Manhattan Transfer*.'

"He let out this huge laugh, and then I started laughing too, because all I could think of was Mother hearing him through the door and how she must be planning to kill me for clowning around with a director who was casting a serious part.

"He asked me if I'd read the novel, and since he hadn't fallen for any of our other lines I told him yes, as much as I could stand. He said they were changing the setting to the Napoleonic era, because he liked the look of the costumes better than the sixteenth century. And they were changing the heroine's name to Madeleine, because the publicity people said they didn't want to spend all their time explaining the difference between Emil and Emily. And we both started laughing all over again.

"He asked me if I thought I could play Madeleine, and I told him no, I could barely walk across a set. Then he said he'd called us only because I was the most beautiful girl in any of the photos. He never once considered me for Madeleine, he figured he could use me in one of the ball scenes. I said, 'Please don't do that. It will only encourage Mother and I'll have to spend another year here at least.' And he laughed some more and said he'd give me a screen test. And if I was truly as awful as all that, he'd tell Mother

I was never going to get anywhere, and she should take me back to Milwaukee and let me read modern novels and get married.

"He tells Mother that he's going to give me a screen test day after tomorrow. She spent the next day trying to get me to move like an aristocrat and act more Napoleonic instead of sixteenth century, and I did everything she asked, thinking this would be the last of it.

"We got to the studio and they put me in makeup and this costume that had obviously been made for a woman with a much bigger bosom. They forgot to pad me out and it was hanging off me, and I didn't say anything because what did I care, it wasn't a real test anyway. When I walked out, Emil did kiss my hand, which thrilled Mother, and for once I didn't mind because he winked at me as soon as her back was turned. And he told her, very politely, that it was best she wait off set. And she left. It was glorious.

"Now you know in those days with no sound, the director could talk to you the whole time. As soon as the cameras started turning, he started telling me what to do. It was a scene between Count Morano and Madeleine, and I was supposed to be recoiling from his advances. The actor playing the Count didn't much appeal to me and I thought that would help, but then I started and Emil ordered the camera off after just a minute or two, and I knew I'd been as terrible as ever.

"And he took me aside and told me that if I didn't at least try, Mother would be able to tell and who knew how'd she react. He said he knew I must have had men trying to flirt with me in the casting offices, and I probably hadn't liked it. He was so kind that I told him about the other director who'd made me lift my skirt, and getting poked and sometimes pinched and having to stand up and turn around so they could comment on my legs or my chest, and how awful it always made me feel. He said fine, think about that. We started over and I realized this wasn't bad. He was going to get me out of there, and I did everything he asked. It took longer than I expected, maybe six or seven takes, and I wondered about that. When the test was over he told me to go out and have a good time. I told him I wouldn't be going anywhere, I'd be going home with Mother, like always. He said I wouldn't have to do that much longer.

"We didn't hear anything for a couple of days, and then a couple more days, and Mother was beside herself. Then a week had gone by and we were at home, I don't remember doing what, and the phone rang in the hallway and Mother went to answer it. And she starts shrieking. 'Miriam,

Miriam! You're Madeleine!' It was absolutely the last thing I had expected. It was a catastrophe. I wasn't blonde, I wasn't sweet, or blushing, or aristocratic, and I couldn't act. Everyone was going to find out I couldn't act. She told me, 'Miriam, he wants to talk to you.'

"First thing he said was, 'Are you terribly angry with me?' I told him, 'Yes. You're making a mistake. I'll ruin your movie, I'll be awful.' Mother grabbed my shoulder and shook it and I had to pull away so she wouldn't be close enough to hear him. He said I should be sensible and realize it would be much easier for a successful actress in Hollywood to get rid of her mother than for an unmarried girl in Milwaukee. I told him—I had to be careful, because if I said much more Mother would have apoplexy—I told him if it didn't work out that way, things would be worse than ever. He said, 'I don't want some actress who already thinks she knows everything arguing with me. I want someone who will trust me to tell her how it should be.' And he asked me if I trusted him. I didn't, I thought he was crazy. But I told him I did.

"The contract wasn't much by the standards of a real leading lady, a few hundred a week. But it was a world of money to us. We moved into a little bungalow and we had the studio car instead of having to take the streetcar all the time. I went out and bought some new clothes and Mother did too, and we thought we were living it up." She looked at the clock, a big brass thing under a dome on the mantel. "It's past 10:30. Time for my cigarette. I know you smoke too, would you like one of mine?" She reached for a lacquered box on the table.

"I didn't know you smoked."

"I have two in the evening." It was the most disciplined thing Ceinwen had ever heard. Miriam took the top off the box, took one and handed the box over. The cigarettes were filters with a gold band around the middle.

"Never seen these before."

"They're St. Moritz." Ceinwen's hand stopped. "What's so funny?"

She took one and snapped the lid back on the rest. "Nothing. I'm happy to set St. Moritz on fire at the moment." Miriam got up and pulled a large silver table lighter off the server, along with a big silver ashtray, lit Ceinwen's cigarette and then her own.

"Did he treat you well on set?"

"Very well. It didn't take long to see that wasn't the case with others. He wasn't a shouter, he told me once he'd had enough shouting in the army. But if he didn't like what was happening he'd walk over to whoever was offending him and quietly tell them what he thought. And he was vicious. I've never known anyone who could be so cutting in so few words. About a week into the shoot he said something to the DP, I didn't hear what. But the man went white and walked off and didn't come back. We shut down for a couple of days while they found someone else.

"But with me he was always reassuring. He set aside a car for Mother during the day and she would go out to lunch and brag to people that I was going to be a star. He knew how to get on my good side. I was the teacher's pet, and all I wanted was to make him happy. But it wasn't a happy set. Push, push, push. We were filming late almost every day, and no one dared complain to his face, although they did plenty behind his back.

"We were about a week into shooting and it was very late in the day, and we were doing a simple scene where I entered a room and collapsed into a chair. I did it once and Emil told me it didn't look right. Still no good the second time. He demonstrated and I tried not to laugh and I could tell he was annoyed. The third time I did it he yelled 'cut' and he shouted, 'Is that how women sit in Milwaukee? Ass first like a dog?'

"He'd never raised his voice on set before, and it was me he did it to. I yelled right back at him, 'If that's how they talk to women in Berlin, you can take your movie and go straight to hell.' I ran to my dressing room and locked the door so I could cry. I threw all my costumes off the rack. But I wasn't very good at tantrums. Costumes cost money, and I didn't think to rip them up.

"People started knocking. The assistant director, the art director, the hairdresser, he was sending anyone I had ever seemed to like. I kept the door locked and I told them all to go away. Finally Emil knocked. Him I told—well, I don't think he had realized I knew that phrase. I took off my makeup and put on my street clothes and sat down to wait until it sounded as though they'd all left for the night. When the set got quiet I walked out and he was by himself, sitting on one of the prop sofas. He asked if I was calm enough to talk.

"He told me he was sorry. It was the only time I ever heard him apologize to anybody for anything. Emil said he had to be the way he was, because Gregory was the biggest skinflint in Hollywood. He didn't want to be von Stroheim, spending too much money and taking too much time, and winding up with his movie taken away from him and no work. He was going to do it his way, but on time and on budget, and if that meant he had to browbeat everyone that was how it would be. I told him I understood, and he kissed me."

"Did you, ah . . ."

For the first time, Miriam looked as though she were enjoying herself. "Did we what?"

"Did you go to bed with him?" Ceinwen winced at herself.

"Not that night. The set was cold and back in my dressing room the costumes were still all over everywhere. I wasn't the only one who didn't want to mess them up. No, he took me home. The next evening I told Mother I had to go to his house to rehearse. She didn't make the slightest objection. That was when we went to bed. You should ash that." Miriam held out the ashtray and Ceinwen flicked her cigarette. "I've shocked you."

"No, why should I be shocked. You were in love."

"Because it is shocking, you know. It was wicked of him. Not much better than Chaplin. I was nineteen and he was thirty-eight. I teased him about that later, him being exactly twice my age. He said he could have waited for my next birthday, to make the difference less embarrassing, but he didn't like waiting for anything. I asked if he wanted to give me more life experience so I'd be a better actress, and he said it was exactly the wrong thing to do. Madeleine was a virgin, that was the whole point to her, and he'd fixed that for me forever, hadn't he."

Miriam wasn't much easier to rattle than Matthew. She might as well ask. "You think that's why he cast you? To sleep with you?"

"I thought about that, even at the time. Of course he said that wasn't it, what else would he say. But I'm sure he thought about it as soon as I walked in the office. Probably even from the photos. That's how it works with a man, just a few minutes."

"I don't think that's true at all," protested Ceinwen.

"You really are a romantic, aren't you." Miriam put out her cigarette. "That's the real reason you wanted to hear all this. If I'd had an affair with a train conductor you'd be just as fascinated."

"I wouldn't say that. I love movies."

"But if the story is as good as a movie . . ."

"Maybe." She thought back. "Did you ever see *Closely Watched Trains*?"

Miriam let out a hoot. "No! A romantic movie about train conductors! You know one!"

"He isn't a conductor, he's a station employee. The girl's a conductor."

"I think," said Miriam, "I can tell why you didn't want to stay in Mississippi. Well, New York usually knocks some sense into romantics. And you'll be better off."

"But I really do think a man can fall in love gradually."

"That's what I mean, dear. I'm talking about sex, you're talking about love. I don't mean they'll instantly try it with any woman who makes them think 'yes,' I mean they don't sit around for months, then decide, 'next week, if I've nothing better to do.' Anyway, I'm sure now that wasn't why he cast me. The movie was too important for him to be that self-indulgent. He wanted the actors to look a certain way; to him they were like figures in a painting. You can imagine how they loved him for that too." She rolled her eyes. "I had the look he wanted. And it was just as he said, he wanted someone who would do as she was told. At Ufa his first movie was with an actress . . ." Miriam trailed off. "What was her name. I used to know it. Something like Lina." She shrugged at Ceinwen. "Name's gone. No matter. I'm sure Lina or Nina or whoever is gone too. She wasn't a big star but she'd made a lot of movies and because he was a newcomer, she felt free to argue every part of every scene. Which he would have found irritating from anyone. Coming from a young woman it was intolerable. He wasn't going to do that again."

"You don't exactly seem like a pushover."

"Don't I? Didn't I just tell you I went to bed with him one night after he kissed me?"

"That's what you do when you're in love."

"That must be good news to your boyfriends."

"*Miriam*," protested Ceinwen.

She smiled. "I had small ways and small moments, like the Chaplin audition, but mostly all Mother had to do was lie down and moan and it was off to another casting call. Emil was shrewd and he saw that. My backbone grew in later. Anyway, after that, for all intents and purposes, I moved in with him."

"What?"

"I know. You would think, wouldn't you, that with all Mother's show of protecting me, she would have something to say about that. And you'd be wrong. I told her that I had to rehearse with him because the work we were doing on my acting was important. And that we were working late, and naturally I stayed over sometimes. And she pretended to believe me. I would stay at our house one or two nights a week and the rest of the time I was with Emil. He was going to make me a star, and if that meant she had to hand me over to him in the bargain, she was willing to do it.

"Of course word got out on the set, and almost everyone started to despise me. I tried not to care, I was caught up with him. But it was dreadful. Edward Kenny, Valancourt, after takes he would tell me how nice it was to work with someone with a lot of life experience. The one who was playing Morano . . ." She rubbed the back of her neck. "Old age. Thought I'd never forget him and here I have. But I remember his mouth well enough. Swearing under his breath as soon as they quit rolling, to show me I wasn't enough of a lady for him to watch his language. Although one day he forgot himself and did it on camera and Emil lit into him. Audiences could read lips and they'd know those words right away.

"Even the crew, they were supposed to be respectful, but the wardrobe woman would say things about my costumes. They were rumpled, what had I been doing in them? There was another man, a set dresser, very low on the totem pole but he was always around sticking his nose into everything, making a big phony show of being friendly, like he thought I'd confide in him or something. And we couldn't do a thing about him because he was cousin to Frank Gregory's wife. The only one who still treated me like a human being was Norman Stallings, the assistant director.

"I could have complained to Emil, but I didn't want to set him off. As it was, I was afraid someone would drop a light on him, they hated him that much. There weren't any unions and he would make everyone stay until he got it right. Half the time we would go home and he would have a few drinks and then we'd just fall asleep.

"It took almost two months, which was a long time in those days, but Emil finished it right on schedule and they started cutting it. And we finally started going to some parties, and I was still staying with him most nights, and it was as happy as we ever were together.

"Now it was the fall. 1928. You know what happened the year before, yes?"

Oh yes. "*The Jazz Singer.*"

"Terrible movie."

"I didn't like it either."

"Jolson." Miriam made a face. "The things I could tell you about *him*. Anyway, it wasn't like *Singin' in the Rain*, not everything changed at once. But anything with sound, all talking, half talking, sound effects, music, whatever, it was packing them in. They were still making silents, but it was different. People were, I don't know, they looked at things in a different way. Once they'd seen talking pictures certain things didn't play to them anymore. I don't think Emil understood that. I know I didn't.

"And they finished the movie and they arranged a preview out in, oh, some dreadful little inland town, very ugly. Emil took me and Mother, and I got dressed up even though I knew it wasn't going to be a fashionable crowd. And Frank Gregory was there and a bunch of men from the studio, and we were all feeling very confident. And then the movie started."

Miriam looked tired, and Ceinwen wondered if she should leave. But Miriam picked up the box of cigarettes again, offered one to Ceinwen and went on.

"I don't know if you've ever been in a theater where a movie was playing, and you thought it was good, and the rest of the audience . . ." She made a waving gesture.

"Sure." She didn't have to think hard. "I saw *Imitation of Life* in a theater once."

"Claudette Colbert?"

"No, the other one, with Lana Turner. I love that movie, I'd seen it on TV and I wanted to see it on screen because it's beautiful. But the audience kept laughing at it. The more tragic it got the more they laughed." The 8th Street Playhouse. She still hated that place. Miriam said nothing. "That was what happened? You liked it and they didn't?"

"Yes. After about ten minutes it was like I was watching a different movie from everyone else. It was slow and pensive, no real jokes or comic relief. There were dissolves and process shots, there were times when he was trying to make the characters' thoughts visible. The novel has a lot of digressions that he'd cut out. He'd used it instead to make a movie about . . . well, about this naive young girl's fear of sex, raw terror of men really. And I could feel people getting restless, and then there were some giggles, and then more. Mother kept trying to shush people until I shushed her."

Miriam lit her own cigarette. "I don't know. I loved him so, and it's been so many years. I hadn't seen any rushes, Emil thought they would make me self-conscious. Maybe it did have more problems than I thought. It seemed to me that on screen he'd made my inexperience look like Madeleine's naiveté. I didn't think I was bad. A couple of years later I saw a Murnau movie, called *City Girl*. I thought, yes, completely different story and setting, but that was Emil's vocabulary." She exhaled and watched the smoke vanish overhead. "From time to time I've wished I could see it again.

Find out whether time passing made it look different to me, better or worse."

"I'm sure it was a great movie," said Ceinwen. She meant it as comfort, but Miriam shot her a look.

"That would be more romantic, wouldn't it."

"I didn't meant that," said Ceinwen, defending herself once again. "Don't you trust your own taste?"

The same look, only longer. Finally, "If I had to put money on it, I'd bet on my judgment, not Frank Gregory's. Yes. I will say that. We'd been sitting near Gregory and his people . . ." Miriam's cigarette burned untouched. "I think . . . I think I won't say more about that night, if you don't mind."

Ceinwen saw it was almost midnight. She was wearing Miriam out, and making her sad, and she felt ashamed of herself. "I'm sorry. You don't need to tell me anything else at all."

"Oh well," said Miriam, her voice regaining the old briskness, "you've come this far. You can't leave at intermission. Not much more to tell anyway." She stubbed out her cigarette and checked the pot. "No coffee left. I think we'd best avoid the brandy straight, don't you? I'll get some water."

She came back with a tray set with a pitcher of water and two more glasses, and put it on the table. "I never drank brandy with Emil. He paid his bootlegger a fortune for the best stuff, but back then I still didn't like it." She sighed and poured the water for them both. "They asked for recuts, of course, and Emil did it because he didn't want them doing it without him. He'd stay out late and then he'd come home and pass out, sometimes on the couch because he never made it back to the bedroom. They finally released it in November and the reviews . . ." Miriam drank some water. "James Quirk at *Photoplay*, he liked it. The way a movie was shot mattered to him, he didn't see them as overdressed plays. But the rest, they just waved it off." She dropped her voice to a pompous baritone. "'A rather tedious romance. It isn't altogether without interest, and perhaps it will appeal to certain distaff segments, but for an intelligent audience . . .'" She set the glass down with a thump. "Meaning men, I suppose. That *idiot* at the *New York Times*, Mordaunt Hall. I wanted to kill him." She gave her half-smile. "I walked around wanting to kill a lot of people. Starting with Frank Gregory. What a monster he was. They were all monsters, the studio heads, but Gregory, he was two-faced on top of it. So kind, so understanding, while he was poisoning your life. He told Emil they believed in the film and then he gave it this piddling release, here one minute, gone the next. Said they'd try to sell it in Europe, never did. Poor Emil, he'd worked so hard to keep the movie cheap. All that meant was the studio could swallow the loss more easily. My contract was for just a year, but Emil's was for two. Gregory could have released Emil, while there was still a chance to get something else, but he was angry his prestige picture had flopped. Thought he'd been made a fool, and he held Emil to the terms out of spite. Kept saying oh, of course there'd be assignments. Then, nothing. Civitas went under in 1932, and the day I heard, I went out and bought a bottle of champagne.

"I knew I was through, and I didn't care, I'd always thought it was a dirty business. But he wanted to work, so badly. And he didn't want to make talkies. I don't know if you know what that was like."

"A bit. They had to put the camera in a box."

"Yes, at first, with big things almost like carpet to mask the sound of the cameras. They hid microphones all over the set. The actors could barely move and the camera couldn't move at all. Emil loved to move the camera, *Mysteries* had all these long, slow shifts. They developed some better talkie techniques pretty fast, but Civitas was too cheap to buy the best equipment, and Emil said if he'd wanted to direct plays he'd have joined a theater. But after six months he went to Gregory and said he'd reconsidered, he could do talkies. Gregory said that was great news, he had just bought a play that would suit Emil, and he came home and we celebrated. But then another month went by without a call from anyone, and Emil knew Gregory was still lying to him.

"He'd drink and then, well. It always seemed to end with him saying I was young and ignorant and I should shut up. One night I told him we should go back to Germany together."

"Really?" Germany in 1929. That didn't sound like a great idea.

"Hitler wasn't in power."

"I know, but . . ."

"Well, yes. I imagine that's why Emil got angry. He told me I was stupid even to suggest it. Everybody knew the man who'd taken over Ufa was a stooge. He was in bed with the Nazis and he knew nothing about film or anything else except money and right-wing politics. I said that didn't sound much different from Frank Gregory. That was when Emil punched a wall." Miriam's eyes slid to the side of the room, as though she could still see a mark. "I was terrified, for a second I had thought he was going to hit me.

I started crying and he told me he was fine, not to make a scene, and went to get another drink. And he couldn't hold the glass while he poured, his right hand was swelling so much already.

"I made him get in the car and I drove us to the hospital. His hand was broken and they spent all night putting it in a cast. When the doctor found out how it happened, he told Emil that from time to time he got patients who'd been fighting with walls, and the wall always won.

"We got back some time after dawn and I watched him get a drink. And then I got the case I'd brought with me, and I packed all my things in it and I called a taxi. And he sat there with his brandy, and he never said a word, and neither did I.

"I went back to the house and when Mother wanted to know what happened I wouldn't tell her. I didn't think Emil and I were finished, but I didn't want to stick around and find out how bad things could get. The first couple of times he called I wouldn't talk to him, but he called a few weeks later when Mother was out and I answered. He sounded sober and he wanted to see me, and I said all right.

"We met at a park close to the house. He told me Civitas was never going to do anything else with the picture, and never going to give him another one. He was going to stay for the ten months he had left on his contract, and then go to France. He knew some people there and thought he could find something. He said if I'd go with him, he'd marry me. I told him I'd think about it. He wanted to drive me home and I told him I'd walk. He got into his car and I asked him how he could drive with his hand in a cast. He said he used his other hand and could sort of brace the wheel with the cast, and anyway it was best to use the hand, he didn't care what the doctor had said.

"Next day, early morning, I heard someone knocking, getting louder and louder. I went to the door and it was Norman. I'd always liked him, he was the one person who was always nice to me on that set. Emil had liked him too. And he was crying, and he told me Emil was dead. Mother was standing right behind me when he said it. And she said, 'My poor dear' or some such blather and reached to put her arms around me, and I pushed her away. I got dressed and asked Norman to drive me to Emil's house. Mother wanted to come too and I told her that was the last thing I wanted. In my mind it was somehow her fault.

"And when we got there, people were all over everywhere, from the studio, from the film, some creditors, I didn't even recognize most of them.

Creepy little nobodies Emil wouldn't have let past the front walk when he was alive. Going through papers, going through his desk, telling me things would have to be sold. They were looking for a will, and it turned out he didn't have one. Why should he, he wasn't even forty.

"They were already piling things in the entrance that they thought would bring some money—a couple of paintings, his suits, the case where he kept his watch and his ring. I wanted to take those but I knew they'd notice. I walked to his bedroom, which was all the way in the back of the house. He'd kept a print of the movie, the original version before he'd had to cut it. He had it in a cabinet, and I opened it up and looked at it for a minute and I thought about taking that. I wish I had. But I didn't know how to get it out, and I didn't have a way to watch it, anyway. I looked at his nightstand and saw a picture I'd given him, and I took that. I thought . . . I wasn't thinking very clearly at all, but I thought I'd be able to come back and get something else when they were done. It never occurred to me it might be my only chance. When I went back the next day, they told me the house had been seized, along with the contents."

They sipped water for a minute, and Ceinwen's remorse swelled once more as she stared at the empty coffee cups. "I should let you go."

"What? You can't possibly. This is the most important part. This is where I tell you life goes on." Miriam was, incredibly, smiling. "So. Life . . ."

". . . went on."

"That's what I was going to say, but then I realized that's a lie, because it didn't, not for a while. I stayed home. For months. The market crashed, we lost money, and I barely noticed. We lived on the last of my paychecks and tried to save. Mother, if you can believe it, wanted to go back to Milwaukee. I'd finally won. Except now I didn't want to leave. It felt like deserting Emil. We moved into a cheaper place, and finally I looked around and realized it was possible to starve in sunny California, and Mother and I were about to prove the point. So we took in sewing, for a couple of years. But times got hard fast, and having your own dressmaker was one of those things people were trying to do without.

"But now, come to think of it, I do have a star story for you. Exactly one. Are you ready?"

"Let's hear it." She hoped that squeak in her voice didn't make her sound too starstruck.

"Norman had been doing well for himself, helped us make rent a few times. He was always good to his friends. He showed up one night and insisted on taking me to dinner at the Cocoanut Grove. And it was as awful as I thought it was going to be. Hollywood failure, you reek of it. Nobody wants even an accidental whiff. I went to the powder room, just to get away, and this beautiful woman was in there, primping. We'd met at a couple of parties before *Mysteries* was released, and she said hello, didn't scamper away or pretend she didn't recognize me. She complimented my dress. I said I'd made it myself and she told me how elegant it was, like something from Paris, and wasn't it wonderful I could sew like that. She asked if I'd ever considered doing it for a living, and I said I was trying, but it wasn't exactly steady. A couple of days later I got a call from the wardrobe department at MGM, and they said they'd been given my name, and asked if I was interested in seamstress work. I went over and spent a few days showing them what I could do, and they hired me. I worked there until 1947." Miriam waited. "You're tired, Ceinwen. There's an obvious question here, and you're not asking it."

"What question?"

"The woman was Myrna Loy."

All she could say was, "I've always loved her."

"Me too, dear. Me too." Miriam checked the clock and moved to the edge of the sofa. "I suppose that really is it. Unless you want to hear about how to sew fake breasts into an evening gown for a flat-chested actress." She put up her hand. "Don't answer that. You probably do. But it's past my bedtime." Ceinwen stood up. "Are you glad you heard all that? You won't feel the need to carry my groceries anymore?"

"I liked carrying your groceries. I'm glad we met."

"I'm glad you're satisfied."

A hug at this point was completely out of the question, and a handshake didn't seem the done thing with Miriam, either. She walked Ceinwen to the door and said, "Thank you again for the present."

"You're welcome." Then, hesitantly, "See you around?"

"I should think so, yes." The door closed behind her.

Ceinwen crept upstairs and went to bed, thinking she'd never sleep again. But somehow she did.

When she went to the kitchen in the morning, Jim was putting away towels, which they kept in one of the cabinets where Ceinwen supposed normal people like Miriam and Donna kept canned soup or something.

"Morning," said Jim. "So it went well!"

"Um, yeah."

"You sure stayed a while. Get any good Hollywood gossip?"

Ceinwen heard herself tell him, "She was a seamstress at MGM."

"Hey, that's kind of interesting. What did she tell you?"

"She sewed a lot of clothes."

He waited, then said, "Okay." He pulled a towel out of the cabinet. "Hope that was worth the scarf. Better get some coffee. You watch, today it'll be everybody who decided overnight that your store is actually a rental place. Get ready to explain the meaning of the words 'final sale.'"

"Thanks for the towels. I think it was my turn, I forgot."

"You've had a bad holiday, I know." She poured herself some coffee and thought about the jewelry counter. Matthew's face intruded, eyes fixed on her when she mentioned Mary of Modena.

"Jim, I want to ask you something." He had his towel and clothes in his arms and his comb in his mouth, ready to make for the bathroom, and gave a grunt. "When you meet someone, do you decide in five minutes whether or not you'd want to sleep with him?"

He set the towel on the stove and took the comb out of his mouth. "You mean you *don't*?"

Talmadge she might have shrugged off, but Jim seemed definitive. "No, I don't."

"It takes a while to fall in love. Sometimes. But either I can imagine doing the deed right away, or I can't."

"That's what Miriam said."

Jim picked his stuff back up and said through the comb, "Uh-huh. Clothes, and sex. Me and Talmadge should have tagged along."

She wasn't going to tell him yet, nor Talmadge. It wasn't as though she could show them anything. The film was gone. Hadn't anyone ever tried to find it?

JANUARY

1.

ONE SUNDAY NIGHT SHE CAME HOME FROM WORK AND THE APARTment was silent, though down the hall she could see the lights in the living room. She found Jim and Talmadge on the floor, Talmadge on a cushion and Jim on the bare boards next to him, their arms around each other. She'd never seen them do that. She knelt next to Talmadge.

"Stefan died," said Jim.

She put a hand on Talmadge's back, then took it away. He wasn't huggy, especially not with girls.

"I'm so sorry," she said. "He's in a better place." She didn't believe it, and she knew Talmadge of all people didn't believe it either, but she said it, because it was what people had said to her.

"Must be," he said. "I've got a lot of friends there."

"I'll make some tea," said Jim. "I think we've still got some oregano." He went into the kitchen while Ceinwen sat close to Talmadge, and neither of them said anything else.

The Gay Men's Health Crisis paid for the funeral. It was on a Friday, a big sales day at the store. Lily speculated about whether or not funerals really helped anybody, since the guest of honor was dead. Talmadge told her that he was going, and if she thought she could replace him that day and all the days that followed with someone who sold as many old, used clothes as he did, she had his permission to find out. Lily let him go, and when Ceinwen found the nerve to say she wanted to go too, to her amazement, Lily rolled her eyes and said all right.

A couple of dozen people gathered in the small funeral home. It only took an hour. Talmadge got up and spoke about going from door to door just past dawn in Brighton Beach, trying to find someone who spoke English and would let him use the phone, and even though they hadn't talked in weeks, Stefan's was the only number he thought of calling.

When they came home the light was flashing on the answering machine. The first message was Talmadge's mother, calling to ask how the funeral went and if there was anything she could do.

Short silence began the second message. Then, "Ah, yes. This is Matthew." Pause. "Calling for Ceinwen." Pause. "I was"—pause—"thinking perhaps we could talk." He left his number, which she had memorized ages ago. The recording clicked off.

"I'm hanging up my coat now," said Talmadge.

Jim still stood there. "Do you think he broke up with Anna?"

"No," she said, and pushed erase on the machine.

They worried that Talmadge might want to drink again, but he came home every night at the normal time, though he went behind his screens after only half an hour. He ate almost two pints of ice cream before bed, and complained every morning that he was going to get fat.

Somehow she saw Miriam only once. Ceinwen told her they'd have to have her over sometime soon, and Jim could cook. Miriam said she'd like that. Ceinwen didn't think either one of them believed it was going to happen. Their conversation had made them like two people who got drunk, fooled around, realized they didn't want to be a couple, but couldn't figure out how to be anything else.

No one was talking much. She went to the movies almost every night, for Bette Davis, for Carole Lombard, for Howard Hawks, stretching her funds to the limit, replacing Jim and Talmadge's voices with the ones on the screen.

Twice in ten days she came home to a note on her bed, the same words both times: "Matthew called," and the number, once in Jim's careful print, once in Talmadge's flashy scrawl. Both times she picked it up and carried it to the trashcan in the kitchen, leaving it uncrumpled on top of the garbage, still legible until somebody threw in food or a coffee filter.

Harry's books on her shelves reproached her. She'd had them since September, and he was leaving for Paris any day now. She wasn't sure of Matthew's schedule this semester, or when he would be at Courant. She decided to write a nice note to Harry and leave the books with the receptionist on Monday. She wondered if Harry could take a pencil and work out a proof for the odds of running into Matthew in the lobby.

She forced herself to wear an ordinary outfit, leggings and a tunic with badly placed shoulder pads that always made Jim scowl when he saw it. She put on her Doc Martens to wade through the slush, although they leaked, and blended her eyeshadow until it was barely there. If she did see him, he wasn't going to think she had made an effort. She loaded the books into Jim's duffel bag.

She told the Courant receptionist she was there to drop off some books for Professor Engelman, and the woman immediately picked up the phone.

"No," protested Ceinwen, "it's the beginning of the semester and I don't want to bother him."

"He went up a while ago," she said. "I'm sure he won't mind." Matthew had said the receptionist was notorious around Courant for her reluctance to do anything, and Ceinwen knew the woman just didn't want a big stack of books behind her desk. But she had trouble coming up with the right objection, and then the woman was saying, "Yes, young lady to see you, a Miss . . ."

"Ceinwen," she said, giving up. She watched the floor as she lugged the books down the hall, kept her head turned away from a crowd leaving the conference room, peeked around the corner to the elevator bank, closed her eyes for a second when the doors opened. Sixth floor, Matthew's office—door shut, lights off. What a relief, she told herself.

Courant's best offices were on the corners, like everywhere else she supposed, and Harry had one, full of windows that looked down Fourth Street and Mercer. His desk was messy but the rest of the office was clean. Sixties-style furniture, shelves covered in math books. A whiteboard was covered with equations in Harry's terrible handwriting; if Ceinwen squinted, they looked almost like the Chinese characters on Miriam's wallpaper.

Harry had moved from cheek kisses to hugs, and his embrace almost lifted her off her feet. Matthew was at the Bobst library, did he know she was coming?

"No," she said. "I haven't seen much of him lately."

His eyebrows stopped moving, which was as significant as when they were jumping around.

"Too bad," he said. "Donna was here about an hour ago. She'll be sorry she missed you."

He stacked the books on his desk and sat down to chat. What had she seen, anything good? Any silents? She told him about *The Torrent, The Thief of Baghdad, The Wind*.

"Seastrom! Oh, that one's marvelous." They talked about Lillian Gish. The greatest silent actress of them all, said Harry. Had she read the bit in King Vidor's book, about filming the death scene in *La Bohème*? Had she seen that one yet? And Gish's mad scene in *The Wind*, genius. "You know who really loves *The Wind*? Andy. He has a beautiful old poster of it. Rolled up, in a tube. Can you believe it? He buys this stuff and he never looks at it!"

"Do you think he might show it to me sometime?"

"He didn't show it to me, he just bragged about it. But then he's never invited me to his apartment. That's where he has all the movie stuff. Here at Courant, we're his math storage area. You should see his office." He stopped. "In fact, why don't you."

"I don't want to disturb him."

Harry's big frame was almost prancing to the door, like a kid on the stairs on Christmas morning. "He isn't there. He's never there. And this is one of the seven wonders of Courant. The others being the view from the thirteenth floor coffee room, the computer lab, Tom Savini's corduroy jacket, although some people say he's got two and rotates them, Dennis Antonik's handlebar mustache . . ." He beckoned madly and kept talking as Ceinwen followed.

Up the stairs they went to the eighth floor. Andy's office was on the far end of the opposite corridor. Harry walked swiftly ahead of her, stopped and pointed at the narrow window in the door. She peered, and instantly forgot her manners.

"Holy shit," she said. Then, "Excuse me."

"No need," roared Harry. "That's what everybody says!"

The office might have been as big as Harry's, it might not. Hard to get a sense of dimensions when a room was this crowded. The bookshelves held journals, extras stacked horizontally across the top of each row, not a bit of space on any shelf. More journal stacks listed in front of the shelves. The back wall was lined with file cabinets, smaller ones balanced on top of larger ones, books crammed in the spaces between. Papers on the windowsill reached to obscure half the view. The desk was so laden she couldn't see if Andy had a chair. All over the floor snaked a maze of folders and journals, some stacked high as her shoulder.

"What is all that?"

"Journals. Papers. Monographs. You name it. I suppose any one of us could have an office like this, if we never threw anything away. See that cabinet against the left-hand wall? He keeps the windows open year round, and one day it fell over . . ."

"Are you looking for me?" Andy was calling to them from the opposite end of the hall.

She stepped back from the door, but Harry didn't budge as Andy hustled toward them. "Of course we are. What else would we hope to find in there?"

Andy's eyes no longer bulged as much. She supposed she was seeing his normal face. "I've thought of you several times since Thanksgiving, Ceinwen. I'm delighted to see you. Did you want to ask me about something?"

She opened her mouth and tried to remember a Vilma Banky movie, but Harry was on the case. "*The Wind*!"

"It's actually a bit better today, Harry. I told you at the staff meeting that I need the windows cracked in there."

"Not that wind," said Harry, "*The* Wind. Seastrom. Ceinwen just saw it."

"How absolutely wonderful. I envy you, seeing it for the first time. Where did you go?"

"The Regency." Oh brother, here we go.

"Not bad, not a bad space at all, and they respect the speeds, although the sound system, I must say . . ."

"I was telling her," said Harry, "about your poster from the film's original release. We thought we'd stop by and see if she could have a look."

"I don't keep my collection here. You know that."

"To be honest, I don't know exactly what you *do* keep in there, my friend. Well," continued Harry, as Andy's mouth tightened, "if you're in the office, I'm sure it's important."

"I could chat for a minute. If Ceinwen's free."

"I'm so sorry, but I have to go. It's my day off and I have some errands."

Andy's eyes seemed to recede. "Some other time, then."

Harry walked her to the elevator and gave her another squeeze, still chuckling over Andy, and told her to come back any time. She was almost all the way through the lobby when someone called, and she turned to see Andy speed-walking to the front desk. How had he gotten down that fast? Seven flights, that was a lot of stairs.

"I'm glad I caught you. I have an idea. If you'd like to see *The Wind* poster"—he paused a bit longer than usual—"I'd . . . be . . ."—stop, a struggle to get the next word out—"*happy* to have you come over and take a look. I live right down the street."

"That's so nice of you. I'd love to, but today—"

"Oh, I don't mean today. Any time." Pause. "I could serve lunch."

She'd rather listen to Roxanne talk about rent control. Ceinwen prepared to say something about Stefan, how her roommates needed her around and would for a long time, when she thought of Andy's office and remembered Harry saying what a movie collection the man had. Stills, posters, books, magazines, the films themselves.

He could have anything in that apartment. Nine reels of *The Crowd*. Or maybe something *really* obscure.

"Did you have a particular day in mind? Because I'm off work again tomorrow."

"Tomorrow," said Andy, "would be *perfect*."

When she pushed through the revolving door, she had a pink telephone slip from the receptionist's pad in her pocket, with "1:00 p.m., 1 Washington Square Village, Apt. 3B" written on the back.

2.

THE RADIATORS WERE BANGING. JIM WAS DRINKING HIS COFFEE IN front of the local news. "High today 23," he announced. Ceinwen decided on tights under pants; she didn't want to dress up for this lunch, anyway. The wind hurt her face; she stopped at two delis on the way, warming up while faking interest in the ramen selection.

She had her long velvet scarf wrapped around her head, and tried to convince herself the effect was Julie Christie in *Doctor Zhivago*. But when it was this cold and the scarf was wrapped this close to her face, it was more like *I Remember Mama*. The wind tore across the driveway between the buildings until her eyes streamed. She put her head down and stared at the pavement, figuring she couldn't collide with anybody because most people had the sense to be indoors. She was halfway to the entrance when she heard her name.

Matthew was hatless and gloveless, wearing just his coat, collar folded up to protect his neck. His nose was red and he must have been even colder than she was. He was crossing to her.

"I was just going out. I have office hours."

"Don't want to miss those," she said. "You'll ruin your ratings."

"My hours are different this semester, the day changed," he said. "We can walk over together, if you'd like to talk."

He thought she'd come to see him. He looked happy. For a second, she felt such a surge of joy she could have dropped everything for five minutes spent walking with him to his office. Then another gust of wind hit her eyes, and the impulse was gone.

"I'm about to be late myself," she said, and started to walk again.

"For what?" He'd maneuvered so she'd have to walk around him.

"I'm having lunch."

He backed up a step, but he was still smack in front of her, the lines on his forehead deepening slightly. "I didn't know you knew anybody else in the building. I mean, except Andy." She stared past him at the building. He stuck his hands under his armpits and moved too close. "You're never here to see Andy?"

"You probably got a big line of students over there already, so you better get a move on."

She moved again and he shifted again. "I'm trying to talk to you. Have I got this right? You're going to Andy's flat to have lunch?"

"Are my lunches any of your business?"

"Who else is going to be there?" Like Granana asking about a Saturday night party.

"Just me," she said. "And I have to go."

As if to stand more casually, he shifted a leg into her path. "Now see here." Calm, teacherly tone. "I know you're oblivious, or so you like to pretend, but even you must have noticed how he was acting at Thanksgiving."

"You mean before or after you invited him to sit next to me?"

"At a table with two dozen people, Ceinwen."

Her scarf was sliding off her hair and her nose was starting to run. The longer they stayed out here the worse she was going to look. "You got some nerve, you know that?"

"I'm giving you advice. As a friend." Slightly sharper version of the office-hours voice. She snorted, but wasn't sure whether he thought that was just her nose. "There's not one female postdoc at Courant who'll let Andy into her office and close the door."

"So that's what, one woman?"

He didn't like that at all. "Two. Two women with common sense."

She yanked her scarf back up on her head and felt her hair bunch. "He's not nearly as weird as you claim he is. He's just this uptight little man who likes to collect movie stuff."

"That uptight little man probably outweighs you by a good five stone."

"God, you're ridiculous. What, he's going to attack me? He won't stop talking long enough."

"I'm not saying that. I'm saying you're putting yourself in an uncomfortable situation." He blew on his hands.

"Well aren't you just the *soul* of chivalry, *Mister* Hill." She pulled a tissue out of her pocket and wiped her nose.

"We'll both freeze to death out here before you see reason," he snapped, then stuck his hands in his pockets and shifted back to Professor Voice. "I'm not saying don't talk to him. Talk to him at Courant or something."

"I want to see his movie collection. Satisfied?"

"Then bring Harry."

"He doesn't like Harry. Jesus Christ Matthew, you're such a *priss*."

He pulled out his hands like he wanted to punch something, but all he did was lunge at her and shout. "You haven't the sense you were born with. How in god's name do you manage?" She stepped back and he lunged again. "I don't know how you hold a job. I don't know how you pay rent. I don't know how you cross Astor Place without fainting because you didn't eat breakfast. You smoke a million cigarettes and you walk around in your little silver-screen fog having mental conversations with Greta Garbo or whoever the fuck is obsessing you at the moment, and common sense never once enters into anything you do."

Seemed he'd been saving that up for some time. That was all right by her, because she'd been saving up some things, too.

"I never asked you for advice and I never will. I'm managing just fine. I make my own living and my own decisions. What the hell would you know about it, anyway? When did you ever have to work a real job?"

"Right." He was still yelling. "Academia is the last bloody word in luxury."

"And as for *me* not having common sense," she slammed on, eager to play her trump, "who is it yelling at me at the top of his lungs practically right outside Andy's window?"

"He can't hear us, Ceinwen," he said, his voice back to normal. "His apartment faces Third Street. You also have no sense of direction."

"I know where the entrance is and I'm going in."

She made for the door as he hollered after her, "You want a nice chat about old movies? I've got the perfect one. *The Collector*."

She swung into the lobby and paused just inside, tossing through her bag for another tissue. *The Collector*. Ooh Matthew, nice work, coming up with a genuine sort-of-old psycho-kidnaps-girl movie just like that. She patted the corners of her eyes, trying not to wipe off the liner. Except Samantha Eggar is a *redhead*, you—

The doorman at the desk called, "Hey, you just missed him. Walked out five, maybe ten minutes ago."

She wiped her nose, squeezed the tissue into a ball and looked at the fingermarks on it for a second until she trusted herself to speak. "I'm here for 3B."

He was confused. "3B? In this building?"

"Yes," she said, reminding herself it was not this man's fault she was fantasizing about hurting one of the tenants. "3B. Evans."

"Evans?"

Was she speaking Albanian, or what? "Evans. Andrew Evans."

With a small, none-of-my-business head shake the man announced her and said, "Go on up."

Her lipstick had dried out, and before she pressed the elevator button she dragged out her compact to touch it up. As she snapped the top back on the lipstick, she was certain she caught him looking at her with an expression she thought a doorman should have learned how to suppress. But it was so fast that by the time she had everything back in her bag, he appeared to be rearranging pens in his desk drawer.

The doorbell gave a muffled clang and a beaming Andy was there in seconds. The door opened directly into a huge room decorated in the same style as his office, Late Compulsive—stuffed with bookshelves, papers piled on top of file cabinets, dozens of poster tubes leaning in a corner. There was very little furniture but what little there was, was invisible, lost under towering stacks of folders.

"I use this room primarily for storage, as you see. I always say, the most precious commodity in Manhattan is space."

"Harry says films take up a lot of space."

"Ah. Yes. I don't keep those here."

There was a couch only half-covered in small mountains of paper, an old chair facing it, and a card table placed between, probably brought out of a closet for the occasion. Andy was saying he wasn't much of a cook—just as well, he probably kept file folders in the oven—and he had ordered from Empire Szechuan, which he thought was quite good for a chain, and he hoped she liked fried rice and egg rolls. She sat on the clear half of the couch while Andy fetched the food and paper plates from the kitchen.

She'd tried to act like this wasn't a date, but Andy was certainly working to turn it into one, fussing to get the right amount of rice on the plate, asking if she wanted chopsticks or a fork, going on about the relative merits of area takeout and delivery speeds. At least she didn't have to say much, although his subject matter didn't lend itself to questions. She decided to steer the conversation away from fortune cookies.

"You sure have a lot of movie stuff." Andy floored the gas pedal before she could add a thing, telling her about a big collector's convention near Syracuse, about some place called Ohlinger's over on 14th and how bad their selection of silent stills was, about other collector events, about bargaining, about deals he'd gotten.

Wasn't he going to show her anything? "So you have a poster from *The Wind*?"

"Oh, of course. You wanted to see the poster. I think you'll be pleased with it, it's very typical of the period." He took out a wet-nap from the Empire Szechuan bag, wiped his hands and made straight for a stack of poster tubes. He pulled out the poster, held it up for her, and she leaned in to look at all the writing. She reached out to feel the paper and he pulled it back slightly. Then he rolled it back up and asked what she had seen lately. She knew he meant silents.

"*The Thief of Baghdad*. Anna May Wong was gorgeous, don't you think?"

Andy went off on Raoul Walsh and was suddenly on another side of the room, taking part of a stack of folders and putting it on top of another stack, and pulling out a folder that was full of stills. He hadn't searched at all, he just knew where it was.

"I'll hold these up too, since you're still eating." He displayed the photos like flash cards, barely giving her enough time to take in Douglas Fairbanks on the flying carpet before Anna May was there in her slave costume. He put the stills back in the folder and reassembled the stack. He perched on the edge of his chair, so far toward her it seemed he might slide off.

"You know, *The Eagle* is on at the Thalia this weekend. Valentino and Vilma Banky, I don't know if you remember me mentioning her." He leaned in. "They had a magnificent screen partnership."

"Gosh, really? I'm so disappointed. I work on the weekends, you know. Nights too."

The doorbell sounded. Andy gave a start and Ceinwen found herself doing the same. No. Had to be the super or a neighbor or something.

Another ring. He went to the door. From where she was sitting her view was blocked by the stacks of folders, but she could hear everything, including Andy's soft, unenthusiastic greeting. The other voice got louder as it came further into the room.

"I'm late, I know, sorry. Had to cancel office hours and couldn't seem to get hold of Angie. Don't know if it was lunch or she was just out." The top of his head had appeared over the stacks. She focused fiercely on her paper plate. "Wound up going over myself, then some of them wanted to talk anyway, and I had to reschedule so they wouldn't get themselves worked up about it. Finally put up a sign to say 'bugger off.' Nicely, of course." She picked up an egg roll and took a bite. "Hello, have you been here long?"

"Ceinwen didn't mention you were coming," said Andy.

"We weren't sure I could make it, were we?" She chewed. "We didn't think you'd mind my tagging along. Ceinwen told me she was coming here to talk about silents and look at some of your, ah, holdings and I just invited myself. Couldn't pass up a chance like that. It's extraordinary, I never thought much about old movies until I came here, but she and Harry have me hooked. Can't seem to get enough."

She had spent eighteen years of her life in Yazoo City. And even if she wasn't much good at it herself, she'd always assumed Southerners were the undefeated champions of social lying, able to tell straight-faced absolute whoppers about how the farm was doing, how the food was, how your hair looked, how your wife looked. Now she reflected, as Matthew nudged some papers aside on the couch with more deference than he'd probably show a cat, that she'd been wrong. The English swept the table.

He sat down. "Chinese?"

"It isn't pastrami," said Ceinwen.

She felt a little sorry for Andy. He knew this wasn't on the level, but he didn't have the equipment to fight off a frontal assault of British. "I only placed orders for two," he said, "but there's some left. Would you like a plate?"

"No idea this was a food occasion, or I wouldn't have eaten. Had a sandwich before I left for Courant. I'm sure it wasn't nearly as good. Did you get tea with it, by any chance?"

"No," said Ceinwen.

"Pity. I don't suppose you have any lying around, Andy?"

"I might."

"Hate to be a bother."

Pause, as Andy tried to grasp what was being asked. "You'd like me to get you some tea?"

"Super. Ceinwen, how about you?"

"No thanks." She grabbed a box and forked some more rice onto her plate. Andy stood for a second, then headed for the kitchen.

Matthew surveyed the rows and rows of folders, the bookshelves, the poster tubes, the stacks of loose papers and magazines, and said, "This is more or less precisely what I was expecting."

"I thought," she whispered, "that you were expecting to find me locked in a closet."

He'd stood up and was opening folders. "You're not very enterprising, just sitting there with the fried rice. Have a look around, isn't that what you came for? What's this?" He held out a sheet of stiff paper with a picture on it.

"It's called a lobby card."

"*Queen of Sheba*. Seen that one?"

"It's lost." She hated to admit it, but he had a point. She should at least see what was on the bookshelves. She crossed to a point on the shelves as far from him as possible, wondered how she could manage to see Andy's bedrooms, squelched the thought, and felt her inward shudder turn into a burst of fury. "How was St. Moritz?" she hissed. She looked at his profile and told herself she couldn't stand the sight of it. "Snow nice and deep? Chalet comfy?"

"It was a hotel." He held up another lobby card. "*Ten Commandments*. Didn't realize there was a silent version." She pulled out a few books to see if they were doubled-shelved; amazingly, they weren't. He spoke quietly. "I called at least three times. Don't tell me you didn't get the messages." She gave him the meanest look she could muster and put back the books. "I must say, last time Talmadge outdid himself. He said, 'Ceinwen's presence is required at work. She is the jewel in the navel of Vintage Visions.'"

She dropped to the floor and tried to get a look behind a stack of papers. "They told me you called. I just couldn't figure out why. What did you have to say? 'Oh Ceinwen, please, let me explain.'"

"I've nothing to explain. I haven't lied to you." There was too much to see in here, yet oddly there wasn't a single thing that even resembled film. Too bad. She could use a reel or two, if only to wrap them around his head.

He'd moved to stand nearby, and she refused to meet his eyes looking down at her on the floor. "I wanted to hear how you are," he said. She fixed her eyes over his head, made a big here-I-am gesture, then crawled over to look behind another row. He squatted next to her and said, even lower, "I wanted to hear your voice."

She stood up, kept her eyes on the floor and walked to the couch. Andy was coming back in with a mug. He looked at the spot where Matthew had been sitting and paused.

"Over here. Thanks," said Matthew, standing up. "I was giving Ceinwen some space."

Andy seemed to accept giving Ceinwen some space as normal practice. He handed over the mug and perched again on the edge of his chair. "I could hear you two chattering away in here," he said, with a note of reproach.

"We were talking about a movie," said Ceinwen. Not exactly an inspired response, but she was having trouble concentrating.

"Sound movie," continued Matthew, checking the bookshelf behind him, then carefully resting his shoulders against it. "Hope you don't mind. Maybe you know it. *The Collector*? Used to pop up on the box all the time."

Screw it. She was going to focus, she was going to get something out of this lunch, and then she was going to leave, and when she did, he could take his friendship and stick it on his office door along with his bugger-off-students note.

She had to say one thing for Andy, abrupt subject changes didn't faze him one bit. "Eh. Late-period William Wyler. I didn't bother with it. His *Ben-Hur* wasn't very good. Absolutely travestied the chariot race. In the Fred Niblo—"

"Actually, Andy," she said, "I have a confession to make. We were looking in that top folder over there. My curiosity got the better of me." He swiveled around to look at the stacks as though she'd told him somebody had a hand on his wallet. "I really hope you don't mind."

"The lobby cards. You were looking at the lobby cards." Like she'd said they were rifling his underwear drawer.

"Yes, and do you know what was the first thing we saw?"

"Top folder? *Queen of Sheba*." Of course he knew.

"Yes, and I was telling Matthew it was lost."

"Heartbreaking," said Matthew, pulling on the string of the teabag as though trying to determine how it got there. "Looked like my sort of thing."

Andy wasn't buying it. "How so?"

"The two-piece costumes, for one . . ."

"It's so sad," sliced in Ceinwen, "that it's gone. And it reminded me of another lost movie I was curious about. *The Mysteries of Udolpho*."

"Emil Arnheim!" Andy exclaimed. "I must say, Ceinwen, your knowledge just becomes more and more impressive to me. That one's known mostly to scholars. May I ask how you happened to hear of it?"

"In a book." For once Andy appeared to be waiting for her next thought. She could sense Matthew's eyes on her reddening chest; he'd figured out where she blushed, and when, some time back. "A big book."

"Big as in, famous?" asked Matthew. "Or big as in, large and hard to carry?" Andy had gotten up and walked over to a stack of folders.

"It had a lot of pages and I don't remember the title." She better not sound too crabby, Andy might notice. She turned up the accent a bit. "That's the thing about me. I remember movies better than books." Andy slipped his hand inside one of the tallest stacks, about one-quarter of the way down. She put a hand up to her neck, then forced herself to drop it in her lap.

"I'm happy to tell you," said Andy, "that I do have two stills from that one. Would you like to see them?" His hand had emerged with one of the folders.

"By all means," said Matthew, before she could get out a word, and he set down his mug and settled on the couch. Andy paused slightly, slid his eyes to Matthew, then took out a still by the merest sliver of an edge.

"Because of the rarity of these photos, I'm going to hold them up for you. Fingerprints can be terribly damaging." Matthew scooted to within a few inches of her thigh. She crossed her legs away from him and folded her arms.

It was a master shot of the castle, tall and towered, with a carriage in front of it. No Miriam, no actors at all, but exactly the sort of thing she'd have taken to her room and pored over just a few years ago, imagining herself in the castle. Maybe she'd do that even now.

"Well done," said Matthew. "Looks real."

"I do not consider 'looks real' to be a compliment," said Andy, "but yes, it's very well done. A matte shot. This was a big production for Civitas, but they didn't build the exterior castle set, to save money."

He put it back and held up the other. Jackpot.

A medium shot of Miriam, in another Empire-waist dress like the one in her publicity photo. She was sitting next to a handsome actor, her head slightly down, eyes looking up at him with shy yearning. They were on a bench in a garden. He was holding her left hand, looking down at her upraised palm as though he were reading it, his eyes seeming to care for nothing but the skin in front of him. Miriam hadn't liked Edward Kenny, but that didn't show in the still, not at all. It was as erotic as a kiss. She found herself checking Matthew's reaction. His expression was the one he wore at the chalkboard in his office when he was working out another equation. "She looks familiar."

She put her eyes back on the still.

"Here," said Andy, "of course, are the two leads, Miriam Clare as Madeleine and Edward Kenny as Valancourt. Although I very much doubt, Matthew, that you have seen Clare in anything else. This was her sole substantive role. Kenny, on the other hand . . ."

"You'd be surprised," said Matthew. "I'm good with faces. For a mathematician." His eyes moved to Ceinwen. "Miriam," he said. "Not what you'd call a common name these days."

"I'm afraid your supposed memory is all but impossible," said Andy, with lordly finality, "unless you remember every face you've ever seen in a crowd scene." He pulled the still away and replaced it in the folder; it was like watching someone snatch away your dinner. "According to Professor David Gundlach, who wrote a monograph on this film, Clare's other credits amount to bit parts."

She knew this lunch was a good idea. "There's a whole book on this film?"

"A monograph, as I said. Not a long one, due to the film's lost status, but Gundlach reconstructs some of the shoot, speculates about the look of it, gives as many names as possible for the cast and crew, and tries to place it within the context of Bazin's theory of the spectator and the ways in which people watched silent films made on the cusp of sound. Which, of course, was a very sad era—"

"Have you read it?" She shouldn't cut him off, but how else was she going to get anywhere?

"Why yes. I have a copy." She reminded herself to breathe out. Doing that reignited her awareness of Matthew and she used the excuse to jump up.

"Would you mind showing me?"

He didn't answer for a moment, then, "I don't see why not," he said, standing up with his hands clasped together, gracious as a cardinal giving an audience. "I'm curious about your interest. Arnheim made two movies at Ufa, is that the hook for you, so to speak?" He walked to the shelves and she followed as close behind him as she could stand to get.

"I'm afraid you'll think I'm silly," she said, "but the truth is, I just love that novel." A kind of throat noise near her shoulder. Matthew was right behind her.

"How marvelous. Shows what an unusual sort of intellect you have," said Andy, scanning the shelves.

"I read it too," said Matthew. "What I remember is a catastrophic number of commas."

Andy pulled out a slim volume, the cover creased, frayed and darkened, and held it for her to see. *In Search of the* Mysteries," by Professor David Gundlach, University of . . . oh come on, fingerprints weren't going to damage this.

"Do you mind if I take a look? I'll be careful." Andy placed it gently in her hands, as though passing along a gardenia. She immediately opened it to the middle. No photos. "Who was Professor Gundlach?"

"Cinema studies at USC. He died a few years ago," said Andy. "I was fortunate to acquire this copy shortly after it was published."

"So this is all the information that exists," she said. An annotated complete cast and crew in the back.

"Oh no, there's also the fragment at the Brody Institute."

Breathe, breathe. "A fragment? Of the film?"

"Yes, just over two minutes. Saw it a few years ago, during a day in which I was catching up with some of the rarer acquisitions. Most intriguing."

"Which part is it?"

Andy paused a fraction longer than usual. "Been a while, you realize, and I saw it with a number of other things. I believe the heroine was being menaced by someone."

"That could be any point in the plot," said Matthew.

Miriam. A scene with Miriam. "How can I see it?"

"Goodness, I had no idea Mrs. Radcliffe still had this sort of fan club. I'm afraid I'm not sure. The Brody Institute for Cinephilia and Preservation is a rather, I'd say, sinister organization with a great many rules. And the *Mysteries* fragment isn't available to the general public. You need academic credentials to have it screened."

Ceinwen began to read the abstract at the front of the monograph. "In December 1927, German director Emil Arnheim was brought to Civitas Studios by Frank Gregory, who was . . ."

Academic credentials. There was no way in hell she was going to look at Matthew, because she knew his face would be a monument to smug. Wellington at Waterloo. Olivier picking up his Oscar. That would be Matthew, and she wanted no part of it.

He was reading over her shoulder, so close she couldn't move without brushing him. She tried to compose a question. Much as she wanted to take them and look at them for hours, Andy would never let the stills out of the apartment. But this book was about busted to pieces. He couldn't be all that attached to it.

"I would really love to read all of this," she began.

"Might I have a look?" Matthew plucked the book before she realized he'd reached for it. She'd seen mothers hand over newborns with less anxiety than Andy showed at seeing the monograph in Matthew's hands.

"It's long out of print," said Andy. "And there weren't that many copies published in the first place. I'd be terribly upset if something happened to it. Maybe you could come here and read it in stages."

"Nothing like a cozy room and a good book." Matthew licked his finger to flip a page. Andy reached out a hand and Matthew peered more closely at the type.

"It's kind of hard for me to get away from work." She gave Andy her sweetest smile. "Retail hours are irregular. But I understand your wanting to take good care of it, considering how valuable it is." Matthew snapped the book shut and ran a finger down the chipped, broken spine. If she concentrated hard enough on his throat, maybe she could make him start to choke.

"I try to take care of things," began Andy, taking the book from Matthew and tucking it under his arm.

"And so you should," she said. "I know Harry feels the same way. That's why I was so grateful when he lent me all those books. Some of them had been out of print for ages, and great photos, too. Things I had never seen anywhere else. I tell you, I was almost afraid to open them. But Harry was so sweet. You know how generous he is. Said he trusted me completely. I brought them back as soon as he wanted. Went right up to his office and we had a great talk." Matthew's eyes had shot toward the ceiling three different times during this speech, so she added for good measure, "He got me coffee."

Andy was chewing on the side of his cheek. "Could you have it back tomorrow?"

"I don't really read that fast. I'm not like you professors." Make all the faces you want, Mr. Hill, I'm getting this book. "It would probably take me at least two or three days."

"Thursday?"

"I might be going to work early . . ."

"Friday then?"

She better quit now. "Friday, sure, Friday should be fine. Thank you so much! I could bring it by your office in the morning before work."

"You two could have coffee," suggested Matthew. "I'd join again but I have a class to teach."

"Unless you put up a sign," said Ceinwen.

"You can't do that too often, they seem to find it irritating," said Andy.

"I have to go now," she said, picking up her coat and scarf. "Although maybe Matthew can stay. I know he's dying to pick your brain about the silent *Ben-Hur*."

"I should walk out with you," said Matthew. "Work to do, I'm afraid."

He moved to help her and she sidestepped him. She threw on her coat, swung the scarf around her neck and grabbed her purse. "We can say good-bye at the elevator, since you're going back upstairs."

"I'm going back to Courant, actually." She took a step toward the door when she realized Matthew had her so angry she'd nearly behaved like Anna. She turned to Andy. "Thanks so much for the delicious lunch and everything else. I've had a lovely time."

"My pleasure," said Andy, both hands still fastened on the monograph. She reached out. Andy put it in her hand, but it wasn't coming away. She gave the gentlest tug possible and at last he let go. She cradled it with both arms and gave him the same smile as earlier. "I promise to return it just as I found it."

He looked borderline distraught, but managed to say, "Eleven okay for Friday?"

"Perfect."

She opened the door wide and fast, but the doors in the building weren't automatic, so it didn't swing back into Matthew's face. He came up behind her as she was pushing the elevator button repeatedly, a very New York habit she'd always promised herself she wouldn't pick up.

"Are you familiar with the Brody Institute?" he asked pleasantly.

She threw her head back and strode toward the stairwell. She opened the exit door, turned, said, "You're a prick," and charged in.

"That was good and loud," he said, following. "With any luck Andy heard that." She was going down the stairs as fast as her damp Doc Martens would permit, but he was right behind her.

"The fact that you're a prick is no news to Andy."

"And now it's no news to the second floor either. Shall we inform the lobby?"

"I don't want to talk to you!" They'd reached the lobby, and she was practically running for the door.

"You should, if you want to see that clip. With Miriam." She stopped. Smug, all right. "She makes an impression, that neighbor of yours."

She said triumphantly, "I'll get Harry to take me."

"Harry's leaving for Paris in forty-eight hours. Plan to wait until he gets back?"

"I will if I have to."

"No, you won't. You can hardly bear to wait for your next cigarette." They were both breathing hard. "You're here anyway. Come up and talk, this is just stalling."

The doorman was concentrating hard on his *New York Post*. She walked to the elevator and pressed the button once. Matthew followed and glanced at the monograph in her hands. "If you're going to keep borrowing books," he said, "you should get a larger handbag."

Ceinwen was about ten feet into his apartment when she felt a hand on her back. She whipped around for her best New York "watch it, buddy" and found herself turning straight into a kiss. Her purse and the monograph fell to the floor and she yanked her head back.

"Oh, so you're worried about Andy. Andy's a weirdo, Andy's going to make a pass at me. Meanwhile you ask me up here to *talk* and now you think—"

"Later," he pleaded, and tried to pull her back.

"Later? Like nothing happened? You left me here—"

"Later," he repeated, talking over her, following every step back that she took. "Please, can't we have the fight later? Shh, no, listen, we're just flipping the equation, that's all." She was keeping her mouth away and he was trying for her neck. "Basic maths. If it works one way, it has to work the other. First we make love, *then* we have the fight."

"You leave me here to go skiing with Ah-nuh . . ."

"The whole fight. I promise. Only later."

"—and then you come back and here you are, trying—"

"Please, please. I've missed you so much." He'd unfastened all three buttons on her coat and she was hanging onto both lapels to keep him from pushing it off. "No, wait, let me finish. We can reverse everything. After we won't have the fight right away, we'll go to Theatre 80—no, listen, and we'll sit through both features, both, even if they're Westerns, and I promise, I swear, you can start the fight as soon as the lights come up. Even before that, if you want. You can start calling me names during the credits." His voice was shaking; they were both trying not to laugh. "Or the fadeout. Music, 'The End,' 'Matthew, you insect . . .'"

She looked over his shoulder and said, "Matthew."

He sighed and let go. "All right."

"You forgot to close the door."

3.

THE BATHROOM DOOR WAS OPEN, SO SHE LOOKED IN. MATTHEW WAS sitting on the side of the bathtub, applying Bacitracin to a welt on his knee.

"What happened?"

"Carpet." He grimaced and reached for a Band-Aid on the sink.

She was willing to apologize to all kinds of people for all kinds of things, but not that. "Can I borrow your robe?"

"Help yourself."

She grabbed it off the back of the door and went into the living room, where the monograph was still on the floor. A page had been creased when it dropped, but maybe she could press it out before Friday. She took it to the couch and started with the contents. BACKGROUND. SYNOPSIS OF SHOOTING SCHEDULE . . .

"Did you want to talk?" He had his jeans back on and was standing a couple of feet in front of her, hands in pockets.

"What about?" Couldn't he see she was reading?

He braced a hand on the back of his head and lifted his face to the ceiling. "Reagan's tax policies. What do you think?"

"You mean, about the sex we just had."

"Yes. That."

She didn't see anything she could use as a bookmark, and dog-earing the page might give Andy a heart attack, so she kept the book open and tried not to look down at it. "I thought you didn't want to fight."

"I don't."

"Awesome. Neither do I." DISASTROUS PREVIEW IN POMONA. CRITICAL RECEPTION. Maybe she should go to that first. No, let's have a look at DEMISE OF CIVITAS.

"I think we should spell out terms." She looked back at him. "To avoid misunderstandings. Like Christmas."

I understand perfectly, she thought. I understand you came back, and I need to bide my time. "Fine. Lay it on me. Do you want to sit down?"

He didn't move. "I think it's obvious neither one of us wants things to end."

"Yep. Got that loud and clear, Matthew." You had such a swell time with Ah-nuh that you jumped on me first chance you had. Got that too, professor.

"But the basic situation hasn't changed. You know that, right?"

"Did I ask you to change it?"

"No, but . . ."

"Like you always said. You do what you want. And so do I." Civitas went into bankruptcy in 1932, along with a wave of other . . . The book slipped out of her hands.

"Why don't we put this aside for one little moment." He placed it face down on the table. "Are you all right with going back to things as they were?"

"I guess not."

He dropped beside her and slid way down the cushions. "Then you'd best tell me now."

"Next time, we have to make it to the couch. You think your knees hurt, you should see my back." She reached for the book.

"Does this call for first aid?"

"Later." The Civitas film library was thought to have little value, but it was part of the assets sold to . . . A hand slid to cover the page.

"We understand each other?"

"I heard everything you said, and I said I understood, didn't I?" Everything. Including when you said you missed me. Don't you try to tell me that was only after St. Moritz.

The hand lifted. "I'm going to start dinner." He got up. The negatives in were stored in . . . "Steak?"

"Don't make too much." She lowered the book and watched him open the refrigerator.

You're mine. I know it. You just don't know it yet.

He started taking things out of drawers and cabinets and putting them on the counter. A bowl, an onion, a knife.

"Isn't it kind of early to start dinner?"

"I'm marinating them. It's all part of the wonderful world of cooking. You should join us here sometime."

"I cooked all the time for Granana, the whole last year before she went in the nursing home." She bent her head back to the book. A fire at the warehouse in 1956 destroyed all known negatives of Civitas . . .

"What on earth did you cook?"

"Quick stuff. Chicken. There was this list of food she could eat. It was only about a page long. Everything had to be low-fat and no-salt on account of her kidneys. Then I'd turn my back for a minute and she'd throw in a ham hock."

He started peeling garlic. "I know better than to ask you to chop anything."

"I can chop!"

"Since you're here anyway," he said, dragging a cutting board from the back of the sink, "and since you passed up the chance to have our fight, why don't you tell me how you found out your neighbor was in a movie."

She didn't want to put down the book, but if she was going to be asking him for favors she supposed it was only fair to tell him why. She placed it face down to mark her place and slipped up on the barstool next to the counter. Her version was shorter than Miriam's, but she kept circling back to details she'd forgotten, like Miriam's hair falling out, and including things she'd meant to leave out, like how mean Emil got toward the end. By the time she got around to Myrna Loy ("The one from *The Thin Man*? She was cute") he'd chopped up the onions and the garlic and finished whatever he was going to use to soak the steaks, having poured in something from every bottle in his cabinet. She was a little afraid of this marinade. He pulled the steak package out of the fridge.

She waited. "Isn't that the most tragic thing you've ever heard?"

He pulled a mallet out of a drawer. "Tragic, not really. Bit depressing."

"A bit? She was in love with the man! Hollywood destroyed him! Almost destroyed her, too!"

"I don't think the sack of Rome would have destroyed Miriam." He was laying wax paper over a steak.

"I think you're being incredibly cold."

"It's sad." He grabbed the mallet and brought it down on the steak with a whump. "But look at it rationally. Let's say he lives. And she stays with him." Whump. "Alcoholic, washed-up director." Whump. "Verbally abusive." Whump. "Potential to get physically abusive." Whump.

"Never," she protested.

Whump. "Could happen. All he has to do"—whump—"is miss the wall one night and connect with her face." He pulled the steak off the cutting board, laid it in a baking dish and grabbed another. "She goes to France with him." Whump. "He drinks." Whump. "She does who knows what to support them"—whump—"sewing, maybe, or laundry"—whump—"and this goes on for ten years"—whump—"until the day his countrymen"—whump—"show up in tanks." Whump. He peeled off the wax paper and stuck the mallet in the sink. "You say that's grand thwarted passion. I say she was well out of it." He laid the second steak in the baking dish. "Quit glaring at me. You've plenty enough sense to know I'm right."

"I thought I didn't have any common sense."

"I didn't say you had none. I said you didn't use it." He picked up the bowl and poured the marinade over the steaks.

"Maybe you have no sense of romance." He stopped, the bowl poised over the sink. Then he lowered it in.

"Haven't seen enough old movies, I suppose."

"Well then, are you going to help me see what's left of this one?"

"I don't see how I can get out of it." He shoved the dish with the steaks to one side of the counter.

"Aren't you going to put that in the fridge?"

"Tastes better if you leave it out." Matthew and Jim were the only men she'd ever seen who washed their hands with the dish soap.

"How long?"

"Couple of hours or so."

"What? It could go bad or something."

"Christ. Americans and their germ phobias." He shut off the tap and shook the water off his hands.

She leaned over to have a look. "I don't even know what you have in there. It could kill us both."

"Wouldn't that be just like a movie?"

"I don't know any movies with a big food poisoning angle. It isn't very cinematic." She slid off the barstool and headed for the couch.

"Where do you think you're going?" He followed her.

She grabbed the book and curled her legs up on the couch. "I have to read this. I only have until Friday. Unless . . ."

"Unless what? Unless I have a better idea? I have *much* better ideas." He was standing over her.

"There's a lot of Xerox machines at Courant," she reminded him. He covered his face with his hands. "What?"

"Yes, there are copy machines," he said from under his hands, "and they're all guarded by harpies."

"Go to Harry's secretary and use your charm," she suggested.

He lowered his hands. "Angie can't stand the sight of me. And I haven't any charm, I'm a mathematician. *And* I'm a priss."

That meant he wanted her to take it back. But if he was going to insult her common sense, as far as she was concerned, he was still a priss. "Sneak into the office when she isn't there, then. Or tell her it's for a big secret conference. Come on. Improvise. Live a little."

This was ridiculous. Every time she picked up the book, Matthew was pulling it out of her hands. Wasn't she ever going to get some time alone with it? "Fine, Miss Reilly. I'll just spend the next couple of weeks perjuring myself for you. No worries. But you have to put this sodding book down *now*." He closed the book and tossed it on the coffee table. Great, he'd lost her place. "And I'll take it as a personal favor if you don't sit there giving it long, yearning looks." He put his hands on the couch on either side of her, still standing.

"I'll need two copies," she told him.

FEBRUARY

1.

THEY GOT COFFEE AT A DELI AND DRANK IT AS MATTHEW WALKED HER to work. She had on yesterday's outfit, but it wasn't the first time that had happened. And anyway, nobody at the store had seen yesterday's outfit yesterday.

Once she found out when Miriam could come uptown with them, he was going to call the Brody. Her anxieties about how he was going to get them in were dismissed out of hand: "If I can't come up with a good reason why a mathematician would want to see a movie clip, they should send me back to Cambridge."

She figured they would have to be honest about who Miriam was. If Matthew tried to claim she was his grandmother or a professor emeritus, his two half-serious suggestions, even now Miriam's face was so clearly the one in the movie that the Brody people might figure it out. But explaining Ceinwen herself would be a snap, said Matthew; "you're my research assistant."

"Doesn't assistant sound kind of suspicious?" she asked.

"Suspicious how?"

"I don't know," she said, unwilling to admit that she thought it sounded like a stripper he'd stashed in an apartment on 42nd Street. "I think secretary sounds more respectable."

"Secretary sounds worse."

"There's nothing dodgy about being a secretary," she said, showing off a word she'd picked up from him. "My mother was a secretary."

"That so. Where?"

"Cotton broker."

"A cotton broker having a secretary is perfectly logical. A postdoc showing up with his own secretary, that sounds dodgy."

He peeled off one door down from Vintage Visions, still refusing to have anything to do with Lily. He had kept the monograph and promised her about five different times that yes, he'd find a way to finagle two copies. She watched his back for a moment, then checked her watch. Five minutes early. Take that, Lily. This year was finally turning around.

She clocked in and breezed over to the counter. Talmadge was on the men's side showing leather jackets to a man she thought was kind of hand-some, but since he was a blond she knew Talmadge wasn't going to linger and try to flirt. And she also knew Talmadge would have something to say to her today. She had called the apartment last night and left a brief mes-sage on the machine to say she wasn't coming home, she was spending the night with Matthew. Sure enough, when Lily disappeared outside for her cigarette, Talmadge sidled over to the counter.

"And how are we this fine afternoon?" he asked.

"We're swell," she said, and took out the Windex so she could clean the counter mirror. "At least, I'm swell. Do you have something you want to tell me?"

"No, gracious no. I have no problem here. Nooo problem at allll." He reached in his pocket and put on his glasses, black-rimmed sixties-style things he wore only when he wanted to emphasize his seriousness, since the lenses were plain glass. "As long as you're doing this for the right rea-son."

"What's the right reason?" She grabbed the paper towels.

"Going back for the sex, that's the right reason. Going back because you're attached to this guy, that would be the wrong reason."

She sprayed the mirror. "The sex is great. For the record."

"That surprises me. I don't know if you know this, but I had an English guy once, too. We lasted maybe a couple of months. All he did was talk."

"No sex?"

"No sweetie, I mean he talked during sex. The whole time. Like he was narrating, I swear to god. So I always thought that must be because most of them are funny-looking—"

"Matthew is *not* funny looking!"

"Oh, Matthew's fine. I told you that. He showers, he shaves, he makes eye contact."

"He's—"

"But come on, England isn't wall-to-wall hunks like Spain or Italy. Let's face it, all most of them've got is the accent. After that, the party's over." She tried to break in again but he forged on. "I figured Julian, that was his name, Julian, and it wasn't the kind of name you wanted to be call-ing out at a big moment—"

"Talmadge—"

"I figured Julian thought if he didn't keep reminding me of what was cute about him to begin with, I could change my mind at any point."

"There has to be a reason you're telling me this." She finished wiping off the mirror and stashed away the Windex.

"I'm telling you to be careful."

"We use condoms, all right?"

"I think you know," he said, removing his glasses, "that's not what I'm talking about."

"He came back. That says it all, doesn't it?"

"It could say all kinds of things." He suddenly turned around. "Shit, there's Lily." She wished she had his ability to sense Lily's disturbance in the force, without even facing the door. "I'll talk to you later sweetie."

Talmadge's shift ended before hers. The day held no potholes, although early February was as dead as it got in retail, and she sped home to see if she could catch Miriam. She galloped up the steps to the fifth floor, but no light shone under Miriam's door. She knocked and waited. No response.

She trudged into the apartment and put her coat away. Jim came out from his room and stood in the door.

"How are you?" he asked.

"Swell," she told him.

He leaned against the doorjamb. "All right then. Do you want to watch a movie?"

Thank god. This was Jim's way of letting her know he wasn't going to give her a hard time about Matthew. "I won't be able to concentrate. I have to go ask Miriam something." Jim's eyebrows rose. "It's a secret," she added. "I'll tell you later."

Talmadge came out of the kitchen with his ice cream pint and a spoon. "All right Talmadge, here's our chance," said Jim cheerfully. "Ceinwen's not watching the movie with us. *Nightmare on Elm Street*, how does that sound?"

She went into her room and picked up the copy of Louise Brooks's essays that she'd just bought at the Strand, flipping through the pages to the tune of muffled cries of pain and horror from the TV set. She kept checking the clock and each time another half-hour or so passed, she walked through the apartment, trying not to look at the TV, and went downstairs to see if Miriam had arrived. The third time she did it, Jim paused the video and said mildly, "You could leave a note on her door, you know."

She could, at that. Ceinwen thought about it. "I don't know, I'd feel funny doing that with Miriam."

Sometime around midnight she gave up.

She woke up early, tiptoed into the kitchen and discovered that even the Cafe Busted was gone. Thrifty would be open. She pulled on her blue Harlow dress and didn't bother with underwear. She added some striped leggings and her Doc Martens. Ceinwen had been wanting to see how she'd look if she mixed up her vintage with new items, like some of the girls who came into the store. Now she had her answer: terrible. Even a bra wouldn't help.

But it was good enough for Thrifty. She put on her coat, picked up her bag and closed the door to the apartment as quietly as she could.

She passed Miriam's door without stopping; too early to knock. On the next landing she realized she was hearing a steady noise. Rattle, bump. Rattle, bump. She slowed and looked down the stairwell. Praise be, it was Miriam.

"Hey!" she called, then looked around, hoping no neighbor would pop out to rebuke her. Miriam waved and paused as Ceinwen scrambled down to meet her. The noise was from Miriam's laundry; she had a bag stuffed in one of those rolling wire boxes that homeless guys used to wheel their stuff.

"Sorry," said Miriam, "do you need to get past?"

"Nah. Let me take this for you."

"I'm not an invalid. I do this all the time."

"I know, but I'm going down anyway." Ceinwen grabbed the basket and lifted. It was a bit heavy even for her, and she had no idea how Miriam was managing.

"I go early," Miriam was saying, with what amounted to cheeriness for her. "No waiting. I used to have a little washer-dryer in the apartment, but the landlord made me get rid of it. Said it was against the rules, because of the pipes." They'd reached the bottom. Miriam held open the door.

"That's terrible."

"Isn't it just. Making a poor broken-down old lady do this every week. The man's a monster." Miriam put the back of her hand to her forehead, then grinned. "He was hoping I'd move out. Ha. Fooled him. Had to give up the washer six years ago and I'm still here, just like that Sondheim song." They were at the street corner now; the closest laundromat was halfway down the next block.

"Why would he want you out? You're the least trouble of anyone in the building."

"Not to a landlord I'm not." Miriam put a hand to her mouth and whispered, "Rent control."

"How did he find out you had a washer?"

"As the English say, somebody shopped me." Miriam stopped just short of the laundromat door. "I'm sorry. These days I don't suppose you care what the English say."

"It's fine," said Ceinwen, feeling happy about it all over again. "Matthew and I got back together."

An honest-to-goodness smirk from Miriam. "I thought that might happen."

"Why's that?"

"You seemed quite taken with each other." Miriam opened the door and braced it with her back. "Thank you dear, but I can handle things from here."

"I'm not in a hurry," said Ceinwen. She wheeled the basket in.

"All right then, keep me company a bit if you like," said Miriam. "Eight o'clock on a weekday morning this place is basically a morgue. Of course," she added, looking around, "it's never cheery at the best of times, is it."

They were the only ones there besides the attendant. The laundromat's floor was covered in chipped, warped tiles, the dusty machines were a hideous yellow and the walls were mottled with scorch marks from a fire that Mr. Rodriguez at the Thrifty Mart said had happened in 1978. Her head felt foggy and achey. If she was going to introduce the topic of the clip at the Brody in anything resembling a smooth way, Ceinwen figured she was going to need coffee. They had pulled up in front of a washer and Miriam was untying the top of the bag.

"Let me put this in the washer for you and then I'm going to grab a cup of coffee," she said.

"Ceinwen," said Miriam, with great firmness. "You have nice manners. I'm sure they were very proud of you back in Mississippi. But I can handle getting the laundry in the machine. I promise you, I will not collapse." Ceinwen hesitated. "Go on, get some coffee."

"You want some too?"

"From where, the Thrifty Mart? Thanks, but no." Miriam was already putting towels in the washer, and Ceinwen gave up and left for Thrifty. She bought a cup of coffee, a can of Cafe Busted and a pack of cigarettes, and while Mr. Rodriguez was ringing her up and telling her she should really get a tan or something, she decided the best approach was to bring up the book first, and then introduce the Brody's fragment.

When she returned, Miriam was sitting in one of the rows of attached plastic chairs, watching the washer swish the soap through the towels. Ceinwen took off her coat, sat down and peeled back part of the coffee lid.

"I've been thinking about your movie," she began.

"That doesn't surprise me."

Miriam always had the same tone when movies came up. "Did you know there was a book about it?"

"A book? No. There was a professor who wrote something about it a while back. Out at USC."

"That's the one," she said, a little disappointed that Miriam already knew. "It's a monograph."

"Eh. Fancy name for a long-winded paper. He contacted me when he was writing it. Gundlach, was that his name?"

"Yes, that's him. What did he want to talk to you about?"

Miriam made a fly-swatting motion. "He didn't want to talk *to* me. He wanted to talk *at* me, the gasbag. On and on about German Expressionism and Emil's influences." Miriam turned and narrowed her eyes. "Hold on, young lady. How do you know about this?"

She had made another major tactical error. She took another sip of coffee and hoped the caffeine would kick in soon. "I, um, well. I was just talking to a collector and I asked if he'd heard of the film. And he's got so much stuff about silent movies that he happened to have a copy of the book."

"You were just talking to a collector." Miriam folded her arms. "I hope you didn't mention me. Did you?"

"Oh no," Ceinwen said, relieved she could be truthful. "I told him I'd heard of the movie because I liked the novel."

"Fell for that, did he."

"I did like the novel!"

"So you said." Miriam shook her head. "I guess it's my fault for not saying so, but I do hope you won't run around telling anyone about our conversation."

"I would never," she said, with a sudden guilty thought of Matthew, cooking dinner and saying bad things about Emil.

"I don't want anyone else coming around and prying, you understand? Not that most people would care. But silent-movie obsessives are an odd bunch. And you never know when some bright young reporter person will hear of you and take it into his head that you're a human interest story.

Happened to an old friend. You know. 'Alone on Avenue C lives an elderly woman, with nothing but memories of a magical, long-lost time in Hollywood to keep her company.'" Miriam pulled a finger across her throat. "No. Absolutely not. I'd rather have hives."

"Gundlach asked about you and Emil?" The monograph hadn't had a word about the affair.

"That would have been a lot more normal. No, he couldn't have cared less about the human element. It was all about using the movie to make a point about the coming of sound." The book did have a section at the end, about how ways of seeing film were changing at the end of the twenties, but since Gundlach's observations about the shifting gaze of the spectator were almost as exciting as Andy discussing projection speeds, she had skipped it. "The only personal thing he wanted to know was whether Emil was Jewish."

That was a brand-new wrinkle. "Was he?"

"Probably."

"You don't know for sure?" She flashed on an image of Emil, smashing his fist against a wall at the idea of going back to Berlin.

"No, and Gundlach never found out anything from me, because that was when I threw him out. He thought he'd offended me and tried to explain that émigré Jews were already shaping a new aesthetic, and I showed him the door. He hadn't offended me at all, he was putting me to sleep. Honestly, the way some intellectuals talk about movies, they could make the Marx Brothers boring."

She swigged her coffee again. "What made him think Emil was Jewish?"

"He tried to get some simple records from Germany and hit a dead end. And of course, that doesn't generally happen with German records. He thought maybe Emil changed his name. I didn't tell him that had occurred to me a long time ago. If Emil wanted to bury the past I wasn't going to dig it up for some nosy academic."

"Why would he want to hide it?" For the first time, she was getting a look from Miriam that told her she'd said something truly dumb. "Of course I understand why he might not want to bring it up in Germany, but in Hollywood he'd have had plenty of company."

Miriam shrugged. "Different times. If people thought nobody Jewish was around they'd say all sorts of things. Sometimes they'd say things even if somebody was right there. And after he was dead, I thought back to how Emil would get very cold and quiet if anybody used a slur or complained about Jewish bankers or studio bosses. He was blond and everybody assumed he was a gentile. But he never talked about his parents or much of anything before the Great War. And I went along with it. I thought he was above petty things like background, because he was so left-wing, and once I fell in love with him I decided I was, too." Miriam raised her voice and shook her fist like a street-corner ranter. "What does it matter where you came from! What matters now is that you stand with the workers!" She coughed. "I can still sing the 'Internationale,' but I never could stay on key."

"And you started thinking he'd changed his name."

"Not until the war. I was reading the newspaper about a battle near a Dutch town called Arnhem. And I thought how Emil's name was just a German version of that, and he'd told me he spent a while in Holland." She shrugged. "It fit."

Ceinwen could bring up the clip now, but with Miriam so chatty she wanted to know more. "Emil was a communist."

"Socialist, more like. Jack, my husband. He was a communist."

The Mississippi in Ceinwen never could get used to this kind of thing. "Isn't that something," she managed.

"What Emil started, the Depression continued, I guess. I went to meetings for years. Met Jack in '34. Poor man had been asking me to marry him for at least ten years before I finally did."

"Marriage is very bourgeois." She figured this was the sort of thing you were supposed to say to a communist.

"That's exactly what I kept telling Jack," chuckled Miriam. "And he kept arguing that it was a perfect cover. No one would suspect a respectable couple of being agents of the revolution. Truth was, he was a respectable sort of man. Born to be a husband, really."

"What made you change your mind?"

"Oh, by '46 or so it became clear it was time to leave Hollywood. Easier to get theater jobs. Although not that much easier." Miriam pointed toward the entrance. Just past the door, a man was sitting on a fire hydrant and downing a can of something concealed in a paper bag. "Hence our eventual gracing of Avenue C. Anyway, you couldn't gallivant around the countryside living in sin, not in those days. The hotel clerks wanted a marriage certificate."

They both watched the washer for a minute.

"I'm going to get a copy of the monograph," said Ceinwen. "I was going to make you one, too."

"Good heavens, don't do that. I won't read it. My good memories won't be in there, and the bad ones I'd rather leave alone."

She inhaled and said, "I found out something else from the collector guy."

"What's that, another scholarly paper about Emil? They must be hard up for topics these days."

"No, he said he'd seen a little piece of the film. There's an archive here in New York that has it. Place uptown, called the Brody Institute for Cinephilia and Preservation."

Miriam put both hands on the side of her chair and pushed herself to her feet. She turned her back and walked away a few paces, then came back with her hand over her mouth. I'm a jerk, thought Ceinwen. I keep forgetting how old she is. I could have given her a stroke. Miriam took her hand away.

"How long is it?" she asked quietly.

"He said it runs about two minutes. I haven't seen it yet. You have to be some kind of student or academic. But I'm sure we can get you in." Miriam's hand was back on her mouth. "Great news, yes?" added Ceinwen, hoping Miriam was going to start looking happier.

She folded her arms tightly. "Which scene?"

"He said you were getting menaced by someone."

She snorted. "That's the whole movie right there."

Ceinwen ventured, "When would you want to go see it?"

Miriam sat again and crossed her legs. "I don't."

It was Ceinwen's turn to jump out of her chair. "Are you crazy?" She checked herself and said, "I'm sorry, but that makes no sense to me at all. You told me you'd always wanted to see it again."

"I said I wanted to see the movie again. The whole movie. Not some itty-bitty little scrap of it. Like the Oscars. God help us." Miriam's voice took on a breathy starlet quality. "'Ooooh folks, here's this little clip from the dark ages, before everybody figured out how it was really done. Don't worry, it's not too long, we don't want to *bore* anybody.'"

The sudden rush of pure hatred in Miriam's voice kept Ceinwen from sitting back down. She said, very tentatively, like she was approaching a guard dog, "There's a lot of people who still love silents. You said you trusted your own judgment, not Gregory's."

"And I do." Miriam's voice was no longer venomous, but it still invited no argument. "Who knows, maybe people would appreciate it now. But I can tell you for sure, nobody's going to see two minutes of *Mysteries* and suddenly decide to give Emil his due, much as I might wish otherwise. I've made my peace with that. Most people labor at things that won't survive. It's pure ego to think you should be any different."

"But this bit did survive." Not even a shrug in response. "It's better than nothing!"

She waved her hand in Ceinwen's direction. "You like that dress, don't you."

Oh for god's sake. Not the fucking dress again. "I wear it a lot, I know. That's because it's *flattering*, Miriam."

"It's lovely on you. Although you do need a bra with it. I'm trying to put this in a way you'll understand." She paused. "Let's say Talmadge took that dress."

On top of everything, Miriam had a completely wrong picture of Talmadge. "That isn't his thing." The washer had stopped. Ceinwen grabbed a laundry cart and pushed it in front of the door.

"Not to wear. He just decides one day that it isn't nice anymore and nobody else is going to want it, so he throws it away. You can't even fish it out of the garbage. But he keeps a little bit of one ruffle. And when you complain, he hands you the scrap and says, 'Here you go. It's better than nothing.'"

Ceinwen yanked the washer door open, caught a towel as it fell out, and reflected that she was never going to get it right with Miriam. "I'd still want to see it."

"That's your youth talking. Old ladies, we ask for more. After a while we decide all that sweet feminine making-the-best-of-things is for the birds." She picked up Ceinwen's hand and gently pulled it away from the basket.

"You don't mind if I see it, do you Miriam?"

"Knock yourself out." Miriam pushed the basket over to the dryer. "How are you going to get in? You aren't a student, are you?"

"No, I'm not. Matthew's arranging it. He's a postdoc at NYU."

"I see." Miriam swung open the dryer door with a thump. "You told Matthew."

How could good news go this badly? "I told him you'd been in a movie in the twenties. That's all."

She could tell just by the way Miriam was throwing in the clothes that she didn't believe her. "I suppose I can't expect you to keep secrets from your sweetie. And those English upper-crust types aren't a gabby bunch, anyway. But please, no one else. The last thing I want is the NYU film department ringing my bell."

"Matthew's a mathematician." Miriam slammed the dryer door shut and started feeding in quarters. "He doesn't know a soul at the film department."

"A mathematician? That's going to sound odd," said Miriam. She hit the button with one short push of her index finger. "How on earth is he going to use that to see a film?"

"He's an academic. They can come up with all sorts of weird ideas at a moment's notice," said Ceinwen, with pride.

Miriam turned and put her hands on her hips. "This should be fun for him, then. 'How Émigré Jews Brought Trigonometry to Hollywood.'"

"That's pretty good. I'll suggest it."

"Go right ahead." Miriam sat back down. "Well, I know you work today . . ."

Ceinwen knew her cues by heart. She said goodbye and grabbed her things. At the door, she turned to look. Miriam was watching the dryer with a face like Garbo at the end of *Queen Christina*, staring off into eternity.

2.

"**G**OOD," SAID MATTHEW WHEN SHE TOLD HIM THAT MIRIAM DIDN'T want to see the film. "One less explanation." He'd managed to Xerox two copies of the monograph and grumbled that it would have been easier asking Angie for a kidney.

When she returned the book to Andy, finding a reason to leave quickly was helped by the fact that there was no place to sit in his office. She told him the best part of the monograph was the section about ways of seeing silent movies, and she swore she was going to pick up some Andre Bazin the next time she was at the Strand. Andy said she could come over to his place and flip through *Cahiers du Cinema*, which he had dating to the inaugural issue in 1951. She pointed out that she didn't speak French and he told her that he'd be happy to read it out loud to her and translate. She told him it might be a good idea, but she needed to wait until her schedule got a little less crowded.

Matthew called the Brody and said the man he'd spoken to, some sort of curator, was a little distracted-sounding on the phone and didn't seem to care why they wanted to see it. He just took their names and said to come in next Tuesday morning at 11:00 a.m. and ask for the director at the front desk.

Ceinwen wore her forties suit with stockings and her best ankle-strap high heels, causing Matthew to point out that the streets were still slushy. "I want to look serious," she told him.

When she caught sight of the building, she grabbed his arm. A townhouse, at last, and not just any old townhouse. Red brick, paned windows, ornate white trim and a staircase that curved to the entrance floor. "Five floors. Look at how wide it is. Aren't you glad I wore heels?"

They were buzzed into a lobby and she had to restrain herself from spinning around to take it all in. The floor was white marble set with tiny black tiles. Dead center was a round, tufted settee like the ones in thirties-movie hotels. Many feet away, at a carved mahogany desk, sat a young woman with red hair and plenty of freckles sprinkled across flawless skin. Behind her a window soared up two stories to show a bare winter garden. On the right a staircase swooped up toward a huge chandelier, on the left more stairs led to the lower floor. Other than that, the hall was almost bare. The settee was the only place you could sit.

"Matthew Hill and Ceinwen Reilly. We're here to see Isabel Chung."

There was a carved frieze running all the way around the ceiling, vines and flowers and people doing things, but it was hard to see what.

The woman seemed puzzled. "Did you have an appointment?" Where, Ceinwen wondered, did you get two-story-tall velvet drapes?

"Yes. I spoke to Fred Creighton."

"Oh," she said, sighing. "Fred." She punched a button on the telephone. "Fred. Did you make an appointment today? . . . Yes, now . . . Yes. Standing in front of me . . . All right. Yes, all right." She put down the phone. "You can have a seat. He's coming down." She took their coats, disappearing with them through one side door and reappearing through another right next to it, which was odd. Ceinwen tried, but failed, to get a glimpse of more interior. Matthew sat down, but Ceinwen kept walking around, partly because her feet were damp and her toes were numb and she needed to get the blood back in them, and partly because she was thrilling to the sound of her heels clicking on the marble. She looked at the poster on one wall—*A Woman of Paris*. She crossed to look at the other—*La Bohème*. Ah wait, that was Vidor. Harry wanted her to see that one.

A man, pale and slight, with intensely dark eyes and a couple of days of beard growth, bolted down the shallow marble steps two at a time. She was still glad she had dressed up, but he must be used to the place, with his faded jeans, sweater, and frayed sneakers.

"Yeah, Kelly, sorry. Isabel's, ah, gonna be late. I'm supposed to, um, fill out some stuff."

"I don't have anything on my calendar."

"I told Isabel but, uh, I guess I forgot to tell you."

"I guess you did." Fred's shaggy hair was damp along the line of his forehead, he was breathing hard and shifting back and forth on his feet, and she seemed to take pity on him. "Telling Isabel's the important part."

Fred shook hands, folded one arm and tapped the other hand against his elbow. "I, ah, filled out the request but there's this, um, form that I was supposed to complete that has some more, ah, details. So I told Isabel, um, she's the director, and she's supposed to be here soon, but in the meantime I'm supposed to take you back and, um, get stuff in order. So. Yeah. We can go to her office."

"Isabel's office?" That was the receptionist, sounding as though Fred were proposing they all meet in the ladies' room.

"That's what she told me."

Kelly picked up a letter opener and sliced into an envelope from a stack on the desk. "All right. If you say so."

They followed Fred upstairs to an office with casement windows over-looking the street. There was a huge fireplace at one end, unlit, and an-other antique desk across the room, an immense leather swivel chair behind it, the desk's surface bare except for a few papers on the blotter. The walls were lined with enough film books to restock the Strand. She craned her neck at one shelf, to check out what looked like every "Films of" book ever published, when she caught a look from Matthew and reluctantly put her eyes back on Fred. He had stopped alongside them, behind the two low-backed gilt chairs in front of the desk.

"Where would you us like to sit?" asked Matthew.

"Oh. Yeah. I'll go back here." They took their seats as Fred walked around to the swivel chair, observed it for a second, sat down carefully, rolled the chair to the desk, placed one hand on either side of the papers without touching them, and squinted down. "Um, right. These are the forms. And, um, I'm supposed to fill in the stuff about the project. I was, um, supposed to do that on the phone, but, well." He looked at the center drawer, drew a breath, pulled it open and came up with an enameled pen. "I, ah, guess it's okay to use this," he muttered.

"Should simplify matters," said Matthew.

She was glad Fred didn't seem to have taken that in. "You're, um, the first request I've had for this one. And my first request from a mathematician. So, yeah. Unusual. But I've only been here a couple of years." He posed the pen over the paper. "Okay. I guess you can, uh, start telling me what you're working on."

"This is a personal project," said Matthew. "I have a notion that there are places where the sciences and humanities intersect. I'm pursuing it in my spare time. But I do hope to publish." Fred scribbled and looked up.

"Come to think of it, I went to film school at Tisch and I, ah, did oc-casionally run into a Courant professor. Name of Engelman."

"I know him well."

"Yeah, he'd show up for screenings from time to time. Never spoke to him. So, um . . . first thing I'm supposed to ask . . ." He trailed off as he read the dense block of small print on the form. Finally he looked up and said brightly, "What's the interest here?"

"The project's about lost films," said Matthew.

More writing. "Trying to, ah, reconstruct this one?"

"No," said Matthew, "not at all. The premise is that lost films fortify our ideal of cinema."

Fred set down the pen. His hand rubbed his stubble a couple of times and dropped back on the desk. "They do?"

"Yes. They're part of the Romantic notion of doomed artistry, that's capital-R of course. The films that are lost are much better in our minds than the ones we actually have. So they're in tune with our Platonic ideals, and in that sense, we need lost films. They're an important element of our conception of cinema as art."

Fred's eyes lit on Ceinwen, as if to check whether she was on board with this. "Don't think I've, ah, ever heard it put that way. Working in an archive, we tend to think of lost films as, you know, a bad thing."

"I'm trying to encourage a broader perspective." Matthew was enjoying himself way too much.

Fred blinked. "Okay." He readjusted the chair and scratched his neck. "So, um, repeat that for me, please." Matthew repeated it, and Fred repeated it back as he wrote it all down, right up to ". . . encourage . . . a . . . broader . . . perspective." He put down the pen and re-read the form. "Um. So. Professor. I have to wonder why you want to, ah, see this fragment, if your thesis is that it's better to just, you know, imagine it."

"That's where the mathematics comes in," said Matthew, slouching back and tapping the side of his nose, as one who's revealing the heart of the matter. "What percentage of a lost film do you need to see, in order to have enough to create a meaningful image of the film in your mind."

This was the longest pause yet, but when it ended, Fred wrote that down, too. Then he grabbed his neck again, recrossed his legs and rolled through an "ah" and an "um," possibly in preparation for telling Matthew he had rocks in his head. Then the door opened and Fred started so hard his chair rolled back about a foot from the desk.

The woman who entered had on a pale-green suit with gold buttons, and a black braid trim. Her height was hard to tell, as her heels were at least an inch taller than anything Ceinwen ever had worn herself.

"I'm Isabel Chung. How do you do." Her shiny, stick-straight hair swayed as she strode across the office.

"Matthew Hill. From NYU. This is Ceinwen Reilly."

"I was filling out the forms," said Fred, holding them up like a shield. He'd already moved halfway around the desk.

"Thanks, I'll have a look." She took the papers from him and they all sat down, except Fred, who no longer had a chair. Isabel laid them on the desk and read intently for a couple of minutes. "Fred. I can't read your writing. It looks like this says lost films fortify our ideal of cinema. Is that supposed to be forfeit? or forsake?"

"No. Fortify." Isabel put her chin on her hand. Fred's foot began to tap and his deep voice took on a slightly higher key. "Fortify. Right, Professor Hill?"

"Matthew. Yes, that's right."

Isabel's black-lined eyes swept from Matthew, to Ceinwen, then back to the paper. "Unusual perspective."

"I like to think so."

"Should you happen to get this published," said Isabel, in a tone that suggested such an event would correspond with raining frogs, "we'll be interested in seeing it."

"I'll send you a reprint."

"Fred, I don't see where you filled in their IDs."

"Oh sh—sorry." He rocked slightly on his toes.

"How did they get in here?"

"I, um, took them upstairs?"

Isabel sighed. "All right. You can give me your IDs now." Matthew took out his wallet. "The university ones."

"I'm not at NYU," said Ceinwen.

"You're not a student?"

"She's assisting me part-time," said Matthew. "It's a project outside my university duties, as I said."

At that, not only did Isabel check out Ceinwen, from the roots of her hair down to her ankle straps, but Fred quit moving and looked hard, too.

"It seems Fred didn't make this clear," said Isabel, "but ideally both parties are supposed to be affiliated with an academic institution. However. Since you're here, and since this project is . . ." She glanced back at the forms. "Since this project is somewhat atypical, I can accept a driver's license."

Ceinwen pulled out her license. Isabel began to write down the numbers, then stopped.

"Miss Reilly. This is expired."

Matthew fastened a hand on the arm of his chair. "Expired. Really. May I see?" He took it. "Aha," he said, with an indulgent little smile for Ceinwen that involved only the corners of his mouth and left his eyes boring into her skull. "I see the trouble. You gave them your Mississippi license. Where's the New York?"

"New York what?"

"Your New York State driver's license. The one you got when this one expired *eight months ago*. Did you mistake one for the other?"

A pro forma wallet search was performed. "Must have, I guess."

"Do you have anything else?" asked Isabel. "A passport?" She caught herself before she laughed and shook her head. "All right." Isabel took the card back and shook her head. "Since your employer's ID is in order, I suppose I'll accept this." Ceinwen told herself she'd imagined the tiny hesitation before the word "employer." "I don't want anyone running all the way back downtown. But if you want to arrange further viewings you'll need proper ID."

They had to sign and date the forms in two places. "Fred, did you bring brochures?"

He shifted his weight from foot to foot. "I was just gonna ask where those things are living these days."

She rolled open a drawer and set out two. "Did you tell them anything about the Brody?"

"Um . . ." Fred was staring out the window, as if to assess how far it was to the sidewalk.

Isabel pushed her hair back and gave a tiny shake of her head. "The Brody Institute for Cinephilia and Preservation was founded eighteen years ago on the death of Herbert Brody, who had an extensive collection of pre-1940 films, stretching well back into the silent era. This was his house. He'd made a fortune in business."

"Safety razors," said Fred, happy to contribute at last.

"Yes. Grooming products," said Isabel, and her eyes stayed resolutely away from Fred and his stubble. "But movie collecting was his passion. He left his money to establish this nonprofit organization to preserve and curate his holdings. The mission of the Institute is primarily educational, hence the viewing restrictions. Mr. Brody believed the collection was best used by those well-versed in cinema. However, in recent years some funds have also been used for acquisitions, in order to further our preservation goals, and the Arnheim fragment was part of a collection we acquired from a gentleman in Vermont whose wife decided he no longer had the space."

A sudden chuckle from Fred. "He was storing them in his tool shed."

"And," said Isabel crisply, "since they were predominantly silents, and on celluloid nitrate stock, we were lucky to get them before they completely deteriorated."

"Before MoMA got there," murmured Fred, steepling his fingers.

"The collection had attracted interest, as Fred says. Was there something else you wanted to add?"

"No," he squeaked.

"Fred's predecessor was involved in obtaining the films, and he transferred some that were in particularly bad shape. This was the only surviving part of one reel, and we found no other part of the movie." Isabel checked her watch. "Fred is reasonably familiar with the rest of the provenance, so if you have further questions you can ask him after he takes you to the viewing room." They got up to go. "Don't forget the brochures."

As Fred climbed another flight of stairs ahead of them Matthew bent to her ear and whispered, "Expired, for god's sake. You're such a *child*."

"How was I supposed to know we needed ID?"

"Most working adults have it as a matter of course."

"Why? This isn't *Casablanca*," she hissed back. "I don't have to have my letters of transit."

"Still on your way back there?" called Fred.

"Right behind you," Matthew called back.

Fred showed them into a small room with blackout shades drawn. A viewing machine sat on a table; it had a reel of film laid flat and connected to a small screen. "So. Yeah. Time to see what's left of this one," he said, as they sat down.

His tone worried her. Fred seemed like a nice guy, in his stammering, perpetually fidgety kind of way, and Matthew hadn't exactly bothered to make a good impression. She said, firmly, "I hope it's clear that Matthew isn't arguing that we want films to be lost. We both admire the work that you do here." A beat. "Very much." She waited again, then added, "Don't we, Matthew."

"Certainly. Don't know how you do it."

Fred looked straight past Matthew to address Ceinwen. "Um, well. Not easy," he said, foot tapping. "Never enough time, never enough money. So we, ah, tend to work on the most urgent cases, and that means the, uh, stuff with known artistic or historic interest. To tell you the truth I'm, um, not sure why this fragment got transferred in the first place. I assume that Chris, you know, must have liked it."

"Do you like it?"

He smiled at her. "You've caught me. I haven't seen it. There's, ah, still some obscure and fragmentary stuff I haven't seen, especially if it wasn't something I worked on." He got up and walked to the light switch. "Ready?" He switched off the light, walked back and punched a button on the machine.

It was Miriam, sitting on a sofa with the man playing Count Morano. His body language was polite, formal even, but she was looking at him like he was a curled-up snake. She put up a hand as if to get him to stop talking, and he took it between both of his. She looked at him and said something, and it was evident that it was taking everything she had not to snatch her hand away. He said something else, and she did pull her hand back this time and crossed her arms against her body. She looked down at the table in front of them, refusing to meet his eyes. He made another move in her direction and she stood up, trembling a bit. She turned, looked at a point just past the camera and seemed about to ask something. The film ran out.

Ceinwen had always admired Miriam's cool, elegant stillness. There were no nervous movements with her in real life, and here was proof that that was also the case sixty years ago. Louis Delgado had made the light play across her, like Gloria Swanson in that *Queen Kelly* scene they showed in *Sunset Boulevard*. The shadows around the edges of the room made it seem vast, although Ceinwen realized the set probably wasn't.

She tried to shove away the feeling, but it wouldn't leave. Disappointment; not huge, but there. Miriam said Emil loved to move the camera, and what was left of *Mysteries* was a standard medium shot. Not so much as a cut. Not a single close-up of that face he'd loved. After all he went through to reject stagey, static talkies.

"Beautiful actress," said Fred.

"Stunning," said Matthew, still staring at the blank screen.

Fred half-smiled and pulled on his ear. "Might be nice to see more, yes? But that's all we got."

At least Miriam was right about one thing, she wasn't bad. A young girl's terror of men, she'd said. But Ceinwen also saw anger in those small, contained gestures.

"What's she doing at the end?" asked Matthew.

Fred shrugged. "Can't know without seeing what came after."

Emil had told Miriam to think about the casting offices.

"Run it again," said Ceinwen. Both men looked at her, and she realized she didn't sound like an assistant. "Please, can you run it again? I want to look at her costume."

With swift, utterly fidget-free precision Fred rewound the reel, looped it back through and ran it again.

"One more time? Please? This time, look at her chest."

"Anything you say," said Matthew cheerfully. This time when the film ran, Ceinwen leaned forward and pointed.

"The bodice is too big. Look how the fabric is sagging over the sash."

"Yeah, I see," said Fred. "What's that tell you?"

"I don't think this is a scene from the film. I think it's a take from her screen test," said Ceinwen. "Her costume was too big. She told—" Matthew's foot nudged hers. "She told an interviewer that. In an article. That I read." Matthew closed his eyes for a second. "I don't remember where."

"Possible," said Fred. "That would also explain why she looks like she's about to ask something here. She, um, might have been asking for instructions. Or someone might have walked onto the set." Miriam looked past the camera again and the film ran out. "If that's what this is, it's a rarity all right. Not a lot of screen tests from this era. Hardly anybody bothered to save them."

"If you found more of the film," said Ceinwen, "would you be able to transfer it so people could watch it?"

Fred's fingers drummed on the machine. "We'd need the funds, of course. Every year we're debating what to, um, allocate to which movies and like I said, we're more or less forced to pick and choose. Triage, basically. With Arnheim, you know, there isn't anything else surviving from him. So, yeah, I guess there'd be a fair amount of interest, even though nobody really knows what his films were like."

"How about you? Would you be interested?"

His hand went back to his neck. "I'm interested in everything. That's why I'm here, right? Framing's good. The lighting is, um, not so typical of the period. Not at Civitas anyway. Shadowy, like actual candlelight. Actress, ah, gorgeous. And if that's just a test, you know, the actual film is probably much better. Yeah, I'd totally want to give it some priority." She smiled at him and he smiled back. "But I'm not the one who decides. There's a lot of layers to, um, the bur—authorization, I mean."

"And you'd have to find the film first," said Matthew.

Fred's eyes finally lit on Matthew, but only for a moment. "Yeah. That's the hard part, obviously. As you were saying, chances are it's gone for good."

Matthew checked his watch. "This has been helpful. Thank you." He stood up. "Do we have to sign for our coats?"

"I'm not sure I remember how to get out of here," Ceinwen interjected before Fred could reply.

"On the way in, I saw signs marked 'exit.' Thought they might be useful at some point," said Matthew.

"I have to take you down anyway," said Fred, looking apologetic. They were opening the door when Fred turned around. "Oh, right. I also, um, have to bring the film."

"In case someone walks in off the street?" inquired Matthew.

At that, Fred stalked to the table where the canister was sitting and said, loudly and fluently, "Listen, I know the rules are a pain in the ass."

"Knock it off," Ceinwen mouthed at Matthew, whose expression changed not a bit. Then, to Fred, "Isabel seems like a stickler."

He opened the canister and set it next to the machine. "Oh, Isabel's all right. She hired me. She's just . . ."

"A yeller?" asked Ceinwen, with a flood of sympathy.

Fred rewound the reel. "No, god no. She's, um, organized. Isabel is very, very organized. And when you're kind of not . . ."

"You're obviously very organized." Fred froze with his hands on the reel, and Matthew's whole face seemed to twitch. "Restoring a movie's precise work. You have to keep track of a lot of different details at once," she continued. "Probably you just don't have a lot left over for other stuff."

Fred flushed slightly. "Thanks. I'll, um, remember to point that out." He laid the film in the canister. "Anyway"—with a short, sharp look at Matthew—"Isabel's been trying to make some changes. Stepped up the acquisitions, a lot. She wants to lend things out more. Maybe even start public screenings. But, uh, there's all this stuff in the trust that she, ah, has to work around."

"You have to admit it's odd," said Ceinwen. Quit looking at your watch, Matthew, I'm trying to find out stuff here. "Film is supposed to be the people's art form, yes? Not some exclusive club for academics."

"Ah. Well. Old Brody, he had some ideas. He though the big ones, um, the *Casablanca*s and *Gone with the Wind*s, those films'd be fine. But the silents, the obscure stuff, eventually it would be academics and, you know, intellectuals keeping them alive. Nobody else would care." He picked up the reel and stuck it under his arm.

"We care," said Ceinwen.

Fred leaned toward her and said, sotto voce, "We're weird."

"I'm sorry to rush," said Matthew, "but Vladimir Arnold's giving a lecture."

"Rock star?" joked Ceinwen.

"For maths, yes," was the curt reply.

"You better go then," said Ceinwen. "I was hoping I could stick around and ask Fred about some things."

Fred shifted the canister from one arm to the other. "Like what?"

"Like, nitrate."

3.

"**T**HEY'VE FOUND FILMS IN ALL KINDS OF PLACES. BROOM CLOSETS. Under porches. That guy in Vermont really did have everything in his tool shed. His wife decided on a big spring cleaning and the guy at the Brody got a tip that there was this collection and she was going to toss it all out, and he went up there and got all this stuff. And sometimes the prints would hit the end of the release period and the theaters never bothered—"

"May I interrupt?" Matthew had his burger in one hand; he'd been taking a bite whenever he gave up temporarily on trying to break in.

"Wait, this is important—they never bothered to return them to the studio. That's how Kevin Brownlow found part of *Napoleon*, see. Czechoslovakia was the end of the line in Europe, and—"

Matthew put a finger to her lips. "I didn't realize Fred was so fascinating. But—what's that grin about?"

"You've been very patient, that's all. Go on."

"I've been trying to figure out why you wanted to spend—an hour and a half, was it?"

"An hour. He had to get back to the lab."

"Pity. An hour, then, talking about film stock and where the Brody finds its films, when all you ever talked about before was watching films. And I have it now. You're planning to look for this one." She looked down and realized she'd only eaten about three bites. Admittedly, at Cozy Soup 'n' Burger the things were as big as her head, but she had to do better than that or she'd never hear the end of it. "Aha. We're not denying it. We're engaging in diversionary eating." She shrugged and continued to chew. "You think you're going to find this film. Finish that, I'll wait."

At length, she said, "Maybe nobody ever looked for it before."

"Maybe nobody else lives in your fantasy world."

"I tend to assume that anyway."

"Nice idea. Belongs in a movie. Like all your ideas. But you won't find it. What you *will* find is the curse of dimensionality."

"You know very well I don't know what that is." She took another bite.

"You will. When you head-butt it so hard you break that cute little nose you're so proud of." He handed her a napkin, and she wiped the lip-stick off her chin.

"All right, professor," she sighed. "You're dying to tell me, so by all means, explain the curse of dimensionality."

"In layman's terms—"

"Oh goody. I don't have a pencil, though."

"In layman's terms, and no talking out of turn please, it means that as a high number of dimensions, or here we can say variables, are added to a problem, there is an exponential increase in volume. The problem becomes unimaginably vast. In this case, for all intents and purposes, it becomes impossible."

She took another bite and pondered. She had him. "You're wrong."

"No, I'm not."

"Yes, you are. There aren't that many variables," she said. "There was a finite number of prints. And not that high a number, because it didn't get a big release."

"But there's a much higher, indeterminate number of hands through which they passed. And sixty years during which the prints could have been dispersed who knows where. Even if there's one left, it could be in Tahiti."

"Well, no. Tropical climate. Probably wouldn't last long there."

"Ceinwen . . ."

"Nitrate should be stored in a cold place. Plus, we know it was only released here in the States. I don't have to go to Czechoslovakia."

"That's a relief. Especially since you don't have a passport. Which reminds me—"

"What time is it?" She gestured to the waitress for the check.

"It's 7:15, and I can't believe you—"

"We better pay up."

"The movie's not until eight. How can a grown woman—"

"We need a good seat. I'm short, remember."

"Stop, I will not be distracted. It's ludicrous, absolutely unbelievable that you let your license expire. How do you expect—"

"Excuse me, but—Ceinwen?" A man had walked over to their table, long-haired, slope-chinned, a coat that needed dry-cleaning in the worst way. She needed an out, fast. "It is you! Hello there! How are you?"

Too slow. Always too slow. She tried for a vaguely preoccupied smile and said, "Hey. I'm fine."

"Good to see you. You're still in the neighborhood?"

"I'm just having dinner." The waitress came over and slipped the bill on the table.

He stuck out his hand at Matthew. "I'm Paul Becker."

"Matthew Hill." They shook hands. Then—friendly, too friendly— "How do you know Ceinwen?"

"From the film department over at Tisch."

"I see. I'm at Courant. Postdoc." Ceinwen examined the numbers on the check. Matthew motioned for her to give it to him, and Paul kept talking.

"Courant? Wow, that's a big switch. Mathematics now?"

"I'm not at Courant, that's just Matthew," she said. "I'm working at the moment."

"That's great news. I know you were worried about having to leave the city. We're all still hoping you can come back."

"Oh," she said, shrugging and keeping her eyes on Paul, "you never know."

"You should definitely reapply. The aid parameters are always changing." He turned to Matthew. "Ceinwen has a fine critical eye for film. Very promising student. But I'm sure you knew that."

"Not really. She's awfully modest," said Matthew.

Paul was the nicest man in the film department, but that gray hair poking out of his unbuttoned collar had always bothered her. Still, if the choice was between a dead squirrel on a man's chest and Matthew's face at the moment . . .

"Hopefully you can give her some advice," said Paul. "It's good to have people familiar with the process. And you know, Ceinwen, like I told you at the time, you're always welcome to stop by the office and I'll be happy to help any way I can." He started patting his coat. "Hang on, I'll write it down. They switched me to another floor this year, all that work they're doing on the building." He was fishing in his pants pockets. "Don't seem to have a pen."

"Neither do I," said Ceinwen. "Don't worry, I can always look it up."

"Here you are," said Matthew. He reached in his jacket and pulled out a pen and his memo pad.

"Thanks." Paul scrawled for a minute, then handed her the pad. "So this is where the office is now, and the phone, and I wrote down my hours. You should definitely come by sometime." She thanked him, closed the cover to the memo pad and handed it to Matthew as Paul walked out.

Matthew opened the cover, tore the paper off the pad and pushed it across the table to her. "Don't forget this. I'll pay up."

"Let me put on my coat and we can go." She folded the paper and put it in her pocket.

"Wait here. I need change for the tip." He was already halfway to the cashier. She decided to put on her coat and pretend they were almost ready to leave. When he got back to the table she was standing beside it, scarf around her neck and bag hooked over her arm. He sat and leaned his back against the wall.

"You're going to stand? You'll block the waitress."

"We're leaving, aren't we?"

"No. We are not. What was that about?"

She sat down. "Paul is a film professor."

"You don't say. Not a lift operator?" She put her purse on the table and spotted a small thread coming loose from the stitching. "You lied to me."

"I didn't lie. You don't tell me everything either."

"You most certainly did lie." So much for his taking that bait. "That first day we had lunch, I asked if you'd read history. And you said, 'I didn't go to college.' In so many words. And you've never said a thing to correct that."

"It was just a semester. I didn't think it counted."

"It counts. I think you know it counts." She tried to pull off the thread and the stitching unraveled some more. "If I'd known you better I'd have known you were lying. You're bad at it. Is that why you picked film, not acting?" The guitar player yelled when he got mad. Matthew's voice got quieter, but meaner. "Are you going to tell me about this?"

She checked her watch. 7:30. "I got accepted but I didn't think I could go because Granana was sick. But then she died and left me some savings bonds and an account she'd been keeping for me. And it was just enough for a semester. So I went. For a semester."

"And you dropped out?"

Sure, that was exactly what she'd wanted to do. "Of course I didn't just drop out. I didn't have the money."

"What about financial aid?"

Lord, this was tiresome. "Yeah, what about it. Spent half my time at that office. Most frustrating thing I've ever been through. That's why I didn't want to talk about it before, and I don't want to talk about it now."

"Your father couldn't pay for anything?"

"No." He was bringing up Daddy? What happened to the Matthew who just let things drop?

"Why not?" She'd pulled the stitching loose along about two inches of the flap now. He pushed her bag to one side of the table. "You couldn't get financial aid, but your father couldn't pay for anything?"

He wasn't going to be satisfied until she came out with the whole thing. "No, he couldn't. He hadn't paid taxes in a while and everything he inherited went to pay them. Except the farm and the house in town. Those made him look pretty good on paper, even though he was always broke. They care about what you've got, not what you owe. And getting forms out of him was like pulling teeth because he was still all paranoid about the IRS. Plus they wanted to know why one minute I could pay and the next minute I couldn't. And I finally did get some aid, just not enough. I got enough to cover half. Maybe a little more. Didn't matter how I juggled it, I couldn't make it work. So I said all right, later, and I got a job so I wouldn't have to go back to Mississippi. I figured maybe I could apply as self-supporting in a couple of years. But I haven't." She remembered her cigarettes and reached for her purse. "Cross-examination over?"

"Wait, you're angry with me? That's rich. You might have asked me about it. I've had to help students with aid this year."

"Why would you know anything? Here they pay you. Back in merry old socialist England you didn't have to pay a cent." She pulled out a cigarette and lit up.

His voice got louder. "Socialist? Ever heard of Thatcher?"

"Wait, she's persecuting Cambridge now? I thought it was just the Irish."

"That's all you Americans ever . . ." He stopped and let out a long breath. "Oh no. No, you're not doing this. You're not changing the subject, Miss Reilly. I didn't design your bloody education system, so spare me the right-wing Southern belle act."

"Well now, speaking of Southern," she drawled. "College wasn't exactly a common thing back in Yazoo City. Let alone film school. I know that's hard for an upper-crust London boy to appreciate."

"Oh for fuck sake, not this again. Upper-crust, too right. Me and Prince Charles, we're *mates*." He pushed her wrist to one side to get the smoke away from him. "What are you talking about? Did you ever try to get a job on a film, instead of standing around behind a counter all day?"

"I happen to be good at standing behind that counter."

"Of course you are. Why wouldn't you be. Reading about James II. Memorizing every line of *His Girl Friday*. Spending all day saying 'may I help you.' Practically the same thing."

"Oh, that's not snobbish. Not at all."

"You're the one always dragging background into it, not me. I guess I'm supposed to agree that you fit right in at a shop. I'm sure that's exactly what you'd like to be doing in twenty years." His voice softened a bit. "Go on, admit it. That can't be what you want."

"What I want," she said, taking her last drag, "is to make rent on time this month. And before that, I want to make it to Bleecker Street for *Children of Paradise*. If I cared about all this I'd have mentioned it in the first place." She stubbed out the cigarette and stood up, but the thought of going to the movie by herself didn't appeal. "I'm sorry. It wasn't a good year, all right?"

He was still sitting. Finally he said, "All right. Have it your way. But don't do that again."

"Drop out of college?"

"Don't lie to me." He picked up his coat. "Or play dumb, for that matter. 'Drop out of college?' Not all men find that cute."

It turned that out that seeing a movie, even a great movie, with someone who was still fuming wasn't all that appealing, either. Like sitting next to Chief Scar from *The Searchers*. "Not only are you rich, you want to be loved as if you were poor," said Arletty. Matthew's expression never changed. She couldn't tell if he liked it, and she couldn't ask.

Somehow they wound up going back to his place and she decided to change in the bathroom. She had the old debate with herself about whether to wash off her makeup, and wound up doing it. She brushed her teeth, still getting pleasure from the fact that he'd never thrown away the toothbrush she left at his place back in November. When she came out in just her underwear, the light was off and he was in bed, breathing deeply; he almost never snored.

"Why have me over if you're going to do that?" she said to his back, not bothering to whisper. She slipped onto the bed. "It isn't enough to be mad, I have to go to your place and see you fall asleep because you're mad?" The breathing didn't change. He really was asleep.

She pulled up the covers and thought about the best way to track down a bunch of old people, until she fell asleep herself.

The sun couldn't have been up long, the light hadn't fully come in the windows; but yet again she couldn't make herself get back to sleep. She went to the kitchen and drank a glass of water while she thought some more.

She walked back into the bedroom. Matthew was on his stomach, both arms under the pillow. Kings sleep on their backs, rich men sleep on their stomachs, Granana had told her. Ceinwen slept curled into a ball; she couldn't remember what that meant. She braced her hands on the side of the bed, then threw herself onto it with a bounce that shook the entire mattress and brought Matthew up on one arm, hand to his eyes.

"What . . ."

"Oh god, I'm so sorry. I was getting back into bed and I tripped. I didn't mean to shake the whole bed like that." He collapsed back onto the pillow. "But now that you're awake, I might as well tell you about this."

"I'm not awake," he said.

"I've solved the curse. Is that what you say in math?" She was pretty sure that what he muttered was "fuck me" but she continued anyway. "What do you use in math to break the curse of dimensionality?"

"Why?"

"Because I have it."

"No, why are you talking to me?"

"Just tell me what you call it, what you use to break the dimensionality. Or solve it or counter it or whatever."

He said something into his pillow like "mmhmshun."

"What?"

He flipped onto his back. "Selection. Selection of features. Are we done?"

"That's exactly what I have. A selection." He was staring at the ceiling. "I'm selecting Emil's print. The one he kept. Miriam said the place was crawling with people the day he died, and she doesn't know what happened to his print. That's the one to look for. It was his original cut anyway, it's the best one." He put both arms over his face. "I can finish telling you about it later."

She was opening the bedroom door when he said from underneath his arms, "The studio people probably took it and it was destroyed along with the rest of their library."

"We don't know that, do we? There were all kinds of people going through his house after he died, Miriam said so."

"What's the purpose of this?" He'd uncovered his face but his voice was almost a moan. "You can't tell me it's for Miriam's sake. We offered to show her what's left of her brilliant Hollywood career and she couldn't be arsed."

"She didn't want to see a lousy two-minute clip."

That got him up on his elbows. "Lousy? I like that, Miss Reilly. I put my academic credentials on the line—"

"I meant from Miriam's point of view, not mine," Ceinwen interrupted hastily. "Lousy, as in not enough. She does want to have the whole film back. She said so."

"Then why hasn't she looked herself?"

"It's too depressing for her, obviously."

"*Obviously*." He sat all the way up. "You really are the worst liar I've ever met. You're pathetically bad."

"Listen." She dropped all pretense of a gentle morning voice. "She said she wanted to see it and see if she was right, that it was good. That's *exactly* what she said and I *told* you . . ."

"'I'm so sorry Matthew, I tripped.' Like hell you tripped, you little . . ."

She walked to the bed, slowly, and put her hands on the edge. "You little what?"

"I demand an apology. This instant." She shook the mattress with all her might, until he threw off the covers and dove after her.

4.

IF SHE DIDN'T SET THE ALARM, AND SHE DIDN'T NEED TO GET UP, SHE woke up around 7:00 a.m. and couldn't get back to sleep. If she needed to get up, but forgot to set the alarm, she slept until noon. So Ceinwen had set the alarm for 8:30. She awoke to Jim shaking her shoulder and the radio blaring. She squinted until the numbers on the clock cleared to say 9:08.

"Did I hit the snooze?"

"No, honey. It's been going since 8:30. I finally came in to ask when the hell you started listening to Bartok."

"What's Bartok?"

"That's Bartok."

Her ears focused on four or five string instruments sawing along something that was definitely Not Beethoven.

"He's a composer?"

"Yes. What did you think this was, the Thompson Twins?"

"I knew it was the classical station." Matthew listened to a lot of classical music and that seemed to be all that Miriam listened to, but this wasn't something Jim needed to know. "I thought it would be a nice way to wake up. Serenity. Ease into the day."

"That'll teach you to stereotype," said Jim. "Do you mind if I switch this off?"

Her head was clearing. She was sure Matthew had mentioned Bartok. She remembered walking down some street in the Fifties after they went to the Carnegie to see *White Heat*, and he had pointed to a plaque on a building where the guy had lived. She needed to stick with it, obviously. Sometimes with Matthew's music you didn't get a real melody until later.

"Let's just turn it down. I like it."

"You do *not*."

"I do." She was going to need Matthew's tidy mind, and if she was pestering him about her own obsessions it would help if he could squeeze in his own every once in a while.

Jim lowered the volume. "Does Miriam listen to Bartok?"

"I am trying," said Ceinwen, reaching for her robe, "to broaden myself."

"Then eat something," said Jim, over his shoulder as he walked out.

She got dressed and slipped one of the copies of the monograph into her messenger bag. She'd intended the extra for Miriam, but she figured both would be useful, one clean, one to mark up. She switched off the radio. She wouldn't see Matthew for another forty-eight hours, which should be just enough time to come up with a compliment. Challenging. Ugh. When somebody said that, you knew he just didn't understand the movie. Different? God no, that didn't even work when the necklace made the customer look fat. Bracing. Bracing had possibilities.

She bet Anna listened to Bartok. Anna probably brushed her teeth to Bartok.

She paused in the living room to check for her keys and noticed Jim and Talmadge were both there, drinking coffee and staring.

"Where are you going?" asked Talmadge.

The best approach to deceit, she had decided, was to latch on to the thing you could say truthfully and stick with that. Since she had a lot of lying on the schedule, she figured she could start with half-truths, and sooner or later she'd work her way up to humongous fibs.

"The library."

"Meeting Pope John Paul?"

"No. He's not the only of us who reads, you know." Her keys were in her coat pocket. "Like I told Jim," she said, "I'm trying to broaden myself."

"Which one are you going to?" asked Jim.

"The library," she said, impatiently. "Long steps. Big lions. Fifth Avenue and . . ."

"Fortieth," supplied Jim.

"I was just trying to remember if I have everything," lied Ceinwen.

"Looking up a movie?"

"Yes," she said. "That's exactly what I'm doing."

The R train came quickly for once and she got out at Times Square, glancing as she always did at the Victory movie theater and wishing it played old movies instead of porn. She sped past the horrid park in back of the library, averting her eyes from the people sprawled on benches and playing deaf to the calls of "Smoke? Smoke?" The first time someone asked her that in Washington Square Park she'd tried to hand the guy a cigarette. He got mad.

Inside the library she stopped on the red carpet to look up at the vaulted ceiling. She'd only walked inside once before to have a look, that semester at NYU when she'd been trying to see every part of the city she'd read about or seen in movies. Every weekend she picked a place, not caring whether it was touristy or not—the ferry, the Trade Center, the Empire State Building, the Chrysler, although nobody had ever told her you couldn't go to the top. The Met, over and over again. But she'd been scared of this place and the books that had been written here, like it was for real New Yorkers, and she hadn't worked her way up to it. Maybe because she'd never gotten a library card, either.

She was a real New Yorker now. You told anybody, even a native, that you lived on Avenue C and you qualified. Why did she feel like somebody was about to throw her out?

"Can I help you?" The security guard was calling to her from a few feet away. She walked over.

"I need to look up some stuff," she said, in a near-whisper.

"You're in luck." He didn't smile, but she did.

"Which floor do I go to for the phone books?"

"Phone books. You run out of 'em at home?"

"I need the one for Los Angeles."

He sucked his teeth. "I'm sure they have those, but why don't you just go to Mid-Manhattan?"

She was disappointed. "This is nicer."

"Yeah, but you gotta fill out a slip, wait for them to bring it up. You got across the street, it's right out where you can get it."

She should probably do that, to save time before work. "Right across Fifth?"

"Catty-corner." He made a diagonal gesture with his hand.

She slipped out the door. No reading room. No making like Betty Friedan writing *The Feminine Mystique*.

Compared with the main library, Mid-Manhattan was positively ugly and seemed filled with old people whose main job was to glare. She found the phone books on the second floor. After two hours of searching, she had seventeen numbers for people named Louis Delgado or L. Delgado in the Los Angeles phone book.

Delgado had been the cinematographer, the main credited one; the one who had walked out on Emil was dead. The appendix in the back of the Gundlach book had an annotated cast and crew, with death dates for anyone who had passed away before 1973. That eliminated more than half of them. She had decided not to start with the next of kin unless she had to. It didn't seem logical that you'd find a nitrate film in Mom or Dad's effects and not, well, do something with it.

So the old people it was. An old person might forget what they had. They might sell something. Or they might have been there with all the people milling around Emil Arnheim's house the day after he died, and seen someone take the film.

And in the meantime, the nitrate stock could have crumbled to dust. The film could have stuck together and solidified into a gelatinous mass, what Fred told her was the "hockey puck" syndrome. It could have ignited.

She didn't care. She was going to do this anyway. She had started with Delgado and she'd keep going from there.

The one that needled her, though, was Edward Kenny. "Last year," wrote Gundlach, "Kenny was still listed 'at liberty' in the Los Angeles casting directory." But there was almost a full page of E. Kennys, and thirteen Edwards and Eds and Eddies. She didn't have that kind of long-distance money.

Wait, wouldn't the library have the LA casting directory? Maybe? She stood in line at the information desk and was directed to the Dewey decimal section. They had the one for 1986. She pulled it down and opened it right there while she was still standing at the shelf.

"Edward Kenny (b. 1899). At liberty. The Poole Agency."

Son of a gun. Good for him, she thought, even if Miriam hadn't liked him. She took the book back to her study carrel and wrote down the agent's number. If he was still acting, he'd be in plenty good enough shape to remember *Mysteries of Udolpho*. She packed up the photocopy and hopped the subway to Vintage Visions.

That night she took the phone into her room, blessed the time difference, and started with the Delgados. The night before she had stayed up late writing a script, and spent her lunch hour trying to polish it. Hello, I'm working on a project with an NYU professor. It concerns lost films of the silent era. I was wondering if you would be willing to talk about a film you made in 1928, *The Mysteries of Udolpho*.

The first number gave no answer. The second was an extremely irritable woman who refused to believe she wasn't selling something. Third and fourth, listed as "L. Delgado," were both women. The fifth didn't know what a cinematographer was. (You're in L.A.? How do you survive? wondered Ceinwen.) Sixth and seventh, no answer. The eighth spoke only Spanish.

On the ninth call, she got a hit. She asked for the Louis Delgado who had been under contract to Civitas Pictures from 1924 to 1930. The man said nothing for a second, then asked, "You want to talk to Louis Delgado, the cinematographer?"

"Yes, is he there?"

"He's dead. This is his son. Louis Jr."

She'd written a separate script in case of this very situation. But she felt like too much of a jerk to reach for it.

"I'm so sorry."

"Yeah, it's okay. You didn't know." His tone was so flat she couldn't tell if he meant that.

"When I looked up one of his movies, the source said he was still alive."

"Really. He's been gone for a couple of years now."

She decided it was time to find her "in case subject is deceased" sheet, but she'd buried it somehow. As she shuffled papers she heard him say, "Which movie?"

"*The Mysteries of Udolpho*. 1928."

"Huh. Don't know that one."

"It's lost."

"I don't know a lot of the early stuff Dad worked on."

"Did he ever mention it?" She dug her nails into her palm to keep her voice even. "Or keep anything?"

"Nah. He wasn't much for scrapbooks or any crap like that. When it was over, he played golf. You'd have had better luck asking him about his handicap."

She'd found her script, but it seemed she didn't need it. "All right, thanks for your help." He didn't jump in, so she added, "I'm sorry for your loss. He was talented."

"Yep. He was. Sorry I couldn't help."

She lit a cigarette and sucked down the first drag so hard the ash grew a quarter-inch. Delgado hadn't yelled at her or broken into heaving sobs, but he was obviously not happy to have some strange woman calling for his dead father.

This is a good thing I'm doing for them, she repeated to herself, as she drew a line through Delgado's name in the monograph. It's a good thing to have your work remembered. I'm not trying to upset anybody.

She decided she'd had enough, and went to bed without going out to say goodnight to Jim and Talmadge.

She waited the next morning until just after twelve, when people in Los Angeles might be getting to the office. The receptionist at the Poole Agency put her on hold for a long time. Then, finally, "Can I speak to the agent who represents Edward Kenny?"

"Who?"

"Edward Kenny. The casting directory says you represent him."

"Let me look." She was put on hold. "I don't see him in our files. Are you sure the directory listed us?"

"Positive." Hold again, longer this time.

Then, "All right, I'm going to put you through to Doris. Hang on a moment."

"Doris Poole here."

"Yes, I'm calling to inquire about Edward Kenny."

"He isn't working anymore. He's at the Motion Picture Home."

That was odd. It was practically a brand-new casting directory. "This wasn't for a part. I'm helping a professor at NYU with a paper, and we wanted to interview him about a movie he once did. Can you tell me how to get in touch with him at the home?"

"He won't be able to talk to you, I'm afraid. He's sick."

"Sick? I'm sorry to hear that. Could I possibly write to him?"

The woman's voice was older, and kinder, than she'd expected from a Hollywood agent. "That won't do you any good either, hon. He's senile. Wouldn't understand a thing."

She looked at the note she'd made in the margin. Edward Kenny. The Poole Agency. "I'm sorry I bothered you then. It's just that he was in the casting directory."

"Is that it? I was wondering, that's why I took the call. I haven't had anyone ask for Eddie in more than ten years, and that was somebody wanting to interview him about the old days, too. His daughter kept paying to keep him in the directory, you see. When his mind first started to go a few years ago, she'd show him the listing every now and again. Felt like it brought him back a little bit."

"That's sweet of her."

"She's a good girl, always was. I repped Eddie for thirty years so I know her well. I'm surprised she's still listing him. He's pretty far gone now."

"I'm sorry," she said again. "Thanks for letting me know."

"I'll tell her someone was calling for him. She'll like that."

When she hung up, she looked at Kenny's name but didn't want to draw a line through it, like she had for Delgado. Instead she wrote next to it, "n.a." Not available.

She pictured the man holding Miriam's hand in the still.

This was going to be harder than she'd thought.

5.

THE WEATHER HAD TURNED TANTALIZINGLY WARM, AND SINCE THEY knew it wouldn't last, Matthew insisted they make the most of it. They were sitting by the dry fountain in Washington Square Park, and Ceinwen was engaged in a vain effort to eat a falafel sandwich neatly, while telling Matthew about the last few days in the library. She had already told him about Louis Delgado and Edward Kenny. She had found Wouten Oberholzer, the producer, by virtue of his being the only one in the phone book, and had been thrilled when he answered the phone. But he had been rather vague and weak-sounding. He didn't remember anything about making *Mysteries* and had to be reminded that the director was dead.

After that she had a good long think, and decided the phone book wasn't the best place to start, after all. She recalled the Reader's Guide to Periodical Literature, which she'd used when she had done her senior English term paper on *A Tale of Two Cities*. She began going through it, in reverse chronological order, month by month, searching for each of the eleven names she had left that were listed as still living in the Gundlach monograph. She was up to 1980 and had discovered that the editor had died and so had the art director.

"In conclusion, then, you have no idea what you're doing."

"I am systematically going through the list of people on *Mysteries* who were still alive in 1973 and trying to track them down," she said. "I think that's a perfectly reasonable approach."

"Has it occurred to you to consult an expert?"

Uh-oh. "What kind of an expert?"

He took a bite and chewed slowly, as if to make sure he had her full attention. Then he said, "I talked to Harry a bit. No, don't panic, I didn't tell him why, it doesn't take much to get Harry talking about film. Have you heard of William K. Everson?"

She rolled her eyes. "Of course. Harry lent me one of his books."

"Then I presume you also know he's here at NYU. Maybe you even had a class with him."

"Cinema studies," she muttered. "Different department."

There was a pause during which she tried to figure out whether or not there was a pot sale going on twenty feet away.

"Are you trying to imply that you won't talk to Everson because you've never been properly introduced? Because that certainly isn't stopping you with anyone else."

"Miriam doesn't like professors. She said so."

"We don't have any evidence that Miriam's liked anyone since she got married. Possibly not even then." Looked like the deal hadn't gone through. Maybe the prices had gone up. Not that she'd know; pot made her sleepy and paranoid. "You don't tell her, for god's sake. Why should you? You're not telling her anything else. Harry doesn't know Everson very well but said he's supposed to be a mensch."

"When did you learn that word?"

"Ceinwen," he said, so loud he startled the pigeons. "There is a man just a few blocks from here who's made a career out of rescuing silent movies from obscurity. And instead of consulting him, you talk to me. I'm a mathematician. Until two months ago I could hardly pick Buster Keaton out of a photograph."

She brushed a falafel crumb off her skirt. Then she said, "It's my project. Everson couldn't possibly care about this obscure movie as much as I do. He's probably out looking for *Queen of Sheba*."

He balled up his wrapper, and sighed. He looked at the wad of trash in his hand and sighed louder.

"What? I'm not hurting anyone. I know you think you think I'm wasting my time, but it's my time to waste, isn't it." She pulled two pickles out of the sandwich.

"I was going to bring up something else." She blotted her fingers and wondered if he realized she had stolen his one napkin. "What is it with you and pickles? No, don't lay them on the fountain, here's the bag."

She dropped them in. "Q.E.D. Pickle problem is solved."

"The pickles are not the problem." He pulled a tissue out of his pocket and wiped the tahini off the stone. "I'm not sure I should mention this. You could be doing something constructive."

"For example?"

"For example, finding a sane person to work for."

"I'll get to that. I'm busy."

"Right. Busy. So then. After I spoke to Harry last night, I started thinking about this scavenger hunt. And it occurred to me that you're overlooking something else."

She decided not to get snippy until he said something even more irritating, but she didn't try to make her "How so?" sound encouraging.

"You haven't thought much about that clip. Screen test, if that's what it was." She threw her stolen napkin into the paper bag. "Here you are, chasing everyone who ever walked onto the Civitas backlot. What about that man in Vermont?"

"What about him? They got everything he had. Fred said his wife even gave them the home movies."

"But why did he have it in the first place? Your friend Fred said hardly anyone bothered to save screen tests." He picked up the paper bag and shot it like a free throw toward the garbage can, where it bounced off the mounds of trash already stuffed there. "If that's the case, then tell me. Who would hang on to Miriam's test?" He waited as her chest began to flare red. "Go on, who?"

"Emil," she admitted.

"Good hypothesis. Logical, even." He walked to the trash can, picked up their bag and balanced it on top, then walked back and straddled the fountain edge. His look was the one that meant, don't mind me, I said something brilliant, I'll give you a moment to digest. But he lasted only seconds before he said, "And you'll have noticed something else." What was there to say, except, you were smarter than I was? She wasn't saying that. "Come on now."

"That was smart," she ventured.

He made a beckoning gesture. "Out with it. Concede the point."

"That was helpful."

"Bloody—" He swung a leg back over the edge and put his face right up in hers, causing her to crane back. "It's the *romantic* explanation, isn't it." He pulled back and folded his hands. "Yet it didn't occur to *you*, did it, Little Miss Let's-drag-Matthew-to-a-Kay-Francis-double-feature."

The rush of happiness was so strong she thought it might hurl her square at him. But she said only, "You liked *One Way Passage*. You know you did."

"It made more sense than *Mandalay*. And that's only because *Mandalay* made no sense at all. Watch it, there's still—" She had already scooted down and snaked her arm through his. In crowded places, especially near NYU, he found an excuse not to do things like that; in movie theaters he never dropped an arm around her shoulders. This time he held still and pointed. "Your coat is going to smell like pickle."

"It's due for a cleaning anyway." He rubbed his thumb near her hairline, probably to get rid of a smudge. "Let's talk about something else," she said.

"My god, do you think that's wise? Shouldn't you wean off gradually?"

"Nope. Cold turkey." They stared at each other. "I forgot to tell you. Last week, I was listening to Bartok."

They stayed up late that night, listening to the third and fourth quartets. He tried to explain something called a Fibonacci sequence. He played something for strings, percussion, and something else, and she kept up a stream of what she thought were positive comments, starting with "bracing" and progressing to "unique" and "daring," until after midnight he announced, "That's enough faking it for one night," and they went to bed.

The next morning she slipped into the living room and fished Fred's card out of her wallet. Kelly picked up the phone and told her Fred was in the lab.

"May I leave a message?" Evidently Kelly didn't remember her. She spelled her name three times.

"And it's pronounced Kine-wen?"

"Yes."

"Wow. That's different. Can I tell Fred what this is regarding?"

"Oh . . ." She paused. She hadn't thought about that. "Just tying some things up."

"Like a package?"

Probably a joke, but Ceinwen had concluded that the Brody was the nosiest place in Manhattan. "No, like conversational loose ends."

She turned to hang up and found herself looking straight at Matthew, who was in his underwear and leaning against the bedroom door jamb.

"I do love American slang," he said. "All that nuance. What does 'cold turkey' mean to a Yank?"

"Means I'm from Mississippi, so don't call me a Yank," she said. "Do you want to get breakfast before I go to the library? I've only got a few hours before work."

He went into the bathroom to shave, which took him twice as long as it took her to put on a full face of makeup, including liquid eyeliner and three coats of mascara. She hadn't told him everything, not by a long shot. She'd combed through the monograph and come up with some studio names. Benjamin Rosber, second in command under Frank Gregory, not listed in the credits but mentioned in passing. Rex Garland, who'd done some uncredited script work.

Best of all, Lucile Pierrepoint, "Gregory's devoted personal secretary," whom Gundlach described as "legendary for her efficiency." Now that sounded like someone who might show up to sort through a dead director's personal effects. Trouble was, women got married and changed their names. So she'd been thrilled to find an article in Beverly Hills magazine, about a dinner the Women's League had given in 1980 for its oldest members. It named "the former Lucile Pierrepoint" and said she'd worked at Civitas. Her name was now Miller, and Ceinwen had groaned at the number of potential hits in the Greater Los Angeles phone book. Even the Beverly Hills phone book had about a dozen L. Millers, and she figured part of the appeal of Beverly Hills would be having an unlisted number.

If Miller had been "devoted," she must have liked the man, figured Ceinwen. So last week she had spent hours composing a letter to what she hoped was a still-living Mrs. Miller, emphasizing that her ever-mutating project included a revisionist view of Frank Gregory as one heck of a swell guy. She enclosed that letter inside another to the Women's League of Beverly Hills, and that one was even harder to write. The Women's League of Yazoo City wouldn't have forwarded a letter for Ceinwen if she'd covered the envelope in gold leaf. They were all the same, women who had once been debutantes and the girls who were about to be, the girls who whispered about her clothes when she walked by and rolled their eyes or giggled every time she spoke up in class. The Women's League was supposedly all about "service," but so far as Ceinwen could tell, service meant standing around in a hoop skirt and twirling a parasol at the entrance to a historic site, drawling, "Welcome to Yazoo City!"

She pretended Granana was standing over her shoulder and wrote the most elaborately polite letter of her life, her script so careful she had a hand cramp for the rest of the day.

She was proud of the whole scheme, and she wanted to tell Matthew. She wanted him to realize she was smart. As smart in her way as, say, a doctor of economics. But it seemed he kept confusing "smart" with "obsessive."

At least the Vermont collector was a good lead. She hoped Fred called her back soon.

She got dressed and decided to buy a newspaper on the way to the coffee shop. They could talk about Iran-Contra. And maybe Kay Francis.

MARCH

1.

SHE HATED THE WAY THE LIBRARY'S LIGHTS SEEMED HARSHER AS SOON as the sun began to go down. The fluorescent bulbs turned her copy of the monograph greenish-gray. Plus, her notes made it look as though it had spent six weeks with the world's most psychopathic copy editor.

She'd called or written to everybody she could locate—everybody, that meant, except Norman Stallings, Miriam's friend on the set. Gundlach said his last known movie credit was from 1942. After that, nothing. She had been working her way back from the current year, she was sitting there with the Reader's Guide for 1942, and she hadn't found a single Norman Stallings that fit for all those years, although she had a good bead on Norman Stallings, chief executive officer of A&R Shipping, and Norman Stallings, author of *King of All Britain*, about Athelstan the Glorious.

She could either start on newspaper archives—she glanced to where she knew the *New York Times* indexes were shelved—or she could give up on Norman. She could try Edward Kenny's daughter, but that wasn't going to be pleasant. And surely a good daughter wouldn't have left Daddy's movies laying around.

She slammed the Reader's Guide to Periodical Literature shut and an old man cleared his throat and glared at her. She knew he was right, but she glared back in true New York fashion. Some detective she was, spending all her time in the library or writing letters and making phone calls. No response from Lucile Miller, messages ignored by the nursing home where Rex Garland lived. People always got back to Philip Marlowe. Even when Dick Powell was playing him. And that was another thing. Ten days had gone by after she called Fred, she'd left another message, and now it had been five days more. What was going on? Didn't he like her?

She put her head down on the book. No, that wasn't the problem, she was sure of it. He didn't like Matthew, but he'd been fine with her. They'd had lunch, after all. He was probably just busy. Or maybe he didn't get the messages, although the Brody seemed like the kind of place that never lost messages.

Fred, though. Fred definitely could have lost a message. Two messages, even.

Maybe she should just show up. Doorstepping, Matthew called it.

She bet Fred worked late. If she hopped on the subway and went up to the Brody, she might get there in time to catch him on the way out. It was a lot harder to ignore somebody who was standing there in the lobby. Even if he couldn't talk, maybe she could get him to make plans. If he wasn't there she could tape a note on the door, although in that neighborhood the locals might think a flapping piece of paper on a townhouse was bad for property values.

It was too dark to see her watch when she arrived at the Brody and rang the buzzer. There was no response, but she could see lights. She buzzed again, waited, then again, leaning hard. The door clicked and she pushed it open. The receptionist wasn't at the desk; instead Isabel, wearing a slim black cocktail dress, sheer black stockings, and red heels, was standing in front of it. She was carrying a massive, full-length, shimmering-black fur coat over her arm, and the other hand cupped a tiny gold purse studded with red gems.

"We're closed for the night," she said. "I realize our hours aren't posted, but given that it's past seven . . ."

"Is Fred still here?"

". . . and we're open by appointment only—did you say Fred? Creighton?"

"That's him. I was walking past and thought I'd come say hey."

"Hey?" Isabel's eyes opened wide and her arm dropped so the coat almost brushed the floor.

"Yes ma'am. That's Southern for 'hi.'" Ceinwen wasn't sure she'd seen sable before, but that coat looked better than mink. Wasn't there a sable coat in *All About Eve*? The party scene, the coat's on the bed, and Thelma Ritter holds it up—

"May I have your name?" Isabel slung the coat across the desk and set down the purse. Either Isabel didn't remember her, or this was a way of putting her in her place.

"Ceinwen Reilly."

She strode behind the desk, punched a button on the phone and waited. "Fred? Miss Ceinwen Reilly to see you . . . I have no idea . . . Is there time for that? . . . One moment." Isabel punched another button and gave her the eye. Too bad Ceinwen's houndstooth coat was covering up today's dress. It was black, too, with brass beading around a deep neckline and more beads edging the peplum, and Ceinwen thought it was as nice as Isabel's. "Fred says you can come up for just a minute. Do you have ID?"

Not again. "I don't think so."

Isabel turned back to the phone. "No can do Fred, she doesn't have ID. You'll have to come down. It's time anyway." She set down the phone with a firmly precise snap and slinked herself into the desk chair. Her dark red nails drummed silently on the arm. "You've been here before, haven't you?"

The round settee was so far away that if she tried to sit there, she'd be calling to Isabel like a mother on the playground. Ceinwen tried to stand straighter. Why couldn't they put a chair in front of the desk like normal places? This was like being brought to Conrad Veidt's headquarters. Ve think ve haf seen you beefore, Meez Reilly. "I came here to see the Arnheim fragment."

"I remember. You didn't have ID then, either."

"I guess," said Ceinwen, "you could say I'm not that organized."

"Neither is Fred."

"He's much more organized than I am."

"That's alarming," said Isabel briskly. "I take it you have further questions about the fragment?"

"I have some matters of a personal nature to discuss," said Ceinwen, in what she hoped was a real Bette Davis get-lost kind of voice. A door opened one flight up, and Fred careened down the stairs, slipped, collided with the banister, gave a small yelp, and continued. He had on dress shoes, Ceinwen noticed, leather oxfords. Also a pair of badly pressed navy pants and a white button-down. She wondered whether for Fred, this qualified as dressed to the nines.

"Hi, um, I'm, ah, sorry I didn't return your call, it's been, um, pretty crazy around here." He was rubbing his elbow.

"You haven't got much time." That was Isabel, putting on her coat. Were they going out together? Fred's stubble was slight. Signs were definitely pointing to an occasion.

"I'll make it," snapped Fred.

"I'm sorry," said Ceinwen, "I didn't realize you had to be somewhere. I don't want to mess up your schedule."

"No, um, it's okay, we can walk out together."

"Did you remember the jacket?" Isabel again.

"In the closet with my coat."

"And the tie?" She flipped out the ends of her hair so they lay perfectly over the coat.

"In the jacket pocket."

"Great idea. Wonder why Hermès doesn't do that?" said Isabel, as she picked up her purse and walked around the desk. The fur was so long and lush it looked as though it was swallowing her feet-first.

"I rolled up the tie. The tie situation is under control, all right?"

Isabel paused and looked Fred up and down. He grabbed his elbow again. "The driver's waiting around the corner. I'd drop you off, but it's in the opposite direction."

"There's plenty of time. I'll make it."

"Don't forget to set the alarm," said Isabel, striding toward the door.

"Good night, Isabel," he called after her, emphasizing the "night." She waved her hand without turning around. Fred laced his fingers behind his head and let out a whoosh of breath when the door shut.

"I picked a bad time to drop by, didn't I," said Ceinwen.

"Nah, it's okay. It's just that I have to go to this meeting, and um . . . let me get my stuff." He opened the door to the closet and Ceinwen followed, once more trying to peek in. He called to her from inside. "I'm, yeah, I'm going to the Bangville Police Society tonight, and they've got a dress code." She wanted to follow him so she could see the inside of the closet, but it was dark and he had disappeared. The other door opened and Fred came out, just like Kelly had when she first came there. How did that work? She really wanted to know. He was wearing a jacket and carrying a black wool coat dotted with pills.

"Did you say the Bangville Police Society?"

"Yeah. Mack Sennett appreciation club." He was fishing in his jacket pockets. His eyes shifted.

"That's a Sennett movie?"

"First true Keytone Cops short." He pulled one pocket open, looked inside like it was a handbag, then repeated the process on the other side. "They um, meet bimonthly and show . . . damn." He felt the jacket's inside pocket.

"Try the coat maybe?" He put his hand inside a coat pocket and his shoulder relaxed. Out came his hand, holding a rolled-up tie. "They show Sennett movies?"

"Whew. Yeah, not just Mack Sennett, they show anything with anybody who ever worked with him. And Sennett worked with everybody. And, ah, I'm supposed to . . . give me a minute, I gotta put this on."

He crossed to a mirror on the opposite wall and pulled the tie around his collar, paused, then unbuttoned the collar buttons. He pulled on one end of the tie, then the other, looked down and touched the tag that was showing.

"Want me to do that?" asked Ceinwen.

"Oh god, would you?"

"Sure." She flipped the tie around and pulled the ends down to the proper length. What was that cologne? He smelled kind of almond-y. "Half-Windsor?"

"Um, what?"

"Never mind." She began the knot. "So it's jacket and tie required."

"Yeah. One time I showed up without a tie, and they lent me one, and, uh, I'm no tie expert, but it was . . . bad."

Since this one was a taupe-and-puce stripe, unfashionably wide and some sort of rayon blend, Ceinwen couldn't imagine what would strike Fred as a bad tie, but she kept her mouth shut and pushed the knot toward his neck like Jim had taught her. "You must really want to see this movie."

"Three movies. I've seen them before. I, ah, have to talk to this guy who's in the New York chapter." He turned and looked in the mirror. "Hey, that looks good. Thanks."

She couldn't agree, since the tie didn't go with the jacket, and the jacket was plaid for goodness' sake, but the knot was fine. "You're welcome. What are the movies?"

"Fatty Arbuckle. *He Did and He Didn't* with Mabel Normand, *The Garage*, uh, Buster Keaton's in that one, and *The Life of the Party*."

"I'm jealous. I've never seen him in anything. Just read about him."

"*Hollywood Babylon*?" She nodded. He shrugged himself into his coat. "Technically, this is open to the public."

"Technically? I could go?"

"Yeah, although if you do, ah, I wouldn't mention *Hollywood Babylon*. They'll freak. Everybody there hates that book. And you, uh, have to wear proper attire. They dress up. Way up."

"Hold on." She unbuttoned her coat and pulled it wide open. "You mean like this?"

Fred gaped. "Wow. That's, um, perfect. They'll love that. Is it old?"

"It's vintage," she corrected him, realized the way she was holding the coat made her look like a flasher, and buttoned it back up.

"Where do you even get something like that?"

"Store I work at. We sell antique clothing."

He was still staring at the coat like it had opened to reveal the Wizard of Oz. "I thought you were a secretary, um, assistant. I mean assistant."

"No, that's a side job." That sounded dodgy. "I work at the store selling accessories. The stuff I do for Matthew doesn't pay the bills." That sounded worse. "You wouldn't mind my coming along?"

"I'd be glad to have company. They're . . ." Another pause. "They're unusual folks."

"Screwballs?"

He looked her in the eye and said, "You have *no idea*." He checked his watch. "Lancashire Hotel on 82nd Street. We better move. It starts at eight and it's a big deal if you walk in after the movie starts."

He was holding the door for her when she looked at him and asked, "Do you set the alarm from outside?"

He tapped his forehead with his fist. "Thanks. Step outside and I'll, uh, set it."

She waited on the staircase and watched Fred mess with a set of buttons near the front door. He emerged, let the door swing shut, beckoned and loped down the staircase and up the street. They turned onto First Avenue and headed uptown, Fred pausing a couple of times for her to catch up.

"So, um, yeah. When you called. You wanted to talk some more about the Arnheim?"

"I wanted to talk about careers."

He pulled up at the crosswalk and squinted at her. "Careers at the Brody? They, ah, don't do a lot of hiring."

"More like film preservation in general," she told him. The light changed, he was off, and she scampered to follow his long legs. "After seeing what you do at the Brody, I started thinking maybe I should try to do it, too." They turned the corner at 82nd. Flattery wouldn't hurt. "I see you as a role model." He stopped.

"You want *my* career?" He was holding his elbow again.

"Sure. I certainly don't want to be standing around a store twenty years from now, saying 'may I help you' all day."

He took off again, still pulling at his elbow. "Okay. I'm, uh, right. We'll, um, go to the Bangville Police Society. And you can, you know, see the kind of stuff I do when I'm not picking over film stock. And, um, if you still see me as"—he seemed stuck—"um, a role model, we can, um, talk about how I got where I am today." He stopped under a large green awning. "Right here." He took a big breath, then held the door for her.

They walked into a vast, tiled lobby, the walls lined with sheets of mirrors, and a woman at a folding table called, "Fred!" Behind her the doors to a conference room had been propped open. Ceinwen could see beyond it to people in padded, straight-back chairs in rows and a red flowered carpet. The woman was enormous, taller than Fred and so wide she seemed to stretch down half the table. Her full-length velvet evening gown was sleeveless, revealing arms like two legs of lamb. She had on long rhinestone earrings and a silver headband, from which a battered feather curled down one side of her face. Her grin revealed at least two chins. "Fred," she repeated. Her voice was an incongruous Kewpie-doll chirp. "You brought a date. That's so *cute*."

Fred put a hand on the back of his head, turned to look at the street door, then back to the woman. "This is Ceinwen. She's a friend."

"Of course she is, baby. Sign in, please." Fred took the pen. A man in a tuxedo had walked over. White tie. She'd never seen anyone in white tie before, not even at a wedding.

"Fred!" The man's hair was combed over his bald spot in a yellow-blond wing, feathered like Farrah Fawcett's. She had a good view of the hair and the bits of scalp under it, because he was even shorter than she was. "I guess I don't need to ask how you are. You're doing much better than all right." He made a giddy-up noise out of the side of his mouth and winked at Ceinwen. "Hi there. I'm Gene. Can I take your coat, Miss—"

"Ceinwen." She handed over her coat.

"Oh-ho-ho. Exotic moniker. I like." Fred handed over his coat.

"I like that dress," proclaimed the woman. "I'm Lorraine, by the way."

"You're a good influence," said Gene. "Fred wore his own tie."

"She's a friend," said Fred, his voice going up slightly.

"I should hope so."

"She has a boyfriend," said Fred, in the same register. "I met him when I met her." Uh-huh. Fred was cannier than he seemed.

"And what the boyfriend doesn't know won't hurt him," said Gene. "You two go on in and find a seat, we're about to start."

They sat in the back. The room was about two-thirds full, maybe sixty or seventy people, and she had a vague impression of more suits, more velvet, little cocktail hats with veils and bows and feathers—where were these dames when she was trying to sell hats at Vintage Visions?

Gene walked to the front of the screen. "Good evening, and welcome to the monthly screening of the New York chapter of the Bangville Police Society. My name is Gene Washington, and I'm the president." Gene could project like crazy, she was having no trouble hearing him at all. "Our group is dedicated to the appreciation of the great Mack Sennett and his comic brethren. And sistren, too. I'm happy to see some new faces this evening. For those who aren't familiar with the proceedings, first off"—he looked around the room and threw up his arms—"we show the movies." Net and feathers rippled across the audience with the small chuckle that followed. "Afterward, in the adjoining room there to my left, various members of our fine society will have tables set up where you can purchase items related to the sacred Sennett, as well as the stars of our pictures tonight and other silent-movie greats. We will also be serving a small selection of refreshments."

"Like what?" whispered Ceinwen, who was getting hungry.

"Punch and cookies, usually," Fred whispered back.

"Tonight we are screening a program of longer movies starring the great silent clown, Roscoe Arbuckle." Gene let the applause die down. "Most of us here know the story of Roscoe, starting with the fact that he hated the name Fatty." Cries of "yes" echoed around the room. "But just in case some of our newcomers are familiar with him only through the vicious smears in that book which I shall not sully your ears by naming"—an outbreak of boos—"let me start by saying that Roscoe Arbuckle was a magnificent comedian, revered by Buster Keaton, admired by Charlie Chaplin, adored by children everywhere. And let me state also that the scandal that tragically ended this man's career should never have happened."

More cries of "yes." This was like going to church in Mississippi.

"Roscoe was the victim of a power-mad district attorney, a lying yellow press, and an ungrateful public hungry to see its idols brought low."

She was certain she'd just heard an "amen."

"He was tried three times for manslaughter in the death of Virginia Rappe. Three times, ladies and gentleman. Where was our constitution's protection against double jeopardy for him, I ask you?"

"He was framed," yelled someone.

"He certainly was!" Gene shouted back, pointing at the man who'd called out. "And when the third jury finally acquitted him, they said he should never have been tried in the first place. But it was too late for Roscoe. He spent years in the wilderness as a broken and forgotten man, and died just as he was starting to make a comeback. Well, we here at the Bangville Police Society have not forgotten, have we?"

The applause went on until Gene put up his hand. "And tonight, we pay tribute by showing three of his best movies." The lights began to go down. "Because that's the way Roscoe Arbuckle would want to be remembered, with laughter, not tears." Gene began to retreat from the screen and bellowed, "ROLL FILM!"

For such a little man, he sure had a big sense of drama.

"I think these people are awesome," whispered Ceinwen.

"They know their stuff, that's for sure," muttered Fred.

It became clear, about two minutes into *He Did and He Didn't*, that this was the best silent-movie audience she'd ever encountered. No restlessness, unless you counted Fred's shifts of his legs and arms, and he always did that. No talking. Every laugh was related to something on screen. They picked up every gesture, no matter how small. The first glimpse of Fatty— Roscoe—got a round of applause, Mabel Normand's pretty face got an audible sigh, Buster Keaton got a shout of recognition. Fred wasn't a loud laugher, but he was completely caught up with what was happening on screen, leaning forward and occasionally giving her a side glance to see if she got the joke. And Arbuckle was a marvel, holding his own even with Keaton, supple and flexible in the way he moved.

When the applause at the last film died down and the lights came back up, she told him, "I don't know what you're complaining about."

"I'm not complaining about the movies. Arbuckle's great."

"I like the audience too. They're so into it."

"I like most of them." She'd stood up to stretch, but he was still sprawled in his seat, legs straight out and hands in his jacket pockets.

Pretty wide variety of ages here, and some big-time vintage clothing. That was a real 1920s sailor dress on that little brunette. That older woman had an alligator bag. And some people had gone all the way into actual costume. There was a Louise Brooks, and a Mary Pickford with a tiered lace dress, flat Mary Janes and cascading blonde curls. No Tramps, but that man had on a zoot suit. She wondered where they were getting all this stuff, because she didn't recognize any of the people from the store. "Do you mind if I go over to the room where they're selling things?"

He stood up. "Sure. You go find yourself a screwball." He gestured toward to the screen, where there stood a block-shaped, balding man in an emerald-green smoking jacket. Fred's whole body seemed to sag as he walked over.

For a moment she watched him twitch and grab his elbow again. Then she went into the other room. There were about a dozen tables set up. Some had posters displayed, some had hand-recorded videotapes. Two of the tables held piles of film reels, but she could tell by the size that they were 16-millimeter, so she decided she had no reason to check them out. *Udolpho* would be 35-millimeter; the reels would be huge. She drifted to a table that was covered with boxes of file folders. A tall man was standing behind it, talking to Gene. She smiled at him.

"What have you got here?"

"Stills," he boomed. "I am the Still Man. Ralph's the name."

"I'm Ceinwen." She shook his hand. He was wearing a chalk-stripe suit, and his was the first handsome face she'd seen all evening, unless you counted Fred.

"Silent movie stills?"

"Yes ma'am. Any silent you can name." Ralph hooked his fingers in his vest pockets.

"Careful of this one," said Gene. "He's a shark. Ralph, be nice to the new lady. We want her to come back. She's with Fred, you know."

"No kidding!"

Ceinwen was suddenly conscious of feeling aggrieved on her escort's behalf. Honestly, who could get a load of this crowd and pick Fred as the only one too weird to bring a girl? "He's a friend."

"That's what they keep saying," said Gene.

Enough of that. She had decided to go with a long shot. "You have anything I could name? Anything?" She narrowed her eyes.

Ralph put his hands on the table and leaned forward. "Try me."

She leaned right back at him and lowered her voice. "Got something from *The Mysteries of Udolpho*?"

He whistled. "That big Civitas flop? You know about that one?"

"Mademoiselle is a connoisseur," said Gene.

"So," said Ceinwen. "Got that one?" Ralph looked at the ceiling and tapped his chin.

"What's going on here?" Lorraine had dropped anchor next to Ceinwen.

"Fred's newcomer is playing Stump the Still Man," said Gene.

"Hey, who says I'm stumped? Give me a minute." Ralph pulled over a box and flipped through the folders, commenting on them one by one. "Nope . . . nope . . . nope . . . nada. Okay. Let me think here."

"He doesn't have it," crowed Gene.

"I didn't say that, my man, I didn't say that." Ralph bent under the table, came up with a box and shoved it onto a clear space.

"What did she ask for?" Lorraine wanted to know.

"*Mysteries of Udolpho*."

Lorraine let out a cackle. "A toughie. I like that in a woman." Ralph had finished with that box and shoved it back under the table. He scanned the other boxes.

"Just admit it," said Gene. "She's got you beat."

Ralph walked to the end of the table and laid his hand on the last box at the end. "Says you." He flipped through a few folders, pulled one out and opened it. He began to turn the stills over one by one as they all watched.

"What do you want this for?" asked Gene.

"I have a personal interest in lost films."

"Not me," said Lorraine. "Too depressing. I try to focus on the ones that get found."

"Ah-ha. Ah, ah, ah." Ralph held up a photo with the back facing out. Ceinwen put both hands up to her mouth. "Who's stumped now? Who's got me beat now?"

He flipped the still around and placed it in her hands. She could feel herself shaking slightly so she set it down on the table.

Lights and wires around the edges of the frame. An on-set still. Miriam in a pale, filmy costume, one hand on the back of a chair. Edward Kenny next to her, hands on his hips. A couple more actors, probably the woman who played Madame Cheron. On the far right a dark, heavyset man in a suit, and a slim, long-jawed younger man with his jacket off, holding a script. Left, a bit apart from the others, a man resting his elbow on the camera. Light-haired, tieless, smiling.

She couldn't remember how much cash she had on her, but she would hand it all to Ralph if he asked, down to the tokens in her change purse. She'd walk home if she had to.

"Where was it?" asked Gene.

"I had it filed with the studio photographer," said Ralph. "Almost forgot because I only got this batch about a month ago."

"How much?" breathed Ceinwen.

"Hmm. Let's say thirty."

Lorraine exploded before Ceinwen got her hand on the latch of her purse. "Thirty? What did you put in your punch?"

"It's an extremely rare item."

"Oh please. Nothing's thirty. Last time you sold a still from *Beggars of Life*, it had Louise Brooks and people have actually *seen* that one, and you didn't even charge twenty-five."

"Twenty-five," said Ralph.

"We want her to come back," said Gene. "She knows her silents. She knows how to dress."

"It's highly collectible."

"Like hell," snapped Lorraine. "Only one in that flicker anyone's ever heard of is Edward Kenny."

"And he's in the shot!" said Ralph, pointing at the photo. "Look, right there. And you have to admit, the leading lady was an eyeful."

"Yeah, yeah, yeah, she's cute. Take ten, you know that's all it's worth."

"I can do fifteen. That's as low as I go. And it's only because I lust for you in my heart, Lorraine."

"I'll tell my old man. Twelve-fifty."

"I can do fifteen." She couldn't stand it anymore, she needed to know it was hers.

"You're getting hosed, doll," said Lorraine.

"She knows a treasure when she sees it," said Ralph. Ceinwen pulled out her wallet. She had been spending so much time at the library she still had cash. Fred walked up while Ralph was putting the still in a folder, then in a paper bag.

"What did you get?"

"*Mysteries of Udolpho*," said Gene. Fred peered at her but before he said anything, the smoking jacket called out from the door.

"Yo, Freddie." Fred jumped at the sound of the man's gruff, nasal voice. "So tomorrow, we gotta date?" The man was going bald in a way that left a Florida-shaped peninsula of hair still jutting down his forehead.

"Yeah, tomorrow at seven."

"Aces." He made a little salute and was gone.

"What in the hell?" asked Gene. "You're seeing Steve?"

"We have some, um, business," said Fred. "So, ah, Ceinwen, you ready to head out?"

She slid the still between the pages of her monograph Xerox, to protect it. "Yes, let's."

As they swung out onto 82nd Street Ceinwen thought about quitting while she was ahead, but then she remembered why she wanted to talk to Fred. He was yanking off his tie and staring bleakly down the street toward First Avenue. She did a half-pirouette to face him.

"Hey. You wanna get a drink or something?"

He stuffed the tie in his coat pocket. "I'd love one."

2.

FRED LED HER UP A FEW MORE BLOCKS AND AROUND THE CORNER TO a downstairs place barely visible from the street. It used to be a speakeasy, he told her. Inside it was tiny, with a long, carved bar and wooden booths along the opposite wall, the seats so high-backed that when you sat down you felt as though you had a private room. They found an empty booth and Ceinwen ordered her usual wine. He asked for a bourbon and downed about half as soon as it arrived. If she wanted to get anything out of Fred before he got what Matthew called rat-arsed, she better figure out why he was so miserable.

"Why do you have to meet with this screwball?"

He took another gulp. "Raymond Griffith, know who he is?" She shook her head. "You've seen *All Quiet on the Western Front*, right? He's the French soldier, the one who dies in the trench with Lew Ayres. He was a comedian in silents, a really good one. We've got a two-reeler of his in the collection and I'm trying to restore it. I got one reel okay but the other one had some heavy damage and it isn't going to look very good. Steve, he's got a big collection and I know he's got some Griffith. On a hunch I call him and Steve's all coy and 'why don't you hop on over to the screening tonight, Freddie, whaddya say.' And tonight he says yeah, he's got it all right. Says his copy is in great shape and I could probably even use his print to make what I've already done look better." Fred was the only person she'd ever met who stammered less when he got a glass of liquor in him.

"That's good news, isn't it?"

"Yeah, maybe it would be if he'd drop off the reels or let us send a messenger like a normal person. But no. He wants me to go to his place." She got it now. She felt herself blushing for Fred. He knocked back all but a half-inch of his drink and gestured to the waiter for another. "I don't usually drink this fast, by the way."

"Are you saying . . ." This was terrible. No wonder he was so upset. He eyed her grimly and she fumbled for the right turn of phrase. "Steve, he, um, he likes you?"

Fred backed himself into the corner of the booth like he was Tippi Hedren being attacked in *The Birds*. "*What?* NO." He swallowed the last of his bourbon and scooted toward her, his voice a bit lower. "I—god, no. No, no, no."

"I'm sorry, it's just that you were saying . . ."

"I didn't mean anything like that. I like silents, I like my work, there's a lot I'll do, but not that." The waiter arrived with the drink and she could have sworn it never actually made table contact before Fred grabbed it.

"Okay, okay. So why do you have to go to his place?"

He propped his head against the booth and closed his eyes. "He wants to show me Topo Gigio." Another hit of bourbon, eyes still shut.

"I don't know his movies." How bad could they be?

He choked and had to grab his napkin. "Topo Gigio isn't a director. He's a mouse. A puppet. He was on TV."

"Oh. Mostly all I watch on TV is movies." She was dying for a cigarette.

"He hasn't been on in years. *The Ed Sullivan Show*. I guess he was on Italian TV too. It took four people or something to move him around on the show. Um, can I bum one of those?" She handed him a cigarette and lit them both. "Steve's obsession besides old movies is Topo Gigio. And he has his own puppet, and he's really proud that he can move Topo Gigio all by himself. And if you go over there to get a print out of him, that's the price you have to pay. You sit there for hours while he waves his fucking mouse puppet at you." She couldn't manage it any longer. The laugh rolled out with the smoke. "He does the voice too." She let out a howl. "It's got an accent, this mouse. I'm glad you think this is funny." She wiped her eyes with her napkin. "Yeah, Isabel thinks it's funny, too. Last year she let me set up a meeting with Steve, by myself, even though she knew I'd have to meet the puppet. Never said a word."

She got her voice under control and said, "Don't you think maybe you're making too big a fuss over this? It's just one night."

"That's what Isabel said. Why don't you ladies try it, then. You should have seen her face. 'I'd go too, but I have an engagement,'" he mimicked, in a pretty good version of Isabel's refined drawl. "And she'll have another party tomorrow, just wait." Another swig. "She likes torturing me."

Something about the way he muttered that last part made Ceinwen give him a closer look. He was taking a drag off the cigarette and coloring slightly under his five o'clock shadow.

Fred had a *crush* on Isabel.

Maybe this shouldn't be a shock. Isabel was smart. And she was beautiful. Admittedly, if she felt like it, Isabel might snap a man's balls off at the crotch and roll them across the floor like Christmas ornaments. But she was definitely beautiful.

"So yeah. Be me when you grow up. Four years at Tisch and, um, two more years for the master's degree. Some training at MoMA, couple of years at Eastman House and then, when you're ready for the big time, you go talk to a puppet. Did I mention that?" She started laughing again. "You have to talk back to the mouse or he pouts."

"At least your honor is safe," she choked out.

He was almost done with this drink, too. "I'd be better off just sleeping with the guy." He paused. "I didn't say that. Never tell anyone I said that."

"You mean Isabel? I wouldn't dream of it."

"Isabel would kill me anyway. She's huge on ethics. And I'm huge on not dying. You want to know my big ultimate career goal, me being your role model and all, that's it. Not getting killed by Isabel."

Ceinwen imagined Isabel wearing a negligee, propped against satin pillows and ordering Fred around the bedroom. Fred was probably imagining the same thing. Maybe that was what all men wanted. Someone to give them a hard time. Matthew hadn't broken up with Anna because Ceinwen was too nice to him. She should stand him up.

She would, too. Next week.

"I wouldn't think Isabel would worry much about ethics. She seems kind of ruthless."

He sat up straighter and gave her a look like the one he'd given Matthew. Watch it, she thought, this is his dream girl you're running down. "She's incredibly ethical. That's how I got hired." He was almost done with the second bourbon.

"She hired you because you're honest?"

"Sort of." She waited. "I shouldn't be . . ." He took another swallow. "All right, if I tell you this, you have to swear you won't tell anybody. Not one person. Especially not . . ."

"Matthew?"

"Yeah. Especially not him. You know Chris Bixby, the one I said got us that Vermont collection and retired? It wasn't true. He was fired. Where's the waiter?" He motioned to the man again.

"Maybe you should switch to beer."

"Good idea." He asked the waiter for a Heineken and another wine for her, although she wasn't nearly finished.

"Was Bixby stealing movies?"

"Not exactly. He had a side deal with some collectors. They'd pay him a fee, couple of hundred dollars, and he'd lend them a negative to print. Well, the Brody doesn't have many negatives. So, um, then he started lending out the prints to copy. The guy running things before Isabel never even noticed. But she wanted to know all about how everything was working, and she was, ah, taking inventory. And when she found some stuff out of order and she couldn't find some other stuff, she got suspicious. So she called in Chris and he, ah, he admitted it pretty quickly. He wasn't a master criminal, just a film geek in an archive."

The waiter set the drinks down and Fred took a swallow.

"She fired him?"

"She fired everybody. Two curators, three lab technicians. She even fired the receptionist. Way I heard it, um, she called them into the lobby and you know, there aren't any chairs, and she stands them up in a row and she says, you're history." He pulled up his arms and fired an imaginary rifle.

"They were all in on it?"

"Just Bixby. But she, um, assumed the others had to know he was doing it, so she fired them for not blowing the whistle."

Whoa. Isabel was one tough hombre. "What was the receptionist doing?"

"I, um, think she just didn't like the receptionist and figured now was her chance. So I'm up at Eastman House and it was all right. I mean, they do great work, but man, I hated Rochester. Rochester, god, it makes Buffalo look like Paris. And I, um, I had been trying to get out but there's not that many places, you know? And I heard the Brody was hiring and I sent my CV. And I included a cover letter, um, it was long and I went on a bit about preservation and film, and how if we didn't keep film history alive everybody was just going to sit around watching, I don't know, *Friday the 13th* and shit like that. And, um, I closed with some stuff about art and about losing a big part of our legacy as American citizens." He picked up his beer, looked at the top of the bottle, and set it back. "It wound up being two pages long. Single spaced. I got carried away, kinda."

"I don't think so at all," she said. "I agree with all of that. I bet Isabel does, too."

"Isabel . . ." He trailed off. Was he imagining something? Like Isabel in a bikini, cataloguing film fragments with him? "Um, I don't know how much she cared about this stuff when she took the job. She was a lobbyist before."

Well, that fit, for sure. "Who for?"

"The American Bar Association."

She better not laugh, he might slam down his beer and leave in a huff. "She's a lawyer?"

"Yeah. Never practiced. Didn't have to, her family's loaded. But, um, she's the kind of person who has to work and she's gotta do everything perfect. And me being so over-the-top made her think I was the same way. She called me and said I had exactly the right attitude, even though I was just an assistant, and she flew up to see me work. I spent a day, um, showing her the stuff I'd done and next thing you know I'm back in New York and I'm in charge of restoration and preservation at the Brody."

He was hammering his beer almost as fast as the bourbon. She drained the last of her first wine and started on her second.

"Did she go after the collectors?"

"Nah. Not worth it. They returned everything, they always meant to. We need them, anyway. I mean, hey, Kevin Brownlow was a collector. Old Brody was a collector. Collectors are the only way a lot of this stuff survives. But archives and collectors, they, um, have this weird relationship. They think we're stuffy academics, and we think they're crazy obsessives."

"Who's right?"

He grinned. "We both are."

She thought of all the people at the Bangville meeting, and the tables piled with reels. "Do you know who Bixby was working with?"

"One of them was Gene."

"Wow. Did you ever say anything to him?"

"Nope. He knows I know, though. And I'm sure he knows who else was doing it. They all know each other, from things like Bangville and that convention up in Syracuse."

Finally, her opening. "Like maybe that guy in Vermont? What was his name?"

Fred squinted, and she was afraid he was going to clam up, or ask her why she cared about the Vermont collector. Instead he put a hand under his chin, blew some smoke into the middle distance, and said, "Anderson. That was his name. I don't know, maybe, but I think Chris wanted the collection so he could feed it to other guys. Not the other way around. A hardcore, big-time collector, he doesn't give up his stuff.

Not unless something forces him to." He stubbed out his cigarette. "Like, you know, death."

No Andersons in the cast or crew, and none that she knew of at Civitas, either. Damn. She'd have to dig more, somehow. At least she had the still.

And she was enjoying Fred. He was working his way up to saying something else; she could tell because he was clearing his throat for the third time.

"Ah, you're not a student, right? Because, you know, I think it's great you want to do restoration. Not that many of us. Everybody wants to run off and, um, be the next Scorsese. But these places want a film degree. I don't think you need it, myself, but they'll want it."

"No, I'm not a student. But I'm thinking of going to film school. I just need to find the money. They tell me the aid parameters are changing all the time."

"I hope so," he said glumly. "I'm still paying off my loans. You, um, you also have to do a lot of physical stuff. There's a lot of chemicals and sometimes mold so you can't have allergies or anything." She had her hand braced on the side of the booth, and he was looking at the curve of her arm. "And, um, you do a lot of hauling things around, like film canisters."

"What, you think I can't carry things?"

"It's not that," he said quickly. "It's just that it's heavy and stuff, and you're . . ." His eyes wandered for a minute and he snapped them back to meet hers. "You're, um, petite." He looked back at her arm. "Your build is petite. You're a very petite woman."

Ceinwen had noticed that when men found an adjective to describe you that they thought was tactful, they liked to repeat it a few times.

"Is there food here?" she asked.

They ordered French fries and calamari and more drinks, and he told her some more about the Brody, about the difference between preserving a film, where you just made sure a copy was made and stored properly, and trying to restore the movie to what it used to look like. He drank his beer, a bit more slowly, and he told her about the places collectors got their prints—a lot of 16-millimeters from TV stations, it turned out. She mopped up some cocktail sauce that had dripped off her last piece of calamari, and she thought of a network of collectors, who all knew each other. And maybe, too, they knew how, and where, everyone got their stuff.

"Isabel's not going tomorrow night," she said.

"No way."

"That's too bad. I can't imagine anyone forcing a puppet show on Isabel, can you?"

He snorted. "No."

This was not a man who was going to take a hint. She pulled out her cigarettes and offered him one. She lit his, then hers, exhaled and said, "Would you feel better if you had some company?"

3.

FRED WAS MEETING HER OUTSIDE STEVE'S BUILDING AT SEVEN, BEFORE her shift ended. That meant she couldn't go to work. The only way you left early from Vintage Visions was on a stretcher. Lily's attitude was that if you could pick up a phone, you could sell old clothes. Ceinwen felt pretty rough already, but she chain-smoked three cigarettes to get her voice to the right level of husky. She cracked her knuckles and dialed the number.

Roxanne put her on hold. Then Lily: "I've got a store to run here."

And good morning to you, too. "I can't make it. I'm sick."

"What, were you drinking? You need to work today. I got no one else for the counter."

"I can't. I've been throwing up." Jim had walked in and was listening.

"You're pregnant?"

"I'm *sick*. I think it's stomach flu."

"You know what I think?" Oh god, another one of Lily's questions. "I think—"

She lost the rest because Jim yanked the phone cord and it crashed to the floor. Before she could speak he put a hand over her mouth. From the receiver she could hear Lily shrieking her name. Jim held up his other hand and counted out slowly with his fingers—one, two, three, four, five. Then he took his hand off her mouth and picked up the phone.

"Hello, Lily? This is Jim. Good to hear your voice again . . . No, I don't want to chat. She dropped the phone. She had to run to the bathroom." He pulled the receiver a little further from his ear. "Are you saying you want me to describe what she's doing? . . . Oh. Okay then . . . I'm sure she'll be better tomorrow. She doesn't want to leave you in the lurch . . . Yes . . . Okay . . . I'll tell her. Have a great—" He looked at the receiver, then hung up. "She says if you don't come in tomorrow, you're fired."

"Thanks."

"Lily's special way of saying get well soon."

"I mean it. That was beautiful. I'm so glad it's your day off."

"Had to do something. Watching you try to lie is painful. There's coffee if you want it." He went into his bedroom.

She carried the coffee back to the living room. Matthew should be at Courant for office hours by now. This was going to teach him a lesson. A lesson in what, she wasn't sure, but a lesson. She said hello and he launched in before she could say anything else.

"Listen, would it kill you if we switched movies tonight? I know it's Walsh, but I'm dying for color. What about *Angel Heart*? You could at least try to keep up with what's new."

"Matthew . . ."

"Christ, when was the last time you saw something made after Eisenhower was president? And before you answer, that one about the MGM musicals doesn't count."

"I can't—"

"Neither does *The Men Who Made the Movies*."

"I can't make it tonight."

"What?" The word was midway between a screech and a bark. "We planned this days ago."

"I know, I'm sorry. There's something I have to do." Jim had re-entered, dressed now, the shock in his face mirroring that in Matthew's voice.

"And what is that?"

She had the phrase rehearsed; she thought it sounded good and British. "I'm not at liberty to say."

"You're—" There was a noise of him shifting the phone, and she heard him say, "Yes, hello there. Can you give me a minute, please? I'm afraid I have to take this." His voice came back, lower but even madder. "You're not at liberty? You sound like the White House press secretary. You stand me up—this is the only night I'm free this week, by the way—and you won't even tell me why?"

"I said I'm sorry, didn't I?"

"You don't sound the least bit sorry."

He was right. She was happy he was pitching a hissy fit.

"I have something I can't do any other night. I'll tell you about it when I can. I promise."

He must have had the receiver right up to his mouth because she could hear him inhale. "Let me guess. The film. What is it this time? Are we exhuming someone at midnight to see if they got themselves buried with the print?" What kind of a person would do that? Well, there was Dante Gabriel Rossetti, he buried a bunch of poems with his wife. "For god's sake don't *ponder* that, I was being sarcastic."

"You sounded serious. It's not like I left you cooling your heels at the Bleecker Street. I'm trying to give you some notice here."

"You're too good."

"Call me when you get some time," she said, adding maliciously, "I'm free Sunday morning."

"I'll bear that in mind." Click.

Jim was sitting on the couch. He patted the seat next to him. "Come here. Sit." She picked up her coffee and perched on the edge. "You just called in sick when you're not. You went to work during Hurricane Gloria, but today you fake being sick. That's surprising, but no problem, Lily deserves it."

"I'm a little hungover, truth be told."

"No kidding. Last night you were out till 3:00 a.m. And it wasn't with Matthew. You disappear nearly every morning with a book bag. Most nights you barely say hello. You take the phone in your room and have conversations you don't want me and Talmadge to hear. You never say who you're calling. Yesterday I got the phone bill, and there's $68 of calls to LA. I don't know anyone there. Neither does Talmadge. I didn't realize you did, either."

Shit, where was she going to find $68? He paused, then went on.

"Correct me if I'm wrong, but you just canceled on Matthew. This time last month you'd have done that right around the same time you made us all watch *Casablanca* colorized."

"He's been taking me for granted."

"I'm not complaining. I'm saying it's unexpected, but go ahead. Cancel him like a postage stamp. By the way, you got a letter from California. I don't think you saw it last night." He pulled it from under the coffee table. She reached and he held it away. "Uh-uh. Nope. Not handing this over until you tell me what's going on."

"Nothing shady, I promise."

"So you say. But whatever it is, you're going overboard." He stuck the letter under his thigh and pulled out a cigarette. "No. Scratch that. You're going ape-shit crazy. You've even lost weight. It isn't like you were eating us out of house and home before, but now I never see you with food. You're too busy making phone calls and writing letters. I never, I mean never, thought I'd say this, but thank god for Matthew, because at least when you're with him I know maybe you're having a meal." He lit up, exhaled, and looked at her. She looked at her hands and tried to remember where her cigarettes were. "I don't get it, honey. We used to talk."

"It's just not my secret to tell, that's all." She picked up his cigarettes and took one without asking. "And Talmadge, I love him, but he isn't very discreet."

"I am. You know that. Try me. We don't have to tell Talmadge."

She lit the cigarette, and she told him. A short version, but all of it, just the same. He listened without saying much, except when she finished telling him about Miriam and Emil, he did quote *All About Eve*: "What a story. Everything but the bloodhounds snappin' at her rear end." She told him about the Brody and Fred and the Bangville Police Society. She told him about her still.

"Where is it? Can I see it?"

She'd been drunk when she got back last night, and she hadn't looked at it again. She fetched it and they sat close.

"This is one of the sets?"

"Must be." Her finger hovered over the man on the left, and she had to remind herself not to touch the picture. "I think the one with his arm on the camera is Emil."

Oval shape to the face, small chin. High forehead—hair maybe receding a little—nose prominent, but in proportion. Big eyes. It was a good face. Not the face of a man who'd be cruel to Miriam, much less a man who would break his hand punching a wall. The smile wasn't wide, but it was confident, a young smile.

The biggest electric-train set any boy ever had, Orson Welles said when he first saw a soundstage. Emil had the smile of a boy who just got his train set.

"Handsome guy." Jim put a hand on her shoulder. "Do I need to get the toilet paper?"

She touched the corners of her eyes. "I'm all right."

He leaned back. "You know I don't like agreeing with Matthew about anything. But I don't see how this is going to lead anywhere. Meanwhile you've got an awful lot invested in this, honey. Too much, if you ask me."

"If I have to give up, I'll know when it's time." She slid the still back into the paper bag. "Things keep happening, like finding this. It's all signs. It all means I'm supposed to keep going."

"You sound like Talmadge." He sucked in his cheeks and worked his fingers through a bit of Talmadge's manual-dexterity exercises.

She didn't laugh. "It isn't right."

"What isn't?"

"All those people. All that money, all that work." She took another one of his cigarettes. "All that heartache. It isn't right that it's gone."

"You think that's what Miriam thinks? It's not right?" She had borrowed his matches and as usual, she was breaking one after another. "What Miriam wants is for you to run around asking everyone where's her movie? Only she doesn't know that's what she wants?"

"She's always wanted to see *Mysteries* again," said Ceinwen. "She told me that."

He took the matches, and with one hand, he flicked one alight and held it out. She'd always known better than to try and learn that technique. "Then why haven't you asked her for help?"

"Well . . ." She lit up. He blew out the match and waited. "She's a pessimist." Jim nodded, like a reporter waiting for an interview to continue. "She thinks it's all dust now and she's resigned to it. So if I tell her I'm looking for *Mysteries*, she'll say everybody in Hollywood was an awful person and she wants nothing to do with them anymore." She paused. "But if somebody finds Emil's whole entire film, that's different." His mouth was shut tight. "She loved Emil so much. You should have seen her face when she was telling me about him. She's still sad about what happened. She wants him to get his due, she said so. But that can't happen just from an itty-bitty piece of the movie." No movement. "You see?"

"I definitely think it's a good idea not to get her involved," Jim said.

"Until I actually find it."

"Uh, yeah. Tell her then."

She blew her smoke toward the ceiling, then sat up, alert again. "Hey. Gimme my letter."

Jim pulled it out from under his leg. "Here you go. I have to run a few errands. When you're done reading, for heaven's sake take a nap. You've got trenches under your eyes."

He told her he would be back soon. She took the envelope into her bedroom. The letter had a nice weight to it, but there was no name, just a return address in Fresno, and she didn't remember writing to Fresno. She slid a finger under the flap and felt the edge cut a line of blood along her knuckle. She finished by ripping, and stuck the finger in her mouth. Sheets of airmail paper, folded neatly around a pamphlet. She picked up the pamphlet, which showed shafts of sunlight shining down on a neatly trimmed meadow. "First

Apostolic Reformed Church of Fresno," it said. Oh brother. She peeled off the last page of the letter and her attitude improved on the spot.

"Very truly yours, Lucile Pierrepoint Miller."

Frank Gregory's secretary, the one she had written to care of the Beverly Hills Women's League. Praise be, the ex-debs had forwarded her letter. She'd have to be nicer about them. A little nicer. She fanned the pages slightly—seven, front and back, covered in a neat, prim hand, the letters round and upright like little balloons. I'm going to read it from the top, she scolded herself. If I try to skim, I may miss something.

"Dear Miss Reilly,

"My old friends at the Women's League were kind enough to forward your letter to me. It has been a long while since anyone asked about the old days at Civitas. I do not know how much help I can give you on your proposed freelance article, but I will answer your questions as best I can. And I hope that my doing so can reinforce your thesis about Mr. Gregory and the influence of the great studio heads. He certainly was one, and I applaud your desire to clarify the record and give him his due.

"However, I must say that *The Mysteries of Udolpho*"—Lucile had underlined the title, the way they taught Ceinwen in high school—"does not strike me as the best topic for a look at Mr. Gregory's life work, and I can't help wishing you had picked something else. Still, it does show some of his unique qualities as an executive, so I will go along.

"The project was a difficult one from the beginning. It is an old-fashioned and not terribly exciting book. I believe Mr. Gregory had wanted to take on a work with more obvious literary merit, such as *The House of the Seven Gables* or *D'Ri and I*."

D'Ri and I? What in the world?

"But when he brought Emil Arnheim over from Germany (at considerable expense, Civitas paid his way) Arnheim was most insistent about the choice of book. And even though the screenplay was by one of the best writers Civitas had, Arnheim also demanded extensive revisions."

No "Mr." for Emil.

"It was the first, but by no means the last time that Arnheim would make trouble for us all. I am sorry to say that he was a thoroughly distasteful person, with all of the bad parts of the German character and none of the good. He did not have much experience, but he was far too cold and arrogant to attempt to benefit from anyone's advice, not even Mr. Gregory's. I experienced this first-hand.

"It was my task to type Mr. Gregory's memos to Arnheim, concerning things that needed to be done in order to make a movie that people would want to see, which in the end of course, he did not manage. I would send the errand boy over to the set and tell him to wait for the message back from Arnheim. The boy would come back in an hour or so and I'd ask what Arnheim had to say. Had he read the memo? Oh yes ma'am, the boy would tell me, I watched him read it just like you told me. And what was the reply? He said to tell Mr. Gregory 'thank you,' the boy said.

"Now what was I supposed to do with that? I would go back to Mr. Gregory and tell him the memo had been delivered, but we never knew if Arnheim was paying them any mind. Mr. G. was seeing rushes, of course, but the high-handedness of Arnheim was still incredible.

"One day I got so angry that instead of sending the boy I went myself. And I walked in and they were setting up a shot and there was Arnheim. I marched over and handed him the paper and said 'This time, Mr. Arnheim, I am waiting for the reply myself, because I am sure you will have something to say other than thank you.' He sat down and made a show of unfolding and reading it. He asked if I could wait another minute, because he wanted to re-read and make sure he had the reply just right. So he read it again, while I stood there on that boiling hot set. And he folded it up again and said, 'All right, Fraulein Pierrepoint. Please tell Mr. Gregory I said danke schoen.' Then he turned his back on me and walked away.

"So you can see what kind of a man we were all dealing with."

I certainly do, thought Ceinwen. She looked to the still, in its paper bag on the table, and gave it a thumbs-up.

"And you can see also what Mr. Gregory had to endure from a man who should have been nothing but grateful to him. Probably you will hear and read a great deal of nonsense from people about Mr. G. But surely you can see how patient he was. Arnheim was very smooth and reassuring, and Mr. Gregory trusted him, and he should not have. That was clear when we held the preview. I went to take notes, as always. And the movie was quite dreadful. The lead actress had never made a picture before"—why, you lying old bat—"and she simply wasn't up to it. Most of the movie was just Arnheim showing off, moving the camera for no reason at all. Putting up a shot of something nonsensical, like dust, if you can believe it. A shot of dust! I assure you, Arnheim didn't have that in the dailies when I was there with Mr. Gregory."

Dust. On a piece of furniture? In the air? Blowing across something? Should she write back and ask?

"When the screening was over, and it seemed to go on for hours, Mr. G. went to talk to Arnheim. Instead of apologizing for refusing his guidance and asking how the picture could be fixed, Arnheim proceeded to insult the audience. He said they were dull people in a dull town, compared them to that book, *Babbitt*, and said that the movie was never aimed at them. That was when Mr. Gregory let him have it. He told him that a movie was made for whoever had the means to pay for a ticket, and since Arnheim couldn't turn the movie into something this or any other audience would like, he would have his own people cut it in half if that was what it took.

"That finally shook up Mein Herr a little. He told Mr. Gregory not to do it, that he could cut it himself. Mr. Gregory didn't want to do it, good money after bad he said, but he finally gave Arnheim two weeks. You see how kind he was? Who else would do such a thing? Why, Mayer would have had the man locked out of the studio.

"So he recut it, and it still wasn't right, and Mr. G. had his editors go in and take out things like the dust and the candles and the mirrors and everything else that was boring people to death. We released it and I believe we did manage to break even, barely."

So what are you complaining about?

"After all that, Arnheim thought Mr. Gregory should just up and give him another picture. For a few months it seemed as though I was fielding a call from that man every day. Then he started coming to the office. I would tell him Mr. Gregory was otherwise engaged, and he would say he'd wait, and he would sit there doing nothing but reading and giving me those cold German stares until he decided it was time to leave.

"At first he thought he could still ask for the projects he wanted. When it dawned on him that he wasn't going to get those, he got off his high horse and said he'd do whatever Mr. G. asked. But we knew he couldn't be trusted. For one thing, everyone knew he was running through his salary, still maintaining a big fancy car and the same house and spending on gambling and drink, which I smelled on him more often than not. Mr. G. gave him a loan against his salary on the contract, just to get him to go away. And Arnheim ran through that too, and Mr. G. advanced the next year's salary, thinking maybe he'd get it back if Arnheim turned out to be a decent director of Bs or something, I suppose. Or perhaps he just felt sorry for him. In any event, by the time Arnheim died, he owed the studio the equivalent of another full year's pay."

Sort of like sharecropping, she thought. Lovely.

"But I am afraid that I am sounding harsh and unforgiving, when that is not so. I could see only how selfishly Arnheim was behaving. It wasn't until a few years later, when Mr. G. had retired and I was no longer working, that I began reading the Bible and I realized that Arnheim deserved my pity. He was a very sick person, sick in his soul. All I could see was how he took advantage of Mr. G., and how bad his behavior was, with all that extravagance and drinking and rudeness. I didn't realize that people turn to alcohol when they must fill a great emptiness inside. That was also the reason he was carrying on with that actress, the one he forced on poor Mr. G. She was a stuck-up little thing, too, no time for anyone but Arnheim. If she had known the love of God, I believe she would have been a far different person."

Don't bet on it.

"It is for that reason that I have enclosed a tract for you. I don't know you, but I always try to spread the word. We can never know who among us might be in need of comfort."

She better read the tract before she tossed it, in case it had real information. Like, "We believe it's a sin to throw away nitrate."

"And that is why, later on, I also felt regret that Arnheim died before he could find the spiritual fulfillment he needed so badly. At the time, I am sorry to tell you, all that I and just about everyone else thought was that his chickens were coming home to roost at last."

She laid the letter down on the bed, went into the kitchen, got a glass of water from the tap, chugged it, set the glass in the sink, and went back. She lit a cigarette and picked the letter up.

"You ask me about what went on at Arnheim's house the day after he died. No, Mr. Gregory did not go. He sent me and Myron Badgley to look through Arnheim's papers. As I said, he owed Civitas a good bit of money and Mr. G. very properly wanted to see if the studio had a way to seek repayment. He also wanted to make sure any studio correspondence didn't fall into the wrong hands. There was no point in damaging Arnheim's reputation any further.

"We went through the house front to back. I was concentrating on my work and the notes I was taking, so I can't tell you everyone I saw. I do remember that Arnheim's actress was there—"

Miriam Clare. You remember all this, you remember her name, too.

"—and she wasn't speaking to anyone, just walking around in silence and trying to put things back even though she knew we were tallying them. I also remember Norman Stallings, the assistant director, hanging around and questioning everything. He had a close relationship with Arnheim. I suppose that wasn't surprising, considering that Norman himself was dissolute in a different way."

Dissolute, but in a different way. Gay, thought Ceinwen, although Miriam hadn't mentioned it.

"One thing I can tell you is that when we got to the bedroom in the back, there was no film there. I hope you understand that prints were studio property and it would have been quite improper for Arnheim to have one. It would have been repossessed, and anyone who found such a thing would have had to notify Mr. Gregory immediately, through me. I can tell you with complete confidence that no print of *The Mysteries of Udolpho* was ever found that day. I suspect that whoever told you such a thing was indulging in gossip, and nothing more.

"I hope this serves to answer your questions, and to give you a better picture of Mr. Gregory and how fine a man he was. I am sorry that the Arnheim film is gone, as indeed I am sorry that anything Mr. G. put his efforts into is gone. But of all the Civitas films that are no longer available, I certainly regret that one the least.

"If you have further questions, you may write to me at this address. I hope you also find time to look at the reading I sent. Without the grace of God, we are all inches away from becoming Emil Arnheim.

"Very truly yours,

"Lucile Pierrepoint."

Myron Badgley, the studio's lawyer, was dead. What the hell happened to Norman?

She took Jim's advice and lay down for a nap, but woke up a couple of hours later to him shaking her shoulder and handing her the phone.

"Hello." Matthew sounded formal.

"Hello yourself. What's up?" Jim began to walk away.

"I've given the matter some thought." Sheesh, this skipped formal and ran straight into stuffy. "And I believe I owe you an apology."

Had he ever once apologized for anything, even stealing the covers? "That's all right, don't worry about it."

Jim stopped.

"I overreacted."

"I understand. You were pissed." More than once he'd told her that to him, pissed meant drunk, but she never remembered until after she'd said it. "I canceled on you, it was natural."

Jim mouthed, "Let. Him. *Apologize*," and disappeared.

"I was being childish. Really, it's none of my business if you have to call off something." That didn't sound good. "I was more disappointed than I would have been ordinarily" (what was she, one of his students?) "because I'm leaving in a week or so."

The chipped paint on her wall slid out of focus, like the camera was telling her someone was about to faint. "Leaving?" she said. "Leaving New York?"

"Leaving for spring break."

"Oh." Waterskiing, maybe.

"I thought you knew it was coming up."

"No, I don't keep track of school holidays. Since I'm not in school." She prayed he hadn't noticed the tiny crack in her voice.

"No reason you should, I suppose."

"Where are you going?" She put her hand over the receiver so she could get a deep breath that didn't sound like a sob.

"USC."

West. The opposite direction. She summoned a vision of Lauren Bacall and tried for a lower key. "Meeting someone there?" Hopeless. She just sounded hoarse.

"Maths professors." She covered the receiver again and gulped air like someone had taken a pillow off her face. "Busman's holiday."

Tears had rolled all the way to her neck. No Anna. He was working. She took her hand away. "I understand," she managed. "Publish or perish."

"Precisely. There's a couple of profs there who have a computer program I think I can use. So that's what I'm doing. For ten days. Starting Wednesday."

"You'll be busy," she said. Her voice wasn't so bad anymore, so she added, "Too busy for anything else."

"That's what I'm trying to say. I have two years here in the States to get as much done as possible before I start applying for tenure track. I won't have time to drop by the film department and reminisce about the late Professor Gundlach. I don't want to be rude, but I do want that up front."

"I've never complained when you needed to work, have I?"

"No. To be fair, you haven't."

"I'm sorry about tonight." She was now, anyway. Very sorry. "Do you have another night? Before you go?"

He let her wait, then said, "Monday?"

"That works. Monday's a bad night for digging up graveyards."

A small, slight laugh. But a laugh. "Monday then. Good luck with . . . whatever you're doing tonight."

"I'll tell you Monday."

"Then why not now?" He didn't sound annoyed or formal anymore. He sounded like Jim had earlier, on the couch.

"It's just that, I'm afraid you'll think it's a bad idea and . . . then you'll explain why. And that will make me nervous. More nervous."

She mopped up her face with the edge of her sheet. He said, quietly, "Is that what I do?"

"Sort of. Sometimes."

"Like that fellow in the Katharine Hepburn movie."

"We've seen a few . . ."

"She's an athlete, and he's a big blond Aryan type. Whenever she's playing, he talks to her and says all the wrong things and before you know it, she's off her game."

"*Pat and Mike.*"

"That's the one," he said, softer still.

"Never," she said, matching his volume. "Nothing like him."

"Good."

What were they waiting for? "See you Monday?"

"See you then."

4.

SHE WAS SUPPOSED TO MEET FRED OUTSIDE, BUT SHE SAW NO ONE. She poked her head in the door, the doorman looked up from his desk, and she ducked back out because she didn't know Steve's last name or the apartment number. She walked back toward the curb and took in the building: tall, set well back from the street, concrete trim, plate-glass windows, shrubbery along the front. She heard a voice say, "Hey." She looked down the sidewalk one way, then the other. "Hey." Louder this time. She stepped to the curb and edged between two parked cars, trying to get a look at the street.

"*Ceinwen*. I'm over here."

Fred was walking toward her from the direction of the plants. She had been looking at that spot not two minutes before. "Were you standing behind the bushes?"

"I wasn't *behind* the bushes, I was *next* to the bushes. Um, have you got an extra cigarette?" He set down a duffel bag on the sidewalk while they lit up. As he exhaled he said, "Thanks. We can't smoke up there. Steve, ah, Steve is asthmatic. Hates cigarettes."

"Good to know." His whole body was rocking slightly, side to side. "I hope you aren't nervous or anything."

"No, of course not." He had an overhand smoking style, very 1940s, except people back then held still when they smoked. "I just, you know, want this over with as soon as possible."

They smoked silently, and she resisted the urge to put her hand on his shoulder to stop his swaying. "Looks like a nice building." Fred shrugged. "Has he got a lot of stuff stored up there?"

"I guess," said Fred, with a sidelong look. "All I saw was, um, the living room. Pretty clean."

She was giving him the wrong idea again. "I was just asking because I went to another collector's place, and you wouldn't believe how crowded it was. Barely enough room to sit. Glad Steve's place is normal."

"Uh, hold on a minute there," said Fred. "Didn't say it was normal."

"What's wrong with it?"

Fred looked at his cigarette, which was almost down to the filter.

"I'm not sure, but, um, I think his decorator must have been Tod Browning." He took one last drag, and with a graceful overhand toss he threw the cigarette toward the street. It sailed between the cars and landed straight in the gutter. He bent down to get his duffel while she tried to imitate his throw. Her cigarette landed a good foot short of the curb. She looked back to see if he had noticed, but Fred was facing the door, still twitching.

"All right," she said brightly. "Let's get this show on the road."

Once in the elevator she racked her brain, trying to remember more Tod Browning. *London After Midnight*, check, *The Unknown*, check, but he'd done sound movies too, famous ones. Why was she blanking? Nerves, must be. She didn't want to ask Fred and make a stupid mistake, like she had with Topo Gigio.

When they reached Steve's door, she waited for Fred to ring the bell, and saw that he was hugging himself. She reached across him and pressed the button. Footsteps sounded, Fred hugged himself harder, and Steve opened the door.

"Good evening! Freddie my man, how it's hanging?" Steve's voice really was something, a honk that sounded like he was blowing his nose.

"You know," said Fred. "Can't complain. This is my friend Ceinwen."

"Howdy!" Steve pumped her hand up and down. "Come in, come in, don't be shy."

She walked in and checked to make sure Fred was behind her in the short hall. He was, albeit at a bit more distance than seemed logical. She took a look at the living room and remembered. *Dracula*. And *Freaks*. Who on this green earth painted three walls black and one wall blood-red?

"So you're Freddie's new friend. Let me take your coat."

"Ceinwen's, ah, interested in film preservation," said Fred, clutching his duffel.

"Yup, yup, yup, and film preservation is interested in her, too. Hey Freddie, wanna hand me your coat there?"

"I'm kind of cold . . ."

"Whoopsie, sorry about that. I'll go turn up the heat." Fred shifted his duffel and handed his coat to Steve, with a far-off expression like Merle Oberon in *The Private Life of Henry VIII*, getting ready to put her head on the block. Steve led them to a sofa placed directly in front of a massive poster from *Nosferatu*. "I was pretty sure I saw you at the Bangville screening, but I didn't get a good look. Then Gene called me this morning and said hey, whaddya know, didja see Freddie brought a girl last night. So when Freddie said he wanted to bring a friend, I figured it wasn't that scary broad he works for." Fred opened his mouth, and Ceinwen tugged on his sleeve to get him to sit next to her. Steve shifted their coats to one arm and put up a hand. "Sorry, I mean lady. But you gotta admit, friendly she ain't."

"Isabel," said Fred tightly, "is professional."

"I so agree," said Ceinwen. She had turned so she didn't have to look at Max Schreck and found herself confronting a gold-framed reproduction of that Goya painting that showed a giant biting a man's head off. She put her eyes back on Steve. "I met her, and she's terrifically professional."

Steve's couch was a bit like theirs at home, but it had all its legs and the wine-red upholstery was in better shape. Fred set the bag on the floor and put both hands on his knees, whether to persuade his legs to move less as they popped up and down, or to have his hands along for the ride, she couldn't tell.

"Let me get you kids a drink," said Steve, picking up some coasters and flipping them on the table like playing cards, still balancing the coats on one arm. "What'll it be? I make a mean vodka tonic."

"Awesome," said Fred. Not only was he moving even more than usual, his sentences weren't long enough for him to stumble over. Ceinwen nodded. Steve disappeared and she swiveled to look at another wall. Sure enough, *Freaks*: "The story of the love life of the side show." To avoid looking at the poster she said to Fred, "You've seen *Freaks*, right?"

"Sure. You too?"

"Kept me up for days," she told him. "Those people crawling toward him in the rain . . ."

"Yeah, so you see it and have nightmares," whispered Fred. "Steve sees it and thinks, you know, lifestyle option."

She turned to look at the last wall, behind the couch, and found a framed lobby card from *He Who Gets Slapped*. She'd seen that, Seastrom, it was a good one, but this room was definitely suggesting a theme, and it wasn't "home sweet home." "I admit it," she whispered back. "I'm starting to get your point." There were low cabinets along the length of one wall, with plants and little statues on top—an Easter Island head, a miniature mummy case. "Is that where he keeps his movies?"

"He didn't open them last time, but, um, I don't think so," said Fred. "Reels'd be too wide to fit."

"Videos then?"

"Yeah, right size for that, I guess." He paused his knees for a moment. "They'd fit all kinds of things. Thumbscrews."

"Fred."

"Shrunken heads . . ."

"*Fred*." She put a finger to her lips as Steve came back in holding three tall glasses against his chest. Fred blanched, but Steve didn't seem to notice as he set them down and said, "Fresh outta swizzle sticks." She tasted her drink and remembered that she hated vodka. Fred took a gulp, tapped the back of his hand against his mouth and said, "So, ah, Steve. We, um, appreciate the hospitality, but we've, um, got a motive here."

"Course ya do, Freddie. Here, lemme take a swallow"—he gulped and smacked his lips—"and I'll be right back with what I know you been waiting for."

Fred looked surprised and relieved as Steve left the room. "Hey, you're a good-luck charm." She smiled. Fred took another swallow and kept his drink in his hand, as though afraid it might be taken away at any minute. She looked past him to the Goya painting. It was even more frightening than she remembered. She was wondering why on earth any man, gay or straight, would pick that Goya instead of *The Naked Maja* that Ava Gardner had played in a biopic, although it was a pretty bad movie, when she felt something brush her shoulder and then her ear. White fuzziness swayed across her sightlines and a furry touch grazed her cheek. She let out a scream—"*What's that?*"—clamped her hands on Fred's arm and felt his drink slosh as she tried to hide her face behind his shoulder.

"Aw, don't be scared," she heard Steve say. "Topo's just trying to give you a kiss."

Fred picked up his napkin with his free hand—she hadn't let go of his arm. She sat up and found herself eyeball to eyeball with a mouse in a prison uniform. Stripes, anyway. It was about ten inches tall, the ears were enormous, its mouth was slightly open to show its buck teeth, and its cheeks were horribly red. Steve was standing behind the couch and holding the mouse in front of her by wires attached to its creepy little arms. She felt Fred prying at her fingers.

"Sorry."

"It's okay, if you could, um, relax the grip a bit . . ." She took her hands away. Fred wiped at her skirt and then his pants leg.

"Topo didn't mean to startle you," said Steve. "He wants to say hello." Then, in some kind of accent, "Hel-lo, Karen!" She wanted to say her name wasn't Karen, but she didn't want to talk to a mouse. Steve moved around the couch, the mouse moved closer, and she backed away. "Aw. You're hurting Topo's feelings. Kiss and make up." It advanced on her once more, and this time she threw her arms over her head and flattened herself face-down on the cushions.

Steve's voice was so cold it almost sounded normal. "What's going on here?" She felt Fred tap her gently and she raised her face. He was looking at her the way Brandon DeWilde looked at Alan Ladd in *Shane*. He winked, so fast she wasn't sure she'd seen it.

"Uh, I'm really sorry about this, Steve. Should have told you. The lady, um, is deathly afraid of mice." She righted herself.

"I am," she said. And it was true. At home, Jim and Talmadge could tell her cockroach scream and her spider scream from her mouse scream, because the mouse scream, Jim said, was like how you'd announce finding a dead body.

"I don't get it," said Steve. "This one is a toy."

"I know, I know," said Fred, like a doctor apologizing for a crappy prognosis. "That's, um, why we thought she could handle it."

"I guess I can't," said Ceinwen. Adding, "It's a phobia. It's not what you'd call rational."

Actually, she thought any rational person would scream if you assaulted them out of nowhere with a mouse puppet, but there was no percentage in pointing that out. Steve looked at the puppet, then back at Ceinwen with an expression that was almost wounded. "All righty then," he said. "I don't suppose you mind if Topo just sits with us?"

"No problem," said Fred. "Does he drink vodka?"

"Ha ha ha, Freddie," said Steve. He arranged the mouse so it was sitting upright in an armchair. "You okay there, Karen? Not gonna run away screaming?"

"No," she said hastily. "I think this is kind of therapeutic, having him around." Fred gave her a look. "As long he isn't moving, he's fine." Steve gave her a look. "He's even kind of cute, just . . . sitting there."

"Okay," said Steve, "I guess I should bring out the other main event." And disappeared.

Fred took another swig, this time with a celebratory air. "That," he said in a low voice, smacking his lips, "was pretty seriously brilliant."

"What was?"

"The mouse phobia. Genius. I'm, uh, sorry it took a minute to, you know, pick up the cue. But, um, you didn't tell me."

"Oh," she said, waving her hand, "I thought it would be better if I didn't. That way you could react naturally. Like improv."

Fred reached over and gave Topo a sharp poke. It tilted to one side. "I never thought about it, but, um, this little guy is definitely scary. Those buck teeth."

"You better sit him back up," she said. "Steve's already annoyed." Fred slammed Topo back into position with a force that squashed the puppet's head straight into its shoulders. They heard a door shut and Fred shifted back onto the couch. Steve walked in holding two film canisters. He placed them carefully on the coffee table, posed with his arms out and said, "Voila. *The Man From Manitoba.*"

Fred popped the lid off the top canister and inhaled sharply. He looked at Steve and grimaced, then pushed gently on the film with his finger. Steve sat next to Topo and smiled back placidly.

"This is nitrate," said Fred.

"Of course, Freddie. I told you, it's a good print."

Ceinwen leaned forward. It didn't look dangerous at all. It was just a big reel of film.

"Last night I asked you. I said, do I need to bring the containers. And you said no."

The film did smell funny, though. Like nuts. Almonds. Ceinwen realized this was what she'd thought was Fred's cologne.

"It's just two little reels. And they're in great shape. Why bother schlepping a container for that?" Fred ran both hands over his face and back through his hair, and Steve rolled his eyes. "Oh my good goodness. Everybody's such a fraidy-cat tonight. First we get all freaked out about Topo Gigio. And now I'm scaring poor Freddie with my nasty old nitrate."

"There's procedures I'm supposed to follow."

"I'm not going to tattle on you. Just take it with you and put it . . ." Steve paused. "Wherever you boys put the nitrate. Someplace safe I'm sure."

"You have nitrate prints back there just lying around?" blurted Ceinwen. Steve waved his hand.

"I've got a fireproof cabinet. With a cooling system."

"Can I see it?" she asked, too fast and too eager.

"No," said Steve, his voice colder even than when she'd screamed at Topo Gigio. "Nobody sees my cabinet."

"Is Isabel going to kill you?" Ceinwen asked Fred, under her breath.

"Not kill, but she might *hurt* me."

"We-ell we don't want that," said Steve, loud. "You don't have to take it if you're afraid you'll up and burst into flames."

"I didn't say that," said Fred.

Ceinwen had never been up close with a reel of old film before. She stretched out a finger and pushed on it, like Fred had. She caught Steve watching her and quailed, but he batted his eyes and said, "See? Your finger didn't fall off."

"It's got a little give to it," she said.

"That's the way it's supposed to feel," said Fred. "When a reel's starting to go it gets spongy and, um, then if it's really far gone the layers stick together and, um, once it feels hard you're in trouble."

"With nitrate, anyway," guffawed Steve. Fred glared at him.

"You mean, at that point it could catch fire?"

"Oh puh-leez." Steve rolled his eyes. "People make such a big fat hairy deal about nitrate. And there were thousands of reels traveling all over everywhere for all those years and nobody gave it a second thought. If it was as bad as they say, all you'd have heard about would have been theaters blowing up like Jimmy Cagney at the end of *White Heat*." He smirked. "Isn't that right."

"Made it, Ma. Top of the world," said Ceinwen, and giggled. Steve started giggling too.

Fred didn't laugh. "I should go back to the Brody and get a container."

"Don't bother. I won't tell. Karen won't tell."

"There's been fires, haven't there?" asked Ceinwen. "I read about one in Montreal."

"That was a cigarette," said Steve. "People and their dirty butts."

"I follow the rules for a reason," snapped Fred. "It wasn't a cigarette in that Scottish theater."

"No, they just put the film on top of a *battery*, for crying out loud. What, Freddie, you're going to take this back to the Brody and do that?"

"Of course not, but—"

"Never never ever, right? We know you're a very, very careful boy."

Fred drummed his fingers on the table for a second, then replaced the lid, unzipped his duffel and laid the reels in carefully. "All the same, I'm gonna take this to the lab right away. I don't want to be running around with it."

An acid taste rose from Ceinwen's chest into the back of her throat.

"You mean now?"

"That's the idea," said Fred, sounding more cheerful than he had all evening. She glanced wildly around the room. How was she going to ask about Vermont? From his chair, Topo kept watch with beady eyes, as if daring her to find a way out of this one.

"You don't have to rush," Steve was saying, and she felt a twinge of liking for him.

Fred was zipping the duffel. "Not, um, really supposed to sit around with this."

Her eyes lit on her glass. "I haven't finished my drink," she said. "I can't possibly waste a good vodka tonic."

"Couldn't agree more," said Steve. "And Freddie could use a refill."

"Rules are rules," said Fred, sounding like a baritone version of Isabel.

"There you are, Karen, Freddie just wants to protect us. One minute we're sitting here next to a two-reeler. Next minute, ka-POW. *White Heat.* No, hang on, maybe Freddie's nightmares are in color. *Zabriskie Point*, that whatcha thinkin', Freddie?"

Fred pulled the duffel bag onto his lap and shouted, "I AM NOT AFRAID OF THE NITRATE."

There was a moment of profound silence.

"In that case, I'll top this off," said Steve, as he picked up Fred's glass and made for the kitchen.

She picked up her own, barely touched drink, and ran a finger down the condensation, refusing to look at Fred.

"What did you have to go and do that for?" she heard him ask under his breath, sounding not so much mad as plaintive. "We were practically out the door."

She took a sip. It was still awful. "I like my drink."

"You don't have to get a drink from Steve."

"It's free. You think I can just waltz out and get a free drink anytime I feel like it?"

"Um, yeah. Actually, I do."

She was still refusing to look at him. "I don't want to make trouble. All I want is a drink." She sipped again.

"Jesus, Marilyn, I'll get you a drink. I'll get you a whole bottle."

"Marilyn?" she asked innocently.

"Come on. 'All I want is a drink.' *All About Eve.*" She glanced at the duffel bag in his lap. He was tying the straps into a knot. She could hear an ice tray cracking in the kitchen.

The silence lengthened. She reflected that she didn't think she had seen any Antonioni.

Finally, in her normal volume, she asked, "Did you like *Zabriskie Point*?"

"I fucking hated it," said Fred.

"Hated what?" Steve had appeared in the door.

"*Zabriskie Point*." Fred took his drink and slurped off the top.

She had better work fast. This conversation was deteriorating in one quick hurry. She had no ideas at all.

"I think *Il Grido*'s pretty terrific," she ventured. She hadn't seen that one either, but she'd read about it in the front section of the *New Yorker* and could fake it if she had to.

"Alida Valli," agreed Steve. "Whatta dish."

That was as far as she could go with Antonioni. Matthew. He could work with this situation. She needed a Matthew remark. "I must say," she said, louder than either man had been speaking, "I'm relieved." Both heads swung in her direction, probably because she suddenly sounded like Mary Poppins, but at least she was changing the subject. "All these years I've been hearing about how frightfully dangerous it is to store nitrate, and that's not the case at all."

Ten minutes ago she was Fred's hero. Now he was obviously thinking she was dumb as a side of ham. "Um, what are you talking about?"

"Steve takes good care of his nitrate. But it seems like it can survive even when you don't. Like that man in Vermont with that big collection out in his barn."

"It was in his tool shed," said Fred. "Some of it was in terrible shape. And, ah, frankly it's a miracle there was anything left."

"Gotta agree there, Karen. Let's not get carried away," said Steve. "In the first place, Otis didn't have it out in the shed more than a year. That wife of his made him put it out there."

"Guess she didn't care about film collecting," said Ceinwen.

"Guess not." Steve shrugged.

"So narrow-minded," she offered, by way of sympathy. "She should have made more of an effort to understand how important collectors are."

"That's exactly how I feel," said Steve. "But it wasn't Otis's collection."

"What?" said Fred. "Of course it was."

"Oh no, Freddie. Nope. It was his wife's."

"But you said she made him get rid of it," she said to Fred.

"That was his second wife," said Steve. "I don't know who the hell she was. No, the collector was his first wife. Lauren, her name was. Her I knew, before she up and died."

She had to get the last name. "How about you, Fred, did you know her?"

"Um . . . a collector named Lauren?"

"Reifsnyder," said Steve. "Lauren Reifsnyder." Bingo. She should write it down, but she'd just have to remember it. "But I guess Freddie never met her. The Brody got the collection before you got there, isn't that right?"

"Years before. I was, um, still at NYU." She took another sip. The melting ice was making the vodka almost palatable. She was mulling her next move when Fred spoke, sounding interested for the first time. "You knew this woman?"

"Sure. Everybody did."

"Stood out, huh." Fred sounded skeptical.

"Ha, yeah, I know what you academic types think about collectors, but trust me, Lauren was a genuine nutcase. First of all, she was about this big around." Steve held up a pinkie. "And she was always cold. Didn't matter what time of year it was. Ninety degrees out, she'd have on two sweaters and a big wool scarf."

"Where did she get all her films?" That sounded nice and casual. Matthew would approve.

"Same places everybody did, I guess. She might have known somebody in the business. No idea. I couldn't believe it when she got married. I mean, she wasn't a bad-looking old bird, but she never wanted to talk to anyone. She'd just scurry around and barely speak. Then she meets old Otis Anderson, brings him to a few events and he stands there looking bored as hell. I used to chat him up just 'cause I felt sorry for him. Next thing we hear, she's up in Vermont. She musta covered herself in blankets up there. I always figured she'd move to Florida. Well, I dunno, she didn't last that long. Maybe the cold did kill her. I don't think she ever made it to the five-year anniversary." Steve crunched some ice thoughtfully.

"What happened to Anderson?"

"He took the tax deduction and dropped dead, like, I don't know, maybe a year later," said Fred.

"I'm thinking Lauren came back to haunt him after he got rid of it," said Steve. "You guys never would have gotten anything out of her when she was alive. She never sold a frame. Oh, you could ask her and she'd pretend she was taking you seriously, or sometimes she'd even offer to sell you something herself. But then you'd get down to the nitty-gritty and she'd name her price and she'd want a fortune, some amount nobody in his right mind would pay. After a while it got to be a known thing and nobody tried anymore. Not even me." He chuckled. "And I tell you, if I'd heard she kicked the bucket in time, the Brody wouldn't have gotten her stuff, either."

"She never sold anything at all? She just kept buying nitrate?"

"I didn't even know she had nitrate." She definitely didn't believe *that*. But she had the name and Steve had made it clear he wasn't showing them anything else.

"Fred," she asked, "are you sure you're comfortable with that bag in your lap?" He straightened up a bit and knocked back another swallow.

"Yeah, careful there Freddie."

"I'm not afraid of the nitrate," Fred repeated, in a normal volume this time. "I work with this stuff all day. It's just, you know, procedures."

She drained the rest of her drink, as Fred did the same, and she came up with a Miriam line. "I'm awfully afraid we're keeping you. Fred and I had better skedaddle." Skedaddle was her own word. She wanted to keep it all natural-sounding. I'm doing great, she gloated. She set down her drink, it tilted over the edge of her coaster, and she re-centered it.

Fred was already standing up. They put on their coats.

"I'll, uh, take good care of Raymond for you, Steve."

"Do that, Freddie."

"I'll be in touch when I can bring it back." He paused and added brightly, "Unless, you, ah, wanna donate it."

"No way."

"Didn't think so."

Steve held open the door. "Hey, when you come back, you can bring Karen."

"Great idea," said Fred, weakly.

Fred hit the lobby button with his palm. The handles on his bag were still knotted. "Phew, that's over." He leaned his shoulders against the elevator wall and let the bag slip to the floor. "And you finished your drink. Happy?"

"Ecstatic," she said, without sarcasm. The doors opened; he heaved the bag back up by the shoulder strap and held an arm in front of the door.

"I'm, um, I know I got impatient back there," he said. "He gets on my nerves."

"It's all right." She didn't want Fred mad. "I just wanted to talk to him some more, that's all. He's interesting."

"He is?" She'd made things worse.

"Of course he is," she said. They were on the sidewalk. She tightened the belt of her coat. "It's different for you, this is what you do for a living. Me, I work in a store all day and at night I go see these movies and nobody wants to come. And then nobody wants to talk about them, either."

He shifted the bag. "What about your project with, um, you know—"

"Matthew?" Shit, she'd forgotten the phony project again. "He's mostly focused on his math. He likes this sort of thing, but . . ." Fred was just standing there. "He, I don't know . . ." Still not moving. "Maxes out?"

"Yeah. I get that from people too."

Something was nagging at her, and she'd better ask while he was still there. "Fred . . . that woman up in Vermont. Did they save everything she had?"

He shook his head. "No way. About half of the nitrate was, um, shot. Couple of them disintegrated before they could even get them out of the canister. Um, do you mind if I—" He paused. "Never mind. Bad idea. Smoking around nitrate."

"You're right," she said, though she was dying for a cigarette too. "I guess," she continued, sounding a little off even to herself, "you wouldn't even know which ones were there."

"Oh, we knew all right. They were labeled."

Labels. She had never thought about labels. She swallowed hard. "So which ones? Are we talking a movie that had been lost?"

He inhaled, rose up on his toes, then rocked back on his heels. "Are you ready for this? Like, ah, really ready? Because it's bad." Oh god. "*Flaming Youth*."

She breathed out. She didn't know that one. "That was the one with—" She groped. Fitzgerald. "The flappers?"

"Yep," he said. "Colleen Moore." He breathed deeply and shook his head, like he was recalling a death in the family. "Couldn't salvage a frame. I wasn't there. It was, ah, before my time, you know. But they told me Bixby put his head down on the table and cried."

She felt like crying herself, and she'd never even heard of this movie. Obviously she needed to stay away from vodka. She settled for shaking her head slowly, like he had. "Was that the only lost film there?"

"Yep. That was it. Except, you know, the Arnheim fragment. That was just one reel. Kinda weird." She was so relieved she figured she'd better clam up for a minute. He put the bag on the ground and started rifling his pockets. "Okay. So, um, right. I gotta get back to the Brody. *Not* because I'm afraid of the nitrate."

"I understand. Isabel."

"Yeah." He took out a card. "And, um, to be honest, it's gonna be, ah, crazy for a while. But um, look, here's my card. And, you know, in a couple of weeks, when the weather's warmer, if you want to come up and, I don't know, look around and, um, talk about Roscoe Arbuckle or whatever, give me a call."

She took the card, though she had one already. This card felt more sincere.

APRIL

1.

Sʜᴇ ꜱᴛᴀʏᴇᴅ ᴜᴘ ʟᴀᴛᴇ, ᴛʀʏɪɴɢ ᴛᴏ ᴅᴇᴄɪᴅᴇ ᴡʜᴇᴛʜᴇʀ ᴏʀ ɴᴏᴛ Lᴀᴜʀᴇɴ Reifsnyder was a dead end. The woman had the screen test, but not the movie print. How on earth did that make sense? She overslept and made it to work just in time. For once exhaustion worked in her favor. Lily eyed her and said she hoped Ceinwen wasn't still throwing up.

As she showed people jewelry, she found herself thinking about the jewelry, which she hadn't done in ages.

When she came home that night, she opened the street door and saw Miriam, getting the mail. That's the ticket, she thought. Bet you anything Miriam is still holding out on me.

"Hello," said Miriam, and began to climb the stairs.

"Oh hey, Miriam," she called. "I was hoping to run into you." Miriam turned and tucked her mail under her arm. She decided to answer the question Miriam was refusing to ask. "That's because there's a new coffee shop over on Fifth Street. I thought we could go and try the coffee." Miriam tilted her head slightly. "Or the doughnuts."

"Why would we do that?"

"To see if it's any good?" ventured Ceinwen. Miriam climbed off the bottom step and walked over.

"No, I mean why would we go together."

It suddenly occurred to Ceinwen that she spent a big chunk of every day dealing with people who refused to act like normal human beings. The elderly, the English. Retailers. "To be sociable?"

Miriam folded her arms. "You can't be much more than twenty."

"Twenty-one."

"I thought so. And yet you keep attempting to, what's the term, hang out with me. I've got more than half a century on you. I'm ancient. I bought a cemetery plot seven years ago."

"Really? Whereabouts?" Next to Emil, or Jack?

Miriam's hand flew to her forehead, then dropped. "Ceinwen. Do you realize that most girls your age would not hear that I'm preparing to die and promptly ask me where I plan to get planted?"

Miriam was implying she was weird. She was not weird, any more than she was obsessive. This she wasn't going to let stand. "I've always related well to old—er people."

"You don't say," said Miriam, flatly. "Why?"

The street door opened and a middle-aged woman came in, holding her child by the hand. They moved to let her pass, and despite the extra time the procedure gave, Ceinwen couldn't come up with anything good. When mother and child had disappeared beyond the first landing she said, trying to sound casual, "They're interesting."

"No. They're not. They eat bland food and check their blood pressure and worry about whether Reagan is going to cut Medicare. They watch CNN and go to bed early."

"You don't do any of those things."

"Oh yes I do," laughed Miriam. "Don't you see what I'm saying? Go to a punk-rock club. I've been past that one on the Bowery. The famous one."

"CBGB."

"Yes!" said Miriam, sounding pleased for the first time. "Go there!"

"I've been there," said Ceinwen, morosely. "I didn't fit in." She'd worn a good dress, too.

"All right then, find another place. Have Matthew find another place. Dye your hair a different color. Find a girlfriend your own age. What's so great about old people?"

"They've lived through history." That was what Granana always said.

"So have we all," was the crushing response.

"And," said Ceinwen, trying to salvage something, "they like the same movies I do."

"I suspect"—Miriam held up a finger—"we have the heart of the matter right there." Miriam didn't want to talk to her again. Especially not about movies.

"You're telling me you're going upstairs to watch CNN?"

"*Nightline*. Since you ask."

Out of patience and with her tact nowhere to be found, she lashed out: "Why the hell do old folks want to watch the news all the time?"

Miriam gave a very slight smile. "It makes us glad we won't be around much longer." She turned to go and said, "Maybe some other time."

"Sure." It was never going to happen.

Monday morning, she made a list. Talk to Gene at Bangville and see if Lauren ever sold anything. Steve said she didn't, but maybe he didn't know. Talk to Steve and see if he knew more about where collectors got things. Both of those ideas involved calling Fred to get the phone numbers, and she better have a good story ready for that. Go back to the library and start working through the Times, to see if Norman Stallings had ever been mentioned.

When she'd finished, she stared at the page for a bit and decided to go to the movies to clear her head. Up to the Thalia for *Waterloo Bridge* and *The Red Shoes.* Tragic ballerina double feature: first the prostitute, then the suicide. The Thalia's floor sloped down, then up. She sat near her favorite spot on the upper slope, a good way down from the inexplicable pillar that blocked the view from some seats. She concentrated on Shearer's hair; that red had to be natural. Just like Kelly at the Brody.

She had some time before she went over to Matthew's apartment. She looked down the street and thought, I have enough clothes, I don't want to look at any more. The Strand is too far away, I'll go tomorrow. She went into a drugstore and strolled to the L'Oréal shelf. Almost time to touch up her roots. She put her hand on the box and paused. It was just hair. Hair grows. Why not try something different.

When she arrived at Matthew's place she put her bag on his counter and he pointed to the Duane Reade logo. "Not getting sick, are you?" She pulled the box out of the bag and showed him.

"Light Auburn?" he asked, as though the box said "Turquoise."

"Change of pace," she said. He was reading the back of the box. "Besides, I've got redhead-type skin. I even get freckles sometimes."

"It says here," he said, "that if you put this over blonde you'll get Bright Light Auburn. You want bright red hair?"

"I'm young and it's good to experiment, don't you think?"

"I think I like it the way it is," he said, and slipped the box back into the bag.

He didn't ask about where she'd gone the night she stood him up, and despite his expectant looks over dinner, she didn't offer. He was trying to teach her to play chess. Or, rather, she already knew how to play chess; Matthew was trying to teach her how not to be terrible at it. Some way into their first game she shifted her castle. He contemplated the board for a moment, then said, "Are you sure you want to do that?"

Uh-oh. "That means I shouldn't?" He was looking at the piece as though it had insulted him. She said, "If I don't move it, your pawn is going to take it." More silence. "I don't want you to take my castle. It's my favorite."

That got his eyes on her. "It's called a rook. Why is it your favorite?"

"It's the prettiest one."

"See here, Greta Garbo. Sentiment has no place in chess. Look, I'll show you. Now I move my bishop. And then you get your knight out of the way, because you like those too—no, don't deny it—and then what happens?" She looked hard at the board. "What have you left open now?"

"My rook," she said. Rook, not castle. I can do this.

"Sod your rook. Look again."

She got it. "My queen."

"Correct." He put the pieces back, including her rook. "Try again. I'm giving you this one."

This game wasn't nearly as reasonable as he'd made it out to be. "How the hell am I supposed to know what's going to happen two or three moves out?"

"You're supposed to conjecture. It's strategy." She didn't have the slightest idea what she should do now. She glared at her queen, who was forcing her to sacrifice her pretty rook, and she heard Matthew say, "It's not a bad way to approach life in general, you know. Trying to think ahead."

Tuesday, after a second look at her list of ways to figure out the Reifsnyder question, she went to the Strand. She was halfway to the movie section when she stopped to reconsider, and a leather-clad, shaven-head kid with a backpack almost collided with her as he stalked to the "Sell Your Books" desk. She shifted out of the way, then walked to the "review copies" table. Twenty minutes later she walked out with a half-price copy of *Money*, by some English writer named Martin Amis. She'd spotted the paperback on Matthew's desk and taken a look, because the cover had film rolls on it. Matthew said she shouldn't borrow *Money* unless she understood that it was definitely not her kind of movie the characters were making. She started it that night and had to underline the slang she didn't know, so she would remember to ask when he got back.

Wednesday morning she went down to the bodega and bought a *Voice*. She spent lunch hour looking at the Help Wanted ads. If she wanted to take the *Waterloo Bridge* career path she was all set. The other ads, the legitimate ones—what did "front office appearance" mean? She didn't know, but she suspected she didn't have it. And why did so many places want a degree? Did she need college to answer the phones at a magazine?

Thursday, the day after Matthew left, she realized as she drank her coffee that she didn't want to go to the library. She didn't want to pore through a movie book or try to call anyone. She didn't want to do anything.

She'd told Jim and Matthew that she wanted to make sure *Mysteries* survived for the sake of the people who made it. She said she wanted to bring back a bit of Emil for Miriam. It wasn't true, or at least it was only partly true. She wanted to see the movie. But how could she know if it was any good? What was so special about this film, when you got right down to it? No one knew anymore if it had been something great, or "quite dreadful," in the words of Lucile Pierrepoint. Even Miriam said she wasn't sure. No one knew if Emil had talent, or if he was just another German with a bad attitude. And a drinking problem. Don't forget that.

She took her notes and stacked them neatly on top of her bookshelf. She spent Monday and Tuesday reading *Money*. It was funny, and mean, but it was also extremely strange to name a main character John Self, and have her thinking for a couple of hundred pages that this was obviously a self-portrait, and then have the writer put himself in the book, with his own name. Martin Amis, right there. She made some more notes in the margins.

Thursday night she came home and was walking toward her room when Talmadge intoned, "Doesn't she remind you of somebody? Somebody we used to know?"

"Vaguely. Such a long time ago, very long ago and far away, and we were all so young and innocent." Jim had the back of his hand to his forehead.

"I've got it, that little blonde we used to live with. Such a sweet young thing. Whatever became of her?"

They were standing next to each other, like a vaudeville act. "My dear, didn't you hear?" said Jim. "She became involved with"—a big pause, then a stage whisper—"a foreigner."

"No! Please tell me—he wasn't—he couldn't be—English, could he?"

"He was. And what happened, it breaks the heart. He imprisoned her in the Tower. And that's where she must live, to this day. She has to stand by the case and when the royal family wants to wear something, she says 'May I help you?'"

"OH MY GOD."

"And that's not the worst of it. They're forcing her to help them with the *costume* Crown Jewels."

"Do you two bozos want to see a movie?" interjected Ceinwen. "Like, in a theater?"

Talmadge came up close and pointed at her, like Bela Lugosi. "From . . . what . . . year?"

"This year, silly. Let's see what's playing."

Jim staggered. "Who are you? What have you done with Ceinwen?"

She wasn't going to see Freddie Krueger, she couldn't go that far. But she wasn't going to see *Radio Days*, either, even though she liked Woody Allen. It was set in the 1940s, and when Ceinwen wanted the 1940s on film, she went straight to the source. She talked them into *Angel Heart*, which wasn't that hard; Jim confessed to having a thing for Mickey Rourke. *Angel Heart*, it turned out, was set in the 1950s, but at least she'd tried. She attempted to argue them into liking it, though she hadn't much liked it herself. They were all in bed by 1:00 a.m.

When the phone began to ring, she tried to look at the clock, but knocked it over. She made her way into the living room as she heard Matthew's voice on the machine saying, "Ceinwen, are you there?"

She picked up the receiver. "Matthew?" The overhead light blazed on. Talmadge was wearing boxers and a T-shirt and scowling at her.

"I'm terribly sorry," Matthew was saying, "did I wake you?"

"Oh please, you know you did." She'd been so miserable all week, and suddenly she knew that all she'd needed was his accent, his voice. Not just Talmadge imitating it.

"Tell him," announced Talmadge, "he can't be much of a mathematician if he can't add up the time difference from the West Coast. Shit, even I can do that."

"Is that Talmadge?"

"Yes, he's just going back to bed. Give me a minute."

She waved good-night. Talmadge began to slouch out of the room and paused at the entrance. "Light on, or off?"

"Off, please."

"Kinky." He switched it off and when he was safely back behind his screens, she pulled the phone into her room, slid down to the bed and put her mouth close to the receiver. "What on earth were you thinking? Poor Talmadge."

"I was thinking you might want to know what the weather was like today here in southern California."

He called to flirt? The timing was weird, but he must miss her, too. She played along. "I'm assuming it was sunny."

"Correct. Sunny. About 24—that's 75 in your money, I suppose. Low humidity, no clouds. And I had the morning off."

"I'm happy for you, sugar," she drawled.

"Are you, *honey*. Perhaps you'd like to know how I spent my one morning's holiday in warm, sunny, dry Los Angeles."

She yawned. "I hope you wore sunblock."

"Oddly enough, there is very little direct sunlight in the archives of the *L.A. Times*."

"Matthew!" She cringed at how loud that came out and went to shut the door. "You were looking up something?"

"Yes."

"Something for me?" It was a second chance at Christmas.

"Yes again."

He wanted her to ask, and he had more patience than she did. "Who, what?"

"Norman Stallings."

She fell flat on her back with a bounce, and spoke without caring what was in her voice. "You're wonderful. Did you find anything?"

"I did. I'm so wonderful, I even made a copy."

"He's alive?"

"Since you're basically an optimist, let's say yes. I found an article from 1984."

"What did it say?" she demanded, then suddenly felt remorse. "This could get expensive. Do you want to tell me when you get back?"

"I do not. I want to drag you out of bed in the wee hours and force you to listen to the entire story. It's called revenge. And it's worth the charges." She heard some papers rustling. "It's about Norman's career as an assistant director. 'In many far-flung corners of the country there live people whose Hollywood ties go back decades, to a more romantic and glittering time. Their names were never in lights, they never won the Oscars, but they were the people who kept the star machine spinning. One such veteran lives alone in a vast New York apartment, his neighbors passing him every day without realizing the memories he cherishes. His name is Norman Stallings. In the days before sound—'"

"I can't believe it! It's him!"

"Since you want to pause here anyway, I have something to say. I know you have a low opinion of the London press. But if you think they'd run this swill in the *Guardian* . . ."

"He's in New York!"

"If he's alive, yes, probably. The article's dated—"

"But he must be," she said, talking over him. "Miriam told me she plays mah-jongg with some old friends uptown. I bet you anything that's Norman."

"It's certainly possible, although it could be—"

"She told me somebody wrote an article about a friend of hers and she didn't like it. I guess she thought it made him out to be sad or something. This was it. Don't you think?" No response. "Matthew?"

"Mm. Still here. If you'll let me finish."

"I'll shut up now."

More rustling. "What was I saying?"

"Swill."

"Right. Anyway, nothing about Arnheim and very little about silents, but he worked for some of your old friends. Lubitsch, Wellman, someone named Bor-zhayj—"

"That's Borzage." Silence again. "I'm sorry. Keep going."

"Bor-ZAY-gy, then. After I made a copy, I had the bright idea of going up to reception and asking if the reporter still worked there. You wouldn't think he would be, writing that sort of prose, but he was and they let me see him."

"Doorstepping," she said, giddy.

He grunted. "I suppose. I don't think it counts if you're doing it to a reporter. He was friendly enough until I showed him the article and then he put his head in his hands. I thought it must be remorse over all those clichés in one article, but no, he said a few days after it ran 'some old bat'— that was his phrase—some old bat rang him up and shouted at him for half an hour. Said she was a friend of Norman's and he should be ashamed of himself, making Norman out to be a pathetic old relic like that. Told him he had no respect for his elders, wanted to know if his mother knew he was out in the streets of New York exploiting people . . ."

She couldn't help interrupting again. "Miriam."

"Most likely, although he didn't remember the name and he wasn't sure she bothered to state it. He said 'Good morning, *Los Angeles Times*' and it was off to the races. I asked him how he happened to write this and he said he'd spent a holiday at his uncle's apartment on Park Avenue up in the seventies and got acquainted with Norman. He was a lowly assistant trying to write features, so he interviewed Norman, and when he returned, they took it. Why, I can't imagine. You heard the beginning and the whole thing's like that. 'In 1932 he met the great Ernst Lubitsch, then and now a byword for sophistication . . .'"

"Park Avenue. In the seventies. Which Street exactly?"

"Unfortunately, I overplayed my hand, because I asked the same thing and he started to get suspicious and wanted to know why I was asking about this article. I'd introduced myself by saying I was trying to track down an old friend and I repeated that, and he suddenly seemed to think I was working for the lady who'd called him. Refused to say another word. Told me it would be unethical."

"That's all right, I can check the phone book." She turned the clock over. It was past 3:00 a.m.

"In any event, Miriam has her revenge. They promoted him, but he's reporting on the bond market." She stared at the door to her bedroom and wondered whether she could grab the Manhattan White Pages from the living room without waking up Talmadge again. "You're not saying anything. Are we happy?"

"You don't know how happy. Thank you." She inhaled and decided there was no point in holding back. "I know you didn't want to be doing this while you're working. What made you change your mind?"

A pause. "I have a feeling Norman may be definitive."

Somehow that didn't sound right. "Definitive?"

"You told me an assistant director knows everything. And we know he was at Emil's house. So if he knows the studio people took the print, well, that's that."

She'd been standing on top of the Ziegfeld Follies staircase, ready to strut like Lana Turner. And now she was bumping all the way down, smack on her derriere. "Yeah. That would be that."

"Ceinwen?" He was trying to get her to give up. Knowing she'd been thinking the same thing for days only made it worse. "Is something wrong?"

"Are you rooting for me to fail here?"

"I'm not rooting—that means something else in some parts of the world, by the way—"

"Like what?"

"All I'm *rooting* for is a final answer, because 'we'll never know' is never going to satisfy you." Obsessive. He was calling her obsessive again. "Ceinwen." Gently. "I'm not saying that's a bad thing. Not being content with a question mark. It isn't bad at all." He waited, then, "It's a scientific sort of attitude, in fact."

"Thank you. I think so too." She felt herself relax a bit. He'd been out there in Los Angeles doing something for her, not Anna. He didn't spend his only morning researching the causes of the Great Depression, or whatever it was you did to help out an economist. "I always thought we're alike in a lot of ways," she said.

"Maaay-be." He thought that was funny. Well, let him. "I don't think I have quite the same obsession with lost causes."

That word. He'd used it. "That's because you're not Irish."

"So you keep reminding me. Not my fault, is it? God, it really is late. Go to bed. No, wait—promise me you won't call this old geezer tonight if you find his number."

"I'm not even going to look for it until this morning."

"Of course you won't. What was I thinking? Good night."

"Wait, I wanted to ask you something." She grabbed the book beside her bed and opened it to the first dog-ear. "What's spunk?"

"*What?*"

"I'm reading *Money* . . ."

2.

OF COURSE NORMAN WASN'T IN THE PHONE BOOK. WHEN HE RETURNED, before he'd even shown her the article, Matthew demanded to know how she planned to go about about her search. Ceinwen told him she planned to divide the blocks of Park Avenue in the seventies into sections, go into each lobby and ask to deliver a letter for Norman Stallings, then see what they said. She was expecting him to tell her this wasn't the way to do it, but instead he said, "That sounds like a nice methodical approach."

His approval was so unexpected she was reluctant to abandon the plan, but she'd spent all day Monday going door to door, and now it was Tuesday, and she was going on her eighteenth building, and she had realized that while Park Avenue doormen and concierges might not be universally un-friendly—some of them were almost charming—they were universally sus-picious. There's no one here by that name, Miss, ah, Miss . . . Reilly? What makes you think Mr. Stallings is in this building, Miss Reilly? "I must have written it down wrong." Nobody looked satisfied with that. She'd taken to crisscrossing up and down the blocks, not letting anyone see her go straight from one door to the next, so they wouldn't think she was . . . whatever they thought she was doing. Dunning Norman, maybe. Serving a subpoena.

The supply of Park Avenue buildings had to end at some point, but progress was slow, and she was tired. She was also afraid that maybe the doormen all had coffee together someplace, and if they started swapping notes about the crazy blonde looking for some dude named Norman Stallings, she might walk in to discover they had two men from Bellevue waiting with a butterfly net.

She stood on the corner and tried to rearrange her thoughts. Maybe being methodical like Matthew was the wrong approach. Maybe she needed to treat this the way she treated everything else, by pretending it was a movie. The camera told you which building would be the important one, no matter where it was in the frame. She imagined herself as Delgado. No, Emil.

Pan left. She turned downtown. A dog walker with about a half-dozen animals on leashes nearly trampled her in a storm of fur and yapping. She stepped closer to the curb and re-focused. Pan right.

That was the one to try. The dark-brown brick, with the Deco entrance and the black-and-gold awning. That was the place to hole up with your romantic, glittering Hollywood memories.

The uniformed doorman waved her in and she strode to the concierge. "I have an envelope here for Mr. Norman Stallings."

"All right. I'll ring him."

No time for celebration. This was supposed to be a delivery, not a meeting. The meeting was supposed to come later, after he'd read the letter.

"You don't have to do that. I want to leave this for him."

The man paused, hand on his phone. "This is a delivery, am I right?"

"Yes, but—"

He spoke slowly. "When we get a delivery, and the tenant is home, we tell them it's here. Do you have something for him to sign?"

"No, this is a personal delivery."

"Then if he wants to accept it, he can do that in person." Was he looking at her scarf? "As long as you're sure he wants it."

"I don't think he doesn't want it." She wasn't making sense even to herself.

"Good. We're on the same page." He dialed. She closed her eyes and heard him say, "Morning, Mr. Stallings. Young lady in the lobby with an envelope she wants to give you . . .Yes." She opened her eyes and found him looking her over. "Yes. Very . . . I'll have her wait." He hung up and gestured toward the waiting area. "Have a seat."

She sat on the edge of an ultrasuede loveseat, trying to look as though she'd stopped by on her way to Henri Bendel. A middle-aged man in the most beautiful black coat she'd ever seen emerged from an elevator and stopped at the desk. His watch shone and so did his briefcase. She contemplated the place where his coat hem hit his calf, thinking it must be tailored. Usually men wore their coats—

"Good morning. I understand you have a delivery for me." The voice vibrated around her ears and bounced off the painting behind her. A slender old man with white hair the same length as Matthew's was standing in front of her. She hadn't heard the second elevator or anything else.

"Yes," she almost whispered, and handed it over. He took it with one hand without looking at what she'd written. Then, "Pardon me," he said, and edged past her to a chair. He pulled up his pants slightly as he sat, and seemed to be shifting his back into a comfortable slouch. Then he eyed her position on the loveseat and scooted up, until he was perched the same way she was. He slid his rimless glasses to the edge of his nose and stretched his arm until the envelope was several feet from his face.

"Norman Stallings," he read. "Check." He looked back at her face, then at her scarf. Did that mean it did look like Hermes, or that it didn't? "Park Avenue," he continued. "Hm. A little vague, but check." He flipped over the envelope. "By hand. Check." He held it up next to his ear and rattled the contents slightly. "I don't suppose this *is* a check, by any chance?"

"N-no," she stammered.

"*Dommage,*" said Norman. "But since this is *By—Hand*"—he pointed to the words one by one, and she instantly felt that writing them was the gauchest thing she'd ever done—"I had better read it now. Are you authorized to await a reply?"

There wasn't anything else she could do. "Sure," she said.

He took a Swiss army knife out of his pocket, sliced across the narrow end of the envelope, and unfolded the paper with a crisp little snap. "This is your letter?" She nodded. "You write a very nice hand."

"Thank you."

She watched Norman read until he glanced over the edge, met her eyes and waggled his eyebrows at her. She stared at the concierge, until he met her eyes too. After that, she looked at the plants.

Norman folded the letter as before and slid it into the envelope. "Emil Arnheim," he said, precisely as she thought a German would say it. He leaned forward—his knees cracked, he didn't seem as spry as Miriam—and dangled the envelope by a corner, letting it swing back and forth. "Miss Seenwhen—am I pronouncing that properly?"

"KINE-wen."

"Ceinwen. When I got up this morning, I had the oddest feeling, and then I dropped a fork on the floor. My late mother—she's been dead for forty years, so I suppose that makes her unpardonably late—she always said dropping a fork meant we'd have a visitor. So I thought maybe the cleaners would be delivering a day early. Not in my wildest did I picture a fetching blonde come to give me a handwritten letter asking about Emil Arnheim." He shoved his glasses back up his nose and slid the letter into his shirt pocket. "Isn't life marvelous. I'm expecting dress shirts, and I get an O. Henry story. By hand. Do you know O. Henry?"

Her mind flailed, then broke the surface with "'The Gift of the Magi'?"

"Excellent. But that's not it. In the one I'm trying to recall, a strange woman thrusts a hot buttered roll in a man's hand and utters one word, 'parallelogram.' Does that ring a bell? No? In any event, I think we know what William Sydney Porter would have said. He'd have said, take the hot buttered roll. Tell the young woman, by all means, come upstairs and let us discuss my old friend Emil." He eased himself to his feet with somewhat more trouble than he'd had sitting down. Granana always did say old people weren't designed to get off the couch.

"Are you sure?" she asked, dazed.

He swayed slightly as he finished pulling himself upright, and when fully straight he looked down at her. "Are you armed?"

"Am I what now?"

"Armed. Switchblade. Revolver. Hand grenade. Armed."

"No," she managed.

"Then yes. I'm sure."

They took the elevator to the tenth floor, and he asked her about the accent. "Mississippi," she told him. "Where are you from?"

"New Jersey."

"*New Jersey?*" she asked, then realized how rude it sounded. But all he said was, "Princeton."

When they entered his apartment, she paused at the entrance and had to force herself to walk in as though it were exactly what she'd been expecting. She felt as though she'd spent most of the past six months in apartments that were better than hers—Harry, Miriam, Paru, Steve, Matthew, even Andy if you could look past the paper, which maybe you couldn't. But this was the limit, the biggest living room she had ever seen, decorated in a style that was almost aggressively masculine—brown, beige, leather, shiny black tables. In a corner a TV set was blaring CNN. Norman picked up a remote control and clicked it off.

"Make yourself at home," said Norman. "I won't be a minute."

She took off her coat, draped it across one end of the sofa and sank into it. Leather was awfully cold. She craned her neck around the room. There was a large, somewhat abstract painting of what seemed to be a biplane crashing into a field. She didn't want to look at that. On another wall was an arrangement of black-and-white pictures, but it was too far away for her to see what they were. She waited a while, wondering if Norman had gone into the bedroom and fallen asleep, which Granana had been known to do when she said she wouldn't be a minute. She stood up and walked to the pictures. Norman and another smaller, stouter man, having drinks, lounging on beaches, posing in front of the Fountain of Trevi. In the center of the arrangement was a photograph of a field with something happening in the distance. She looked closer. The something was a horse in mid-canter, and a man's backside, high up in the air next to it, about to crash to the ground.

"Which one are you looking at, the middle?" Norman was setting a silver tray on the coffee table.

"Um, yes. Who is this?"

"That's me," he said. "I used to ride."

She walked back and sat down. "Do you have other pictures from your riding?"

"What's wrong with that one?"

"Nothing," she said hastily. "It's just that it's hard to tell it's you."

"Anybody can have their picture taken *on* a horse," he said. The tray had a crystal pitcher of what looked like lemonade, two cut-glass goblets, cloth napkins, sterling-silver forks, gilt-edged china plates, and an unfrosted loaf cake.

"You don't have to go to all this trouble," she protested.

"Oh, but I do. It's our mutual friend's training." She shook her head in bewilderment—did he mean Miriam? "Emil," he said. He picked up a silver-handled knife, cut off a good two inches of cake, and slid it onto a plate. "Emil always said if you had champagne and a dozen eggs in the house, you could entertain anyone at a moment's notice." He handed her a napkin and a fork. "It's a little early for champagne. I'm not quite that louche anymore." He poured out a glass for her. "So lemonade it is." He gave her the plate. "And Emil never said I couldn't put the eggs in a cake."

He served himself and she tasted the cake. It seemed to be made almost entirely of butter. It was delicious.

"Are you settled?" She nodded because her mouth was full. "Excellent. While you're occupied, I wonder if I should refer back to the letter. It was so well done."

She swallowed. "Thank you."

"Perhaps that won't be necessary, though. The idea was simple enough. You heard about Emil through Miriam."

"Yes. Did she ever mention me?"

"Afraid not," he said.

It was absurd to feel so disappointed. And worse to have it show, because he said, "You mustn't think that means anything. Miriam never mentions anyone. Did she mention me, aside from the movie? For instance, that I'm still alive?"

"No," she admitted.

"And there you are. So you live in her building."

"One flight up."

"I'm sorry. What a catastrophe that place is. The noise! The last time I was there, someone was out in the hallway having an absolutely deafening argument about beer."

"You've been there?" She was sure she'd never seen him before. "When was that?"

"1973, must have been. Miriam invited Ira and me to watch her gloat over the Watergate hearings. When Ira died—Ira was my roommate." He paused.

"I understand," she said.

"Oh, good. Young people do. Yes, when Ira died I asked Miriam to move in. Logical, yes? This place is a stadium. Everything is at least fifty feet from everything else. Suppose I slip in the bathtub one day and break my—hm. What I can I break in the bath?"

Did he want her to answer that? It seemed he did. "Your hip?"

"Perfect, a hip. I break my hip and agony renders me helpless, and if Miriam were here, she could hear my cries and call the hospital. If we managed to stay healthy we could bake together and play mah-jongg. But she wouldn't hear of it."

"She's very independent," said Ceinwen.

"That, plus she's convinced this building is full of Republicans. She doesn't care that Republicans are *quiet*. So, because Miriam's as far left as she ever was, if I shatter my hip I'll have to make my own pain-wracked way to the telephone. And if that happens, I hope the guilt causes her many a sleepless night. But it won't." He sipped his lemonade. "So you live one floor above her, and you somehow parlayed this into an acquaintance deep enough to hear about *The Mysteries of Udolpho*."

This was evidently another question. "We just got to talking one night," she said.

"I rather doubt that. Miriam doesn't just get to talking with anyone. When she's really in a mood I can barely manage to find out whether or not she wants coffee. And yet you got all of 1928 and most of '29 out of her. Are you sure you're not a reporter?"

"No," she said firmly. "I'm someone who feels that film is an important part of our legacy as American citizens."

He nodded solemnly. "Something to reflect upon the next time I watch *Cobra Woman*. I believe I'll consult your letter again, after all." He adjusted his glasses and read. "'Miriam was reluctant to talk about certain details, and I didn't want to press her. But I think our project would be a fine tribute to Mr. Arnheim's talent, and a way to keep his memory alive. Still, it is probably best not to inform Miriam until such time as our work has a more definite shape.' That's sensitively put. Let me see if I understand. I'm not to tell Miriam until you can present her with a *fait accompli*, because otherwise she's quite likely to strangle us both with her bare hands."

"That's about the size of it," said Ceinwen.

"The wrath of Miriam. No light matter." He took another bite of cake and contemplated the chandelier. "Still, I'm not rejecting the idea out of hand. Miriam . . ." He laid down his fork and his voice took on a gentler tone. "Ah, well. Miriam blamed many people and many things for Emil. And the movie she blamed most of all. But I was very fond of Emil too, you see. All my life my friends have usually been women and . . . my own kind, you could say. Emil was an exception." He patted the letter in his shirt pocket. "Once Miriam and I are gone, it'll be almost as though he were never here. That doesn't bother her, the little Marxist. But it bothers me." He sat up and folded his hands. "All right. I'll answer whatever you like, as long as it's off the record. No, not merely off the record, I can't have Miriam in a state. Deep background. That's the ticket."

She had no idea what deep background was, but she said, "Sounds good." He beamed at her. She scrambled in her bag for a notebook and came up with her address book. She poised her pen over the blank XYZ section and said, "First, I'd like to ask about the atmosphere during filming."

"Tense," he said promptly, as though firing off the answer to an exam question. "The atmosphere? Really? This is deep background, you know. You don't have to be nearly that boring. Why not ask me if I slept with Emil?"

She felt her entire chest flare red as she said, stammering like Fred, "Um, okay, sure. Did you?"

"Of course not. He was in love with Miriam. I didn't sleep with her, either."

"Was that an option?" she asked, stunned.

"No, it wasn't. I tried to propose it one year. Don't remember which one, but it was still the Depression and we were hard up for recreation. She told me to find a hobby."

"That's good to know," she said, battling the sense that she had lost her grip on the conversation and possibly her entire day. "Sort of adds texture. But I really had in mind more the professional interactions, because it's more relevant to the movie."

"Professional," he repeated, sounding almost disapproving. "For example?"

"For example, how was it to work with Emil, if the atmosphere was tense?"

"Emil was fine. It was everyone else who made things difficult."

"How did they do that?"

"By not doing what Emil wanted them to do."

Now that she finally had him talking about the movie, he had turned into Mr. Brevity. "You were on Emil's side?"

"Certainly. Emil cared a great deal more than they did. Miriam cared, too, but it was only because of Emil."

"They didn't care how the movie turned out?" That would explain the level of interest she'd encountered so far.

"Not ex-actly." He sat back and crossed his legs, and she realized who he'd been reminding her of. William F. Buckley. Same accent. Almost the same vocabulary. "You have to understand the sort of place Civitas was. It wasn't one of the big studios. The budgets were strict and so were the schedules. A factory. And that was the approach they were accustomed to. They didn't want a bad product, but they didn't see why they needed to fuss more over this one."

"But I thought this was Frank Gregory's prestige picture."

"Gregory." It was the first sound of venom in his voice. "He thought prestige meant a literary property and a larger budget. He couldn't wrap his flat little head around the notion that prestige comes from making a bloody effort." He sniffed. "He was such a crass individual. Before Emil arrived I overheard him saying that if Paramount and Fox were importing Germans he figured he should, too."

"Was he joking?"

"No. Gregory did not joke. He was anti-humor. In the sense of anti-matter, or the antichrist."

She decided to take a chance. "Lucile Pierrepoint thought he was wonderful."

"How do you know?" His brows snapped together and his eyes narrowed.

"I wrote to ask her about the movie."

"How creative," he responded, his face relaxing. "So few people would think to contact the studio secretary."

"We're trying"—she made a note, to show him this was important—"to get a sense of how everyone is affected when a film is lost."

"Poignant," he chirped. "Since this is deep background, I'll be blunt. Lucy was Frank Gregory's mistress from her first day of work to the day he died. The rest of the world saw a pockmarked gargoyle with the soul of an abacus. Lucy saw Sir Galahad." He rolled his eyes. "You know how some women get about men they can't have."

"I bet Miriam never did," she said, feeling somehow that her gender was being maligned.

"No, Miriam had the opposite problem. How to get rid of them. Before her first day Emil showed me a picture and I thought ho-hum, another good-looking girl, never seen *that* before at a movie studio." He waved his arm. "Then she walked on the set and the lighting men nearly fell out of the flies trying to get a better look. Lovely as she was on camera, in person she was not to be believed. The legs were good, but she didn't have a figure—that was Lucy's department. Miriam was shaped like a yardstick. But that face! The camera could only capture about half of it." He chuckled. "Edward Kenny was standing right next to me, and I thought he was going to have a stroke."

That was a surprise. "She told me Edward Kenny was mean to her."

He laughed louder. "Of course he was mean to her! He was hell-bent on deflowering her. And then Emil, who was older, not a star and not as handsome, got there first. Eddie was absolutely beside himself. He never forgave either one of them."

"How did you get to be friends with Emil?"

"Oh, I liked him right away. He'd asked for me, because he'd heard I could speak German. My mother was German. From Hamburg. He could speak to me and get things off his chest about whatever was going on that he didn't like, and he rarely liked anything. Trouble was, people assume that if you're speaking a foreign language you're talking about them. In hindsight all that Deutsch-ing away didn't enhance our popularity. But we had tastes and opinions in common. I'd been working for hacks before, mostly. That was the Civitas specialty, hacks. I liked Emil for having some vision. He could *see*."

She might as well jump ahead. "Miriam said she only saw the movie once, at that preview."

"Yes, she refused to go again. Me, I saw both versions. I looked at the last cut before the preview, but I didn't go to the preview and I still think that was a good choice. Not a pretty scene, from what I heard. Then Emil cut it, and Gregory cut it again, and afterward I saw it twice. Place was maybe a third full the first time. Second time, not that much later, there were maybe five people besides Emil and me."

"You went with him?" Norman nodded. "What did he think?"

"He was devastated," said Norman. "I shouldn't have gone. But it was his idea. Called me one night, he'd already had a few. Said let's go down to the Rialto and see it. I knew it was a terrible idea, but then he said he'd go by himself and I knew that was the worst idea possible. And then I had to sit next to him. They'd taken out a little more than ten minutes."

"About a reel." She made a note and saw that Norman approved.

"Yes, that's right. The lady knows. Not that much in terms of time, but in terms of the screen, they'd butchered it. Rearranged a lot of his scenes, went back and inserted things he'd discarded. Took out everything that didn't advance the plot, and the trouble was that the plot was one damn thing after another."

She put her fork down, her appetite gone. "It was bad."

"Now now, child, I didn't say that. It was a still a handsome picture. But the first cut was better. It was good, a good movie. And I stayed in the picture business right up to the war, and I know what's good and what's not. The trouble wasn't that the first cut was bad, whatever they thought of it in Pomona. The trouble was that it was *strange*. He took this old Gothic novel and made a movie that was permeated with sex. Von Stroheim had nothing on Emil. This was almost two hours of everybody in the world trying to, excuse me, trying to fuck one virgin. The villain, the hero, the rejected suitor, he also implied it about her female companion and the *maid*."

She smiled. "That was how Miriam saw it."

"Yes, although I bet she didn't put it that way."

It was time to edge up to what she needed to know. "Did anybody from the movie come around to pay their respects the day after he died?"

He put his hand on his chin and let his index finger rest on his cheekbone. Then he said, slowly, "Why would they do that?"

"It's what people do," she said, huffily. Why couldn't he cooperate? "Back home people would have brought Miriam a casserole or something."

"A casserole!" he exclaimed, as though she'd just handed him one. "For an actress who'd been living in sin with a foreigner who was twice her age. Mississippi has gotten so progressive. I'm delighted."

"The woman's gotta eat," she muttered. She picked off a crumb stuck to her lipstick and was completely off guard when Norman said, "Let's get back to that in a minute. After you've told me what this is really about."

She swallowed the dregs of her lemonade so she could speak. She didn't want to look Norman in the eye, so she addressed his top button.

"As I said. I'm working on a project about lost films." She tried to continue and he cut her off.

"No, no, no. You're good at asking questions. Southerners can be so nosy and still sound polite. But when someone asks you a question . . . all right, you're not entirely hopeless. But you're close."

"I don't understand what you're asking," she said, with no conviction at all.

"I think you do. I should tell you, I have some experience here. During the war—that would be the Second World War, of course, I had nothing to do with the others—I worked for Army Intelligence, because of my German. Also French. And at the time my Russian was all right too, although it's rusty now."

She was flabbergasted. "You were in Army Intelligence? *How?*"

"I joined the Army," he said, patiently. "There was a war on. Seemed like the thing to do."

"Yes, but . . . doesn't the Army . . . as a general rule . . . sort of . . . frown on . . ." She couldn't finish the sentence.

"Aha. I see where you are now. Yes, they do." He dropped his voice to a deep, macho rumble. "But, if you think about it, *who better to keep secrets?*" He gave her a huge grin. She smiled back. "As I was saying. They put me to work translating, and after Normandy they sent me over to interrogate prisoners of war. And here's my point. The ordinary soldiers, the enlisted men, they always tried to hold out. But if we captured an officer, that was a different matter. I'd walk in and he'd ask me for a cigarette. Once he got a light he'd say, 'What do you want to know?' The men in charge, you see, they knew it was all over." He waited, then said, "Wouldn't you rather be an officer?" She decided another bite of cake might buy her some time. He leaned forward. "Would you like a cigarette, too?"

"Yes, thank you," she said. He brought a glass ashtray, a brass table lighter and a pack of filterless Pall Malls. She lit up, eyed him and said, "What do you want to know?"

"I'd like to know what you're doing here."

She tapped her tongue with her fingertip to get a piece of tobacco off, like she'd seen Bette Davis do, and said, "I'm trying to find the film."

"What on earth makes you think you can do that?"

He sounded as though she'd told him she was trying out for the Olympic discus team. She let her annoyance show for the first time. "First off," she said, "as far as I know I got ahold of every last person who's still alive and had anything to do with the movie. And I don't think a single one of you folks ever looked for it. Did *you?*"

He stroked his chin. "No."

"Exactly. Second of all, I'm trying to find Emil's print. Miriam saw it there in his house the day he died and then it vanished. It must have gone *somewhere.*"

He dropped his hand and stared at her. "Emil's print?"

"The one he kept in his house," she said, still impatient.

"Emil kept a print? Miriam told you that?"

She nodded. Norman was shaking with laughter.

"You didn't know? She didn't tell you?"

"No, she did not. Not at any point in all these years. And yet she told you. What an impossible woman she is." He gasped a minute, and continued. "But I have to say, you're quite something yourself."

She wasn't crazy about being laughed at, but at least she wasn't having to beat around the bush anymore. "Look, you were at his house the day after he died. Miriam said he had the print in his bedroom, she saw it there. Did you go in the bedroom?"

His laughter was tapering off into a hiccuping sound. Finally he got ahold of himself and said, "Oh god. I can't remember. I'm so sorry, child." He gave a sigh. "It was a terrible day. One of the worst of my life. I've spent a long time not thinking about it."

"I'm sorry," she said, "I'm trying to—"

"Find the film, yes, I understand. It's a good cause. You're out of your mind, but it's a good cause. Let me see." He put his hand over his eyes, like a psychic at a sideshow. "I got a call at maybe 6:00 a.m. from somebody at the studio to say that they'd found Emil. And I went right over to Miriam, because I knew nobody else would. And we went to his house, and you never saw anything like it. Only a couple of reporters at the edge of the lawn—Emil wasn't a big shot and there was no mystery to how he died. But my god, it was a circus. A circus of worms. Every single peon from the studio, carrying things out like it was a rummage sale. I know he owed Civitas money, but there's such a thing as decorum. I think there were studio people at the house before his body even reached the funeral home."

"So people were taking things out."

"Yes, and if I remembered someone carrying a film I'd tell you, but I'm afraid I don't. I just remember Miriam. By the time we got there, there were other creditors besides the studio, including his bootlegger, if I recall. They're tossing things around and arguing, and Miriam never looked one of them in the face. They would take books or a painting out into the hall and leave to fetch something else, and she would put the things back without a word." He shuddered. "They even took out a desk. It was Empire, I believe."

"What were you doing, helping her?"

"No, I went into his office to argue with Lucy Pierrepoint. What a piece of work she was. And she hated Miriam. I'm telling Lucy that Emil's papers could have something important and she said, 'Why yes, Norman. That's why I'm examining them.' And I said, 'Not important for the studio, you bitch, important for the people who actually gave a damn about Emil.' And instead of getting all prissy about my language, she looked at me and said 'I think you'll find the other one of those people out in the foyer. Why don't you go keep her company.'"

It was worse than she had imagined. The warmth and humor in Norman's face were gone. "Waste. Such waste. He wouldn't have had to hang on that long. A year or two at most. Miriam wasn't going anywhere. By '31 I had some connections. All he had to do was spin out that Civitas contract, then I could have helped him. We'd have found something. I know Miriam says all the bosses were philistines, but that isn't true, not by a long shot. People recognized talent. And Emil stayed on time and under budget. They all appreciated that." He sighed and turned his head away. "I never did try to talk to him about the drinking. Except once, after . . ."

"After he broke his hand."

"Miriam told you that, too. My, my. Yes. He called me the next night, absolutely raving drunk. I couldn't understand a word he was saying. I went over and poured coffee into him until he was sober enough to talk. I told him to pull himself together. Frightening a woman like that, it's not *done*. He wanted me to call her, and I told him he'd have to do that himself." Norman lit a cigarette and blew the smoke away from her. "I was at a loss. All I ever did was offer him food and coffee when the evening got late."

"Miriam said he didn't talk much about himself. Not his family, not his growing up, nothing. She said he might have been Jewish, but he never even told her that."

"I know she thought so. It's possible. There always was something sub rosa about Emil. Part of our bond, perhaps." He gave her a wan smile. "Miriam told me much later she thought he'd changed his name. I could have told her that. Arnheim sounds phony, doesn't it? He liked to joke that he asked for a 'von' at the border, but they told him Stroheim and Sternberg had cleaned them out." He offered her another cigarette. "Of course, a lot of people changed their names. Like that ghastly Leon Whitman. Running around, pretending to be a set dresser. He said he did it because his real name wouldn't look good in credits, not that anyone would have put any of his names on the movie. But we all knew the reason. He was hoping no one would realize he got the job because he was Gregory's wife's cousin."

"What was his real name?" she asked. They were both trying to collect themselves, and this was as good a topic as any.

"Reifsnyder."

3.

"CHRIST. ARE WE IN CANADA?"

The street was dotted by cement planters with no plants and lined with short, plain putty-colored buildings housing 99-cent stores and cheap groceries. Matthew was determined to point out, repeatedly, that the moment they exited the subway station, they had found the precise Euclidean middle of nowhere.

Norman knew where to find Leon Reifsnyder. The man had written him a letter, out of nowhere, after Ira's obituary appeared in the *Times*. "A condolence letter, if you please," said Norman. "Full of all these 'my, that was a time we had' sort of remarks. You could say I was taken aback. When we were working on the picture, he all but called me a faggot to my face. And the last I heard of Leon, he was fighting real-estate fraud charges out in Arizona."

The letter had been written from the Cadwallader David Colden Home in Queens. She bolted to a pay phone, got the number from information, then scrambled downtown to catch Matthew's office hours so she could beg him to call. This was too important for her meager deception skills. Plus, the accent couldn't hurt, she told him.

It turned out, however, that were some instances in life where sounding like Laurence Olivier was not an asset. Matthew called, reluctantly, the home put Leon on the phone, and it soon became clear that the two men had something approaching complete mutual incomprehension. She blocked the office door with her back so students wouldn't keep barging in. As the conversation stalled Matthew sounded more Masterpiece Theatre by the minute, his volume rising until he was almost shouting into the phone.

Finally, Leon put a nurse on the line, and she explained that his hearing aid didn't work well for phone calls. They agreed to stop by on Monday for visiting hours. The journey involved two fares, subway and bus, and Matthew, who'd been to Turkey and Japan and Australia, behaved the entire time as though she'd insisted they go backpacking in the Arctic Circle.

At the bus stop, two women with high heels and high-teased hair were having a loud conversation. "I told him, I said, you were standin' right there with your hand on her ass and you're tryin' to tell me there's nothin' goin' on here? What am I, a moron or somethin'?"

"That's it right there, Lisa. He thinks you're a moron. No respect."

"No respect at ALL. So I says to him . . ."

"I wonder if everyone out here sounds like Leon," said Matthew.

"You understand them, don't you?"

"Barely. He was worse. Like something out of *Mean Streets*."

Matthew still hadn't gotten over Leon's reaction to the accent, she thought, with amusement. "That was Little Italy," she told him, to see his face get more annoyed.

They asked the bus driver to tell them when they got to the stop. The bus meandered down a highway, across a park, down rows of identical brick houses. Finally they pulled up to a stop and the driver yelled, "You getting off or what?"

The home was easy to spot, a wide, tall building in a block of single stories. They were led to the visiting room, a pink-carpeted, ammonia-smelling holding cell, furnished with stuffed, flounced, floral-fabric chairs. A fake-bamboo dining set showed the streaks of the last cleaning still smeared across the glass-top table. A big TV in the corner was switched off at the moment, and besides them, not another soul was there. The nurse told them to sit at the table because it would be easier for Leon, and Ceinwen wondered if that meant he was in a wheelchair. But a few minutes later he entered, and he had one of those canes with the four feet on the end. His shoulders were hunched, he was unevenly shaven, and he was wearing a tracksuit that smelled as though it had been worn several times in the past few days. Leon shook hands; the nurse helped him settle into a chair and left.

"Glad you two could come out," said Leon. He had a tremor in his head that made his voice shake a bit, but the accent wasn't that bad. It really was pitiful, being stuck out in a place like this.

"Not at all, it's very kind of you to meet us. I hope you aren't having as much trouble understanding me now," said Matthew.

Leon touched his hearing aid. "Nah, loud and clear. It's the phone, I tell you. Years and years I spent on the phone, makin' deals. Now I can barely use it."

"You did understand what we wanted to talk about?" Matthew was speaking louder than normal, but not by much.

"Yeah, movie days. Project for your college, right?"

"Yes. NYU."

"I only worked on three movies. Went out to Hollywood in '27 because, I, ah, had some connections. My cousin was married to Frank Gregory, ran a studio name of Civitas. Nobody's heard of it now."

"We've heard of it," Ceinwen assured him.

"Yeah, every once in a while someone has. I got a job dressin' sets. You got a room, you gotta put stuff in it to make it look lived-in, right? That's what I did. Wasn't hard so long as you didn't make too big a fuss about it. You go in, you throw around some vases and candlesticks and stuff, you're done."

Emil must have loved Leon to death.

"And that's what you did for Emil Arnheim," said Matthew.

"Yeah, except he was a pain in the neck about it. Like he was about everything." He cleared his throat with a loud, wet rumble. "Arnheim? You wanna talk about him? That's what I thought you were sayin' before, but then I figured maybe I heard wrong."

"If it isn't too much trouble," said Matthew. "We're interested in *The Mysteries of Udolpho* and what happened when he died. As long as you still remember."

"I remember fine, I'm sorry to say," said Leon. "I don't guess you mind my askin' what for? This place isn't exactly crawlin' with people wantin' to ask me about Emil Arnheim."

"We're working on an academic paper about lost films," said Matthew. "And we decided it would support our point if we focused on this one."

"Lost films." Leon ran his tongue over his teeth.

"Meaning," she said helpfully, "ones where no prints survive."

"Uh-huh. Don't think Arnheim's your man."

"Why not?" burst out Ceinwen. Matthew squared his shoulders and she knew that meant "put a sock in it."

"First off, 'cause he had no talent. His movie stiffed. Cold. You know that, right?"

Matthew's voice was rolling smoothly along before she could even inhale. "In all fairness, it's difficult to know how good it would seem now. Tastes change."

"Yeah, and crap stays crap," said Leon. "But second of all, that picture's not lost."

She held still.

"We haven't spoken to anyone who saw a print past the movie's release."

Leon wheezed. "I had one. Haven't had it for about fifteen years. But somebody's still got it."

"Who?" Ceinwen almost yelled. Under the table she felt Matthew drum his fingers on her knee. Leon pulled back in his chair and gave a phlegmy laugh.

"Nobody ever wanted to know," he said. "Well, almost nobody. Trouble is, I don't know exactly where it wound up. I can tell you why I don't have it anymore, but that's it."

She willed herself not to throw her purse across the room. With a flourish, Matthew pulled his pen and memo pad out of his pocket. "What you know is what we're here to find out," he said cheerfully. "How did you happen to get a print?"

"Long story," said Leon. "You know I worked on *Mysteries*, right? Worst seven weeks of my life. First off, you're working on the decorations, everybody figures you're queer. Even the queers. Like the assistant director. Big sissy-la-la."

"Norman Stallings?" Steady voice, she told herself. Not angry, steady. "You're saying he made a pass at you?"

Leon snorted. "Nah, he knew I'da clocked him. He kept telling me my work showed a nice delicate touch." Ceinwen failed to suppress a chuckle. Fortunately Leon took it as a show of support. "Exactly. How the hell else am I supposed to take that? And him and Arnheim, always off in a corner talkin' Kraut. I'da thought those two were an item, but Arnheim was bangin' the lead actress, even though she was young enough to be his daughter. What a set. He kept us working all hours of the day and night. But I tried to be polite, because that's how I am. I'm a *friendly* person." He paused for affirmation.

"I can tell," said Matthew.

"Arnheim couldn't. Every time I turned around he was yelling at me."

"I heard he didn't yell," protested Ceinwen.

Leon shrank a bit in his chair and his voice took on a querulous note. "Not loud. Question of the way things sound. Maybe not real yelling, but cold. Sarcastic. 'Would you be so good, Mr. Whitman . . .' 'If you're sure it isn't too much *trouble* . . .' That kinda thing."

"Maybe," said Matthew, "we should skip ahead to how you came by the print."

"Got it the day he died," said Leon. "Got a call from my cousin."

"Gregory's wife," said Ceinwen.

"Yep, Sally. Callin' to gossip, that's all. But I got to thinkin' maybe it would be worth goin' over to his house. I was already decidin' movies weren't for me, and the real money in California was real estate. So it occurs to me, it was a pretty good house. Maybe they'd have to sell it in a hurry. Worth checkin' out, anyway."

Matthew gave her another micro-glance, but she knew she shouldn't open her mouth, for fear a word like "ghoul" would pop out.

"Guess I got there before lunch and there's all these people there and I kinda wandered in and looked at the layout. Nice spread. Guess that's why the creditors were the first ones to show up. So eventually I got to his bedroom out in the back of the house. I wasn't really lookin' for anything, I was curious. I mean, the movie, it wasn't much good, but it had all kinds of, what would you call it. Where you're talking about dirty stuff but tryin' to seem like you're not."

"Innuendo," said Matthew.

"Yeah. That. Hope you don't mind my sayin' so."

"No worries. We're all worldly adults here."

Leon grinned at Ceinwen, revealing teeth that made her want to stop smoking. "Yeah. A guy who's got sex on the brain like that, who knows what his bedroom looks like, know what I mean? But it was all normal stuff. And that didn't seem right. I figured, hell, he's gotta have some whips or something in the closet. At least some magazines."

Creepy little nobodies Emil wouldn't have let past the front walk, Miriam had said.

"I opened up this big wardrobe thing he's got there. And whaddya know, there's the film. All labeled and everything, pretty as you please. And there's a coupla suitcases in there too. And I started thinkin', maybe somebody's gonna want this. I mean, the studio couldn't know he had it. Technically all the prints belonged to them. It was already stolen property, so I figured passing it along once it was hot already wasn't that big a deal. Civitas wouldn't wanna use it anyway, after the bath they took on that thing. If I knew Frank, he was still so mad, he might melt it down for the two bucks' worth of silver in the nitrate. So I took the suitcases and I loaded them all in. Jesus, they were heavy. And here's how crazy it was that day. I lugged that thing out inta the hall and nobody looked at me or said a word, except Eddie Kenny. He was walkin' in right then. I don't know what he was doing there, movie'd been over for ages and I know for a fact he hated Arnheim too. If you ask me, he was hopin' to give Arnheim's skirt a shoulder to cry on. Anyhow Eddie says, 'What have you got there, the silver service?' And I told him 'None of your goddamn business, I'm taking back somethin' that belongs to me.'"

"Did you try to do anything with it?" asked Ceinwen. Matthew shook his head at her, almost imperceptibly. But Leon was already well warmed up.

"Oh yeah. Now if I went to the studio they were gonna make me give it back just on principle, and that didn't do me any good, I'da darn near thrown my back out for nothin'. I already had an idea, see. I waited a couple of weeks and I called up the actress, Miriam her name was. And she never called me back. So I went over there one day and her mother answered the door and I said I was there to pay my condolences. And her mother takes me to the parlor and I wait and I hear 'em arguin' and then the Miriam dame shows up and she stands there. Doesn't say a thing. I told her I knew there'd been some bad blood while we making the movie, but I wanted her to know it was all water under the bridge, and it was too bad to see a man cut off in his prime like that. She says something like, 'I can't tell you what it means to see you here.' Yeah, she was almost as snooty as her boyfriend. I told her I had something of Arnheim's I thought she'd want. And she put out her hand like I was gonna give to her. And I said, no, it was a big something and it was a lot of work and so maybe, you know, for my trouble and all, she'd be willing to compensate me a little bit.

"And holy mackerel. You never saw such a change. You never heard such screamin' in your life. Starting yellin' that people like me were the reason the guy was dead. Sure thing, doll, he had *nothin'* to do with that himself. Said anything of his I touched was automatically filthy . . . no, not just filthy, what was it. Big fifty-cent word." He stuck his tongue in his cheek.

"Contaminated?" suggested Ceinwen. "Corrupt?" Matthew's jaw, clenching. One more. "Profane?"

"Profane! That was it. Anything of his I touched was filthy and profane and she couldn't stand the thought of it. What a nutcase. Huh? I ask you." He paused again for the expected agreement.

"High-strung," was Matthew's contribution.

"You can say that again. I'm tryin' to get a word in while she's screamin' her fool head off and then her mother comes in, and if you ask me the mother was even screwier, and she points her finger at the door"— Leon was trying to mime a big Victorian gesture, but his arm was trembling—"and she says I'm not welcome in their house. I tried one more time to tell them, and the girl kinda doubles over with her arms over her head and the mother says, ve-ry dramatic-like, 'Mr. Whitman, can't you see that my daughter is on the verge of a nervous collapse?' Yeah, lady, I figured that out all by myself. So I left. Not much else I could do."

"And then you were stuck with the print," said Matthew, in a commiserating tone, as though Leon hadn't been able to return a defective dishwasher.

"Yep. You got it. I was so mad I left it in a back closet for a good long while. Nobody wanted it, nobody asked about it. And I went into real estate and I got married and I coulda gotten rid of it. But my wife, she was all impressed that I'd worked on some movies, even though I made more dough selling houses than I ever would have runnin' around decoratin' sets. I thought maybe my son would like to see it one day, but he was never interested."

"What was he interested in?" asked Ceinwen.

"Dunno. We don't talk. Once me and his ma got divorced in '58 I never heard from him." Leon wheezed slightly. "Meanwhile my sister Lauren, she's all proud of our family connection, that's what she called it, the family connection to the movies. And she starts buying all this old-movie stuff, what for I don't know. All that nostalgia crap doesn't appreciate, not like real estate. I'd moved the print around with me and I kept it out in the garage and I didn't think about it much until Lauren started buggin' me. Why didn't I give it to her. She knew how to store it. So finally I said fine, hang onta it for me and if I ever find somebody who's interested in payin' some real dough for the thing, she had to hand it back over. She says fine.

"So it's about, I dunno, '74 or so and outta nowhere I get a call from some professor who's decided Emil Arnheim is some kinda forgotten genius." Leon gave a little bark of laughter. "And he says he's been talkin' to people, I know he mentioned the DP and Eddie Kenny. And he wants to know if I know whether somebody mighta kept a print."

"'74?" repeated Matthew. "Professor Gundlach called you in 1974?"

"Nah, that wasn't it. Don't remember exactly. Common kind of a name."

"Do you remember the university?" asked Ceinwen.

"Yeah. Pretty sure it was Enn-whyy-yewww," he said in an affected mid-Atlantic, holding up an imaginary teacup, pinky crooked. "Sorry. I know you're affiliated and all, but me, I never went to college."

Matthew had his face arranged as sympathetically as a TV interviewer as he wrote something down. She shifted so she could pretend she hadn't noticed his warning posture. "Could the name have been Evans?"

Leon's eyes went to the ceiling, and he moved his mouth from side to side. "Maybe. Sounds right. Evans. Yeah, could be. Why, you think you know him? 'Cause I got a few choice words for that guy . . ."

"Not really." Matthew cut them both off as she began to interrupt Leon. "It's a guess. Someone we know who collects films. There are thousands of NYU faculty. And if you think about it, Ceinwen," he said, his don't-fuck-this-up voice so crisp you could wrap a present in it, "I'm sure if our acquaintance had a lost film, he would have given it to the film department."

"You're right," she said. "It was probably wasn't him."

Leon shrugged, his tremor showing more. "I dunno, it's been a while. I know I been sittin' here talkin' about a movie I made in '28, but it's a funny thing about gettin' old. I remember '28 a lot better than '74. Guess it was a better year." He laughed again.

Matthew said, "So this man. Whoever he was. Did you refer him to your sister?"

"Yeah, I told him she had it. And I was in the middle of a crisis, know what I mean? I had some Arizona investments that were kinda, going south, so to speak." His chest heaved with another chuckle. He sure did like his own jokes. "So I had to go out to Tucson, couldn't get out of it"—subpoena, she thought—"and it took me a little while and I sorta forgot about it, I had stuff on my mind, like I said. Then I finally get back inta town and I called Lauren up in Vermont where she was livin' with that friggin' apple farmer. And get this. She tells me she don't have it. I said, what did you do with it, Lauren. She says, I didn't do anything, it musta got lost in the move. I let her have it. I told her if she thought I just fell off the turnip truck she better think again. I said I had a guy who was tryin' to buy it and I told her straight out I thought she'd sold it to him and pocketed the dough. She told me that was an awful thing to say. 'How could you accuse me of such a thing, Leon.' I'll tell you how. After she got married all I ever heard from her was how much money you need to run a farm." He splayed both hands on the table. "Then I hear through the grapevine that she and that husband of hers went and fixed up the barn." He brought one shaky fist down and the table glass rattled. "Cheated. My own sister. I never spoke to her again. Hell, I didn't even go to her funeral."

"Did you try to call the professor and tell him it wasn't your sister's film to sell?"

"That was the hell of it. Been gone a while and I couldn't find his name. Not like Lauren was gonna tell me, either." She started to speak to fill the silence, caught Matthew's eye and waited for Leon to continue. "Like I said. I had my own troubles. Bringin' a lawsuit, it's a pain in the neck." Especially if you've been sued for fraud in another state, she thought. Another bark from Leon, and a wheeze. "Eh, it's just as well. You get to be my age, you're sittin' in an old folks' home, you get to be philosophical-like. Arnheim gave me nothin' but grief when he was alive. So it kinda makes sense he was still at it fifty years after he croaked." He waved a hand at nothing. "I decided to forget about it. Enough already. Enough trouble from that drunken bum. He was no good." His volume dropped a bit, like he was talking to himself. "I knew he wasn't gonna make it."

"His career was pretty much over," said Ceinwen. She wanted to get out of there, she had dozens of ideas already about what to do next, but he didn't want to stop talking.

Leon shifted in his seat and almost spat. "Career? He never had a career. All he had was some people willin' to throw some dough at him for a little while. I knew he wasn't gonna make it home from that speakeasy."

She could feel the ammonia burn down into her sinuses when she inhaled. Matthew said, polite as ever, still running their own personal talk show, "You were with him that night?"

"Course I was with him, he'd been showing up nearly every night for at least a coupla weeks. I couldn't get away from him. All that time on set talkin' to me and everybody else like we were dirt, and now we were pals. Bought my drinks, even. With what I don't know, everybody knew he was broke. Brandy, that was his, and it'd better be a good one too. One after the other. He was always lit but that night he was really something." Ceinwen put her hand on the table and Matthew covered it with his own as her fingers began to curl toward her palm. "Tellin' me he was gonna get it turned around for our movie. *Our* movie. Chaplin was still gonna make silents, he said. People were still watching them in Europe. They'd understand it there if he could get it released. Then why didn't he go the hell back, I wanted to ask him. Ha, that wasn't going to happen. He was gonna get his due right where he was, if it took him forever. Arrogant bastard. Off he goes in that fancy car of his. Still had that, he wasn't giving that up. So drunk he couldn't hardly open the door, even if he hadn'ta had a busted hand. Told me he ran into a wall. Yeah, I believe *that*."

"You let him go," said Ceinwen.

He was surprised, nothing else. "Why shouldn't I? I hated that Kraut sonofabitch. None of my business if he wraps himself around a tree. And then he did. Ran off the road, anyway. Only time in his whole stinkin' life he ever did anything to oblige somebody else." He began to laugh again. "Take it from an old man, honey. There's some justice in this world." The laugh got louder. "Even in Hollywood."

"I'm afraid we're keeping you," said Matthew.

"Hell, I got all day. Not like there's a lot of visitors here."

"Hard to believe," said Ceinwen, "with all the stories you have to tell."

Matthew stood up. "We'd love to stay, but it's a long way back to Manhattan." He helped her into her coat.

Leon stayed seated. "Well, I've enjoyed the chat. Nobody's ever come out here and wanted to talk about Hollywood. Gives an old guy something to do." He held out his hand to Ceinwen. "Been a pleasure."

Ceinwen plunged her hand in her pocket and fished out her gloves. "Thank you for talking to us," she said. Matthew took Leon's hand and shook it. "Yes, thank you very much."

They were nearing the bus stop when Matthew spoke up. "Maybe Harry's right. Andy really does own every silent film ever made." She kept walking. He said, "I don't want to go to New Jersey." They were at the stop and Ceinwen took the last seat at the end of the bench. She pulled out a cigarette and lit up, and when the woman sitting next to her made a face she scowled right back.

Matthew squatted next to her. "I didn't like the man either," he said. "But he has a point. Nobody poured brandy down Arnheim's throat and forced him to drive."

She took a deep drag. Then she said, "I used to hide Daddy's car keys." She finished exhaling and the woman next to her waved her hand. "I always hated driving." The woman got up and Matthew sat down. The bus was visible a block away. She threw down the cigarette and ground it out, barely smoked. "I guess you could say I'm not objective."

They had to stand on the bus, and she looked out the window at Queens. When they got to the subway the train was there almost as soon as they hit the platform. They got on and found seats.

Matthew put his arm around her. "Aren't you the least bit happy? Andy might have the film."

She nodded. Then said, "Poor Miriam," and buried her face in his neck.

4.

SOMEWHERE AROUND 42ND STREET SHE PICKED UP HER HEAD AND began to touch up her makeup. Matthew watched her run the edge of a tissue along her lashes, and said, "Better now?"

"Better," she said. Then, "The movies in your head are always better." She blew her nose. "Lost films fortify our romantic notions of the cinema," she snarled. "In that sense, we need lost films."

"I admit, it fits."

That was the extent of the conversation to West Fourth Street. She charged up the subway stairs and shot across West Third.

"I have just the thing. Nice bottle of wine." For once Matthew was struggling to keep up with her. "Better than our usual plonk. It's early yet but I think we could use it." At the corner of the park she crossed against the light and barely stopped in time for a van. "*You* could use it, let's put it that way."

They turned into the lobby at Washington Square Village and she pounded the elevator button. They got on and Matthew gently pressed for the sixth floor. As soon as the elevator began to move, she punched three.

"What are you doing?"

"What does it look like I'm doing." As it opened on the third floor he whirled and half-pushed, half-backed her into the elevator.

"You can't charge in there and accuse him of hiding the movie." The doors shut behind him.

"*Watch me.*" They got out on the sixth floor, Ceinwen moved for the stairwell, and he slipped in front of her, eyes glued to hers like he was trying to coax a horse into the stable. She kept eye contact, stretched out an arm and pushed the down button.

"He'll deny it and you can't prove he's lying. He might not even *be* lying. It's completely stupid."

"And I'll threaten to . . . to . . ."

"To what?" The elevator sprang open and she found her feet dangling. He'd picked her up by the waist and was holding on tight until the doors shut. "Will you please stop a bloody minute and *think* for once." He set her down. "You have nothing to threaten him with. Nothelllllooo, Jessica." A woman had emerged from a nearby apartment and checked herself dead in front of her door. There was no telling how long she'd been there. Matthew was trying for an ingratiating smile, but the effort was undermined by the fact that he was still panting.

"How are you, Matthew." She was clutching her purse and keeping her eyes away from Ceinwen.

He flapped his arms to indicate a happy-go-lucky attitude and said, "Fine. Thanks. We're just going in." He stuck his key in the lock. Ceinwen didn't budge. "Going to relax. And talk." Neither did Jessica. "And sit. Relax while we're sitting."

The woman nodded uneasily and began to move toward the elevator. "Enjoy yourselves," she said. Matthew was holding open his door. Ceinwen walked past him and sat on the couch, still wearing her coat. He paused, hands out to avert a sudden bolt.

"Are you going to stay there?"

"For now."

He backed slowly to the kitchen, opened the wine and poured two glasses straight to the rim. She took a glass from him and stared at the carpet. He sat beside her, poised on the edge of the couch, legs positioned to carry him forward at a moment's notice.

"Ah. This is more like it." She slurped the top down to a less precarious level. "Not bad, yes?"

"It's *smashing*."

"Cute. Keep at it until you're ready to discuss matters in a nice, rational manner."

She took a mighty gulp. "I'm rational. I've never felt more rational in my life. Don't I look rational?"

"You look like Miss Havisham ten seconds after she's left at the altar."

She pushed her hair off her face and drawled, "You always know *just* what to say to a lady."

"It's my charm." He hammered back a couple of swallows and said, "Right. How does one approach a madman about his film collection. Let's think this through, shall we?"

"All I want to think about is where he's got it. He told me he doesn't keep his films in his apartment."

"He could have the lost continent of Atlantis in there. And you didn't see the bedrooms. So it could be there. Or I suppose he could have it downstairs in the storage. It doesn't matter, does it? We have to think of a way to persuade him—"

"There's storage in the basement?"

He didn't answer. She got up and he sprang to block her again. "Now where are you going?"

"To the basement."

"What for?" She darted around him and dashed for the elevator. He followed. "What's the point? It's all locked."

"You never know," she said. The elevator opened. They got in and Matthew put his hand over the third floor button. She glared at him and jabbed the button for the basement. He kept his hand there as a man got on at the fourth floor, gave a cough and said, "Excuse me." Matthew lifted his hand and moved an inch or two, his whole body still between her and the panel. The man paused, then slid his arm past Matthew to push the lobby button. When the elevator stopped at the lobby, he gave Matthew one short glance and was out before the doors finished opening.

"I don't know what you're expecting to see, I really don't." The base-ment's three cinder-block halls spread away from the elevator.

"How do I find his space?"

"As far as I know, they're numbered like the flats."

They trailed down one hall, then the other, and she noticed Matthew still had his wine. In the back of the center hall was the door marked 3B. It had a combination padlock on it, like a locker. She yanked on the lock and it didn't budge. Matthew groaned and took a swallow.

"What now? Do we wait for the movie spirits to sense our presence?" She held out her hand, he passed her the glass, and she drank too.

"Does this look like a big space?" she asked.

He stood back, checking out the next door. "Bigger than mine, defi-nitely. In this section the doors are spaced much further apart."

She took another sip, bent at the waist and looked to see if there was a light under the door. "It's pretty chilly down here. Is it like this during the summer?"

"It isn't warm, as I recall." She handed him the wine and pressed her face up to the crack of the door, trying to see inside. "If anyone spots you, they'll think you're bonkers. You realize that."

She kept her face where it was. "You'll look crazier," she told him, "standing there drinking a glass of wine and watching me."

He took another swig. "You're right. Let's go." She inhaled. "Ceinwen. You're worrying me. Come upstairs. We can make a list." She breathed deep. "A nice list of options. Nothing like a list for ordering the mind."

She pulled her head away.

"Take a whiff."

"A what?"

"Put your face right where mine was," she said, "and smell." He handed her the wine and did as she asked. "What do you smell?"

He wrinkled his nose. "Vinegar, maybe?"

"Try again." He put his face back and breathed in with a loud, theatrical snort. "Now what?" she asked.

He sniffed once more, leaned his back on the door and took his wine out of her hand. "Vinegar, and nuts."

"Not just nuts. Almonds."

"Lovely. Now we're Miss Marple." He pointed a finger at the ceiling. "Cyanide! The scent of bitter almonds!"

"This time I know what I'm talking about, and you don't. Almonds. That's the smell of nitrate. And the vinegar is the smell of the safety film, getting old." She took the glass out of his hand and drained it in one go. "Now we can go back upstairs and have that rational little chat."

Once they were back in his apartment, she took off her coat and a visibly relieved Matthew did the same. She picked up her glass and he refilled his own. Side by side they sat on the couch in silence.

"Talmadge told me once," she said, "that those combination locks aren't very secure. Practically anybody can pick them."

He set down his glass and put his hands behind his head. "That's intriguing. But I think we can do much better. Here's a thought. You lure Andy to my apartment."

She didn't think she liked where this was going. "How do I do that?"

"I shouldn't think that would be any problem at all, do you? You say to him, 'Hello, Andy. Come up and see me sometime.' There you are. Instant Andy. You crook your finger"—he demonstrated—"and beckon him out to the terrace, right there. I'm hiding behind a potted plant we've purchased for the occasion, and POW! I hurl him over the rail."

"Very—"

"Then, with a bit of luck, he screams out the precise location of *Mysteries of Udolpho* before he hits the ground."

"Very funny."

"No funnier than nicking it from his storage." He leaned forward. "By the way. Since we're on the topic. Does that flatmate of yours have *any* ethics at all?"

She sprang to her feet, yelling. "What are we supposed to do? Let him hog the movie where nobody can ever see it? Keep it down there till it's a pile of dust?"

"Calm down, I didn't say that." He put a hand on her arm and she sat and put her head on her knees. He left his hand where it was. Then he took it away.

"Didn't you tell me nitrate film is dangerous?"

She sat up and shrugged. "Oh, you know. Kind of an exaggeration."

"An exaggeration? You told me they quit using it, it was so dangerous."

Now was not to the time for him to get all fussy about the nitrate. "In theory. They used nitrate for years and years. All the way up through the forties. If it was all that bad, going to the movies would have been like the climax of *White Heat*."

"Well damnit, it *was* like *White Heat* a few times, wasn't it? You said there were cinema fires." No, she didn't like this at all. He poked her chest. "That is exactly what you said. Fires that killed hundreds of people."

"You have to account for human error."

He was on his feet. "I like that. Oh, that's brilliant, that is." He grabbed his wine and knocked back some more. "When I moved in here, I decided I wanted to cook like an American. And I got one of those gas grills, propane. For the balcony. I wanted to put a couple of tanks down in my little space, which is probably about one-*tenth* the size of Andy's by the way, and when I was taking them in, the super spotted me."

"I don't think there's any reason to worry."

"And the super said, 'I'm sorry Mr. Hill, but you can't store propane down here. It's a fire hazard. Regulations.' So my two little tanks of propane are going to engulf the building in flames." He waved the glass to mime an inferno and wine splashed on his hand. "But a entire room full of nitrate film, that's perfectly all right." He stalked to the kitchen and wiped off his hand.

"There's obviously some safety stuff in there, too."

He grabbed the wine bottle. "It's true. It's really true. Once you have tenure, you can do what the fuck you like."

She rolled her eyes and opened her purse to look for her cigarettes. Matthew planted himself in front of her, wine bottle in one hand and glass in the other.

"You want a real idea, Miss Reilly? Here you are. *We shop him*."

"Shop him for what?"

"For having a fire hazard in a block of flats, that's what." He banged down the glass and the bottle and charged for the bedroom.

"What are you talking about?"

"I'm writing to the management," he called, "to report the little bastard."

She rushed to the bedroom. "How's that going to help?"

"They'll tell him it has to go, and then we'll talk him into selling it. Or donating it. Doesn't much matter which. We can see if Harry wants *The Crowd* back. With a bonus." He was rolling a sheet of paper into his typewriter.

"What do we say?"

"Don't worry about it. I'm writing this. Not you. And then, if you don't mind, we're spending the night at your place."

5.

EMPTY BED AND A DEAD-SILENT APARTMENT. WHEN SHE WALKED into the kitchen she jumped and gave a little shriek. Matthew, wearing yesterday's shirt and cords, was drinking coffee with Talmadge and Jim. Talmadge was giving her a 10,000-kilowatt smile. He knew. They'd been discussing her. They couldn't have looked more guilty if she'd caught them having a three-way on top of the stove.

"Morning," trilled Talmadge in his Auntie Mame voice. "Lovely day for a hunt." Jim pursed his mouth and Matthew gazed deep into his coffee cup.

"Is there any coffee left?" she asked, and her voice came out in a croak.

Matthew said he had something to take care of first thing, and he had to work all day too. "I'll see you at the end of the week. We'll see what happens." He made her promise, several times and with the most explicit phrasing possible, that she wasn't going to confront Andy while they waited. They'd slipped Matthew's anonymous note under the super's door before they left.

She spent the day cleaning the apartment, scrubbing so thoroughly that Jim and Talmadge gave her a round of applause when they got home. That night she pulled out a second-hand video of *Stella Maris*. A minute or two in, Jim spoke up.

"When was this made?"

"1918."

They watched for a few more minutes. Talmadge shifted his legs around and Jim lit a cigarette.

"Don't you like it?" she asked Jim. "Pickford was great."

"It's a little slow . . ."

She changed the tape to *Johnny Eager* with Lana Turner.

The next morning she decided to call Fred before she went to work. Matthew hadn't said word one about contacting Fred. She thought she could prepare the Brody for the possibility of another Vermont-type stash, only right here in New York. Easier commute, she wanted to tell him. Kelly didn't make her spell her name. But Ceinwen was informed very firmly that Fred was in the laboratory, and they didn't take calls there.

At Vintage Visions she thought she was doing well, and she even sold a hat, but then a snippy customer handed her the receipt and pointed out that she'd moved a whole decimal point in the price. She had to void the transaction and endure Lily's interrogation, since Lily always assumed a void meant you had your hand in the till.

That night she bought a pizza and beer for the house, and Jim picked the movie, *Cat People*. A remake, but all right, considering that she watched it with her ears tuning in and out like a radio. She really wanted to finish *Stella Maris*.

The sun on the blinds was heating up the room, and when she awoke she raised them and opened the window. A breeze curled in, half warm, half cool. The clock said 11:38, and spring was here.

The phone rang. She stuck her head out the window and breathed deep. It was probably for Jim or Talmadge, and they'd have left for work. Two more rings and the machine kicked in.

"Ceinwen, pick up the phone. Now. This is important . . ." She picked up just as Matthew was saying "Where are you?"

"Hi, I just woke—"

"Get over here." Panic. Matthew, in a panic. "*They're throwing them out.*"

She tried to walk with the phone to her room but the cord was tangled. "The films? Andy had them in storage?"

"Yes of course the sodding films. All of them. The fire department is here and they're going to throw them out."

"What, without—"

"Don't dawdle, don't bother with make-up, don't stand around deciding what to wear."

"Without even knowing what's there?"

"Stop *talking* to me. Get something on your back and *come now*." He hung up.

It couldn't happen. She wouldn't let it happen. She threw on the first clothes she found and checked her purse for her keys. At the bottom next to them was Fred's card.

"Brody Institute for Cinephilia and Preservation, may I help you?"

"I need to speak to Fred Creighton. Tell him it's Ceinwen Reilly calling."

"Oh my goodness. Did he not get back to you? That Fred. He's in the lab again."

"Get him out, please, this is an emergency."

"An emergency? Is someone sick?"

"Tell him," she yelled, "that this is a film preservation emergency, that some things may be lost forever and I need to talk to him."

She couldn't tell if she'd scared Kelly or just puzzled the hell out of her. "All right. Hold on." Ceinwen lit a cigarette. She tried to untangle the phone cord, but she'd have to unplug it to get the knots out. A film preservation emergency, wow, that was inspired. Nobody except another freak like her was going to be alarmed by that. She should have said she was bleeding to death. This is Ceinwen Reilly, I just cut myself on a reel of *Four Devils* . . .

"Hello?"

"Fred, thank god. I need you to come down to NYU."

"I was going to call you back—"

"There's a bunch of films that a collector was storing at Washington Square Village, and the fire department's been called, and they're going to throw them away." Silence. Not even an "um." "Did you hear me? I know for a fact that there's some rare stuff down there and the fire department is going to throw it all out. You need to get down there." She added, "Please."

"You're, um, sure about this?"

"I'm telling you, these are silents, I know these could be important films, and they're just going to get rid of them, I don't even know where they want to take them . . ."

"Okay, okay. Calm, okay? Stay calm." She couldn't find the Kleenex or the toilet paper. "I'm, uh, not sure how much I can argue with the fire department, but I'll go down there. Um, are we talking a lot of stuff?"

"Probably a whole lot. Nitrate."

"*Whoa*. Nitrate? In Washington Square Village?"

"Yes, Fred. That's why they're going to throw it out."

"Hey, don't get mad, I'm on your side." Silence again.

"Fred? Are you leaving now?"

"This, um, sounds like a legal thing."

"Hell yes, it's a legal thing."

"Okay. So I should get Isabel."

"Bring anybody. Bring Kelly if you want."

"I don't think I can. Somebody's gotta stay at the front desk."

"Fred . . ."

"I'm coming, I'm coming. Stall 'em for half an hour or so. I'll be there."

On the last flight to the lobby she slipped, almost fell, discovered she was still holding her burnt-out cigarette, and tossed it away. On Avenue B she saw a cab, which was miraculous, and ran into the street hollering "TAXI!," willing to play chicken if that was what it took to get him to stop. She slammed the door getting in and barked "West

Third and Mercer." And added something she'd always wanted to: "Step on it."

He couldn't pull up next to the complex because a fire truck was blocking one lane, lights flashing. She paid up, overtipping, because she didn't want to wait for change, and because he did kind of step on it. She bolted down Third Street.

There was a crowd of people around the entrance. Firemen in their gear were bringing out reels and climbing the stairs to the garden, putting the films in the middle under a tarp. Another fireman was keeping people away. Matthew was off to one side, pacing. Harry was arguing with a man in a jacket and tie and a fireman's hat.

"You're approaching this the wrong way," Harry was saying. "This isn't just a bunch of old chemicals nobody wants. Think of it more like, the Mona Lisa happens to be *really* flammable."

"I'm approaching this like there is a major, potentially explosive fire hazard in a building of almost a thousand residents, that's how I'm approaching it."

"I agree, Captain, there's no question of leaving it here."

"Thank you *so much*, professor."

"All we're asking for is adequate time to get these films to a place that can handle them." He gave Ceinwen a brief wave.

"Unless you've got somebody lined up, as in this minute, that's exactly what I plan to do." She was trying to interrupt but they were going at each other too fast.

"You may not be aware of this, but we do have a film department here at the university. Rather a well-known one in fact. And I've placed a call to Paul Becker, the department head."

"And what did he say?"

"He's out. So then I tried to call William Everson, he's over at—"

"I have somebody coming," Ceinwen finally shouted over Harry. "From the Brody."

"And what in the almighty hell," said the fire marshal wearily, "is the Brody?"

"The Brody Institute for Cinephilia and Preservation," said Ceinwen, trying to make it sound like a big deal. "I've already called them and they're coming down to see what they can do. They have a lot of experience handling nitrate. Safely. They can take it and store it, they have a whole facility uptown." The marshal wasn't looking impressed, so she added, "State of the art."

That made him no happier. "And when are these people arriving?"

"They should be here any minute."

"They better be. And they better have some credentials, and some preparation, and some way to transport these things. Because in one hour, we're sticking it all in barrels of water, it's going in a fireproof truck, and we're driving it out to a hazardous-waste dump."

"But not all of it's nitrate," Harry was protesting as she turned and ran over to Matthew. She could hear the marshal saying, "Look, professor, I know a lot of it is, and I'm not sorting through a couple of hundred goddamn film canisters . . ."

Matthew pulled her over to a bench, away from the crowd.

"Fred's coming," she announced, to show she was on top of the situation.

"Super," he said. "That's all sorted then."

She scowled. "He's bringing Isabel, okay? You at least respect Isabel?"

"I'm scared to death of her, if you consider that respect." He was watching Harry and the fire marshal, still at it.

"Where's Andy?"

"He's upstairs. Crying, I think. He got so upset he couldn't talk anymore. I woke up this morning around eleven, I was awake all night thinking about that tinderbox in the basement, and then I hear this huge racket and there's a fire truck outside. I went down to have a look, along with everyone else in the building. And the firemen and some NYU security people were coming out of the basement and arguing with Andy. At first he was saying there wasn't any nitrate, then they showed him a reel—"

"Do you know which movie it was?"

"No, Ceinwen, of course I don't know which bloody movie it was. Andy claimed he'd no idea it was any different from his other films. They told him it all had to go, right now, and he said he was going to call a lawyer. And the marshal said go ahead. He said by law he has a perfect right to dispose of anything creating a distinct fire hazard, and he didn't have to ask permission from anyone. That was when I called you. Then I called Harry." Matthew gestured toward to the pile of film under the tarp, still growing as firemen were carrying it out. "They told me it was almost stacked to the ceiling. So many rows they couldn't wedge themselves between them."

"I don't understand. When you wrote to the super, what did you say?"

"All I said was, we had reason to believe that storage space number 3B had a number of celluloid nitrate films. But I also . . ." He paused.

"You also what?"

"Tuesday morning I typed another letter and I taped it to the door of the firehouse. I wasn't sure—"

"You what?" she yelled.

He put a finger to his mouth, then hissed, "Try to get this through your skull. He's *got tenure*. I couldn't be sure NYU would do something even if I said Andy was storing a severed head in a hatbox. I had to make sure the fire department saw the note and realized it was something that could blow up the building."

"Looks like they realized that, all right," she said, as evenly as possible.

He put a hand over his eyes. "I gather the letter landed with an old-timer who once had to put out a fire from nitrate storage."

When a man was this wretched, it wasn't nice to point out his mistakes. In football they called that a late hit. "Did you get a look at the labels? Any of them?"

"I think I saw Harry's *Crowd*. That was it." He glanced down at her legs. "Do you realize this is the first time I've seen you in jeans?"

Her sweat-dampened hair was sticking to her forehead. She pushed it off her face and said, "I need a cigarette."

"I'd say it's rather obvious they won't let you smoke it here."

"I'll walk over to Third Street."

"Your friend Fred better hurry up," he called after her.

She stood on the sidewalk, smoking, watching rubberneckers stream in and out. "I don't care what they told you," one student was saying, "that's a drug bust."

She lit another cigarette off the butt of the first. Where was Fred? She was halfway through her third when a cab pulled to the corner and Fred and Isabel exited opposite doors, like cops hurling out of a squad car. Isabel reached Ceinwen way ahead of Fred; it was really something how fast she could move in those shoes.

"All right," she said, "who do we talk to?" She was carrying a briefcase. Ceinwen threw down her cigarette as she pointed toward the entrance, and Isabel barely broke stride. Ceinwen and Fred fell in behind her.

"I know we're late. Sorry," said Fred. "Isabel said we needed some, you know, forms. And then I didn't know where they were, and she, ah, wasn't happy about that, and then, um, we had to ask Kelly . . ."

One of the firemen told them the marshal was inside. When they got to the lobby, he was hanging up the doorman's phone. The doorman had abandoned all pretense of caring who came in or out and had pulled up a chair to watch the activity. At the sight of the canisters under the tarp Fred let out a whoop.

"Thirty-five millimeter. Just like you said. I love it." He was tapping one sneaker-clad foot against the window.

"I take it you're in charge here," Isabel was saying to the marshal, loud and with a side glance at Fred.

"You take it right," said the marshal.

Fred set down his foot and leaned on the glass, hands positioned like he was doing a push-up. "Man, this bird's even crazier than old Brody."

Isabel raised her voice a little more. "I'm Isabel Chung, and I'm the supervisory director of the Brody Institute for Cinephilia and Preservation."

"Never heard of you," said the marshal.

Fred had his face so close his breath was frosting the pane. "If he's got a carbon-arc projector I'll *plotz*."

Isabel turned her back to the marshal, gave Fred a look that caused him to stand up straight and drop his arms to his sides, and turned to face the marshal again. "We're a film archive, and we're here to see if we can salvage these films you're thinking of discarding."

"Okay," said the marshal. "If you want these things, I need some ID, for starters."

"I think you'll find we have everything you need." She pushed the doorman's coffee cup and newspaper aside and unlatched the briefcase. Ceinwen looked at the straps and thought, real Hermès. What else would Isabel carry? "Here's my work ID."

Fred inhaled sharply and said, "Oh shit."

"And here is Fred's." He exhaled. "That's Fred Creighton, our head curator, over there staring out the window, for some reason."

"Did you *see* this, Isabel?"

"Here is the documentation we have from the fire department regarding our nitrate storage facilities at 669 East 75th Street. We have all the necessary approvals. Here, since you mentioned a lack of familiarity, is a brochure with a brief description of the work we do at the Brody. If you're interested."

"I'm not interested," said the marshal.

Matthew had entered. "That's quite all right, you can read it at your leisure. We have our assistant at the Brody calling now for transportation from here to uptown. It may take a little while longer."

"Better not be too much longer. It's warm today. If you know nitrate, I assume you know that's not a good thing."

"We're on it, Mr., ah—"

"That's Captain Sullivan."

"Captain. Our usual service has small trucks, and it may take two trips."

"Usual service?" whispered Ceinwen.

"She's got Kelly calling every trucking company in town," Fred whispered back.

"You can't just throw this in a U-Haul," the captain was saying.

"We have our own steel containers for transporting nitrate. Those are also fire department-approved, by the way. The time factor will depend on getting the truck to pick up the containers at our labs, then getting them down here. So my suggestion is that you let Fred examine the canisters. Given his well-documented experience . . ."

"All an ID tells me is he can look at a camera with his eyes open."

"But of course. Here's Fred's CV."

"Fred's what?"

"His resume. Right here. And here's mine."

The marshal took out his glasses. "This isn't gonna help him go through nitrate with his bare hands."

"You do realize, Captain, that movie projectionists used to do that all the time."

"Sure, sure, lady. They stored it under the sink. This is 1987. If he hasn't got gloves he's not going near it. And a mask. He needs a mask."

"Oh shit," said Fred. Isabel unzipped her shoulder bag and took out a pair of gloves and a face mask.

"Fine, knock yourself out," said the marshal. "Meantime, you're gonna need this guy's permission to take his stuff."

"I thought you said you didn't need anyone's permission," said Matthew.

"I don't need it. *She* does."

Isabel brought out some more papers. "I have some temporary forms here, pending a more formal agreement between us and Professor—"

"Evans," said Matthew.

"Evans. Friend of yours?"

"Good *Christ* no." Isabel frowned at him. "Sorry. Andy is upstairs. Harry—another professor is trying to talk to him. 3B. I can take you up if you like."

Isabel put the papers back in her case. "No need. I'll go up myself. I've handled this sort of situation before."

"Has she?" Ceinwen asked Fred under her breath.

"Um, no," said Fred, "but I'm not worried. Are you?"

Isabel left and the marshal resumed looking at the papers she'd given him. Fred put on his gloves and mask, and she and Matthew followed as a fireman escorted him to the center of the plaza. They pulled back the tarp. Fred looked at a label, gently opened the canister, set down the lid and pumped both fists in the air. "Hey, Ceinwen! IT'S NOT A HOCKEY PUCK!" She pumped her own fists right back at him. The fireman folded his arms and stared intently at Fred, as if wondering whether this man was safe to leave alone with a fire hazard or anything else. Fred spun on his heel to get a look at the rest of the canisters and gave the top of one stack a loving little pat, like it was a puppy.

Matthew tapped her shoulder. "It's Thursday."

"Yeah, I know."

"Ceinwen. You *work* on Thursday." She yanked up her sleeve. No watch. He checked his. "Five till two."

She whirled around. "Where's my purse?"

"You had it when we were in the lobby." She ran to the lobby where the doorman was putting her purse in a drawer. She'd spent the whole day running, and for the first time ever, she thought maybe Matthew and Jim were right. She really did smoke too much.

When she got to the store Roxanne shook her head and put up a hand, but Ceinwen kept weaving through customers, trying to reach the clock room. She saw Talmadge at the back of the men's side, waving his hands too, then she stopped midway through the store when Lily came through the passage to the women's side. And Lily stood there. Waiting until every eye was on her. Talmadge's hand went to his mouth.

"So you've decided to join us today," said Lily.

"I've been sick," began Ceinwen.

"Sick? You know who's sick? I am. I'm sick of you."

"I can make up the time—" Talmadge's hand had moved to his eyes.

"I'm sick of you coming in any time you feel like it, I'm sick of you picking up men at the counter—"

"*What*? I have never, *ever*—"

"Yeah yeah, that English jerk, he was here for the bangles. And when you finally decide to come in, you look like SHIT. Jesus, who would buy anything from you when you look like this?"

Not a customer nor a salesperson in the entire store was moving. She hated too much attention, that was probably why she'd never wanted to be an actress.

But what the hell.

"I'm not here for my shift. I'm here to tell you something."

"I have something to tell *you*."

"I'm here to tell you," she said, raising her voice so the women's side had a shot at hearing too, "that you're a bitter, pennypinching cow, that you abuse me and every other person who works at this store, and I quit." Talmadge had both hands on the top of his head and his mouth open. Not bad. Missing something, though. She was glad she hadn't used any swear words, but . . .

"You just saved me the trouble of firing you," yelled Lily. She started back towards the women's side. Ceinwen followed.

"One more thing, Lily," she hollered after her. "Wearing all black all the time doesn't make you look any skinnier."

"Get out of my store!" bellowed Lily. Ceinwen pulled her purse up on her shoulder and walked out as slowly as she could will herself. As she passed the register she looked back at Talmadge and saw him giving her the power salute.

She had never had a perfect dramatic exit in her life, and she was feeling proud that Lily was going to be it, until she was in the middle of Broadway and had to turn around, the light changing and horns blaring as she skittered back. When she walked back in, Roxanne looked up from the register and of course, Lily was next to her. Ceinwen said, "I have a paycheck back there."

"What makes you think—"

"New York State labor law, that's what," said Ceinwen. "Give me my check." Roxanne reached in the drawer.

Whatever Lily yelled afterward was lost as she sped through the door.

The check-cashing place was all the way over on First. The line went on and on, everyone seemed to have problems and money orders. After an hour she left with the $180.92, less $2.50 in fees, that was supposed to see her through the jobless future, and made her way back to Washington Square Village, stopping at Smelly to get more cigarettes, a cup of coffee and a package of Dipsy Doodles. She hadn't eaten a thing since the morning, and she wondered if Matthew was right about that too, that she was going to faint one of these days.

The fire truck was gone. Instead there was a small truck parked and some containers were being wheeled toward it by a couple of men. When she got closer she saw Fred jumping off the back.

"Your boyfriend said you went to work," said Fred.

"Work . . . didn't work out," said Ceinwen. "So what have we got?" He was grinning at her. "What's so funny?"

"You. Not, 'is all the nitrate safely away from this, um, apartment building' or 'where's my boyfriend' or, um, 'is the collector guy having a nervous breakdown,' just, you know, 'what movies did you find.' So, yeah. The films."

Get to the point. "The nitrate."

He was still grinning. "Yeah. About one-quarter is 16-millimeter. Rest is 35- and from the look of the canisters I'm gonna guess more than two-thirds of that's nitrate. Hard to tell what we've got here. Definitely, um, a lot of two-reelers. Some of them pretty interesting. The condition, you know, varies. And, um, of course the fire guys were just hauling it out any way they could and nothing's in order. Not always a great idea to open up nitrate canisters outside the lab, so most of the time I was trying to guess from the label, but, um, this professor, his labeling, I, uh, I don't get it. Sometimes the studio, sometimes the director, there's a bunch that just have numbers, some of them aren't marked at all. I mean, it's, um . . ."

"Crazy as he is."

"Yeah. This load is the last of it. Gonna take a while to go through all this, um, maybe a long while. I can let you know. If you're interested. For that, um, project."

Maybe they weren't even there for Fred to find. Maybe they'd been in bad shape and Andy had to throw them out even before he tried to put them downstairs. She wanted to ask Fred if he'd seen a word like "Mysteries," but then she'd have to explain why she thought *Mysteries* was there in the first place. At least they were all out, she reminded herself. They weren't in the basement rotting, day by day.

"Thanks. I'd like that." She tore open the bag of chips with her teeth.

He was knocking his right foot against the curb. "You could, um, stop by if you want. I should have a list going by this time next week. I, ah, can't remember which days you work . . ."

"I'm unemployed."

His foot rested near the gutter. "Is that recent?"

"As of about two hours ago." She crunched some Dipsy Doodles.

"Oh man." Fred looked stricken. "I'm really sorry."

"I'm sorry I'm going to be broke," she said with her mouth full. "But I'm not sorry I'm out of there."

"Okay. It's, um, good to stay positive." He pulled on his ear. "Why don't you come by a week from Monday. Like, noon, all right?"

"Sounds great. Where's Matthew?"

"Said he had to go to the office. The other professor, uh, Engelman.

He's trying to make peace with Isabel and Paul Becker. Becker, um, seems to feel they got cut out."

"You went to NYU. Do you feel bad for them?"

"If I did all I'd have to do is, um, go home and look at my loan stubs," he said. "Isabel's in there pointing out that they, ah, don't have our kind of lab and storage anyway."

She took a huge swig of coffee that burned her tongue, sucked on her teeth, and asked, "Andy agreed to a donation?"

"Isabel got some agreement from him. He's donating the nitrate and, you know, taking a tax deduction, and the safety stuff, he's kinda, loaning it to us. She said he was yelling, then he was crying, then he was yelling again, took her half an hour just to get him able to talk. Finally she said we'd put his name on the collection, I don't know how we're gonna do that, but that, um, got to him."

She might as well see what Matthew was doing. Fred climbed back in the truck, and she walked to Courant.

His door was open and he was at the chalkboard, staring as if it had just turned him down for a date. In a not-terribly-hopeful voice he said, "Lunch hour?"

"I'm officially unemployed," said Ceinwen. "Like half the city."

"Not the worst that could happen. Considering how much you loved your work."

"Yeah, but there's this thing called rent."

"We'll think of something." He put down the chalk. "I don't suppose there's any good news."

"Andy's labeling is all over the place. Fred has no idea what's there, for the most part. We won't know anything else until a week from Monday. And not all of it can be saved." She sat down on the desk. "I feel bad for Andy."

"You're not serious. The man was hoarding nitrate in a block of flats."

"He doesn't have much in his life. Those films were like his kids. And we just forced him to put them up for adoption."

"The fire marshal said his kids are so flammable they even burn underwater. He's a nutter."

She'd had something else on her mind all day. "Andy won't be able to figure out who dropped a dime on him, will he?"

Matthew collapsed on his chair and rested his arms on his desk. "I doubt it. Forensic analysis on an anonymous tip, not much point to that.

Probably looked illiterate anyway. I never could type." He ran his hands over his face. "I'm sorry."

"What are you sorry for? It's all at the Brody now. If there's anything there, they can take care of it. I should have written the note myself. For one thing, I can type."

He picked up a notebook from his desk and started to flip through it. "I should try to work this evening. Harry and I are almost done with this proof and if I finish tomorrow I can give it . . ." He stopped.

"Give it to who, Harry?"

"No, the secretary. To be typeset." He shut the notebook. "You can type?"

"Yeah." She'd impressed him, that was always nice. "I'm pretty good. Used to be almost eighty words a minute. Got an A in high school."

He swiveled around in his chair. "You can type like that, and you were working in a shop?"

Oh god, not the why-are-you-working-retail routine again. "There's more to an office job than typing, you know. For one thing, they want a 'front office appearance.' Me, I just look weird." What was this look? She tried to lighten things up. "Of course, some people find weird attractive."

"They don't care what the secretaries at Courant look like."

"Yeah, I noticed."

"And Angie is retiring. Finally."

"That woman who works for Harry?"

He rolled the chair closer. "Yes. He'll need a secretary. To typeset papers and do his correspondence."

She almost laughed. "Come on. I love Harry, but no way. I got an A in typing, but do you want to hear what kind of grades I got in algebra?"

"You don't need to understand it, you just type it. You learn the program and you type it like anything else."

This was sweet of him, but the day they'd had was obviously affecting his brain. "That sounds like the most boring job in the world, to be honest. Vintage Visions was a hellhole but at least I was around pretty things."

"Stop. Listen to me. If you work full time at NYU you get remission." She shook her head in bewilderment. "Tuition remission," he said, drawing the words out like he was repeating them for someone who didn't speak English. "Free classes. Two a semester. Six a year. Anywhere at the university. Does that make it less boring?"

"Yes," she said, after a moment. "I guess it does."

"I'm going to see if Harry's back."

6.

HARRY WAS SO EXCITED HE MADE HER COME BACK THE NEXT MORN-ing. She arrived, carefully dressed in a suit, and he asked her nothing about her qualifications. He said Donna wanted them all to have dinner again soon, then escorted her down the hall and introduced her to Tania, the professor he shared a secretary with. Tania was the highest-ranking woman in the history of Courant, a diminutive Russian topologist who sat in her chair like someone had strapped a two-by-four to her back. She seemed skeptical and kept asking Ceinwen about her office background. Ceinwen would have been a nervous wreck, what with Tania, and Tania's posture, and having to admit that she'd never worked in an office in her life—except that with Harry there, she barely had to talk at all.

"The important thing is that Ceinwen is intelligent."

"I don't doubt that, Harry, it's a question of aptitude for this specific work."

"So she has to learn the typesetting program," said Harry. "All you need is a good memory. Ceinwen has a great memory."

"That's a little difficult to test in an interview," observed Tania.

"It's easy to test," bellowed Harry. "Ceinwen, who was the cinematographer on *Night of the Hunter*?"

"Stanley Cortez."

"*See?*"

Tania looked from Harry, to Ceinwen, and back to Harry. "Let's see how she does on the typing test."

After that, Harry took to letting her into Angie's office after hours, handing her science copy to type, and having her practice, since she hadn't typed in ages. There were no equations, but there might as well have been, for all she understood what she was typing. But she discovered that you really could look at the letters almost one by one and hit the keys; you didn't have to know what anything meant. It wasn't what you'd call interesting, but it required concentration. It kept her mind off Fred, up at the Brody, going through the film.

Jim, though it looked like it cost him physical effort, allowed as how Matthew pushing her into a secretarial post at Courant was "an awesome idea. Pretty much."

"I'm getting nervous about it. Typing tests are a bear."

"You need to do directed breathing before," said Talmadge. He pushed one nostril shut, breathed in, pushed the other shut, and breathed out. "Like so. It's very soothing."

"We'll give her a thermos of chamomile for the road," said Jim.

She pushed a nostril shut, breathed, and was already bored. She let go of her nose. "Tania seems like a tough article."

"You've worked for the toughest of them all," Jim pointed out.

"Second-toughest," said Talmadge. "You could always apply at Bargain Bernie's. He'd hire you. You're cute."

"That's what I'm afraid of," she said. "I've heard the same stories about Bernie as everybody else."

"Plus," said Jim, "at least half your clothes are way too good for Bargain Bernie's. Don't you agree, Talmadge."

Talmadge smiled enigmatically and went behind his screens. Jim whispered, "Whatever you do, don't tell him you need more clothes for this job. Grand theft, power suit, here we come."

Matthew was working all week, too busy even to explain what it was. They agreed on an early dinner at Caffe Pane e Cioccolato, on Friday after the typing test, because they had so rarely seen each other on Fridays before. She barely touched her omelette and he didn't say a word about it. He told her that he had to go back to Courant after dinner, and she couldn't hide her chagrin.

"I thought you finished the proof. You told me you did."

"And now I'm working on another one, and one with Paru."

"I have needs, too," she muttered. "It isn't just men."

"All you need at the moment is to concentrate on getting this job."

"I don't know," she said glumly. "I'd have been so much more relaxed for the typing test if Harry had been there instead of that admin whosits lady." She'd tried Talmadge's breathing technique, but got confused about which nostril was supposed to be shut when.

"Sixty words a minute isn't bad at all. That's a good deal faster than me."

"You only use two fingers." She set down her fork and gave up on the food. "And I had seven errors. That's a lot."

"Harry wants you. And he's a star, remember that."

"Did you get a good look at any of the other women applying?"

"Reasonably good look at one, I'd say."

"And? Did she look like a serious person?"

"Oh, very. I'd go so far as to say she looked grim." He looked up. "I don't think she's any competition. She was wearing trousers."

At least he was joking. But he didn't seem to be eating much, either. She felt a rush of sympathy; all she had heard in Matthew's voice this past week was anxiety, and she'd barely asked him what was going on, because the wait to see Fred and hear what he'd found was killing her. She needed to do better. "Harry said the proof you two did is very elegant." It was an odd word to use for a math paper, but she figured Harry knew from elegant numbers.

"That it is. What it is not, is significant."

Not for the first time she wished she could read Matthew's work, tell him that he was a genius, and have it mean something to him. She'd asked him once, in a fit of temper, if Anna knew what his papers were about. She had a vague notion, he'd answered calmly, but to understand it fully, you had to be another mathematician. She'd thought then that this must be why Harry and Andy had such a thing about movies. You had to find another love, if you were a mathematician, or you'd have nothing to talk about with regular people.

Of course, getting obsessed with old, obscure movies wasn't necessarily a big help with your social life, either.

"I'm sure it's extremely significant."

"It is to me, because we've finished it." He picked up a swizzle stick and rolled it between thumb and forefinger. "Did you call Becker yet?"

"Yes, he said if I got the job I should come by the film department and he'd give me all the forms. But I still have to re-apply."

"They'd love to have you back. I was right there when he said it."

"I hope he wasn't just being nice." She pulled a pen out of her purse and grabbed a napkin. "How many credits do I need to graduate?"

"126."

"Okay, so I have some credits already," she said, scribbling on the napkin. "But let's say six classes a year, two fall, two spring, two summer, starting this fall . . ."

"About six years." He was tying the swizzle stick into a knot.

"I'm impressed."

"That's just what Cambridge said. 'Multiplication tables all down? You're in.'" He reached for another swizzle stick and tied it around the first.

"What's that going to be?"

"A few more straws and it becomes a fractal. If you're working for Tania, you'll know all about those."

"I'll know how to type things about them." He tied on another stick. "What would I be typing for you?"

"Anything I do with Harry, I suppose. The secretaries don't work for the postdocs."

She waited for him to look up. She said, a bit tentative, "We'll be on the same floor."

"For one more year." He hadn't mentioned Anna. Why the hell did she pick an Italian restaurant, come to think of it? She tried to relax her shoulders.

"Wouldn't you want to stay at Courant?"

The swizzle sticks were starting to look like Siamese-twin spiders. "Of course I would. Doubt they'd have me once the postdoc's done. The better the town, the more desirable the post. I'm not a star."

"Do you want to go back to England?"

"I wouldn't mind. But at the moment there's no jobs." He checked his work.

"So what kind of town do you think you'd rate?"

"Not New York. But maybe not Boise State either. Mid-range. Oklahoma perhaps. SUNY Buffalo."

He pulled off his last straw and began to re-attach it. She tried to think of something positive to say about Buffalo, but all she could come up with was Niagara Falls and bowling alleys.

"They tell me Buffalo's much nicer than Rochester," she said finally.

"Good to know."

"Personally, I think Buffalo would be fine. I like snow."

"Of course you do." Eyes still on the fractal. "You just never learned to dress for it."

"Southerners love snow. We appreciate it. Yankees don't. And you don't have the right clothes either, by the way."

"If I get tenure track in Buffalo, believe me, I'll buy them."

"We'll go shopping together," she blurted, put a hand on her neck, and when he looked at her, she forced herself to drop it on the table. He put down the fractal and slid his hand over hers.

He was going to say it soon. She'd been waiting ever since he came back, and for the last month she'd been expecting it almost every time they saw each other or spoke. The night after they found the nitrate, when he dropped his work after saying he shouldn't, and they split a bottle of wine at his place and laughed like maniacs while Matthew drunkenly mapped her post-secretarial career as the Indiana Jones of film preservation, doorstepping doddering old people world-wide. The night he phoned from

Los Angeles, when they'd spent a half hour talking about Martin Amis and neither one of them knew how to end the call. All those times he'd pushed her hair away to get a better look at her face. And now, when he left his hand where it was as the seconds ticked by, until he took it away and went back to his fractal.

She was so close to hearing it, sometimes she felt as though she'd already said it back.

MAY

1.

ISABEL WAS BULLETING THROUGH THE LOBBY. "HELLO, CEINWEN. KELLY, ring Fred and tell him his appointment is here, please. Have to dash now. Meeting a potential donor. Let's talk at some point."

No ID. How about that. At last, she was in with Isabel.

Fred was up in a matter of minutes and took her down to the laboratory. She lasted until her foot hit the top step and then she barked, "What did you find?"

"Silents," said Fred. She was walking ahead of him and had to wait for him to catch up when she realized she didn't know which door it was. "Lots and lots of silents." Andy storing silents, who'd have thought. She bit down hard to keep from bursting out with Emil's name. "Great nitrate of *The Crowd*, for one. *The Wind*. *The Silk Bouquet*, Chinese-produced thing with Anna May Wong. A Colleen Moore, not *Flaming Youth* unfortunately. *The Magic Flame*, that's a Henry King—heard of it?"

"No."

"Ronald Colman and this Hungarian actress, name of Vilma Banky. Lots of Chaplin. Couple of Arbuckles. Harry Langdon. *Wedding Bills*, that's a Raymond Griffith we didn't have. And, um, the 16-millimeters were also silents and, ah, it was stuff we already had in the collection. All of it. Some of the rarest titles we've got." He pulled up a seat for her. He had a reel on his desk. Thirty-five millimeter.

"That's interesting," she said, hoping she sounded noncommittal.

"Yeah," he said, grabbing one elbow and squinting at her. "That's *just* what I said. Interesting as all hell." He tapped the canister. "And here we go. The most interesting of all. Check it out."

He grabbed a pair of gloves from a drawer and pulled them on. He took the film out of the canister and carefully unfurled a tiny bit, then a foot or so. It didn't look fragile. He pulled out another foot and held a frame up to the light, then grabbed an eyepiece off the desk.

"A loupe," she said.

He screwed it into his eye. "It's like one. How do you know that word?"

"One of my roommates is a jeweler."

He held the film close to the eyepiece, and lowered it. "Take a look." He handed her the loupe, and she put it against her eye; it wouldn't stay put, her face muscles weren't cooperating, so she held it with one hand and thrust out the other for the film. "I'd better hold it," he said. She held the eyepiece in place, and he moved a bit of the long ribbon in front of it. And kept it there, for longer than she'd have thought possible for him to hold anything without moving.

A title frame. White letters curled next to decorated Gothic capitals. *The Mysteries of Udolpho.* From the novel by Ann Radcliffe. Starring Edward Kenny as Valancourt. Introducing Miriam Clare as Madeleine. Directed by Emil Arnheim.

All those other frames to look at later. Right now, this one was enough.

Fred lowered the film and she put down the loupe. He still wasn't twitching.

"I'll be," she said, at last.

"Yeah. Great find." said Fred. He started winding the film back against the reel. "Thought you'd like to see for yourself."

"Incredible," she said. Was this what shock felt like? "After all these years."

"Thrilling," said Fred, with absolute calm. He laid the film back in the canister and replaced the lid. "This has the potential to be, um, a pretty big deal." He peeled off the gloves. "And what I can't get over," he said, "is this is the very film you and Matthew came here to research. How about that, huh?"

She looked back at the reel. "When do we get to see it?"

"That's really something, isn't it? You guys come up here and look at the fragment. Next thing you know, here it is." He threw up his hands. "Wow!"

"Is it going to take a while to get it ready to be shown?"

"A while, yeah, kinda hard to say exactly how long. I'll explain in a minute." He rested his elbow next to the reel. "But, ah, back to what I was saying. You and me, we have a chat about how to store nitrate, hypothetically speaking, and then, um, we get kinda drunk one night and talk about Chris Bixby and that collector up in Vermont. The one, um, the one who had what was probably a screen test for *Mysteries of Udolpho*. Then we go see Steve and whaddya know, we talk about Vermont that night, too. And *then*, all of a sudden, this lost film turns up. In your boyfriend's building. Yeah. That's just, um . . ."

"Incredible," she supplied.

"You said that."

"Like a movie, almost," she ventured.

"I thought so too. The kind of thing you see in a movie and think, ah, no. That wouldn't happen." He ran a finger over the remnants of the glue on the canister, where the label had fallen off. "Not exactly like that, it wouldn't."

All she could come up with was one of Granana's favorite lines. "That's my story, and I'm sticking with it."

A long, motionless look; but she had finally learned how to outwait men. "Okay, then." He gave the canister one tap of his finger. "Even your clichés are vintage, you know that?"

Her favorite part of a musical was always the moment right before Judy Garland or Fred Astaire broke into song—that instant when everything rose from their lungs and rushed into their eyes, and then they were singing, and dancing, and it seemed that anyone who felt something that strong could conjure an orchestra, just like they did. She bet she could. They'd found it. They'd saved it. She wanted to tell Matthew, she wanted to tell Norman and Harry, she wanted to tell Jim and Talmadge and Donna and Roxanne and hell, she even wanted to tell Lily if she ever saw her again. Most of all, she wanted to tell Miriam.

"The whole movie," she burst out, drumming her heels on the floor. "Sixty years, nobody sees anything except a two-minute screen test, and now we have the whole movie."

Fred uncrossed his legs. "Um, well. Not so fast. I've been through almost everything. And, ah, I'm pretty sure that what we have is six reels."

She rested her feet. The orchestra had barely tuned up. "Oh no."

"I'm sorry," he said. "This one, *Mysteries*, none of them were labeled. And the first one I found, I think it's the third reel, and I recognized the actress, from that fragment we saw. What's her name . . ."

"Miriam Clare," she said.

"Yeah. She's, ah, she stands out. That reel was starting to go, but barely starting, you know? I can work with it. Once I realized what I was looking at, I, ah, I was really hoping it would all be there. I called down Isabel, and we looked at what little we could on that reel without damaging anything. And, um, it's pretty hot stuff. Considering everybody's wearing these old costumes. So then when I reminded Isabel that this was probably all there was of the Arnheim, she, ah, she got excited. We kinda had everybody going through everything else looking for these."

Hot stuff? Could he be any more vague? "*How does it look?* How does the camera move? Were there any unusual shots? Like of dust or something?"

He pulled back, almost laughing. "Whoa, whoa, whoa. We can't project it yet. All I personally saw were a few feet of frames. The ones I found, um, showed this woman, um, I guess she's the maid, spying on Miriam Clare while she was in bed. Nice shot, like it was framed between, um, some panels or something. Lighting looks good, like they were going for the candlelight effect. Once it's cleaned up it'll be easier to tell." He paused. "Dust? That would be weird. It's not *Greed*."

Once again, she had to wait. And she better change the subject before he got any more suspicious. "So," she said. "You've got assistants." Four reels gone.

"Yep, three of them. You'll have to meet them sometime."

"I'd like that," she said. Only six reels left.

"Oh, they'd like you too. Trust me. Um, as I was saying, ah, this first reel is in great shape. Like it was barely screened. Fantastic. We've got just a very little decay on the third and the others, um, I think we got those just in time. I mean, we can do it. But it's gonna be a job. Probably at least a year."

"The missing reels—do you have any idea what happened?"

"Could be they were some of the ones that were so bad I couldn't tell what they were. There were maybe a couple dozen or more unlabeled and just . . . dust. Some of them crumbled as soon as we opened the can. Or, ah, could be they were just never there at all. I tried to call Evans as soon as I figured out what we had. Been trying all week, but, well. He doesn't pick up his phone. Or his messages at work either, I guess. But, um, I knew six reels couldn't be the whole movie."

"No," she said sadly. "Nine reels after the cuts. Emil's copy would have been ten."

"Emil?" She realized what she'd said. Fred put his elbows on his knees and said softly, "What makes you think this was Arnheim's print?"

They were in the back of the building, but she could hear what sounded like the traffic outside. "I don't. But I read that he had a print. When I was doing research. For Matthew's project."

"Right. The project." Fred sat up and grabbed his neck. "Yeah. One thing I can tell you about your project. And, ah, Matthew too. With old movies, the really old ones, you gotta take what you can get."

He'd shaved today, she noticed. Fred thought this was a big enough deal to merit his razor. He didn't look unhappy. She picked up the loupe and weighed it in her hand.

"Six reels is better than nothing," she said.

He smiled, very slow and very broad. "Much, much better."

He was taking her back up when she paused on the stairs. "Fred? Andy—Professor Evans isn't going to make trouble, is he?"

"I'd like to see him try. I've seen some crazy people in my time, I mean, look at Steve. But storing nitrate in NYU faculty housing, that pretty much takes the cake." He started to walk, but she didn't. "Hey, we got a signed agreement. Isabel told me, um, she said if Evans didn't answer his phone at some point, she was willing to go down and crash one of his classes."

She giggled. "Let me know if she does. I'd like to see that."

"Heh, I already told her there was no way I was missing it myself. I wasn't sure she'd wanna give this a lot of priority, but she totally does. Man, she's on fire. She wants to put out, you know, a press release in a few weeks."

Oh god. Leon. What if it made the papers and Leon saw it? "Is that a good idea? Are you sure you have all the rights?"

He leaned against the banister, hand tapping while he furrowed his brow at her. "Not my job, but um, I don't think the rights, ah, they're not really a factor. Novel's public domain and Civitas hasn't been around for years."

"We don't know how Andy got it. Maybe there was something dodgy involved."

"Dodgy?" he repeated.

"You know, shady. Obviously there was something weird going on, and what if he didn't come by it honestly?"

For an instant it seemed he was going to pat her shoulder, but he grabbed his own shoulder instead. "It's ours. Okay? Nobody else is gonna get it. And if somebody tries, well, Isabel can handle it. She, um, she'd probably love to sink her teeth into a big fat legal dispute."

"Isabel can handle it," she echoed, trying to convince herself.

Fred smiled again. "Of course she can. That's what Isabel is *for*."

She felt herself melting a little at Fred's look when he said that. The only possible word for it was tender. Ceinwen wondered whether Isabel was ever going to realize that there was a man in this world who loved her not for her beauty, but for her ability to scare the ever-loving crap out of everybody.

As soon as she was on the sidewalk she found a phone booth and called Matthew at his office.

"Four reels missing. My god, Andy. That useless git. What good is it being a compulsive if you can't even hoard a complete set of something?"

"We still have six. We'll be able to tell a lot about the film. And it's Emil's cut."

"I know, you should be proud. I'm tired, that's all." He sounded exhausted.

"You better perk up. We're going out to celebrate."

"What, tonight? I can't possibly. I think I've finally got something and I have to stick with it." Not even tonight? As if to answer, he said, "You don't want to see me anyway. Go see Miriam. She's the important one. Isn't she."

She walked down the sidewalk, then turned around and went back to the pay phone. Jim picked up.

"Champagne! Champagne for everybody!" he sang out when she told him.

"Except Talmadge."

"Come on, Talmadge too. We'll tell him one little old social drink won't hurt."

"That's not funny."

"It is too. Does Matthew want to come?"

"He's working."

"What, again? All righty, bring Miriam. There's one lady I'd like to see drunk."

There was plenty of time on the subway and the walk to Avenue C to think about exactly what she'd say. But when she knocked, and Miriam opened the door, it was Miriam who had to speak first.

"Are you trying for coffee again?"

"I have something to tell you," she said, pleased with how steady her voice sounded. "Something important."

Miriam waved her in. "I just made my own coffee. I suspect it's better, anyway."

The same pot, the same cups. No brandy. Ceinwen picked hers up and ran a finger along the rim. Miriam had her legs tucked neatly to one side, just like Christmas. Except now she was the one with a story to tell, not Miriam. Get right to it, had been Jim's advice. Don't try to ease her into it, it's too big.

"I've been looking for the film."

A long silence. Miriam said, "Have you really. And what did you find?"

"Six reels."

Miriam's cup hit her saucer and for a few seconds Ceinwen just watched her breathe. "You're telling me you have six reels of *Mysteries of Udolpho*? Where, in your closet?"

"Not here. At a film archive. The Brody Institute for Cinephilia and Preservation. It's uptown."

"I think," said Miriam, very slowly, "you had better tell me exactly how this happened."

She told her about going through the Gundlach monograph, about Edward Kenny and Louis Delgado Jr. and all the people who had died, and writing to Lucy Pierrepoint. She told her about the Vermont cache and Fred and going to see Norman.

"You talked to Norman. I see. Norman likes to talk."

She's in shock, Ceinwen thought, just like I was. "Yes. He told me about Leon Reifsnyder. Whitman, you knew him as."

"Ah. Leon." She picked her coffee back up. "I hadn't thought about Leon in almost sixty years." And she didn't sound pleased to be thinking about him now, but that was natural. Ceinwen had decided long ago she wasn't to going to tell Miriam anything about Leon except that he had taken the film from Emil's house.

By the time she told Miriam about going to see Fred today, and looking at the title frame, she'd finished her coffee. Ceinwen gestured toward her cup. "Do you mind if I pour myself some more?"

"Yes."

She stopped with her hand on the coffeepot. "I beg your pardon?"

"Yes, I very much mind your coming in here and accepting my hospitality, for all the world as if you weren't a lying, conniving little witch."

No one had ever said anything like that to her before, not even Lily. The words hit so hard she felt her eyes sting. "Miriam, do you understand? We found the film. Emil's work, the thing you made together."

"I understand perfectly well. I understand that you've spent weeks, no, *months* scurrying around behind my back. I admit, from the start I had you pegged as exactly the sort who might waste her time on a lost film." Miriam's coffee jostled and splashed as she braced her hands on the table to stand up. "But I thought once I quit answering all your questions you'd get bored and write a fan letter to, god, Joan Fontaine or whoever else isn't pushing up daisies yet. I thought you were a film buff, not a lunatic. You *knew* there was a reason I never once tried to see any of these people after the movie was done."

"I couldn't tell you." Her voice was quavering, she sounded like a scolded child. "It made you sad, you didn't want to talk about it. I thought that—"

"Who gives a *damn* what you thought?" Miriam was on her feet and pacing. She *never* paced. Ceinwen wanted to tell her to calm down, but she was afraid that would only make things worse. She could picture Miriam keeling over, like Gladys Cooper in *Now, Voyager*. "Did you think I'd burst into tears of gratitude? Say you're the daughter I never had or something?"

That slapped her into responding in kind. "I never expected anything from you, Miriam. Believe me, I don't even expect good morning."

"You and your pitiful act over your boyfriend, and me falling for it, giving you what you want so you'd be happy and go away . . ."

"Pitiful? I was curious, that's all."

"You were curious all right. So you come in here and you drink my coffee and smoke my cigarettes and you wheedle the most intimate details of my life out of me, all in that smarmy Southern voice of yours. 'Oh Miriam,'" she mimicked, making Ceinwen sound like one of the Yazoo City debs. "'Ah'm jes' dyin' to know what it was lahk to make a gen-yoo-ine motion pick-chur.'" Miriam was standing still now, but this time she didn't look steady doing it.

"I didn't say that. I asked you—"

"And then you *use* that to run around digging up things that are absolutely none of your business. Writing to Lucy Pierrepoint, that god-bothering bitch. Asking her about Emil, when she never missed a chance to harass and humiliate him."

"I was asking her about Frank Gregory."

"Oh really? Did you ask whether he was a good lay, too? Going to see Leon Whitman. Did Norman happen to tell you what we called him? Did he?"

"No, he—"

"Uriah Heep. Crawling around that set, bowing and scraping. He was a toad. I'm amazed you didn't get that out of Norman too, while you were busy going behind my back to him. How did you manage to track down Norman? Did you sneak a look at my address book when I was out of the room, like you nosed around my photographs?"

"What gives you the right to accuse me of that?" Ceinwen was finally on her feet and raising her voice, too. "You didn't even tell me he was alive. Matthew had to go all the way to the *L.A. Times* archives and—"

"But of course, get your boyfriend involved too. He's even sneakier than you are and his accent is better, too."

"He only did it because of me!"

"I believe that. I believe you'd ask the man for his right arm if you thought it would do you any good."

She was, to her relief, much too angry now to give any thought to tears. "I wasn't doing it only for myself. I was doing it because if people work hard on something it deserves to survive."

"And you deserve to be Joan of Arc, running in and saving all these pathetic old people, isn't that it? Your incredible selfishness, your *conceit*. If you can't make movies, you can at least worm your way in with people who did." She stood up. "Get out."

Miriam was still shaking, but Ceinwen was no longer worried about that. She was staring at Miriam's face, the blotches that had never marred it before. The way her mouth was showing wrinkles that Ceinwen hadn't known were there. "I'm a liar? That's rich. You aren't upset that I was nosy and went around talking to people who used to think you were a slut. You're afraid the movie's no good."

"If you think I won't call the police to get you out of here, you're wrong."

"You only saw it once," she shouted. "Practically nobody else alive ever saw it, and if they did they're too old to remember it. And now if it gets restored and people watch it, maybe they'll react the same way they did back in Pomona. Maybe a critic will see it and say the same things as that guy from the *Times*." She breathed deep and spat out every adjective. "That Emil was a lousy director and the movie's a silly, pretentious piece of trash."

"I'm picking up the phone right now," said Miriam, and began to walk.

"You don't want anybody to see you act." Her voice was emerging so loud her throat began to burn. "You're afraid you really were terrible. You call me selfish? You got your nerve, Miriam Clare."

"My name is Gibson!"

"You'd rather have Emil's last movie gone for good than have anybody look at a few reels and think he was a fool to put you in it!"

"Dear god," shouted Miriam, "what does it take? What do I have to say to get you and your bleach-blonde hair out of here? Leave. I'm standing here with my hand on the phone. Leave!"

The door slammed behind Ceinwen with a force that knocked a paint chip off the jamb. She stood there, trembling herself, looking at the other door on the landing and wondering if there was a neighbor behind it, listening. She walked upstairs and discovered that Jim and Talmadge were standing in the open door to the apartment.

"That went well," said Jim.

"I guess everybody in the building heard," said Ceinwen.

"Possibly," said Jim. "Kind of hard to catch all the details, but I don't think she likes you anymore."

"We came out here to see if we needed to break up a fight," said Talmadge. "I thought you could take her, but Jim was afraid she might try a sucker punch."

"She called me conniving. And a witch. And selfish and conceited," said Ceinwen.

"Now *that* makes me mad," said Jim. "I say you march right back down there and get that scarf back." He paused. "After we finish the champagne."

They went to the kitchen. "Talmadge made himself some tea," said Jim. "What's the herb tonight?"

"Chamomile," said Talmadge. Ceinwen stood next to the kitchen table, hugging herself and staring at the stove. "Very soothing," he added. She grabbed her neck. "You two can have some after the champagne. To cleanse."

Jim paused at the fridge. "Maybe Ceinwen doesn't feel like celebrating."

She drew herself up. "Of course I do. Just because Miriam's crazy doesn't mean I'm not gonna celebrate."

Jim poured the champagne into their one set of highball glasses and they toasted. "To Ceinwen's obsessiveness," he said, cheerfully, and she drank to that without a second thought. They sat for a little while, Ceinwen telling them about how long it would take to restore the film, and leaving out the technical bits when Talmadge started to do his cheekbone-popping exercises. She drained the last of her glass. "I have to call Norman," she said.

"Didn't you talk to him enough?" asked Talmadge. "And *oh*. By the way." He draped an arm along the back of the couch with an air that was almost flirtatious. "I think Matthew is a lee-tle jealous of him."

She stopped halfway to the phone. "Jealous of Norman?"

"Just a feeling I had," said Talmadge, eyes crinkling and voice getting deep and mysterious. "The way Matthew said you went all the way uptown so Norman could show you his films and, ah, how to clean them up."

"That's Fred," said Jim, "not Norman. Norman is the eighty-something-
ır-old gay guy. Try to keep up, Talmadge."

"I thought the old guy was named Harry." Talmadge sounded annoyed.
"He's the old professor."

"The one who had the movie?"

"*No*. Jesus. Harry is the one—"

Talmadge put up his hand. "This is way too complicated for me. Of
urse, if Ceinwen had told me all this stuff from the beginning instead of
eping me in the dark—not that I'm hurt about that or anything."

"I thought Miriam would be mad at me if I told people," said Ceinwen.

"Pshaw, you're paranoid," said Jim.

She found Norman's number, dialed. Busy signal. She hung up and
nt back to the living room. They finished the bottle of champagne and
e took some chamomile tea, tepid now. Talmadge and Jim began to de-
te ways to get her scarf back from Miriam. Jim was hoping Miriam would
ve enough class to wrap it up and leave it on their welcome mat. Tal-
ıdge was talking about the People's Court. She went back to her room
d dialed again. This time, it rang.

"Am I speaking to Norman Stallings?"

"My dear lady adventuress. Are you yet living?"

"I was trying to call you. The line was busy."

"That it was. It was turning blue, as a matter of fact."

"What?"

"I haven't heard that kind of language from Miriam since the day this
ın scandal broke. Which, come to think of it, wasn't that long ago. Maybe
e's always had a low-down vocabulary and I never bothered to notice."

"She hates me now," said Ceinwen.

"I could deny it, of course, but that would be deceitful. I didn't think
iriam could surprise me anymore. But this was . . . unexpected."

"I'm sorry, Norman," she said. "I totally did worm Leon's name out
you."

"Yes. But you weren't exactly subtle. I could have told you to buzz off."

"I didn't mean to get you in trouble."

"She'll get over it. She isn't really mad at me, anyway. She was going
ı about how helpless I am, a regular babe in the woods, out there getting
ken by reporters and conniving blondes. I reminded her of all my time
Army Intelligence spotting shady characters, and let's not forget Holly-
ood, those folks could have outfoxed Rommel. She told me I'm a sucker

for a pretty face, male or female, and that's why when I met Eve Harrin
ton, all I did was feed her cake."

"Eve?" That was what Miriam thought of her now, Eve? Now she d
feel like crying.

"Yes. Don't get too upset. Eve makes out all right."

It was so unfair. "Did you point out that Emil *wanted* people to s
Mysteries?"

"Certainly. I told her that was why I talked to you. She said even Fran
Gregory didn't cut away four reels, and Emil wouldn't have wanted tha
any more than he'd have wanted to live with all four of his limbs cut off
asked her to consider the possibility that she was being an itty-bitty teen
weeny bit melodramatic, and at that point she became quite hostile."

"That's not true. It can't be true. A director doesn't put his heart in
a film so—"

"Shh, I know. I told her to pour herself a drink and call me when sh
was ready to be reasonable."

"That was that?"

"No, she told me never to mention your name again and *then* that w
that." Ceinwen sniffled. "She's been mad before. She'll climb back dow
to earth sooner or later. And she won't kill me, I'm too old. She's a practic
sort, she'll just wait for the day I drop in my tracks." She wondered if she
outlive Miriam, or if Miriam would live on into the next century, waitin
for Ceinwen's smoking to take its toll. "Pull up your garters, girl. You'v
saved part of our legacy as Americans, wasn't that your goal?" Maybe, sh
thought. I think my goal has hockey-puck syndrome. "All right then, te
me, when do they unveil this multiple amputee?"

"The Brody says it could take a year, maybe more."

"That should be just enough time for Miriam to calm down," sai
Norman. "Meantime, do watch out in the lobby. Icebergs, dead ahead."

She told Norman she'd keep him apprised of the Brody's progres
since clearly Miriam wasn't going to do it, and hung up. She could sti
hear Talmadge and Jim out in the living room. George had given Talmadg
the air a couple of weeks before, and Talmadge was complaining abou
Jim's lack of sympathy. She scanned her bookshelves, not looking for any
thing in particular, and her eye lit on the paper bag that held the *Mysteri*
of Udolpho still, sitting on top of a row of books. She took it down and ca
ried it into the living room.

"How's Norman?" asked Talmadge.

"He's good. Would you like to see what he looked like, when he was ung?"

She slid the still out of the wrapper and cautioned Talmadge not to get gerprints on it.

"Wait, so this one is Norman? Well, looks aren't everything."

"He looks fine," sighed Jim.

"This one's gorgeous, who's he?"

"Edward Kenny," she said, "the star. He's at the Motion Picture Home w. They told me he's senile."

"Time and chance happeneth to us all," said Jim.

"What's that, Shakespeare?"

"It's the Bible."

"Oh, *excuse me*. Which one is the director, the one with his elbow on e camera?" Talmadge held it a little closer. "Not bad. Hm, kind of a small in. Northern Europeans."

"I was going to give it to Miriam," said Ceinwen. "To celebrate finding e film."

"I'd say it's yours now," said Jim drily. "You should frame it."

She took it back and looked again. Miriam. Edward Kenny. Norman, lding a script. Probably Louis Delgado. And Emil.

"I'll do that," she said. "I'll do it when the film is preserved. And I'll ng it up."

They all looked for another minute. "The men's side at the store just t some picture frames in," said Talmadge.

"No," said Jim.

"Art Deco style. Perfect for an old photo."

"Talmadge, I am telling you, *no*."

2.

HARRY WAS SITTING BEHIND HIS DESK FOR ONCE, INSTEAD OF ON TO of it. "I called the Brody today. Talked to the director, Ms. Chun And I asked her what they had. My *Crowd*, for one thing. I told you Anc would keep that one. But get this." His brows were straining to reach h cheekbones. "She said that they were very excited, because there was a fil in there that had previously been thought lost."

"A lost film? You're kidding." She hoped that sounded surprised.

"I know! Of course I asked her which one and she said they aren't for mally announcing it yet. Cool customer, that one. Fits right in at the Brod they always were a strange bunch. But, more importantly"—he braced h hands on the desk—"can you believe that lunatic?"

"Which lunatic?"

"Andy! That so-called colleague of mine! Not only was he storin nitrate, piles and piles of nitrate for god's sake in his own building, but h had a lost film down there and he hadn't breathed a word to a soul. Min you, I always knew he was off his rocker, all you have to do is look at h office, although this is a math department, everyone's a little odd. But lost film?"

"Maybe he didn't realize it was lost."

"Of course he realized. He probably wanted it *because* it was lost. An he was going to let it sit down there until either it crumbled to dust, or th whole complex burned to the rafters, whichever came first. If there wer any justice in the world the building would evict him and Courant woul toss him out by his hair."

"Is that what's going to happen?"

"Not a chance." Harry made a little grunt of disgust. "Tenure. The wrote him a stern rebuke. I'm sure he was crushed. But"—he held up hi finger—"I've fixed him. I've fixed his little red wagon. There was a facult meeting today, and of course Andy wasn't there. Can't be bothered with meetings, they're boring. God forbid Andy should be bored. And do yo know what I did?"

"You voted to censure him," she guessed. Harry shook his head. "Yo docked his pay?"

"No! I moved to make him department chair for next year! And it ssed on a voice vote. No nays, no abstentions." Harry threw back his ad and let out a great, booming laugh.

"But, isn't that an honor? Department chair?"

"An honor, she says. It's the biggest pain in the tokus you can *possibly* nagine. And it's a four-year appointment. Four years of memos and letters d budgets and meetings and you better believe, I mean you should bet ur life that I will be breathing down his neck every step of the way."

"That's great," she told him. Wasn't this supposed to be a final inter- ew? "Um, Harry . . . my test. Weren't we going to . . ."

"Oh, that. You're hired."

She blinked. "I am?"

He waved his hand like the pope blessing the crowd. "Sure you are. ongratulations."

"Tania is fine with that?"

"Tania left it up to me."

She had to ask. Harry was too good a person to have a lousy secretary. Harry, you saw my typing test, right?"

"Sixty words a minute! You're a speed demon. You start training a week om Monday."

"I, uh, made seven errors."

"Errors, schmerrors. It's all on computers nowadays. You go back and x them before you print it out. Problem solved." He peered at her. "Be- eve me, that's plenty good enough. Angie used to make twice that many nistakes on one page."

"I'm sure I'll get better the more I do it," she said.

"Of course, of course. Besides," said Harry, "it would be a novelty to ave a face around here a man can look at without shuddering." He looked t her, waiting.

"*His Girl Friday*," she said.

His eyebrows were working. "Director?"

"Oh come on. Howard Hawks."

"Who played Diamond Louie?"

"Abner Biberman."

"And that," he shouted, smacking his hand on the desk, "is why you're ired. Get out of here. Go get that limey a drink."

The light was on in Matthew's office and the door was open. She eeked in; he was at the blackboard, chalk in hand, writing out something at the bottom of an equation. She grabbed the door jamb and swung herself into the room, a real MGM musical move. "Hel-lo theah," she chirped in her best British.

"Hello," he said quietly, and put down the chalk. "All done with Harry?"

"Mm-hm." She perched herself on the desk, crossed her legs and twitched up her skirt. "I start training a week from Monday."

"That's wonderful."

"And the remission kicks in for the fall semester." She swung one leg over the other. "But that's not why I'm here. There's a Michael Powell series at MoMA starting next week."

"I don't know about that." He was walking to the door.

"Don't be a bore, this is your native country we're talking about. All I've seen is *The Red Shoes*."

He shut the door. "I can't make it."

"You can't work all the time, not even Harry expects you to. The first one's *I Know Where I'm Going!*"

He leaned against the door. "Anna will be here in about three weeks."

She uncrossed her legs. "So?" He was looking at the floor. "Did that not sound right? How about, so *what*?"

He put a hand through his hair.

"You're going back to her?" No response. "Even after you came back to me?"

"Nothing's changed."

"That's ridiculous. How can you say that?"

He looked at the ceiling. "It's the same story it's always been, do we need to go back over it?"

"Yes. You don't love this woman."

"I do."

"Then why are you telling the fucking light fixture and not me?"

He bent over the back of the desk chair and looked at his hands, fingers laced. "My postdoc ends after next year. After that I go wherever I can get a job. You'll be working for Harry and going to film school. Anna and I planned what we'd do after postdocs for a long time. We're the same age, we have the same way of looking at things, we have years together."

"What do you want, a medal?"

He flinched. "I know you don't like her."

"I don't know her. What I saw was snobbish, cold, and boring, but I n't know her."

"She's moving here. We're getting married." She put her arms across r stomach. "I'm sorry. I truly am."

She rocked forward. "You don't," she gasped, "have to use words to , you know."

He was still looking down at his chair. This was a new expression he d, she didn't know it, but she must have seen something like it some ne, after all these years and all those movies. In her mind she projected se-ups, flipping through them like stills in one of Andy's folders, trying name it. Not pity. Not anger. Not sadness.

The frame paused. Longing.

She had nothing to say. She stood up and walked out.

Go ahead and long.

When she unlocked the street door on Avenue C, she had no idea what res or doorways she'd passed, what men had whistled or ignored her, ho'd tried to sell her anything or whether she'd jaywalked or waited at e corner. She mounted the stairs, looking at cracks under the doorways d listening for TVs. There was a light underneath Miriam's door. She pt walking.

Talmadge called to her from the living room. "Ceinwen, is that you? me and look at this. I moved the couch. I think it looks so much better er here between the windows." She stood in the entrance; he was facing e couch and holding his hands up as though to frame it. "Check out w . . ." He turned to her and trailed off. "Oh sweetie."

She started to talk and couldn't. He put his arms around her. A first. ter a while she raised her head and checked the mascara she'd smudged a his T-shirt.

"Jim was right after all," she said.

"Ha. Let me tell you, Jim's not as smart as he thinks he is. Last night e told me maybe he was wrong." Talmadge brushed at his T-shirt, then opped his hand. "Let me make you some tea. I have linden. It's like, a ee or something."

"I'm okay," she said. And remembered she needed to take off her cket.

"No, you're not."

"I'll be okay." She started walking toward the bedroom. "I'm going to e in the bathroom for a while, do you need it?"

"Not at all."

She undressed and wrapped her robe around her. She grabbed an o[ld] towel out of the stack in the kitchen cabinets and went into the bathroo[m.] The box of hair dye was still in the medicine cabinet. She mixed it up a[nd] started applying with the pointy tip of the applicator, like the instructio[n] said. But she got tired of making parts in her hair, so she unscrewed t[he] top and slopped it on. Then she sat on the toilet seat and waited. She didn[t] have a watch and she didn't put on a timer. She let the fumes sting her ey[es] and watched the light go down in the bathroom until she had to switch o[n] the overhead. When the dye started to itch she stepped into the show[er] and rinsed it out. She got out, dried off, wrapped the towel around h[er] head, and slipped back into her robe. Talmadge hadn't had to see her nake[d] since Christmas.

Jim had come home while she was in the bathroom. When she cam[e] into the living room he just said, "Let me see." She took down the towe[l.] "That's going to be gorgeous, honey." He pushed his cigarettes at her an[d] she took one.

"I moved the couch back," said Talmadge. "Jim told me it would b[e] too hard to see the TV."

"I know exactly what we need," said Jim. "Sit right there." She sat o[n] the couch and Talmadge lit her cigarette. Jim came out of her room wit[h] a tape in his hand.

"In honor of your new hair," he said. He put the tape in and pushe[d] play. He sat down and they watched.

"You need a hat like that," said Talmadge.

Ceinwen concentrated on the glasses on the bar. "How many drink[s] have you had?" Myrna Loy was asking, and William Powell was saying[,] "This will make six martinis." And Myrna was asking the bartender, "Wi[ll] you bring me five more martinis, Leo? Line them right up here."

"Do you have any of the sequels?" asked Jim.

"I have them all," said Ceinwen.

"Good," said Jim. "Line 'em up, right here." She put her head on hi[s] shoulder and settled in for the night.

AUGUST

1.

"THIS ISN'T MY FAULT."

"Then precisely whose fault is it, Ceinwen?" Matthew held up a
ge and jabbed it so hard he left a crease down the middle.

"It's not my fault you have bad handwriting."

"There's nothing wrong with the way I wrote this. Look." He flicked
e page across her desk, picked up his handwritten copy, and slapped it
wn beside her keyboard. "That is a delta. It is very clearly a lower-case
lta."

"If it looks like an alpha to me then what the heck am I supposed to
pe?"

His voice was rising. "You could start by looking here, where I wrote
t the word on first reference. Delta. D, E, L, T, A."

"After that, for the rest of the paper you put little tails on them, like
alpha."

Louder. "You're from Mississippi. I shouldn't have to explain a delta
you."

She picked up her LaTex manual and began flipping to the index with
vage concentration. "Okay, okay, don't have a cow. I'll look up the com-
and for a universal change—"

A full-on shout now. "Which will do neither of us any fucking good
hatsoever because there are in fact alphas in this paper, which you did
mehow manage to spot."

"Listen mister," she said, pulling the manual to her chest. "Where do
u get off swearing at me? I don't have to type your bloody paper for you
I don't want to. You're a postdoc."

"You have to type it because Harry told you to."

"He *asked* me to do it. Harry *asks* me to do things, he doesn't *tell* me."

"Good for Harry. Now fix it and for fu—" He inhaled. "Just—get it
ght this time." He paused at the door. "And for the record, Americans
und *ridiculous* saying 'bloody.'"

She got up and closed the door behind him. She sat down and looked
the printout he'd thrown on the desk when he walked in, smudges where
e pressure of his hand had smeared the ink, alphas shot through with

lines that left dents in the paper, the word "delta" scrawled again and aga
on each page. There was a soft knock at the door.

"Come in." It was Harry, breathing a little hard, as he had all we
when the weather became unbearably hot.

"What was that I was hearing?"

"Matthew was correcting his paper," she said.

Harry walked in and sat down heavily in the spare chair. "I gather
something like that."

"I messed up the Greek letters."

"Yes. Well. Ordinarily I would be taking a stroll down the hall rig
now to tell Matthew that here at Courant we don't yell at the secretarie
Least of all mine." He cleared his throat. "But I'm giving him a pass. Ju
this once. He's got a lot on his plate."

"I wouldn't know," she said. "This is the first time I've seen him in tw
months."

The paper had shown up on her desk last week, with a note from Har
asking her to type it as a favor. She'd left the draft in Matthew's mailbo
downstairs.

"He's leaving Saturday," said Harry.

"Yes, that I knew." She touched the dented lines on the first page, an
managed to say steadily, "And there's the engagement party next week."

In London. She'd heard Anna burbling in Harry's office, all the wa
back in May. When Anna was walking to the elevator Ceinwen had spotte
the ring, just before she ducked into her office to cry. "It can't be two carat
And even if it is, that's not *that* big," was Talmadge's comfort.

"That, plus there's the dinner tomorrow night."

"What dinner?"

"8:30. Il Primo Cerchio," said Harry. "That fancy-schmancy plac
down near the financial district." He was watching her from under h
brows.

"Big dinner?"

"No, just me and Donna and Paru and Radha. Intimate. Or as intimat
as you can get there. They tell me it's the size of an airplane hangar."

"Have fun," she said. "I hear the food's good. Talmadge has been see
ing one of the waiters sort of off and on."

Harry's eyebrows inched lower. "That could come in handy," he saic
"For last-minute reservations. Matthew said Anna booked this about
month ago. She's very keen on the place."

"I guess because it's Italian."

"You'd think she'd want to branch out. Japanese, Thai, even French. ut no, Il Primo Cerchio." He paused, and continued. "At 8:30. Table for x. On a Friday night."

"Sounds cozy," she said.

She picked up the paper. "Don't bother with that tonight," said Harry.

"He said he needs it before he leaves."

"You'll have plenty of time tomorrow morning, and he can look at it efore this dinner tomorrow night. At 8:30. Downtown." He reached over d tapped her copy of the *Voice* on the corner of the desk. "If you leave ow, you could still make the Mizoguchi at the New Yorker. You were lling me you hadn't seen much from Japan. *Street of Shame*, it's a great ne." He waited. "His swan song."

She'd never heard of it, but the title alone sounded like a barrel of ughs. "I'm going home. I have to figure out what to register for next se-ester."

"All right. See you tomorrow." She picked up her purse. Harry seemed be waiting for something, but then he heaved himself to his feet.

Talmadge and Jim were arguing about where to position the fan to atch a breeze. They fell silent when she walked in.

"How was your day?" said Talmadge.

"Don't ask." She threw her purse on the floor and the couch shifted as he collapsed on it. "And I don't want any tea."

"Excuse me, Missy Thing. Did I offer any?"

"I'm sorry." She pulled the rhinestone clip out of her hair. She'd been rying to wear it wavy, in a halfhearted attempt at Rita Hayworth, and with ll the humidity it was always bedraggled by day's end. Not that Matthew ad noticed. He was looking at his fucking deltas.

"Will you see him tomorrow?" asked Jim.

"I doubt it. He has a big dinner. Him and Anna, Harry and Donna, his professor from Columbia."

"How do you know, he told you this?"

"No, Harry did. It's down at that place where Sammy works."

"Well, whoop-tee-do," said Talmadge. "Sammy says you can't get out f there for less than $100 apiece. Even if you order water."

She made a face. "Yeah, and I guess getting a reservation's a bit deal, ecause Harry kept telling me over and over it's 8:30 on a Friday night." he grabbed her purse to get a cigarette.

Jim sat down on the floor. "Now why would he do that?"

"How should I know. The heat's making everyone weird." She drew finger across her upper lip to get the sweat off. "It's supposed to break to morrow. Rain." Good. She hoped the restaurant flooded. She hoped Wash ington Square Village flooded.

"Why else?" said Jim.

"Why else what?"

Talmadge said, "Sweetie. Get your mind in gear. Harry wants you t crash."

"How am I supposed to do that?"

"You show up," said Jim. "It's a restaurant. Not Buckingham Palace.

"Then what? When I saw him today all he did was yell at me about h paper."

"You sit at a table and look good," said Talmadge.

She snorted, the cigarette trembled, and she brushed the ash off he skirt. "I've been right there on the same damn floor as him looking th way I always do for almost four months now."

"Yeah, well, the closer he gets maybe the colder his feet get," said Tal madge. "Marriage is a big deal for Catholics. Just ask Jim."

"What's that supposed to mean?"

"Jim doesn't even like Matthew," said Ceinwen.

"I like him fine."

"Oh please."

"Let's say I'm resigned to him. Anyhow I can't stand to see you mopin around the apartment anymore. You're reminding me of that Garbo movi you made us all watch last year."

"She's shown us, like, six," said Talmadge.

"The one where she's a hooker. But a high-class hooker." They looke at Ceinwen and she rolled her eyes. "Come on, I'm totally blanking here She gets sick at the end." It was *Camille*, but she didn't want to talk abou it. "What's wrong with you? Did you eat dinner?"

"This is what low blood sugar does to a person," said Talmadge.

"Y'all were always the ones telling me not to call," she reminded then sharply. "Now all of a sudden I'm supposed to crash his dinner."

"You're not there to throw your arms around his knees or something," said Talmadge. "You're just *there*. To jog his memory."

"If I just show up out of nowhere I'm going to look pathetic," said Ceinwen. "Believe me, I feel pathetic enough."

"Not gonna lie, honey," said Jim. "I don't see what difference it'll make ther. But your big-deal genius boss knows Matthew better than I do."

"A math genius. That doesn't mean he's a people genius. It probably eans the opposite."

"I give up," said Talmadge. "You work on her. I'm calling Sammy."

"You better have some actual pull with this one, Talmadge."

"He told me he could get me in anytime. He just couldn't, you ow, pay."

Jim plopped next to her on the couch. "Here's how I see it. There's noth- g to lose at this point. We go. If nothing happens, and it probably won't, u promise me you'll accept it and *move on*. Nobody expects you to get over m right away. But I want you to get out of the house every once in a while. ease. You haven't even forced a John Ford movie on us in two months."

Talmadge had already dialed the phone. "Darling, how's your evening ing . . . Oh, mine too . . . Yes, definitely . . . Remember when you said . . ."

Jim pulled the cigarette out of her hand and stubbed it out. "We're orking with what we got, dress wise. So that means the halter."

". . . But could you swing a table for two even if you're not working? . . . u said before . . ."

"You said the white washes me out."

"That was when you were a blonde."

". . . That's fine, just call me back . . ."

"I can't go to this place. I don't have enough money to pay my own ay, let alone two."

"I've got a credit card," said Jim.

"When did you get that?"

"Last year. I figured we should have at least one adult around here."

Friday night the rain began as the sun went down, a steady, quiet pour at was supposed to build as the night progressed. The temperature had ummeted and she wore a thin raincoat to protect her dress.

Il Primo Cerchio was at the top of a twenty-story building way down ear Centre Street. The elevators opened into a marbled foyer, coat-check rea on the right, the passage to the dining room just beyond it. On the ft a bank of windows showed an empty terrace furnished with lounge hairs and benches. People were handing their umbrellas and the occa- onal raincoat to the fellow working the large, half-empty cloakroom, a uy about her height who seemed even skinnier and younger than she was.

It was one swank crowd. Eau Sauvage and Coco, jackets and ties,

teetery heels, flashing rings and watches, those quilted Chanel purses sh
couldn't stand, a lot of lipstick even by her standards.

"Oh look," said Jim. "It's the Armani trunk show. We're just in time

She checked in her coat and her cheap umbrella, which had bee
falling apart ever since the last big rainstorm, in May. Jim told the attenda
that they were supposed to see the maitre d'. She smoothed down her dres
"Do I look okay?"

"I'm reconsidering my entire lifestyle."

"You don't have to lay it on that thick."

"Hey, my sister says all it takes is the right girl." She thought he looke
better than any of these Wall Street guys. That double-breasted suit Ta
madge gave him for Christmas practically made Jim look like a mode
albeit a bookish, ever-so-slightly uptight sort of model.

"Good evening."

And there stood one of the best-looking men Ceinwen had ever see
in her life. Must be forty at least, hair barely turning gray. Still. This wa
Harry Belafonte territory.

"How may I assist you?" She barely managed not to giggle at th
butler-like greeting, but good lord, he sounded good, too. His voice wa
so deep she felt her chest vibrate.

This was Jim's cue, but he wasn't picking it up. He was staring, an
the man was staring back. Finally they said, almost in unison, "I know you,
and started laughing.

"Palladium, right?" asked Jim.

"Yes! That's it! I knew it. You were with a blond guy . . ."

"My roommate," said Jim. "He's a friend. He knows Sammy." H
looked both ways and added, in a conspiratorial whisper, "That's how w
got the reservation."

"No trouble, I'm glad you could get in," said the man. "Remind me o
your name?"

"Jim. This is my friend Ceinwen."

"I'm Rodolfo." They shook hands while Ceinwen fought back mor
giggles. Rodolfo. It simply wasn't possible. But hey, if anyone could liv
up to a name like Rodolfo, it was this guy.

"Ah, can I have a minute with you? I'm wondering—I know it's th
rush right now . . ."

"My pleasure." Jim motioned for her to wait and the men moved to
ward a desk near the dining-room entrance.

And there was Matthew, helping Anna out of her coat. Burberry. Anna s British. She knew Matthew had spotted her, and she waved timidly. dently his slight nod was supposed to substitute for waving back. Anna ied to see who was on the receiving end, and anyone seeing the slow, sfied smile that proceeded to crease her face would have thought her ch happier to see Ceinwen than Matthew was. The coat-check man ped his arm, and Matthew handed him their coats. Anna's dress was pless, lilac. Why were brunettes always trying to wear that color?

Anna said something and strolled straight toward Ceinwen. He foled a few steps behind. She hadn't realized he owned such a beautiful . Italian, probably. When Anna pulled up, Ceinwen sucked in her eks for a second to keep her mouth shut. Her earrings. The woman wearing her earrings, the ones Matthew bought that night at Vintage ons.

"SeenWEN, isn't it?" She and Ceinwen both kept their hands at their s.

"Ceinwen," she corrected. "And you're Anna," she said, not bothering h the vowels. Screw with my name and I'll screw you right back, lady.

"That's right." Still that big, contented smile.

"What brings you here?" asked Matthew. He didn't sound as though really wanted to know.

"I'm having dinner," she said, in a tone meant to suggest that she'd dly be here for Jazzercise.

"What an interesting dress," said Anna. "I can't quite . . . is it *old*?"

"It's vintage."

"1950s," said Matthew. A statement, not a question. He'd learned nething, after all.

"That's right. Early decade."

"I don't think I've ever seen anything like it," said Anna. "And the hair, a bit fifties too, isn't it?"

"More forties," said Ceinwen. "In the fifties they usually wore it short." er Anna's shoulder she could see Jim with his back to her, and Rodolfo cking a massive book at the front desk.

"I'd no idea. It was a different color when we first met, yes?"

"I was blonde," said Ceinwen. Matthew said something low and fast, Italian. Anna's eyes barely flicked his way.

"I don't mean to be rude. I think it's quite daring."

"Red hair?" Jim, get back over here before I strangle this woman.

"No, I mean, to go from so very blonde to so very red, it's so—w
word do I want, Matthew?"

"Nice," said Matthew. "How's that?"

Same expression on Anna, but mouth a bit less mobile. "Yes, very."
tucked her evening bag under her arm. "Excuse us, we should see if
table is ready."

"Sure," said Ceinwen.

"Enjoy your meal," said Anna.

Ceinwen watched them walk away. He didn't look back once.

Jim had a hand on her arm. "How'd it go?"

"She's still a major bitch," said Ceinwen.

"Well, *I'm* doing great," said Jim, turning toward Rodolfo as the n
navigated the crowd to get to them.

"This will take a few minutes," said Rodolfo. "You could wait at
bar if you like. We usually tell people to wait outside with their drin
but"—he waved down the passage at the rain pounding the terrace.

"It's too bad," said Jim. "The view is supposed to be fabulous."

"It's the best part. Aside from the food, of course. You should co
back on a clear night."

"I plan to," said Jim. "Should we get a cocktail?"

"I don't want anything," mumbled Ceinwen. She was staying sol
tonight and besides, she figured alcohol was going to double their bill, a
there was no way she was letting Jim take the whole hit for this schem
even if it was his idea.

While they waited she tapped her foot and bit her nails, until J
grabbed her hand and reminded her that she started smoking in the fi
place so she wouldn't do that anymore. She reminded him that he'd ma
her leave their cigarettes at home. He tweaked at her neckline.

"Messing around with my dress doesn't make you look very straigh
Even though Matthew knew he was gay, Jim was supposed to be on esc
behavior for appearance's sake.

"Maybe I don't want to look straight until I absolutely have to."
shot a look at Rodolfo, who was talking to a couple of waiters.

Who knew what they were doing at their table for six. A toast to t
happy couple. She wanted to die. No, she wanted to march in there a
tell Anna exactly what she thought of her manners, her hair critiques, a
how she looked in those earrings. Then she wanted to die.

Rodolfo was beckoning. The vast dining room gleamed with blac

hite, and chrome, flowers everywhere, the tables spaced far apart to show
ff the fact, she thought, that they made so much money they didn't need
o pack 'em in. The views from all those windows would have been heart-
opping without the rain and fog. Matthew's party was near the far win-
ow, and every table within twenty or thirty feet of it was occupied. Why
id she come, why? So she could watch Matthew sip champagne from the
ther side of Grand Central Station?

Rodolfo motioned for Jim and Ceinwen to follow and walked straight
o the clear space next to Matthew's table. They stopped and Rodolfo beck-
ned to an unseen someone.

She was close enough to hear Harry joking about Andy at the last fac-
lty meeting. He'd tried to adjourn early, but Harry had marched Andy
hrough every item on the agenda, including the pastry selection in the
hirteenth floor lounge. Paru spotted Ceinwen and gave her a somewhat
uzzled nod. Donna looked up and waved, big and eager, like a little girl.
he seemed ready to come over, but Harry touched her elbow and whis-
ered something as his brows gave Ceinwen one big, slow raise.

A side door opened and out came two uniformed busboys carrying a
able, two more carrying the black leather chairs. They set down the table,
ositioned the chairs, another uniform appeared with a tablecloth and nap-
ins, flowers and cutlery materialized . . . all within a few feet of the big
ound table for six, Rodolfo directing everything with only a few gestures.
nna still hadn't turned their way, and neither had Matthew.

Rodolfo pulled out her chair, handed them menus and in an instant he
as gone. She wasn't even sure which exit he'd used. She leaned over to
hisper, "What on earth did you tell him?"

"I didn't tell him anything, I swear. I just said we really, really wanted
table with a good view of the Hill party." Jim twisted slightly to take in
he side of Anna's head and turned back with an evil little chuckle.

The menu was in Italian. All she could make out were the prices. "My
od. I've never seen numbers like this on a menu."

"It's worth twice what they're charging. The maitre d' is James Bond."

Matthew's group was on their salads and appetizers. There was cham-
agne in an ice bucket and the conversation seemed lively, especially on
he part of Anna, who was laughing and offering comments on every dish.
nna swept her eyes over Ceinwen, then Jim, then turned her back to say
omething to Radha about a store in London.

Ceinwen ordered by pointing at the first things she saw. Over at

Matthew's table they were bringing more champagne. Jim ordered a glass of wine. She could barely talk, but Jim had no such problem. Was she ever going to work up the nerve to ask Miriam to give back her scarf. This year they needed to buy an air conditioner even if it blew every outlet in the place. He'd forgotten to tell her Fred called today and she should call him first thing Monday.

Suddenly it wasn't hard to keep her eyes off the other table. "Did Fred say he's ready to project part of *Mysteries* for me now?"

"He said, 'Um, this is Fred Creighton, could you, um, tell Ceinwen to call me, um, when she gets a chance.'"

"Sometimes you have to drag things out of Fred, you know. Just interrupt him during one of his 'ums.'"

"I did. I asked him if he wanted to leave his home number. And frankly that seemed to scare him. His voice got all high and squeaky."

"So he didn't give you the number."

"No, he didn't. Said Monday would be fine. Maybe you should quit calling him every week like you're his mother and let the guy do his work."

"If they didn't have so many rules at that place I could probably watch him work and I'd have seen something by now." Jim looked skeptical. "I bet MoMA would let me watch."

The appetizers were arriving, and she saw she had somehow managed to order raw beef. She braced herself and discovered it didn't taste like much of anything unless you ate the greens with it. As she tried to get a bite of bread in there, discreetly and without opening her mouth to show the beef she was still chewing, she saw Matthew glance at her as he knocked back a bigger gulp of champagne than was strictly polite. Her peripheral vision took in Anna looking, too, so fast she nearly missed it, then a flip of Anna's hair. Now Matthew was talking to Paru, something about long-haul airplane flights.

That's it, she thought. That's what I get to live on from here on out. One kind word by the coat check. One turn of his head. The only word for me is pathetic.

Since that was the case, no reason to pretend she wasn't watching. She sat up straight to get a better view, and when Jim hissed that she was being obvious she told him to watch for Rodolfo.

Some sort of pasta was happening over there; she heard the word "classic" from Anna. When they set down the plate in front of Matthew, Anna laid her hand on his arm.

"Let the expert . . ." she heard Anna saying. Anna took the pepper
nder from the waiter and gave it a few precise twists. Then she took
 cheese and the grater and shaved a very little bit. She asked
tthew something, and she said, "Oh, that's too much, much too
ch . . ." A few more shaves. She handed the grater back without a
nce at the waiter, and the man left. She picked up the salt shaker and
shook his head slightly, still talking to Paru. ". . . just as you want it,
o? Are you sure?"

Matthew said something, then "Thanks."

"My pleasure," was the reply. With one swift move of Anna's hand,
 plate went vertical, the entire contents were sliding from Matthew's
st to his lap, and the plate was back in its spot on the table.

"Holy fuck," breathed Jim.

The logical next move would be to storm out, but some credit was
 here. Anna was not so obvious. She put her elbows on the table and
ded her hands. Harry and Donna, Paru and Radha were frantically try-
 to find a comfortable place to rest their eyes. Matthew was matching
na, glare for silent glare. He seized his napkin by the corners to pick
 as much of the pasta as possible and dumped the pieces on his plate.
ith two hands he began scooping noodles off his lap, picking them off
 lapel and his tie. Anna stood up, plucked her tiny bag off the table like
 was grabbing it out of a fireplace, and walked out, hips swinging and
ad high.

The waiter had arrived to hand over some napkins. A busboy was dis-
etly sweeping near the chair. The conversation in the vicinity, which for
 past few seconds hadn't included even nervous laughs, had resumed,
d it seemed everyone was going to pretend that what had happened was
 accident. Matthew wasn't looking anywhere, least of all at her. He stood
d walked out, too.

She moved to get up and felt Jim grab her arm.

"Here's where you do what I say. Give it ten minutes."

"He could be gone by then," she pleaded.

"It's going to take him at least that long to clean up in the men's room,
d if she's confronting him out there you don't want to be anywhere near
I'm telling you, ten minutes."

"But—"

"No. Just be glad *we* didn't go for the pasta course."

Somehow their main courses had arrived while they were watching

Matthew get his food thrown at him. Fish, with a sauce that she didn't l
the looks of. She'd thought it would be breaded. Donna's voice drift
their way.

". . . a misunderstanding."

"You could say that." That was Paru.

". . . couples, there's all this pressure when you're planning . . ." Rad

And Harry now. ". . . no reason to come all this way and not see w
the *Times* is so ga-ga . . ."

Jim was whispering. "I figured, absolute best-case, miracle scenar
he looks at you for a few hours, he gets drunk, he goes home and says"
his Matthew imitation was almost as bad as Talmadge's—"'Anna, Brit
honor forces me to tell you that I still fancy little Ceinwen like ma
THEN she throws something at him. But right here?" He sat back a
shook his head, lost in admiration. "That was badass. Food fight a
three-star restaurant. This could make Page Six."

"Page Six doesn't care about some mathematician," she said. S
picked off a few flakes of fish and when she put the fork in her mouth,
was still way too much to chew.

"You do." She tried for a bit more fish. "Would you cheer u
This is great." He drained his wine. "You can't say he didn't have
coming."

She didn't feel triumph, she didn't feel hope. She just felt awful f
Matthew. But she didn't have to admit that, because Rodolfo had glid
up. "Hello." Jim's expression was more ravenous than any he'd directed
the food. Rodolfo put a hand casually on the back of Jim's chair and sa
at precisely the volume needed to ensure his voice didn't travel beyo
their table, "I'm told the view here was more exciting than expected. Th
we expected, anyway."

"Really?" asked Jim. "What happened? We've been concentrating
our food."

Rodolfo smiled serenely. "I won't bore you with the details. You'
made good progress. How about the lady?"

"It's delicious," she said.

He cocked his head. "Are you sure? You've barely touched it. Do
be shy. If it isn't what you want, I'll take it straight back to the kitchen."

"This meal has been everything we could possibly want," said Ji
She'd known Jim almost four years, and she'd never seen such flirting fro
him. Talmadge, sure. This would be subtle for Talmadge.

"That's what we like to hear." She checked her watch. Eight minutes.
was rounding up, goddamnit.

"I'm afraid I have to go."

Rodolfo was dismayed. "So soon? You really must let me change that.
uld you like lamb, like Jim?"

"She has some work she has to finish," said Jim. "But I'm sticking
nd."

"I'm glad someone can. All these sudden exits are making me paranoid."

"No, no, I'll be right here. Eating my dinner. All by myself." She
ed up her purse and pecked Jim on the cheek. "Go get 'em," he said.

"Get what?" asked Rodolfo.

"Whatever's out there," said Jim.

Rodolfo was still chatting, and Paru and the others were ignoring the
empty chairs—except Harry, who looked up and laid one finger against
nose. She wasn't sure what that meant.

Outside the dining room, only a few people were waiting for their
es. No Matthew. If Jim was right, he'd still be in the men's room. Surely
hadn't chased after Anna, that wasn't his style. No one getting a coat.
e man came from behind the counter to help her. He handed her the
brella and she asked, "Was there a lady here a few minutes ago—strap-
dress, light purple? Burberry raincoat?"

"Yep." He sounded glum. She opened her purse to get out her wallet
the tip and looked in the bowl to see if she could figure out the going
. Two quarters lay on top of some singles. She glanced up and he im-
diately rolled his eyes to indicate his opinion. Her smallest bill was a
. At least she could improve one person's night. She laid it in the bowl.

"Was there a man with her?"

He grinned. "You don't have to act casual, just ask. You mean her date?
n't know what happened to *him*. Must have run into one of the waiters
ning out of the kitchen. Walked right past me after she left. I still got
coat."

"Which way did he go, toward the men's room?"

"Nope. Coming out of the men's room. Went thataway." The man
nted to the terrace.

"Out *there*?"

"That's what I thought," he shrugged, "but I don't think he wanted
ice."

"Thanks."

As she walked away she heard him say, "Anytime. I mean that. Co[me]
again."

All she could see through the double-glass door was the rain descen[d]-
ing and the wind blowing it into whirling patterns. She scanned in ev[ery]
direction and was about to give up when she spotted a chaise lounge w[ith]
its back to the door and looked closer. Two feet stuck out at the end[. A]
jacket-clad arm dangled over the side. She opened the door and pause[d to]
put up her umbrella, fighting the wind to get it open. She had to hold [the]
umbrella to the wind side to keep it from reversing. When she got cl[ose]
she hesitated.

"I know you're there." Matthew, head still hidden, was raising his v[oice]
over the wind.

"You do?" she called back. "Who am I?"

"I know it's you, Ceinwen."

"How?"

He leaned over the armrest to look at her and pointed back at her [re]-
flection, barely visible in the plexiglass shielding the wall along the terra[ce.]
He laid back against the lounge.

"I can also see," he called, "that whatever you're trying to h[old]
there isn't what most people would call an umbrella. So if I were y[ou]
I'd go back in."

She crossed to stand at his feet. He couldn't have been more sopp[ing]
wet if he'd been thrown into a swimming pool. A wide pink stain fan[ned]
down the length of his shirt and tie. A bit of spaghetti clung stubbornly [to]
his belt buckle. "Why is it okay for you to be out here? What are you doin[g?]"

He waved his hands at his shirt. "Laundry."

"What's wrong with the men's room?"

"I used half the attendant's towels and I started to feel sorry for hi[m.]"
Another gust of wind hit her umbrella. "Don't stay out here, you'll cat[ch]
your death."

"Colds are caused by viruses. You were always telling me that."

He closed his eyes for a second. "Go back in. I'm fine."

"Anna left," she heard herself say.

"Yes, she told me. Me and whoever else happened to be anywhere ne[ar]
the toilets."

"I don't see," she said in a burst of anger, "where she gets the ner[ve]
to act like the injured party. She's the one who made a scene, not you[.]"

"If she were here, she'd say she had her reasons."

"Reasons?" Her voice was far louder than the competing rain and wind required. "It's not your fault I showed up. You were treating me like a human being, that's all. She should try that herself sometime."

"She was angry."

The wind reversed her umbrella and she snapped it back, causing a ray to hit him smack in the face. He didn't flinch. For once she didn't care what she said about Anna or what truths she had to force on him. "She humiliated you. In front of Harry and Paru, in front of that whole damn place. If she was so angry I dared to show my face in a public restaurant she should have thrown the plate at *me*."

He'd discovered the piece of spaghetti on his belt and was working to detach it. He shook it off his hand onto the ground and said at last, "Wouldn't want that, would we. Think of your dress."

She sagged from the blow. "I guess I deserve that."

"Deserve what?"

"The sarcasm."

He picked up his head. Hair soaked to the scalp, eyes locked into hers. "I don't do sarcasm anymore. New York's killed my taste for it." The same tune. The same lines. He said, slowly, "If I had my way, nothing bad would ever happen to you. Not even a mark on your dress." He swung his legs to the side of the lounge. "I think the rinse cycle's done. Why do you have your coat on? Weren't you going to have dinner?"

"I already did."

"If you say so." He braced the balcony door against the wind. "One of these days you really must master the whole eating concept. I'll walk you out."

She could hear his shoes squish as he walked. Back at the coat check the man was handing umbrellas to a group of five loud and rather boozy men. She looked at the floor and noticed small puddles collecting around Matthew's feet. Even his plastic coat ticket looked wet. As the man retrieved the coat Matthew reached in his suit jacket and pulled out his wallet, brown leather, now with a big water stain wrapped halfway around it. He tossed a couple of bills in the bowl as the man came around to help him.

"Thanks. We'll take it as done," said Matthew, and put the coat on himself. "I have an umbrella back there, don't I?"

The man gave a little cough. "The, ah, other lady took it."

"I see."

"She took your umbrella?" blurted Ceinwen. Of all the low—

"We were sharing it."

"Burberry, I guess." Maybe he'd sworn off sarcasm, but she hadn't, n
where Anna was concerned.

"Longchamp," he said. "It's all right. She bought it. I always hat
the thing."

At the elevator he said, "This is different. A coat soaked from the i
side out."

"I was thinking that, but I've been working on my tact." They got c

"You've always been tactful," he said. "Your trouble is saying tact
things in a believable way."

He refused to share her umbrella, saying it was barely enough to cov
her. By the time they got to the corner, the wind had popped another r
Matthew took it gently from her hand. "I think we should let this die wi
a little dignity, don't you?" He stuffed it into a garbage can and they beg
to walk in the direction of the subway. On a night like this, he'd never
able to put her in a cab.

She moved to hop across a vast puddle over a blocked drain and f
him grab her elbow to steady her. His hand was gone almost instantly.
the next corner he looked back. "How far do you suppose we've gone?"

"Two blocks, maybe?"

"That's three blocks, you mean. I know that. I meant distance. Meters
He made a face. "Although why am I asking you of all people?"

"Good question."

He pointed across the street to a building shrouded by scaffoldin
"Over there." He took off, got ahead, and waited for her.

"The subway's that way," she pointed. "I know that much."

"We're stopping here." He stepped into the frame of a deserted doo
way under the scaffolding.

"Are we waiting for the rain to let up?"

"We'd be here all night."

"Then what?" He leaned against the door and for only the second tin
that night, he was holding eye contact. She tried to smooth her hair, tuc
ing the wet strands behind her ears. "What?"

"It's hard to explain to someone who's never been engaged."

Oh brother. It never ended, it never would end, him and Anna. "Sing
people can't find the 6 train?"

He crossed his arms tight against his chest. "Right." He took anoth
pause, then, "You're at a restaurant, and you have a fight with your fiancé
But you realize that doesn't bother you. Not the way it should." He dre

long, uneven breath. "No. In all honesty, it doesn't bother you at all." He shifted his legs. "Probably won't ever bother you again." She waited. "But, if you have a fiancée, even in the technical sense, then no matter what you want at the moment . . . you can't . . ." He was focused on a point somewhere over her head. "Not while you're actually, physically in the same restaurant she was in. It's . . ." His hand traced a few cartwheels while he searched for a term, and at last he came up with, "Tacky."

"Good Southern word," she said.

"Yes. Even in the lobby it's tacky. Still tacky one block away."

A pause. "Four blocks," she said.

He moved closer and looked past her shoulder, to the street. "Eight hundred meters. At least."

Like someone watching from the last row, she saw herself put a hand on his chest to push him away.

"I don't want anything to happen," she said, "if all you're going to do leave again."

He folded her hand in his. "Neither do I." He laid his other hand against the side of her face. And then they were kissing, water running from their hair down to their mouths, hands moving anywhere they could reach, pressing against each other until she felt the damp of their coats work through to her skin.

She opened her eyes and saw a flash of yellow behind his shoulder. "Matthew! Cab!" He spun and bellowed, "TAXI!"

They crouched under the bars of the scaffolding and sprinted to the cab that had stopped in the middle of the street, Ceinwen hitting the puddles so hard she felt splashes at her hem. He held the door and she scooted across the seat, leaving a smear of water on the vinyl. He slammed the door and they sat united for a moment in panting New York triumph, the winners of the big rainstorm cab lottery.

The cabby's turban bobbed. "Hello there."

"Evening," said Matthew. Ceinwen jacked up her hips so she could pull down her skirt and coat.

"Where to, please?"

Matthew appeared to be contemplating the world's hardest theorem. "Washington Square Village?" he ventured.

"That is where exactly?"

"Mercer and, ah, Third." The cab took off.

"But," said Matthew.

"Anna's there?"

"She does live there. As of this morning."

"Think she's maybe putting landmines around the living room?" Matthew choked.

"Mercer and Third, right?" The cab turned and kept going.

"Maybe. Give us a minute," said Matthew.

The driver gave an exasperated groan as the cab continued to move uptown. "You seem like you are nice people. I know it is not fun to be out in a storm. But in my opinion it is best to decide where you are going *before* you hail a cab."

"We're going to her place," announced Matthew, in his Britishest voice.

"Great. I am happy for you. Where does she live?" They were kissing again and she was somewhere else. Theatre 80, Kiev, a train coming back from Paru's. "You did not plan this at all, did you?"

"Avenue C and Fourth Street," said Matthew.

"That was not so hard, was it?" The cab turned east.

He put one arm around her shoulders and the other across her lap. He brushed his mouth near her eyebrow and left it there.

"Did you get your paper? I redid it this morning. I put it in your box."

He pulled back only a tiny bit. "Yes. I know I was a shit. I'm sorry."

She was going to take that as meaning only the paper. "I did it deliberately. You knew that, right? I knew they were deltas. I wasn't trying to make you as mad as all that. I just wanted to see you."

"I wanted to see you too. That's why I was shouting." His mouth slid down to hers and he tightened his arms.

After a while she said, "Are you staying in London?"

He groaned. "Oh god. No. After the party we were supposed to go to Nice." The cab had hit traffic. She ignored her stomach as the driver kept tapping the brakes. Raw beef. Who on earth eats that? "I'm not going anywhere. Obviously," he said, his head trying to burrow under her chin.

She laid her hand on the back of his neck. "You're sure?"

"No comparison, is there? Who'd pick the south of France when they can have Manhattan in August?"

He straightened and she rubbed her cheek against his shoulder. "That's an awfully big ticket to waste."

"Oh, this little evening will cost a bomb. There's no doubt about that. I paid the restaurant in advance. There's the plane ticket. Tickets, that is. There's the hotel deposit. There's calling my mother to cancel that bloody ty, and that doubles my phone bill right there. There's this suit. And tie. And the shirt." He banged his head hard against the back of the c. "And the ring."

"She'll give it back, won't she?"

"Even money. Place your bets."

"So you'll be poor for a while," she said cheerfully. "No problem. If body can show you how it's done, it's me."

He pulled his arms away and leaned forward with his face in his hands. hrist I'm a shit."

"That's the second time you've said that and I don't like it. If you're a t, what does that make me?"

He didn't move. "There's nothing wrong with you. I thought I was ng all the right things, and no matter what I was doing it turns out I'm nit. I've attained the absolute summit of shitdom."

She pulled at his hands. "Once you're at the summit, there's nothing do but leave."

"That's wrong, you know. I could pitch camp here for a very long time."

There was a loud throat noise from the front seat. "You said Fourth 1 C, that is correct?"

"Correct."

"If you look out the window," said the driver, "you will see that is where are."

When she unlocked the street door, Ceinwen found herself con-nting Miriam, who was banging a tall umbrella on the floor to shake off water.

"You two look like hell," said Miriam.

Those were the first words she'd heard from Miriam since the night y fought about the film.

"Good evening, Mrs. Gibson," sang out Matthew. Ceinwen sneezed, n sneezed again.

"What were you doing," asked Miriam, "fording the Hudson?"

Ceinwen examined the drips on the floor tiles for a second, then said, mergency."

"Oh?" Miriam was fastening her umbrella with deft precision.

"Movie emergency," offered Matthew. "That's the only sort Ceinwen er has."

There was silence as they passed her. Then Miriam's laugh, the same e from Christmas night, chased after them as they climbed the stairs.

AFTERWORD

NEW YORK CITY IN THE LATE 1980s WAS REAL, MUCH AS SOME OF
may look at the present-day city and wonder if we dreamed it ↄ
This is a work of fiction. Real places such as Theatre 80 St. Marks and ▸
Courant Institute of Mathematical Sciences on Mercer Street are fre⤸
mixed with others, such as the Brody Institute and the Lancashire Ho◂
that exist only in my imagination.

Aside from the obvious historical figures mentioned, I made
everybody in this book. That is true of the cast and crew of *The Myster*
of Udolpho and the studio that supposedly produced it; the staff and cɩ
tomers of Vintage Visions (no such store); the employees of the Bro◂
Institute (there isn't one, though I wish there were); the true-blue meɩ
bers of the Bangville Police Society; and the dedicated waitstaff of
Primo Cerchio.

And it is certainly true of NYU, where I have, in addition to creatɩɩ
fictitious faculty, set aside the 1980s presence of numerous distinguish
scholars of both film and mathematics. Buildings have been borrowed fro
NYU, but all other realities of that institution (my alma mater) have be
stubbornly ignored. There is not, and never has been to my knowledɡ
anyone storing highly flammable nitrate prints on any part of New Yoɾ
University's property, and certainly not in 1 Washington Square Village
don't believe there is even a storage area in that building, at least not aɩ
have described it.

I borrowed the surname of a famous film theorist, Rudolf Arnheiɴ
for my imaginary director. I also made up the Raymond Griffith two-reel
The Man From Manitoba, gave the long-missing Colleen Moore sile
Flaming Youth a brief shot at resurrection, located the firmly lost *Weddiɩ*
Bills and *The Silk Bouquet*, and implied that *The Magic Flame*, which exiꜱ
only in a fragment, had been recovered in its entirety. I apologize to aɩ
silent-film lovers left crestfallen over those last four. Like Ceinwen, I'
basically an optimist.

In his book *Film Crazy*, writer Patrick McGilligan asked Raoul Walꜱ
about one of my favorite films, the 1941 version of *The Strawberry Blonɖ*

also set in New York, but in the 1890s, when Walsh was a boy. "A jolly
:, good times, nice people," said Walsh. "That's the way it really was,"
:d McGilligan, "or that's the way you want to remember it?" "It's the
I want to remember it," replied Walsh.
I hope that lovers of New York and the movies can overlook the liber-
I've taken. It's the way I want to remember it.

ACKNOWLEDGMENTS

I AM DEEPLY GRATEFUL TO JAMES WOLCOTT AND TOM SHONE, the their fellowship and constant encouragement during the writing of novel; to Rusha Haljuci, who read the manuscript at every stage; and the great Kevin Brownlow, whose chance remark to me inspired the p Profuse thanks to Hooman Mehrman, Dave Kehr, Lou Lumenick, La Harnisch, and John McElwee, who patiently answered my questio usually without knowing why on earth I was asking. Thanks to my edit Mark Krotov and Dan Crissman; and to my wonderful, indefatigable age Gary Morris.